D1460452

The Prince's Man

The Five Kingdoms, Volume 1

by Deborah Jay

Published by Deborah Jay, 2013.

The Prince's Man
First Edition. 29th July, 2013

Copyright © 2013, by Deborah Jay.
Written by Deborah Jay

Cover art by Jennifer Quintenz
Map by Deirdre Counihan

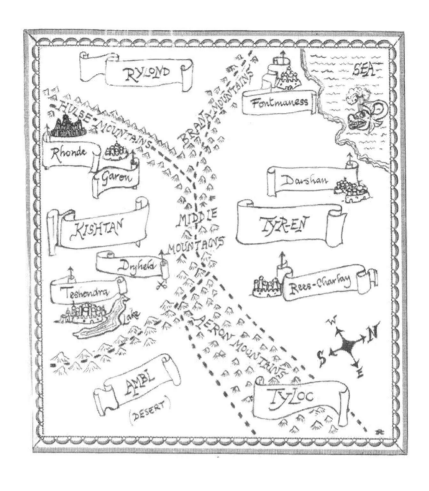

The Five Kingdoms

Prologue

DOMN

Risada tiptoed across the darkened bedchamber and felt behind the tapestry for the hidden niche. Her tiny fingers located it and she grinned as the lock tripped with a faint click.

She heard voices in the outer chamber and light flickered around the doorframe. Heart thudding against her ribs, she dropped to her knees and scuttled forward through the swinging panel into the secret room. This was such fun!

Careful to close the panel behind her—Daddy said you must always lock doors when you were going to have your back to them—Risada wasted no time clambering onto the chair she had positioned beneath the spy hole. Her nose wrinkled at the smell of dust. It seemed like ages since Daddy had shown her how to work the hidden catch. Certainly it had been before *that woman* had arrived.

At thought of Mistress Chalice, Risada scrunched her face up into a ferocious scowl. How she hated her dancing tutor. Oh, the woman was very polite, and she was very beautiful—all the servants said so—but Mummy didn't like her so Risada didn't either. And the maids were saying such wicked things about Mistress Chalice and Daddy. Well, tonight Risada was going to see for herself.

Jaw jutting with determination, Risada stretched up to put her eye to the spy hole. Darkness loomed on both sides of the hole, but she knew precisely where everything was: first rule of the game—always know your surroundings intimachlee.

Some word like that, anyway.

Mummy didn't like Daddy teaching her about the game, but he said it was never too early to start, so now she knew all the hiding holes in the house and the one in the stables too. She knew which guards she could talk to and which she mustn't. Daddy had even given her a little dagger of her own, a pretty silver one with tiny green jewels in the hilt, which she kept hidden in the sash of her dress. Mummy wasn't supposed to know about it and Risada liked keeping secrets.

The bedchamber door swung open. It was to one side of the spy hole and Risada couldn't quite see who was there. Someone walked across in front of her and she caught the glimmer of candlelight on silvered hair. That was Daddy. He stopped beside the dresser, unbuckled his belt and laid his sword down.

But there was someone else as well. Risada leaned across as far as she could without losing her balance and grinned in triumph. It was Mummy. It must be because Mistress Chalice had red hair and Risada could see a head of pale blonde, almost white hair done up in braids like Risada's own.

So much for those prattling maids. Risada began to imagine all the tales she would tell Daddy about what they'd been saying when they'd thought her safely asleep. Carefully she got down from the chair and felt about for the catch on this side of the panel. But what was that? Mummy was shouting at Daddy!

Spinning around, Risada lunged in the dark for the chair and banged into it. She held her breath. Had they heard? As quietly as she could she clambered back up to the spy hole and peered out. Mummy and Daddy were standing directly in front of her, but they couldn't have heard because they were glaring at each other, not at the hole.

"Keep your voice down Arton, you'll wake the baby."

Risada peered downward and now she could see that Mummy was cradling her baby brother, Iain.

"I didn't start this Sharlanne. You shouted at me!"

"Of course you started it! You were the one who brought that woman into our household."

"Mistress Chalice is an excellent tutor for Risada. Hal sent her with the highest references."

"For doing what?" snapped Lady Sharlanne. Then she sighed. "Arton, Prince Halnashead might be your cousin, but does it not occur to you that he might be making some play of his own? There's every good chance she's one of his spies; she's certainly served his House for long enough."

"Why in all Five Kingdoms would Hal want to put a spy in our House? He knows we're loyal to the crown. Besides, I refuse to believe that he would use such a defenceless young woman for that sort of task."

Sharlanne laughed; a short, sharp bark of disbelief. "You dare to say that? You, who've started teaching our daughter—our *six-year-old* daughter—to be a player? And don't think I don't know about that dagger either."

Risada could bear it no longer. She hated Mummy and Daddy arguing, and now they were arguing about her! She slipped down off the chair and opened the secret panel. She was going to make them stop.

"It's for her own safety," Arton was saying as Risada struggled up from behind the low sofa that squatted in front of the tapestry. "You've heard the rumour."

Sharlanne made a most unladylike noise. "You take that seriously? Really, Arton, no House has dared make a final play against another Family in over seventy years; not since the King made such an example of Sencarten House."

"Sencarten was careless. But if nothing could be proven? Just suppose it were true: do you think they'd spare the children?"

As if Arton's words had conjured up just such a play, something dark moved in the shadows beside the window.

"Arton!" screamed Sharlanne, but the Lord of Domn barely had time to turn before a flicker of light—a knife, realised Risada in horror—embedded itself in his neck. Something gushed from around the blade, and Risada smelled a sharp taint in the air. She whimpered and her mother looked around wildly. Sharlanne's eyes lit upon her daughter standing frozen beside the sofa.

She thrust the sleeping baby at Risada. "Take Iain. Quickly: hide!"

Risada clutched her brother but stood rooted to the spot. Her mother had turned back to face the assassin over the body of her husband. In her fist was a silver dagger with emeralds in the hilt; a larger version of Risada's own.

"Guards!" cried Sharlanne, but no one appeared.

The assassin, a short, powerful figure clad entirely in black with his face anonymous behind a mask, stepped silently over his first victim. Sharlanne wove her dagger back and forth menacingly, but the figure seemed made of smoke and where she struck, he faded away. Sharlanne lunged again and finally made contact. Her silver blade slashed through the mask, the fabric parting to reveal blood welling from a deep cut to the assassin's jaw, but it was Sharlanne who gave a strangled cry as the crimson-stained tip of a blade appeared in the centre of her back. She sagged forward, collapsing into the arms of her killer.

The assassin cursed as he staggered back and was pinned momentarily against a settle by Sharlanne's weight. Blood dripped from a ragged gouge along his jaw line, but it was the man's cold black eyes that snared Risada's attention as he looked across the room, straight at her. The child's heart lurched against her ribs. In panic, she spun and dropped to her knees, fumbling for the niche. The tapestry seemed to wind itself around her arm and she sobbed with fright, but she could hear the man still cursing as he struggled to free his sword from the body of her mother.

At last she had it. The panel sprang open and Risada shuffled awkwardly through on her bottom, clutching the baby to her chest. She slammed the panel behind her and snapped the lock, then collapsed against the wall, gasping for breath as tears streamed down her face.

"Mu, Mu, Mummy," she wailed, and then clamped a hand over her mouth, eyes wide, staring into the blackness as she heard the telltale sounds of someone on the other side of the wall hunting for the hidden catch. She stayed that way all the while he hunted, and even when she knew he was gone, just in case. She was still sitting there, cradling the sleeping baby, when the panel slid open and Mistress Chalice poked her head in, preceded by a guttering candle.

"Praise the goddess; they're in here!" she cried to someone behind her, and other voices joined her in thanks to the goddess Chel.

"Come on Risada, it's safe now. You can come out. Here, let me take Iain."

The little girl shook her head and clutched her brother so fiercely he woke and began to cry. Reluctantly she crawled back into the blood-soaked bedchamber.

Ignoring the weeping maids and grim-faced guards, still cradling the wailing baby in her arms, she walked over to the bodies of her parents and stared down at them. No one was ever going to do that to her or Iain, she vowed silently. Then she glared up at Mistress Chalice.

"I hate you! It's all your fault!" she screamed.

1. THE GAME

Twenty years later...

Rustam Chalice eased his way down the rose trellis. His hand closed around a thorny stem and he sucked in a sharp breath, stifling a curse. He exhaled slowly and looked up.

No lights.

Good.

He could not see far enough to be certain, but reckoned he was around man height above the flowerbed. In many ways this moons-dark night was ideal to his purpose, but a little illumination would have helped just now. He let go the trellis and jumped.

His estimate proved a touch short, and as his feet hit dirt Rustam tucked into a roll, clutching the precious glass bottle tightly to his chest. He swore under his breath and picked himself up. The bottle was undamaged but he doubted the same could be said for his clothes. Burrs from a dantseg bush clung to his sleeves and the right leg of his breeches was sodden.

Brushing himself down, Rustam glanced back up at the Fontmaness's mansion. Still no lights. The goddess Chel must favour him this night.

A warm glow of satisfaction suffused his chest, and he allowed himself a minute smile. Prince Halnashead, the kingdom's spymaster, would be pleased with his work tonight.

He felt his way forward, remembering the barbed throne tree he had nearly walked into two nights earlier. That foray had been after his official departure from the estate, on the first of his clandestine visits. Then, the young and delightfully attractive Lady Betha had hung a lantern from her bedchamber windowsill so that he might see his way. She had also sent the guards to investigate a fictitious noise on the other side of the mansion.

Tonight Rustam had no such assistance.

The throne tree loomed before him as a darker patch against the faint sparkle of stars. He skirted it and stepped out onto the gravel path bordering the lawns, wincing as each step crunched rudely into the still blackness. The smell of dew-drenched grass beckoned him on and at the first feel of the cushioning, silent turf beneath his feet he broke into a sprint.

As he reached the cover of the trees, his luck deserted him.

Rustam's heart lurched as a hound bayed in the dark. Lady Betha's elderly husband, Lord Herschel, had taken him on a grand tour of the estate when he had first arrived to take up his position as Dancing Master to her Ladyship. He had seen the guard hounds then. His most vivid recollection was of the size of their jaws, but he had the uneasy feeling they had legs to match. And now they had scented him. He gulped a deep breath and ran for it.

Goddess have mercy, he pleaded as the baying closed on him, only now there were two, with men shouting somewhere behind.

Rustam burst out of the trees. Every breath seared his lungs, and his vision tunnelled until all he saw was the ghostly white perimeter fence ahead. He gathered his last shreds of energy to make the leap.

Agony shot through him as teeth tore into his leg and he was thrown to the ground. Locked together, Rustam and the hound skidded along the damp grass and slammed into the fence.

In a world turned black and white and laced through with pain, time seemed to slow. Rustam slipped his dagger from its wrist sheath, swung an arm that moved with the speed of an obstinate mule, and plunged the narrow blade into the looming bulk of the hound. The beast fell away, howling.

A hammer bird drilled inside Rustam's head and something vile threatened to erupt from his stomach, but his body began to move again with some semblance of speed. Teeth clamped firmly against the nausea, he grabbed hold of the fence, dragged himself up and over. A horse whickered nearby and he gasped in relief—good old Nightstalker, always where she was most needed. He could not see the black mare, but she found him and he clambered into the saddle just as the second hound leaped the fence.

"Go girl, go!"

Nightstalker surged forward with Rustam clinging to her mane. Only when they were half a league away, well beyond the outlying estate farms and into the wild hills did he slow down long enough to tear a strip from his silk shirt—*damned expensive bandage*, he thought sourly—and wrap it around his bleeding leg. It was still too dark to see but he could feel warm fluid trickling into his boot and, *Charin's breath,* it *hurt!* He would have to stop somewhere soon and build a fire, see what the damage was. But not here. Not yet. He clenched his teeth and rode on.

* * * * * * * * * *

The palace guard frowned at the tall, slender, brown haired young man limping towards him through the early morning shafts of sunlight that pierced the colonnaded walkway with military precision. During his duties on this particular entrance to the private wing the guard had seen many odd characters pass, but in time they had all become known to him. He had been in Prince Halnashead's employ some years now.

This man, though; his even, fine features looked familiar, as did the expensive cut of his breeches and velvet doublet, but that limp—

"Master Chalice! Whatever happened to you?"

Rustam grimaced. "Took a damned stupid fall from my horse. I know it's early, but is His Highness available, Dench?"

"To you, sir, yes," Dench replied, frowning as he studied the pallor of Rustam's skin. Dark rings framed the deep blue eyes, and the easy grin that the ladies found so appealing was absent from the dancer's generous lips.

"Are you sure you're well, sir?"

"No, Dench, I'm sure I'm not. But the prince is expecting me so, here I am."

"As you say, sir. He's in his study."

* * * * * * * * * *

"Rusty, you look dreadful!"

Rustam collapsed gratefully into the depths of a plushly upholstered chair. "Well thank you, sir! I did it especially for you; it's about the only chance you'll ever have of knowing for certain that you look better than me."

Prince Halnashead threw back his head and guffawed. He was a large, ruddy-faced man with an impressive girth which shook with his amusement. Rustam watched in fascination as the silver buckle of the prince's belt leapt up and down with the regularity of a metronome, and then vanished suddenly as Halnashead leaned forward to peer across his vast desk. "It can't be so bad if your vanity is still intact, lad. I presume it's all in your report?"

"It will be, as soon as I've had time to make one."

"You've come straight here? Then you have it?" The prince's voice rose eagerly.

In answer Rustam reached inside his doublet and withdrew a velvet-wrapped bundle. He levered himself wearily out of the chair and leaned across the desk to hand it to the prince.

"At last," breathed Halnashead. "You've outdone yourself this time, Rusty."

"You may not say that when you see my tailor's bill," muttered Rustam beneath his breath as he sat down again, but Halnashead was too busy extracting the glass bottle from its protective layers to notice.

He held it up to the light and swirled the carmine fluid thoughtfully. "So this is it: the so-called 'elixir of eternity'."

"That's it," confirmed Rustam tiredly. "Doesn't look like anything special, does it?"

Halnashead turned his head sharply from the bottle to Rustam's face. "Did you discover how much Herschel paid for this?"

"Not exactly, Your Highness. But the Lady Betha was bemoaning the loss of her diamond tiara."

"*That* much?" The prince looked startled. "That could pay the wages of ten mercenaries for a whole year! Multiply that by the number of sales we know about, let alone the ones we don't..."

He allowed the thought to trail away but the implications were clear to both men. The political stability of the Kingdom of Tyr-en relied largely upon the certainty that in a land where manpower was in desperately short supply, the only House wealthy enough to support an army was the Royal House itself.

Halnashead looked grim. "It seems the situation may be worse even than we suspected."

"Mmm," Rustam agreed. "But surely the real question here, is does it work? And if so, what is eternal life worth?"

Prince Halnashead shook his head as he re-wrapped the bottle and placed it gently in the bottom drawer of his desk. "Rusty, of this I can assure you: it doesn't work. There are no elves left in Tyr-en to part with that secret. They either took it with them through their accursed magical Gates into Shiva, or to the grave."

My prince, I know your instincts are most often true, thought Rustam worriedly, *but what if this time you're wrong?*

"Are you absolutely certain?" he questioned aloud. "We're talking about something many would kill for."

Halnashead leaned back in his massive leather chair and drew a heavy breath. "Yes, m'boy, I am. It was a death that alerted me to the elixir's existence in the first instance. One of my agents witnessed a perfectly natural death staged to look like an accident, to deny age as the culprit. This whole operation is a masterful undertaking in deceit, but of this I have no doubt—the potion is a fake.

"What must concern us is where the money is going. *Goddess preserve us*, we may be facing a private army!" The prince scowled angrily but Rustam knew him well, knew the incredible depth of feeling was not directed toward him, rather at those who would threaten the fragile peace of the kingdom ruled by Halnashead's young nephew.

"Rusty, in this century alone, the people of Tyr-en have survived the tyranny of my grandfather, the drunkenness of my brother and two generations of Shivan Wars; I simply will not permit them to be subjected now to civil war!" Halnashead slammed a meaty fist down on the desktop. "I must know who is selling this concoction and what they are doing with the proceeds. Did you find any clues?"

"None, I'm afraid. I don't believe Lord Herschel confided that information to his wife."

"Or you would have been able to persuade her to tell you, hmm? Oh Rusty, I know how skilled you are, but this is one of the most frustrating cases I've ever had the misfortune to handle, and the lack of information points to a highly skilled player in the game."

"Well sir, if the suspected client list I've compiled so far is any true indicator, the supplier must be one of the major Houses."

"Hmm. That we are agreed upon. Ah, and that reminds me." The prince sifted through a pile of parchments, drawing one from near the bottom. "Something I doubt you've heard yet, Rusty: the De Launays have moved up from Sixteenth to Fourteenth House."

"How did they do that?" asked Rustam in surprise. He had been too long at Fontmaness in the goddess-forsaken wastes near the sea. Important moves in the game had passed him by.

Halnashead scowled at the parchment. "It seems the widowed Lady of the Fifteenth was tricked into a grain contract she could not fulfil. Being rather naïve in such matters, she was unaware of the difference in yields between this year and last."

"And De Launay offered to save her honour by fulfilling the contract," Rustam finished for him. "In return for land."

The prince nodded. "De Launay's new holdings raise their ranking above the former Fourteenth. An astute move, if callous."

Falling silent, Halnashead began distractedly rearranging the heap of parchments, deep in thought. Rustam's tired eyes wandered to the huge tapestry behind the desk, as they always did while the prince cogitated upon his next move. The early morning sun lit the threads with a blaze of glorious colour somewhat at odds with the dark scene depicted—that of a crowded ship being pulled beneath the waves by a huge, tentacled horror while helpless refugees either threw themselves to their doom from the crazily slanted deck, or clung hopelessly to the masts and railings. At the far edge of the weaving the rest of the fleet sailed into the distance.

Was this, Rustam wondered, Halnashead's way of reminding his agents that once in the field they were on their own, without hope of rescue should a situation turn ugly? Or did he keep it as a true memorial to all those lost during the Crossing—the mass exodus when humankind fled the magic-ravaged land of their birth to arrive in straggling handfuls upon the shore of this remarkably hospitable continent four hundred years earlier.

Perhaps it was a token of hope, illustrating that even the grimmest situations could prove to have unexpectedly good endings.

Halnashead slapped his open palms down on the desk, decision reached.

"Rustam, I want you and Dart to work together on this."

Rustam jerked upright in his chair. Surprise and indignation warred with curiosity. "My prince," he said. "If you have a task you want doing, you know I am your man, but why would you want me to work with a hired killer?"

Halnashead's face hardened, though Rustam fancied there was a hint of amusement in the prince's flinty grey eyes. "Because I'm ordering you to," he replied. "And Rustam, an assassin is a lot more than just a hired killer. Despite your years as a player, you've no idea who Dart is, have you?"

"No, but I could make some educated guesses."

"And they'd all be wrong, I guarantee it." The prince rubbed his large hands together and smiled slyly. "I do believe I'm looking forward to introducing the two of you. Meet me here at the second hour. Most of the guests will have started to drift away by then."

Rustam groaned. "The Solstice Ball's tonight? I thought I had another day yet."

"You've lost a day somewhere, Rusty. Perhaps the Lady Betha was more absorbing than you expected, hmm?"

Rustam snorted. "Betha? Absorbing? Sweet, perhaps, but I've had more interesting dinners than—"

"Please! Spare me the details. Now go and get that leg seen to. Did you have any other misfortunes on this mission?"

"Apart from two shirts and a pair of breeches? I half killed my horse getting back here in two days instead of five."

Halnashead smiled indulgently. "That beast means more to you than all the ladies, doesn't it?"

"She doesn't have a jealous husband to avoid."

* * * * * * * * * * *

The wretch strapped to the table screamed again; a hoarse, mindless howl that ended in a bloody gurgle. Lord Melcard Rees-Charlay backed up to the wall of the dungeon and dabbed with distaste at the flecks of foamy blood marring his white lace cuffs.

He glared down at the torturer and enquired in a slightly nasal voice touched with impatience, "Are you quite finished?"

"Nearly, my Lord," replied the squat figure bending over the hapless victim. Doctor Hensar, the Fourth Family's retained physician, was more practically attired than his master. All in black, he resembled nothing so much as an overgrown beetle, the only point of colour about his person the glittering crystal that dangled from a chain around his neck. As he turned to replace the gore-smeared bone cutters on the tray beside the table, the pendant swung and spun in the torch light, refracting tiny rainbows that chased each other endlessly across the stained walls of the torture chamber.

Selecting a far more precise instrument for his final manipulation, Hensar turned back to the quivering mass of flesh that had once been a man—a guard to be precise; one whose odd personal habits had led to accusations of magic-wielding—and looked up at his master dispassionately.

"There is little left to be done now. You need remain no longer."

For a moment it looked as though Melcard would take his advice, but the Lord squared his shoulders and shook his blond head. "No, Hensar. I ordered this execution. I will see it to its end. Proceed."

Masking a scowl of annoyance, Hensar turned and replaced the tool he had chosen, reaching instead for a glowing poker that rested in the brazier near the foot of the table. The stench of burning flesh was usually enough to drive Lord Melcard from the close confines of the dungeon, but today, despite the sickly green shade that tinged his already waxen face, the Family Senior stayed obstinately put.

When even the doctor's most expert ministrations failed to raise more than the faintest of moans, Melcard's patience reached its limits. "Enough!" he snapped. "It is finished. Slit his throat and be done with it."

"As you command, my Lord." Hensar swept a respectful bow, and then made one final attempt to remove his unwanted observer. "Might I suggest you leave before I perform this last duty, or your clothing may suffer greater soiling than can be repaired?"

"Hensar! I am still head of this Family and I will not be treated as a gutless weakling. Do it, and do it now!"

The doctor smothered his anger. His time would come, but that day was still in the future. For now, he must play the faithful servant. He nodded shortly and picked up the knife. One quick slash and it was over, but Hensar could not resist the tiny smirk that twisted his lips as Lord Melcard shrieked, doused by the apparently random spray of blood. Hensar had long ago learned just how to angle that particular incision.

Cursing everything to Charin's hell and wiping blood from his eyes, Melcard finally left Hensar alone with his grisly handiwork. The doctor seized the slim chance that something productive could still be salvaged from this afternoon's labour. Paying little attention to the finesse he would have employed earlier had he had the opportunity, he plunged a hand into the open body cavity of the corpse. His face took on a detached stillness as his fingers sifted through the internal organs for a mass the size and shape of which he knew intimately. When he found what he was searching for, he simply closed his fist and yanked.

Hensar examined the small yellow gland that lay cradled in his gory palm, but even as he watched the colour faded to the indeterminate shade of grey that told him it was useless. He flung the dripping lump of cells against the wall in disgust and watched with jaundiced eyes as it burst like an over-ripe fruit and slithered down the wall.

What a waste! To be of any use it was essential to remove the gland before the donor died. Melcard's stubborn insistence on remaining to the bitter end had robbed Hensar of his carefully planned harvest.

He stepped over to the bucket of water set beside the brazier and fastidiously rinsed his hands while he reviewed his requirements. If he was careful he could make his current supply last for at least one more batch, possibly two. More than that, no. He shrugged his shoulders. Beyond that, the apparent efficacy of the elixir would diminish, and that might make Melcard suspicious. Not to mention the clients.

Which gave him barely enough time to engineer the disgrace of yet another vassal of the House of Rees-Charlay. And next time, to ensure Lord Melcard's co-operative absence, he would have to be just that little bit more inventive.

2. SOLSTICE BALL

"Lord Iain Merschenko vas Domn!"

Rustam craned his neck to gain a better view of the sweeping marble staircase. For hours now the nobles of the higher Houses had been making their grand entrances down the curving steps, but none had caused such a stir of anticipation as the arrival of the Lord and Lady of the Second House.

The Lord of Domn stepped forward, and Rustam's eyebrows lifted in surprise. In the half year since winter solstice Iain seemed to have aged considerably. Then, he had been a dashing young man full of energy and zest, an annoyance to his elders with his frequent pranks and a huge frustration to the unattached court Ladies to whom he paid scant attention. Now he looked tired and old, with the first hint of silver frosting his dark hair.

We're almost the same age, thought Rustam, *yet he looks ten years my senior.*

For once, Rustam was glad he had not been born a noble: the responsibilities obviously had harsh results. Iain had recently ascended to Lordship of his Family, finally being deemed ready to take over from the estate's trustees. Now as a *younger* son one might have far more freedom...

"Lady Risada Delgano vas Domn!"

A hush fell as the crush of guests turned to stare up at the balcony. Ladies eyed their husbands in irritation before glancing upward themselves. What would she be wearing tonight? How would her hair be coifed? What jewels would grace her swan's neck?

Lady Risada glided to the top of the stair. She did not disappoint. Six years older than her brother Iain, she looked barely out of her teens, yet with an air of grace and maturity to which most Ladies aspired but never attained.

Dressed in ivory silk embroidered with gold and pearl beads, her pale hair rolled low to frame her oval face, she looked to be the queen the Kingdom yet lacked. Ladies sighed in admiration or envy, their Lords captivated by the most eligible and desirable woman in all Tyr-en.

A tug on Rustam's sleeve drew his attention back to the portly woman beside him. Lady Merisa Stormsel was not one to lose out on an evening's enjoyment and her plans included Rustam. "A trifle overdone, don't you feel?" she whispered sourly. "All that cream and gold. One might think she was the after dinner dessert!"

"I wouldn't mind a taste," muttered Rustam under his breath.

"I beg your pardon?"

"Oh, I agree absolutely, Lady Merisa. Simplicity is the essence of style."

"Quite so, Rustam." She patted his arm approvingly. "You have uncommon discernment for a Craft Master. Surely Lady Risada—ah, here comes the king, may Chel guard and guide him."

King Marten's entrance was as reverently received as Lady Risada's, though the quiet was broken by the rustle of expensive fabrics as the massed nobles of Tyr-en made obeisance to their young ruler. Privately, Rustam thought the king looked terrified, though he hid it well enough from all but a highly trained eye. Prince Halnashead stepped forward to greet his nephew, and led him away through the throng which quickly resumed its mind-numbing chatter.

Lady Merisa linked her arm through Rustam's and tugged, none too gently. "Listen Rustam, the orchestra is tuning up. Shall we make our way to the ballroom? No Ball would be complete without at least one dance with the Kingdom's finest, so I am forced to claim you now, before the more highly placed ladies come to command your attentions."

Rustam deftly disengaged his arm and made a slight, apologetic bow. "Alas, Lady Merisa, I shall be doing no dancing tonight."

"You jest, surely?" Merisa snapped, unaccustomed to having her wishes refused, and certainly not by one who was, after all, merely a dancing Master.

"Sadly no, my Lady. I took a fall from my horse not two days since, and I can barely walk yet, much less dance." He displayed his silver shod walking cane, chuckling inwardly at the frown of annoyance that marred Lady Merisa's chubby features. He had had cause to tutor the lady some months ago and was much relieved his toes were to be spared a repeat bruising. As for what else his duty had demanded of him during that time—he shuddered in remembrance.

"What's this I hear? Fallen off your horse, Chalice?"

Rustam's heart jolted, and he took care to school his expression before turning to answer Lord Herschel Fontmaness.

"Indeed, my Lord. During my return to Darshan following your excellent hospitality."

"Damned shame. Betha was so looking forward to dancing with you tonight. Evening Merisa."

"Good evening, Lord Herschel. Excuse me, Rustam. Perhaps we will have the chance at Winter Solstice?"

"I trust so, my Lady. Have a pleasant evening."

Lady Merisa's place at Rustam's side was quickly filled by the eager Lady Betha, whose pretty, childlike face fell in disappointment as her elderly husband informed her of Rustam's indisposition.

"I wish you'd travelled with us, Rusty. A carriage is so much safer than a horse!" The fragile Betha shivered at the very thought of riding such a dangerous beast.

"It was kind of you to offer, Lady Betha, but I needed to attend to some family business on my journey. It was an unfortunate accident."

A harassed-looking servant in Fontmaness's livery of green with yellow chevrons appeared out of the multitude at Lord Herschel's shoulder. "Pardon the intrusion, my Lord, but there is an urgent message from your estate."

Rustam's attention sharpened, though he let no more than mild curiosity show on his face. Lord Herschel took the parchment and peered short-sightedly at it. "Betha, my dear, read this for me, will you?" He handed the scroll to his wife.

"My Lord," read Betha, "I regret to inform you there has been an attempted burglary—"

"What!" roared Lord Herschel and snatched the scroll back. Holding it close to his face he scanned the writing, muttering to himself. Lady Betha glanced at Rustam, confusion in her eyes. "I don't understand; we've nothing of any real value. It's not as if we're a major House."

"My dear Lady Betha," said Rustam, "it may appear that way to you, but I'm afraid that to a guild-less outlaw even the most humble of your belongings would seem priceless."

"I suppose so," conceded Betha, not sounding convinced.

"Dear me, trouble at home, hmm?" interjected a new voice. Rustam moved to allow Prince Halnashead to join them.

"I fear we must leave, your Highness," said Lord Herschel. "I do hope you will not be offended."

"No, no. Of course not, Herschel. You must attend personally to such a disgraceful affair, and your lovely wife seems quite upset. I will provide an escort, if you wish?"

"You are too kind, Highness, but I fear it would serve little purpose. The thief is probably long gone, but it would be unthinkable for me to leave the investigation of this outrage to an underling."

"As you say. I trust nothing valuable is missing?"

Rustam's eyes sidled to the prince's face. Halnashead was enjoying every moment of Herschel's discomfort.

Herschel shifted uneasily. "I cannot say, Highness. It seems the thief only entered my study before being disturbed—"

Disturbed? Rustam thought. *That's a good tale from a bunch of inept guards.*

"—so he could not have had time to remove anything of great import."

Rustam smiled inwardly at the beads of sweat that had sprung out on Lord Herschel's brow. Halnashead beamed openly. "Good, good. Then off you go. And don't forget to comfort your delightful wife."

The prince kissed Betha's hand, and inclined his head to Herschel's bow. As Herschel turned to leave, Betha hesitated and crowded close to Rustam. Her slim fingers slipped a small scroll into his hand before she hurried after her husband's retreating back. She glanced back once, a tiny, conspiratorial smile on her delicate face. Then she vanished into the crowd. Rustam tucked the scroll up his sleeve, well aware that Halnashead had marked the exchange.

"Well, m'boy. That courier wasn't far behind you, was he? I trust you weren't followed here."

"Your Highness!" said Rustam indignantly, matching the prince's low voice. "You know me better than that. And if the Lady Betha suspects? Well, she can hardly tell her husband, can she?"

"I cherish your confidence, Rustam. Now, you haven't forgotten our meeting, have you?"

"As if I would. I'll be there."

"Good, good. See you later then." And the prince wandered away, calling loudly for another glass of wine.

Partner-less for the moment, and unlikely to be anything else if Merisa had spread the tale of his injury, Rustam limped through the crowded state chambers, drawn to the banquet hall by the delicious mingled aromas of roast poultry, baked fruits and pastries. He picked at the sumptuous buffet and meandered from group to group, ears open for any titbits of information. The scrutiny of the guards posted at intervals along the banner-draped walls, he ignored. Tonight their swords were ceremonial only, for to draw a weapon in the presence of royalty was to invite swift execution, and it had been many years since any House had made an overt play in the game. Not since the bungled Sencarten affair. Even though it had occurred years before Rustam's birth he knew the story, as did all players and nobles. The annihilation of everything to do with that misbegotten House, even to the razing of their manor, was a clear warning to any who might dare to move so openly against another House.

At least something good had come out of that dreadful business, mused Rustam as he perused the assembled nobles in all their finery. The current rounds of social gatherings had been instigated by the king at that time—Halnashead's great grandfather—to prevent his major Houses from hiding away inside their heavily guarded mansions, scheming against one another and splitting the countryside into miniature kingdoms that were all too often at war. The parties and fests obliged the Families to interact socially and maintain the standards of ethical niceties by which they were supposed to live.

Coincidentally, the new social structure had created vast opportunities for agents like Rustam, and the whole spy network had burgeoned until the noble Houses were awash with players. Information gleaning had become such a well realised art form that moves in the current phase of the game were more likely to be financial or face-saving than military, although it was not unheard of for a minor player to turn up dead once in a while.

Yet now it seemed one of the major Houses was preparing to move against the king. May, in fact, have been preparing for years. Rustam found himself struggling to believe that such a possibility could become reality.

Meandering amongst the trestle tables so artfully arranged with foods from each of the Five Kingdoms, Rustam popped another sweetmeat into his mouth and studied the little clusters of highborns; those members of the twenty major Houses who formed the highest levels of the nobility. Respectful circles of privacy surrounded each gathering, and Rustam could not help but covet their conversations. What treacheries did they plan? What secret coups were they celebrating? Which House was plotting treason?

Rustam loved the game—the intrigue, the danger, the thrill of being one step ahead of an opposing player. He had always known the part he would play, and the House that would command his loyalty. The prince had been good to him, even paying for his tutoring after his mother disappeared, but it was not the money which had bought his allegiance, it was the importance of working for the Royal House and so, in a way, for Tyr-en itself. Halnashead's players assured the security of the kingdom, and the Chalice family had long been his finest.

Other craft Masters and minor nobles drifted amongst the guests and eventually Rustam found a seat and settled down to watch their movements. Any one of them could be a spy like himself. Most probably were. And there were the servants too, many of whom had access to nobles of all classes. For a while, Rustam amused himself trying to figure out the identity of the assassin, Dart.

He wondered if it would be anyone he knew. Certainly to be effective Dart must be free to move in even the highest circles, so no mere Craft Master would fill the role. No, he was more likely to be a well-positioned servant, or just possibly a noble of one of the twenty Great Houses.

A bell rang once. Another hour still to go. Halnashead was certain Rustam would not deduce the assassin's identity, and Rustam respected the prince's judgement. With a wry smile he turned his attention to his surroundings, and checked that he was unobserved before slipping Betha's scroll out of his sleeve. He raised it to his nose. Sure enough, her favourite lavender perfume permeated the parchment and its lilac ribbon. Rustam smiled. If he had an oat for every one of these he had received, he could have fed Nightstalker for a month.

The contents were much as expected, although the young and apparently fragile Lady Betha obviously had more imagination than most. Perhaps the Fontmaness mansion would merit another visit after all.

Tucking Betha's letter safely back into his sleeve, Rustam became aware of a pair of gossiping Ladies seated in a nearby alcove. The acoustics of the Great Halls had been carefully considered during construction and a number of places existed where one could sit and hear conversations from further away than normal earshot. Out of habit Rustam had chosen to sit in such a spot.

He identified the tattlers as a pair of minor nobles, one of whom he had had the misfortune to be required to interact with in his professional capacity, early on in his career. Her sharp tongue showed no improvement.

"—of the Fifteenth, or should I now say, the Sixteenth House? Do tell all, my dear," invited her companion.

"Darling, you haven't heard yet? She's just given birth!"

Rustam could hear the malicious glee in the lady's tone, and pictured the nasty little smile that would go with it. Her friend was obviously shocked.

"But how could she? Her husband has been dead for over a year!"

"Ah yes, but she's taken no end of lovers since then. But can you imagine? How could anyone, even someone so witless, become pregnant by one of them and not do something about it? For Chel's sake, it's hard enough to keep a pregnancy even when you want it!"

Rustam winced in sympathy. Not for the Lady in question—he was in absolute agreement about her stupidity—but for her child, who throughout life would bear the appalling stigma of bastardy.

No woman should be that thoughtless.

In his mind, Rustam gazed up at a slim, elegant woman with long auburn ringlets that seemed to have a life of their own. He reached up with a four year old's pudgy hand to pull one and the woman laughed; a clear, bell-like sound engraved on his memory. She stooped to plant a kiss on the top of his head then turned away and walked out of his life forever.

Soria Chalice.

His mother.

"Wine, Master Chalice?"

Rustam glanced up, startled out of reverie. An exceptionally pretty girl wearing the low cut, puff-sleeved white blouse with the purple and white striped skirt of a royal servant stood in front of him, proffering a tray of drinks. He glanced appreciatively from her masses of fair curls down her trim figure and back up to her freshly scrubbed face.

"Thank you, but no," declined Rustam with regret, and raised his glass of fruit juice by way of explanation. "Achieving a drunken stupor on my own isn't quite my style."

"Do you have to be on your own?" the girl asked huskily, moving closer until her thigh brushed Rustam's knee.

He smiled. "Is that an offer?"

"Have you had a better one this evening?"

"I haven't had one at all. But, my dear, appealing though you make it sound, I fear I must decline."

The girl raised her chin and looked down at Rustam with an air of arrogance at odds with her position. "Oh? I'm not good enough for you?" she demanded.

"I have a reputation to maintain."

"So I've heard," she said acidly and moved away, casually kicking Rustam's walking cane well out of reach as she did so.

Rustam smiled to himself, and thanked a passing waiter who returned the cane. *I wonder who she works for, and what they want from me,* he mused. It was unusual for a woman to become a player, but even if the offer had been genuine, Rustam wasn't going to risk taking her up on it; consorting with a peasant serving girl, no matter how attractive, could tarnish his image irreparably.

He glanced around at the crowd. The multitude was beginning to thin out, the older and less energetic guests drifting homeward, or to one of the many guest rooms within the palace itself. Nearby, Rustam noticed the king, a youth barely old enough to grow a beard, hide a yawn behind his raised glass. Marten's brown hair was tousled and his eyes shadowed, yet he struggled to appear interested in the conversations around him. A great improvement on his late, wine-sodden father, thought Rustam.

The king's group was joined by a tall, fair-haired figure in unadorned maroon, and Rustam's distaste for the man turned his fruit juice bitter on his tongue.

Lord Melcard Rees-Charlay. If ever there was a candidate for Dart's attention, the ruling Lord of the Fourth House was surely it. Insular and secretive, Melcard always came out of awkward political incidents in ostensible support of the Royal Family, yet all the intelligence Halnashead could lay his hands on—pitifully little where Melcard was concerned—suggested that the Fourth House itself was more often than not the instigator of those very situations. Combined with the fact that Melcard's rivals always seemed to be the ones ruined or disgraced, there was little doubt of Melcard's mastery of the game.

Rustam's reasons were more personal: Melcard made his job harder. On more than one occasion it had taken Rustam far longer and every minim of his skills to win the confidence of ladies who had previously been courted by the older but still handsome Lord Melcard. Rustam had yet to draw out of any of them exactly what Melcard did to hurt them, but whatever it was, the marks he scored into their lives were slow to fade and Rustam doubted any of them would ever truly trust a man again.

He wondered if Melcard had been different before his wife and infant son died in childbed.

Drawing his attention back to the present, Rustam strained to hear Lord Melcard's words as Marten's already pale face turned white. He caught mention of King Saimund—Marten's father and a contemporary of Melcard's—and the words 'drunk' and 'wine'.

The bastard! Rustam felt his guts clench in impotent rage. Melcard was taunting the king about his father, in public, and with such a commiserative demeanour Marten could not even retaliate. Outraged but helpless, Rustam could only watch as the young monarch raised his chin defiantly, and endured the thinly veiled insults with all the dignity he could muster. As the other members of the group excused themselves with embarrassed faces, Rustam's eyes searched the hall for Halnashead, but Marten's salvation came unexpectedly in the form of a vision in ivory and gold that glided to his side amidst a cloud of exotic fragrance.

Lady Risada Delgano vas Domn exuded such an intoxicating air of vibrant sensuality that she drew others simply by her presence, and the flock of highborns that trailed endlessly in her wake spread quickly between Melcard and his victim. Rustam lost sight of Lady Risada's tall, elegantly dressed—despite Merisa's assertions—slender form until she emerged from the crowd with one arm linked through Marten's, leading her cousin towards the safety of Halnashead's company. As they passed close to Rustam, he heard the Lady's softly musical tones murmur words of comfort and encouragement to the humiliated king, and he watched in envy as her long, delicate fingers stroked Marten's tightly clenched fist.

Rustam drew a deep breath and tugged ineffectually at his highly starched collar. What he wouldn't give for just one night with the ravishing Lady Risada.

He smiled to himself and shook his head. One could always dream.

Rustam Chalice limped away down the long hall with the sound of refined gaiety at his back.

* * * * * * * * * * * *

At the second ring of the bell, Rustam knocked on the door to Halnashead's study. He glanced uneasily up and down the empty corridor. Where were the guards? Perhaps Halnashead had sent them away to protect Dart's identity, but the back of Rustam's neck prickled, and that was a warning sign he never ignored. He slipped his small dagger from its wrist sheath, and eased the door open. The room was mostly in darkness, with just a row of candles flickering on the front edge of the prince's substantial desk. There was someone behind the desk, though Rustam could not make out who stood there.

Wending his way between the high backed chairs and ornate tables that cluttered the main floor space of the study, Rustam trod as lightly as he could with his injured leg, balancing on the balls of his feet, prepared to dive for cover at the slightest hint of trouble. He held the walking cane poised in his left hand like a javelin ready to throw, the dagger nestling coldly in his other palm. His eyes roved the room for signs of a third person. If that was Halnashead behind the desk, then Dart could be anywhere. And if it wasn't...

With a rustle of ivory silk, the figure behind the desk sat down, bringing her face clearly into the candlelight. Rustam stopped in confusion, hastily lowered the cane to a more conventional position and made a small bow. "Your pardon, my Lady. The prince asked me to meet him here..."

Rustam's voice trailed off as the Lady Risada Delgano vas Domn laughed; a resigned, self-mocking sound.

"My Lady?"

Risada shook her head. "Ah, Chalice. I suppose it had to be you, with your pretty face and your courtly manners."

The study door opened, and Rustam spun around. Silhouetted against the light from the corridor was Halnashead's bulky figure. The prince shut the door and strode across the room. "Splendid," he said, rubbing his hands together. "I see you two have met at long last."

"What?" blurted Rustam, his famed manners deserting him. "You mean—"

Lady Risada vacated the prince's chair, and moved around the desk, preceded by her exotic perfume. Rustam's breathing became rapid, though whether in response to the heavy scent or the lady's proximity, he wasn't sure. Halnashead sat down and beamed at them.

"Dart, meet Charmer. Charmer, meet Dart."

Rustam looked pleadingly at Halnashead. "You're joking, surely? You must be. She can't be Dart; she's—"

"What?" cut in Lady Risada. "A woman?"

"No! Well, yes. I suppose so." Rustam shifted uncomfortably, his mind reeling as it tried to adjust to the concept of a noble*woman as* a player. Female servants on occasion, yes. But a *lady*?

He glanced aside at the lady in question. She stared coldly back.

"Please, please!" Halnashead drew their attention. "I want you two to get on with each other. Does it surprise you so much, Rusty?"

"*Rusty?*" echoed Lady Risada derisively.

Taken aback by the lady's obvious animosity, Rustam considered the prince's question. "I suppose it shouldn't. With her court position, the lady has access to all levels of nobility. Certainly a great asset to your Highness."

"And don't you forget it, dancer boy," muttered Risada.

Halnashead frowned. "Be nice, Risada. Rustam is my most skilled agent."

"Most skilled womaniser, you mean!"

"Risada, enough." Halnashead did not raise his voice, but his displeasure was clear. The corners of Rustam's mouth quirked up, but he quickly dropped the smirk when the prince scowled at him.

"You *will* get on with each other. This is a serious matter and you are both professionals; I expect you to behave as such. Now sit down. This could be a long meeting."

Rustam fetched two chairs while Risada stood stiffly, staring into the darkness behind Halnashead where the great tapestry hung. She took elaborate care to arrange her bulky skirts before sitting on the chair Rustam held for her, yet managed to ignore him utterly. Rustam shrugged to himself, and sat down to her right.

"Now, Risada. You know the background to this affair?" asked the prince.

"An interesting choice of words considering the company, but yes, I do."

"And you, Rustam. You've done much of the information gleaning. What you may not know is that a second vial of elixir has found its way into our possession this evening."

"From who?" queried Rustam.

"From a highborn noble of the Eighteenth House. Incidentally, Risada, we have since bought his loyalty."

"Will he stay bought?" asked the lady, sounding sceptical.

"I think so, yes. You see, he committed an indiscretion with a certain young lady of a higher family."

"One of yours, I assume."

"But of course." Halnashead beamed, his good humour returning. "My daughter, Annasala, as a matter of fact. It was good field experience for her."

Rustam stared in open astonishment. The princess too? To mention nothing of the fact that she was barely seventeen.

"You seem shocked, Rusty. Sala is a very confident young woman."

"I don't doubt it, Highness. I was merely surprised that you would choose to use her in such a capacity."

Halnashead laughed. "Rusty, I doubt anyone could use Sala in any capacity in which she didn't wish to be used. It was her suggestion."

"Oh."

"Might we get back to business?" enquired Risada rather tartly.

"Quite so, quite so. Unfortunately we are no closer to discovering the supplier of this substance. He meets with his clients only in a darkened room and speaks through a servant. As to the elixir itself, our alchemists have done some tests on the bottle you brought in, Rustam. So far all they can tell me is that the fluid is rich in iron, and that it has been distilled from a living creature—something quite unusual, possibly unique. Certainly nothing they have come across before."

"Any signs of magic?" queried Risada, her voice heavy with loathing at the idea of arcane involvement.

Halnashead shook his head. "Praise Chel, no. But it does give you two a starting point. This living source, whatever it is, must be tracked down. It must either be secured or destroyed."

"And that is why you want me," concluded the lady assassin as she inspected the set of perfectly shaped nails adorning the tips of her long, slender fingers. Rustam wondered how many lives had been terminated by those impeccably manicured hands.

"Indeed, my dear," confirmed the prince, "though a more pressing point prompted me to this decision even before we obtained a sample of elixir. The resolution of this matter may be crucial to the survival of the Royal Family. I am convinced that whoever is supplying this concoction is gathering money for military purposes, and it may become necessary to make immediate decisions in the field without the opportunity to refer back to me."

"And as I am cousin to the Royal House, you rely on my personal motivations to make the most advantageous decisions for both our families?"

"You see it truly, my dear."

"Excuse me," broke in Rustam. "Does this mean I'm working *for* the lady, rather than *with* her?"

Halnashead frowned slightly and propped his elbows on the desk, fingers steepled before his face. "In a sense, Rustam, yes. Risada is, after all, of the Second House. But I'm sure she won't interfere in your areas of expertise."

"I have no wish to come that close," said Risada, fixing Rustam with a warning glare. "My friends have warned me about you."

Thoroughly irritated, Rustam's mouth got the better of him. "You have *friends*?"

"That will do!" roared Halnashead, his open palms slapping heavily onto the desktop. "Rusty, I tolerate a fair degree of familiarity from you because it amuses me to do so, but you will remember Lady Risada's position." He frowned at them both. "You are my two best operatives and I'm relying on you."

"Sorry."

"I apologise."

"Good. That's settled then. I don't expect to hear any more bickering from either of you." The prince folded his arms over his belly and Rustam knew he would brook no further indiscipline.

"Your Highness, does the king know of this matter?" Risada enquired.

"No. And I don't intend that he should until it is resolved."

"Surely—"

"Risada, I have been in charge of royal security since before you were born. My brother was a fool and our father a tyrant. So far, Marten is neither. But he is beginning to learn about the game and to develop his own moves. Only ten days ago we uncovered an agent of his within my own staff."

Risada raised a delicately arched eyebrow.

"Oh, I've left the man where he is," Halnashead continued. "It gives me the opportunity to feed the information I want to Marten without him realising. But the point is, if he found out about the elixir, he could start interfering and that might prove disastrous for such an infant player."

"Not to mention for us," muttered Rustam.

"So where do we begin?" Risada asked, ignoring him.

"We know the elixir is coming from one of the more highly placed Families, yes? So. The annual round of Family fests begins shortly. It has been on my mind for some time to send Annasala as our representative on the circuit this year, but as she is still of tender age, she will require a chaperon."

Risada folded her long white hands demurely in her lap. "A cousinly chaperon, I presume."

"Precisely, my dear. And Rusty, m'boy; it's time your social standing moved up a notch. I fancy Sala to be in need of her own personal Dancing Master. What do you say?"

"Your Highness, how could I say anything but yes?"

"You couldn't, of course, but I'd like to know you won't consider it an onerous duty, with Sala being so young."

"Rest easy, your Highness. Princess Annasala must have the best, so no other would do."

Rustam noticed Risada's eyes roll upward. Well, there was no point being modest when it was the truth.

"Fine, fine. We are agreed. It is imperative that you locate this living source and deal with it, one way or another. As I see it, this is the best possible opportunity we have for a thorough investigation of all twenty Families."

Risada frowned. "I'm reluctant to be away from Domn—from Iain—for so long, but I see no suitable alternative. And I suppose it will provide further opportunity to screen the Families for signs of the Bastard's presence."

"My thoughts also," agreed Halnashead, and Rustam's mind flicked over the quest that had been ongoing for longer than he had been alive—the search for the rumoured third son of Halnashead's father, King Belcastas. Hints and whispers kept the hunt alive, and whilst no firm evidence for the Bastard's existence had ever been found, the possibility of a hidden pretender to the throne was too great a threat to ignore.

"And now," said Lady Risada, "If you will excuse me, I must return to my brother."

"Go on, go on. We can discuss this at greater length with Sala. I'll arrange a meeting."

Lady Risada stood, smoothed the many layers of her gown, and then swept to the door amid the rustle of silk and a trailing waft of scent. "Good night, cousin. Master Chalice."

The prince inclined his head. Rustam rose hastily and bowed, but she was gone before he straightened.

"Well, Rusty, were any of your guesses near the mark?"

Rustam shook his head. "No, Highness, but I should have known. There's nothing more dangerous than a beautiful woman."

3. FEST

The elaborate mansion of Rees-Charlay, home to the Fourth
Family of Tyr-en, sprawled comfortably in a fertile valley in the
foothills of the Aeron Mountains. To the west, the taller
snow-capped peaks of the Middle Mountains could be seen rising
above the pine forests that filled the intervening land, while beyond
the screening northern hills, rich tracts of arable land lay fallow
after the summer's harvest.

Today, the mansion's extensive grounds swarmed with guests
and servants, musicians and entertainers. Trestle tables dotted the
lawns, heaped with the sorts of delicacies only the wealthiest of
Families could provide and with crystal goblets of wine in all shades
from palest amber to deep ruby. Tonight, the fest hosted by Lord
Melcard would culminate with the Grand Ball, but for now the
guests took their ease in the beautifully tended formal gardens, or in
the opulent apartments provided for each of the visiting Families.

Midmorning sun slanted through the tall windows of the
practice hall to cast broad bands of light across the polished wooden
floor and enrich the sweet smell of freshly applied ondal oil. The
small orchestra of ten squinted in the bright light that bounced off
their burnished instruments and the brass buttons of
Rees-Charlay's maroon livery. Their be-whiskered conductor
divided his attention between his sheet music and the sole couple
on the dance floor. The man—an exquisite dancer, noticed the
conductor with approval—was clad totally in the season's latest
shade of powder blue while his partner, daintily attired in a

full-skirted gown of peach trimmed with gold, seemed about to lose her balance.

The music built to a crescendo. Rustam winced as the heel of Princess Annasala's shoe stamped hard on his instep. Sala jumped back, hands flying up to cover her mouth.

"Oh Rusty, I'm sorry!"

Rustam sighed, unable to decide whether Halnashead's daughter was laughing or dismayed behind the concealing hands. "How is it," he complained, "that one of your undoubted talent with a fencing blade can be so clumsy with simple footwork?"

The hand dropped away and Annasala burst into laughter. "Oh Rusty, you look so serious! No, don't take offence, please." With an effort the princess controlled herself, took a deep breath. "It has to do with which I find more interesting. Now, if you were teaching me a new fencing move—"

"But I'm not, Sala. I'm here to teach you to dance delightfully so that any man you set your eye upon will be powerless to resist you."

A breath of cool air warned Rustam that someone had entered the practice hall, and the heady floral scent it carried told him who. Glancing over his shoulder, he saw the Lady Risada bearing down on them. As usual she looked stunning, today in a gown of rose pink that set off her pale honey coloured hair and the flowers woven into it.

"Master Chalice," she hissed. "Kindly remember who your pupil is, and show her the respect due her position."

"But Risada—" began Sala in protest.

"I'm sorry, Annasala, but it's important for a servant not to become overly familiar."

Abruptly Risada turned to consider the orchestra, her attention lingering overlong upon the conductor—Rustam had noticed that the Lady of Domn bore a fascination for men with beards, and wondered if he should try growing one—before waving a languid hand in dismissal.

When they were gone, she beckoned the others closer. "Must I remind you that anyone could be a player? There must be no suspicion that you are anything other than princess and tutor. Sala, you are young, but your father is relying on you to play the game as a trained professional. Chalice should know better."

Gritting his teeth, Rustam bit off the retort that threatened to leap out of his mouth and drop him even further in Risada's estimation. If that was possible.

Instead, he bowed and asked, "Lady Risada, was there something you wanted?"

"It is time for Her Highness to come and choose a gown for the ball tonight and you, I believe, have a liaison to keep with a certain lady of the Third House."

"Not another one," groaned Rustam.

"What's the matter, Chalice—can't stand the pace?" queried Risada with a venomous smile.

Rustam treated her to his best pained expression. "Not at all, my dear Lady Risada, it's just such a bore; they're all so tediously similar I tend to forget which ones I've bedded before and which I haven't."

"Just don't get their names wrong!" snapped Risada and whirled around, her many layered silk skirts rustling like a hive of angry bees. She swept to the door then paused, looking back. "As soon as you've bathed, Annasala, attend me in your dressing room."

"Yes, cousin," said Sala with a dutiful curtsy. When Risada was gone, she rolled her eyes skyward. "Not another ball!" she moaned.

"At least you have the afternoon to relax," Rustam pointed out. "Think of me, wearing myself out in the pursuit of my duties."

Sala chuckled. "You can't tell me you don't enjoy it."

Rustam grimaced and glanced around the empty hall, half his mind trying to work out the acoustics of the high ceilinged construction while the other half considered the vivacious young princess beside him. "Sala, you've got a lot to learn about this business." He shrugged. "But then again, you're a woman; perhaps it's different for you."

"Meaning?"

"I don't know. I'm not a woman. I don't understand women; never have."

"We're not so different, Rusty."

"No? Well, anyway, I have to go. Mustn't keep Lady Denia waiting, must I?"

He bowed and turned to go, but Sala snagged his arm. He looked down at the girl. Her slender figure was frail compared to her father's bulk, yet her round face showed all the same features, and the strength in her grey eyes equalled his. Heavily waved brown tresses fell to her waist and Rustam found himself wanting to stroke them, as he would the coat of a beautiful horse. He shook his head, bemused by his sudden desire to protect this girl—woman, he reminded himself—from the ugly realities of survival in Tyr-enese society.

"Walk with me, Rusty. Later, in the gardens."

He made his most courtly bow. "Your Highness, it will be a pleasure."

* * * * * * * * * * * * * *

Lady Denia stretched lazily across the cream silk sheets of her huge bed and gazed hungrily up at Rustam. "I trust I shall see you again, Rustam? At Highmeadows, for Lord Banar's fest?"

"Nothing could keep me away, my beauty," Rustam declared, bending down to fasten his shoes. "Except perhaps that brute of a husband of yours."

The lady pouted slightly. "Rupet's not so bad you know. Oh, he's nothing compared to you, lover. Let's face it, nobody compares to you. Annasala's a lucky girl."

Rustam straightened. "Princess Annasala is my pupil," he corrected sharply. "Besides, she's little more than a girl."

"And you like your women a trifle more—mature," purred Denia, running her hands over her amply endowed, naked body.

"As you say," Rustam murmured and bent over to stroke the smooth, milky white skin of Denia's breasts. Her perfume mingled enticingly with the musky scent of sex, and Rustam's breathing quickened as he planted a swift kiss on each jutting nipple. Denia curled up with a delighted giggle, and then snared Rustam's hand as he tried to move away. "Annasala doesn't know what she's missing, but what of Risada?"

Gently, Rustam pried Denia's fingers open. "Risada? She thinks I'm something that crawled out from under a sundial."

"Then she's a frigid fool. Rustam darling, are you certain you have to go now?"

Rustam bowed and let himself out of the bedchamber. Denia's maid discreetly averted her eyes as he crossed the reception chamber and slipped out of the guest suite.

Preparations were in full swing for the ball that night, and Rustam mingled easily with the crowds of busy retainers rushing to and fro in the corridors. As he made his way back to his own somewhat simpler rooms, he considered Denia's words.

Risada, frigid? Unlikely. She could turn her charm on and off at will, and Rustam doubted it failed when the bedchamber door was closed. A fool? No. And Denia was a fool to think so.

He turned a corner into a quieter quarter of the house. As he approached the end of the corridor he shifted onto the balls of his feet, stepping lightly, making no sound as he neared his own rooms. He grimaced slightly as the skin pulled tight across the bite scars on his leg. Too much exercise and too little time spent caring for one of his greatest assets. He made a mental note to arrange for a full body massage as soon as this ball was over.

A careful inspection of the door to his modest apartment found the two hairs he had stuck in place earlier—one across the handle and one high up, stretching between the lintel and the door itself—still in place. He relaxed, reassured that no one had entered the rooms while he was away.

Rustam washed and changed, critically inspecting his image in a looking glass before leaving to meet Sala for the promised stroll around the gardens. Not for the first time he wondered how different his life would have been had he been born with a plain, or even an ugly face. No matter how beautifully he danced, it was his boyish good looks rather than his figure that endowed him with his attractive power. What would he do when his charm grew too old? He ran a hand through his thick, dark locks and laughed at himself. He was twenty years old; plenty of time to worry about the future.

He turned side on to the glass. Was he putting on weight? It would hardly be a surprise considering how many banquets he had attended recently. What was this—the fourteenth? No, the fifteenth fest of the tour. And not a taste of elixir yet. Well, there were only five left to go, and one of those was the Royal House. That left few possibilities. Perhaps tonight, with Chel's good favour, they might strike fortune.

Sucking in his belly, Rustam tightened his belt an extra hole and turned to leave. He paused just inside the door, and plucked two hairs from the crown of his head. He winced and looked back at the glass: any signs of balding? No, not yet. But at this rate....

He shook his head. Bald was preferable to dead, and this trick had saved his skin before now. Perhaps he should try saving the hairs and re-using them. He smiled self-mockingly and opened the door.

Stepping through, he glanced left and right, but the corridor was empty. Deftly he moistened the handle and door frame with spittle and stuck the hairs in place. Then he assumed the swaggering walk so readily associated with him and made his way to the sumptuous apartment provided for the royal guest.

Guards snapped to attention as he approached, but before he could enter the door opened and Sala, resplendent in green and gold with matching parasol, swept out. Rustam offered his arm and at a leisurely pace they made their way along a sun spangled corridor towards the gardens. Walking with one hand cupped against the side of his face saved Rustam from being unsighted each time they passed one of the huge windows, but even so he and the princess nearly blundered into the short, black clad figure of Doctor Hensar, Lord Melcard's personal physician.

Amongst other things, Rustam thought to himself, recalling a number of unpleasant rumours.

"I'm so sorry!" Annasala backed up two steps and crowded close to Rustam. It was the first time he had seen the princess's composure rattled.

"Your Highness." Hensar bowed obsequiously. "Please, do not apologise; the fault was all mine." The corners of his fleshy lips lifted in a smile that made Rustam's skin crawl. The doctor reached for Annasala's hand, apparently intent upon kissing it, but the princess kept her fingers laced tightly together around Rustam's arm. Hensar allowed his hand to drop, his broad shoulders lifting in a small shrug.

"Until tonight then, Your Highness. Master Chalice." He bowed again and as he inclined forward, Rustam's eyes were dazzled by scintillating shards of light refracted through the crystal pendant hanging around the doctor's neck. Rustam blinked to clear the afterimage.

Annasala tugged him back into motion. "Ugh!" She shuddered, and added in a low voice, "I have no idea why, but that midget makes my body want to climb out of its skin. He's even creepier than his master."

"Melcard?" said Rustam in surprise. "Don't you find him attractive? He's almost as handsome as me, surely?"

Annasala punched him playfully on the arm. "Nobody is as handsome as you, silly; all the girls know that." She paused, considering. "You speak truly, though. Melcard is handsome. But his eyes, ugh!" She shuddered. "There's something unclean about the way they undress you, yet at the same time they're utterly passionless."

The doors to the garden balcony opened before them, and the princess practically dragged Rustam out into the fresh air. She paused at the top of the steps, apparently surveying the scenery and took a deep, cleansing breath.

"Shall we?" she invited as though nothing had disturbed her, and descended the stair. Rustam followed her lead.

Other couples and some small groups of unattached ladies strolled about the grounds, or sat on blankets on the lawns. Politely they bowed their heads as Annasala passed by, and she smiled graciously back.

Deliberately ignoring the glances directed his way, some envious, some pretending at a hauteur he knew would vanish if he danced with them that night, Rustam gazed beyond the magnificent gardens to the nearby foothills clothed in the last flush of autumnal grass. He and the princess strolled in companionable silence across the formal lawns and on, following closely clipped walkways threading between bushes and shrubs before emerging finally into open parkland.

Sala tugged gently on his arm to gain his attention. "Alone at last!" she declared.

"Indeed, Your Highness," replied Rustam guardedly. Sala fixed him with an imperious glare no less effective than her father's, for all that it came from a slight, seventeen year old girl.

"And what is wrong with that, Master Chalice? Don't tell me you're afraid I might try to seduce you? I had very strict instructions on that point from my father before ever we left Darshan."

"Aren't you worried someone might notice we've vanished? Rumours—"

"Rusty, please!" Sala broke in. "The rumours began the moment my father engaged you. Why, I've even been asked if you're as good as your reputation! I hardly think that walking alone with you in the gardens is going to cause any scandal. Besides, it's good to get away from everyone once in a while."

"And what do you suppose Risada will say?"

"Nothing she hasn't said already," Sala replied with a shrug. She patted Rustam's hand. "As a matter of fact, it's Risada I want to talk to you about."

"Oh?"

"Yes. She's afraid of you, you know. That's why she's so hostile."

"Oh, come on Sala—the woman despises me."

Annasala shook her head, her face a study of patient understanding, as though she tried to explain something simple to a rather slow child. "You're wrong, Rusty. It's your easy way with women that frightens her. She's afraid she might fall for your charms despite herself, and Risada's terrified of losing control. It's all to do with what happened to her when she was a child—she's been in control of everything since her parents were murdered. Until recently, that is, with Iain becoming Lord of the House. I don't think she finds that easy to accept, you know. It's certainly thrown her fully into her work. Have you noticed how she scrutinises every man with a beard? She's looking for the assassin. Her mother cut him on the jaw with her knife before he killed her and Risada's looking for the scar."

Out with the beard growing idea then.

Rustam put a hand to Annasala's arm and stopped her. The flow of words ceased abruptly.

"Has she actually said any of this to you?"

Sala glared at him. "No, she hasn't, but I'm not imagining things. Charin's teeth! What do you think I am—a dreamy child?"

Rustam studied the princess's stormy grey eyes—so like Halnashead's—then turned away. "Women!" he grated. They always had a way to twist things around to their own advantage, to make it seem like you were the unreasonable one.

Sala turned to face him. "Just what is it with you and women, Chalice? You court us and bed us like a gentleman, but you really can't stand us, can you?"

"You wouldn't understand. You're too—"

"Too what? Too young?"

Rustam could hear the royal temper rising and reminded himself of Annasala's rank. "I'm sorry, Your Highness. I didn't mean to imply—"

"Of course you didn't, Master Chalice," Sala said in a sickly sweet tone. "But don't try your charms on me—I'm immune. And remember what I've said when you're next at each other's throats. Your lack of focus on the situation at hand could be enough to kill us all."

With that, Sala turned on her heel and strode back towards the house with Rustam trailing in her wake. Whispers and titters followed them as they proceeded across the lawns, all eyes upon the enraged princess and her dancing Master.

As Sala swept up the steps to the open garden doors, a hand snagged Rustam's sleeve.

"Turned her down, did you Rustam? Poor child," murmured the Lady Denia.

"That's all I need," muttered Rustam as he hurried after Sala's retreating back, but the doors to the royal suite slammed in his face, and he could see the guards struggling to contain their mirth. He did not deign to glare at them, but turned away with what dignity he could muster and marched out to the stables to see Nightstalker. She might have mareish moods, but at least he understood her.

And she never answered back.

* * * * * * *

Feeling much calmer after grooming the now gleaming black mare, Rustam made his way back to his rooms. As he walked, he puzzled over Sala's motives.

Admittedly the girl was still young and lacking real life experience, but he would be a fool to discount her words entirely. She had been tutored by the best in the kingdom, both socially and clandestinely. Was she trying her hand at romantic matchmaking? Or was she really trying to make some sort of peace between himself and Risada for the good of the mission? After all, it was the survival of Sala's House that was at stake.

Or had she really meant what she said? Rustam found that hard to believe, but determined to be less provocative at his next encounter with Risada and see what transpired.

Instinctively Rustam moved into his silent step, pausing to inspect the door before opening it.

The hair across the handle was still in place, though it looked to have slipped. The one above was missing.

Rustam stood, breathing lightly. Was someone still inside? He listened for a while but heard nothing. Perhaps the intruder had been and gone, but he was taking no chances; whoever it was had been professional enough to spot one hair even if they had missed the other. If they were waiting inside for him, they would not be about to give him warning.

Rustam slipped his knife from its wrist sheath, and took a deep breath. Flexing his muscles in preparation, he focused his thoughts in the peculiar fashion that seemed to be the exclusive preserve of the Chalice family. His mind shifted into high speed.

As the world around him seemed to slow to a crawl, Rustam lunged forward.

The door sprang open and Rustam shot through at floor level, coiled into a rolling ball. He fetched up behind a heavy sofa he had positioned earlier for just such a manoeuvre, and quickly scanned the room. A shadow moved in one corner.

"Well done, Chalice. I'm impressed," said Lady Risada.

"You could be dead!" spat Rustam, his senses snapping abruptly—and painfully—back into normal time.

He picked himself up off the floor and dusted himself down. Another outfit for the laundry, he thought in annoyance.

"Oh, I doubt that. You were too keen to see who it was. If I'd been acting in my official capacity, you would be the corpse."

Ready with a sharp retort, Rustam stopped himself, recalling his resolve of only moments earlier. "My Lady." He bowed. "To what do I owe the pleasure?"

Risada stepped out of the corner and shook out her voluminous skirts. The fragrance of spring flowers preceded her as she crossed the room, and Rustam could not help but compare her coldly perfect beauty with the lush ripeness of Denia. He had the uncomfortable feeling that Risada was likening him to something less favourable.

She stopped and eyed him suspiciously. "Business, Chalice. Something to which you should be attending more often."

Again Rustam bit back the words that sprang to mind. Then his attention sharpened. "You've discovered something?"

"Yes. While you were enjoying yourself, I was entertaining Lady Chayla to luncheon. I made the usual moans about the passing of years—"

"And she took the bait."

Risada paused just long enough to make her annoyance at his interruption evident before continuing. "She did. She was very careful not to say anything too plainly, but she implied that she might be able to supply me with something known to stave off the effects of age. She also hinted that it was likely to be *very* expensive.

"So how do we proceed?"

"Chayla was going to speak to her husband. I propose we keep a close watch on him and see if we can get any nearer to the source."

"But you can't be the one to do the watching."

Risada raised an eyebrow. "My! That brain of yours can actually focus on something other than your appearance or your next conquest. No—" She held up a hand to silence him. "I apologise for those comments. I've never known Halnashead to be wrong, so I suppose I must trust his judgement of you regardless of my own opinion.

"As you say, I cannot be the one; our target will be watching for such a move from one so close to the Royal House. But you, as a mere craft Master, would be beneath his notice. Chayla was meeting with your Lady Denia before returning to her suite, so she has probably just spoken with Ranjit now. If you pick him up when he leaves their rooms we may, with Chel's favour, uncover his contact."

Rustam raised his hands in mock horror. "Now? Just look at me: I'm covered in dust!"

"Well brush it off, you popinjay! Here, turn around."

Rustam turned as Risada stepped forward, but instead of stopping he spun on round and caught her by one wrist. Their eyes locked, their faces so close Rustam could almost taste her lips.

"Don't play games with me again, Lady Risada," he warned. "You might not be so fortunate next time."

Risada's lips curved venomously upward. "Nor might you, Chalice. Look down."

Keeping a tight grip on Risada's wrist, Rustam obeyed. Her other hand was at his side and in it, a needle. Poison tipped for certain. He smiled sweetly back. "Then we might both lose out, my Lady."

As he spoke, Rustam delicately pricked her skin with the tip of the small dagger he held against her throat. "Impasse, I would say. Wouldn't you agree?"

The door burst open and the two combatants leapt back. Sala strode in and slammed it behind her. She glared at them. "Might I be the one to remind the two of you that we're here on a serious matter? If you want to kill each other just leave it until we're finished. I'll even furnish the weapons."

"Your Highness—"

"Annasala—"

The princess shook her head. "Leave it for now. I've just witnessed, quite by accident, a meeting between Lord Ranjit and our host. It seems Lord Melcard can supply something you want, cousin."

"Elixir!" breathed Risada and Rustam together.

"Ah, unity at last!" observed Sala facetiously. "I only hope it lasts. Melcard has sent for his personal physician. I suggest someone follows them."

* * * * * * *

Seven nights earlier....

Prince Halnashead ran both sets of fingers through his greying hair as he read the newly delivered scroll. His gold and onyx signet ring gleamed dully from the depths of the grizzled strands.

Dench studied his prince critically. Were those new lines of strain around Halnashead's eyes, or was it just the study's flickering candlelight that made him look so tired? As the prince's most trusted guard, Dench was used to seeing more than just the public face of his master. Of late, the divergence between the public and the private had widened drastically until Prince Halnashead and Halnashead, Chief of Security for Tyr-en, were increasingly different people.

Much of the change, Dench believed, was courtesy of the rising frequency of hints about the Bastard's whereabouts, and the growing reliability of the sources from whence those hints came. Dench knew that for years the Royal Family had hoped the rumours of a further son of King Belcastas to be false. Apparently they needed to revise that desire.

None of this showed in Halnashead's flinty grey eyes when he finally looked up. Dench was struck, as always, by the strength of purpose in that gaze, but now there was something else—a curious relief.

"Highness?"

"It begins at last, Dench." Halnashead leaned back and stretched his arms above his head, arching his back until his belly pressed forward and met the edge of the desk. His belt buckle shone momentarily, and then vanished as he sat forward.

"Someone has made the first move: Tylocian troops are reported descending the mountains."

"Anything to do with *him*?" asked Dench.

Halnashead shrugged in reply. "Tyloc is certainly where the most recent intelligence places the Bastard, but if this is his move?" The prince shook his head. "Whoever has been gathering funds for mercenaries is working within one of the major Families and considering the extent of the plot I am fairly certain this is a move by an entire House. It could be on behalf of him, but that is not the impression I've formed." He shrugged again. "Of course, I could always be wrong."

Dench shook his head once, firmly, in negation. "That's an extremely rare occurrence, Highness, and this is not the time to be entertaining self-doubt."

Tyr-en's Chief of Security glanced up in surprise at the familiarity of his servant's words, and Dench held himself ready to be reprimanded. But he stood by his speech. Now was not the time for Halnashead to begin questioning himself.

Apparently the prince agreed, for a wry smile touched his lips, reaching just to the corners of his eyes. "Perhaps you speak truly, Dench, and I thank you for your confidence in my abilities, but just now it matters little precisely who is behind this move. My first task is to decide how to respond, and for that I need to consult with others."

Throughout the night, Dench watched a steady stream of people come and go past his station beside Halnashead's study door. Finally, just before daybreak, a number of couriers arrived to take the prince's orders to their intended destinations. When only one remained, Halnashead called him in.

The prince looked up as Dench approached the desk.

"I recall you mentioning a courier arrived from one of the minor Rees-Charlay holdings. Is he still here?"

Dench nodded. "I put him in one of the waiting rooms. I expect he's asleep."

"Fetch him, would you, there's a good fellow."

The courier was indeed asleep, but responded quickly to the summons and appeared only a trifle crumpled as he delivered his scroll to the prince. Halnashead dismissed him with orders to take himself off to a proper bed.

52 Deborah Jay

Once the man was gone, the prince scanned the message and smiled grimly. "At least this gives me the excuse I need to send a messenger to Rees-Charlay." He called in the remaining royal courier. "You will deliver two messages. Publicly, you are to convey my condolences to Lord Melcard upon the death of his cousin, Mendel, in such a tragic accident. The coastal seas are not the safest place for pleasure yachting.

"You will also pay your respects to my daughter and, only when you are alone, give her this," the prince held up a scroll sealed with his personal device. "And this." So saying, he slipped the heavy gold and onyx signet ring from his index finger and dropped it into a velvet pouch. Both items disappeared inside the courier's tunic whilst the prince wrote a brief letter to the bereaved House Senior and sealed it with the royal crest. He inserted the roll of paper into an official message tube and handed it over.

"Goddess speed you," he bade. "Yours may be the most important message of this night's work."

They all knew he was not referring to the scroll intended for Melcard.

As the courier left the room, Dench turned to follow. He had made no more than two steps when Halnashead recalled him. He hesitated, turning reluctantly. "Come here, man," demanded Halnashead. "There's more to be done before this night reaches its weary conclusion."

Obediently, Dench retraced his steps to his master's desk. Obedient, but frustrated.

He had had private business with that courier, business he really needed to attend to. And now the man would be gone with no chance to intercept him before he left the palace grounds.

4. ELIXIR

Rustam stepped softly along the dark, musty passageway. Behind him Risada moved noiselessly. No rustling from this gown, Rustam noted with approval.

Ahead of them, in the secret interior of the Rees-Charlay mansion, Lord Melcard and his personal physician strode purposefully along the ill-lit corridor.

Moments before, Rustam's skills with a lock pick had been tested. Feeling patiently for the delicate trip of the locking mechanism, he'd thanked Chel that the demands of the fest engendered an absence of guards. Despite the extra staff drafted in for this busy time not even Melcard had, or dared show he had, sufficient retainers to waste precious manpower on guarding a locked door.

Must have been much harder for my profession in the old days, back on home continent, thought Rustam. Imagine having an unlimited supply of men instead of having to use each one for at least three jobs.

He whispered the same prayer now, as they traversed the empty corridors with their unwitting guides drawing them on by the sound of their voices—voices which abruptly drew closer. At the next junction of corridors Rustam stopped and knelt down, peered around the corner at ankle height, quickly withdrew. Just around the corner, beneath one of the infrequent torches, stood Melcard and Hensar, glaring at each other.

"You must let him rest!" protested Hensar in a low voice. "He could die if you insist on so much so soon after the last time."

"But I must have an ampoule tonight," insisted Melcard. "I have a very important client: a very *wealthy* client."

Rustam glanced round at Risada; in the gloom he could just make out her tiny smile of triumph. Footsteps sounded on the stone flags and Rustam risked another peep. Melcard and the grumbling doctor had moved further along the passage to another closed door. This particular door was distinguished by the presence of a uniformed guard whom Melcard addressed.

Rustam was too far away to hear the words, but he flinched back sharply as the man left his post and turned towards their concealed position. Straightening to face Risada, Rustam raised one finger, indicated approach, and slid a hand across his throat. Risada nodded her understanding. As the footsteps approached, Rustam's wrist dagger slid smoothly into his hand. A quick glance showed something small, and no doubt deadly, in Risada's fingers.

All unknowing how closely he passed death by, the fortunate guard walked straight along the corridor, not taking the side turn that concealed the interlopers.

When his footsteps had faded away to nothing, and no more sounds invaded the silent passage, Rustam crouched down again and sneaked another look. The corridor was empty. He sidled around the corner, Risada close on his heels. The previously guarded door stood closed and locked.

"They went in?" whispered Risada. Rustam shrugged for answer. "Open it," the lady ordered.

This deep inside the mansion's interior the silence was so profound that Rustam winced at the tiny noise of the tumblers falling into place. The door opened onto the top of a flight of downward spiralling steps. A rank, stale smell wafted up the stairwell and Rustam quickly pinched his itching nose between finger and thumb to stop from sneezing. Lamplight bobbed faintly below them and Risada pushed past him, descending after it. Expecting a waft of floral perfume, Rustam was gratified to smell nothing. A true professional, this lady, even if she was an arrogant vixen. He paused to shut the door behind them, careful not to trip the lock, and then followed the lady on down.

Two turns of the stairs down he came upon a stationary Risada. He put one hand to the slimy damp brickwork to steady himself, and craned over her head to get a clear view of what lay below. The cavern appeared to be a natural formation, the rough rock walls throwing jagged shadows in the light of two torches set in sconces at the foot of the stair. Beyond that, the moving light of Melcard's lantern revealed more detail and Rustam felt his eyes widen in disbelief.

Metal bars fronted a cell that occupied almost the entire cavern – an area about the size of one of Rees-Charlay's better guest apartments and furnished to resemble just that. Some years ago the prison would have been extremely comfortable, luxurious even. Now, though, the draperies were faded and shabby, and everything lay beneath a thick layer of dust. Melcard put his lantern down on a table by the further wall beside a bed.

An *occupied* bed.

A bony, ragged figure with long pale hair lay huddled in the middle of a filthy bedspread. It barely raised its head as Melcard came to stand over it.

"It stinks down here, Hensar!" complained Lord Melcard. "Where's the maid?"

"Don't you remember, my Lord? She wanted to leave the job so you let her. Permanently."

"Haven't you replaced her yet? Someone has to look after him."

"It's not easy, my Lord. We've used up all that type of girls for one task or another. The rest all have family to ask after them."

"You'll just have to look further afield then, Hensar. Now get on with it; I have a fest to oversee."

The doctor put his case down beside the lantern and began to unpack his instruments. The bundle of limbs and rags on the bed subsided into renewed indifference. Something flashed in the doctor's hand as he shuffled over to the figure and tied a tight rope around his victim's upper arm. The light flashed again and Rustam realised it was a blade at the same moment as the doctor nicked open a vein.

That elicited a small whimper of protest and Hensar signalled Melcard to hold the arm still while he positioned a small glass jar beneath the trickle of blood. It dried up quickly and Hensar swore.

"You see? He barely has any left to give."

"That's not enough," observed Melcard coldly.

"I know, I know," mumbled the doctor as he made a second, deeper cut.

"N'more, no!" moaned the now writhing figure. Lord Melcard held tightly to the arm while Hensar determinedly collected his gory prize. When they were finished, the doctor bandaged the wounds, and then lifted the lantern so he could examine the figure more closely. He dragged the filthy, matted hair back from the gaunt face and Rustam could at last see clearly.

Lord Melcard's prisoner looked as though he might be young—he was certainly beardless—but the features were too pinched and the growth of hair so extensive it was difficult to be sure. His eyes were squeezed shut against the harsh lantern light and the skin looked sallow, even greenish. He moaned again and turned his face away protesting the light, but Hensar reached out and caught a handful of hair, jerking him back again.

Rustam frowned. There was something odd about the man's head: something sticking up out of the mats of hair at the sides. Something like—*tall, tapering ears.* Rustam's mind balked. *I don't believe this, it can't be true*, wheedled a plaintive voice in the back of his head. He felt Risada stiffen in front of him and knew that she, too, had seen.

They had their answer at last. The elixir of eternity was blood drained from an elf.

Rustam's time-sense flickered and the world slowed in response to his shock. He forced himself to look again in the desperate hope he had been mistaken but his breath died in his throat as his eyes met with those of the elf, staring straight back at him. The dungeon around them vanished, the damp brick walls of the stairwell receding to leave Rustam floating in a sea of nothingness. There was only himself and those eyes; pale blue, almost silver, begging with him, pleading...

The clang of metal brought him back to himself. Risada nudged him hard in the ribs and he turned, hurrying up the stairs as quietly as he could, flickering lamplight at his back. He pushed the door at the top hard, hoping to surprise anyone standing outside, but the passage was empty and, as soon as Risada was out, he snicked the door shut, allowing the lock to catch.

Two steps into their retreat the sound of marching boots beat a rhythm towards them. They turned and fled in the opposite direction, deeper into the labyrinthine interior of the mansion.

Sconces bearing lit torches became more frequent. As did guards.

"Looks like Halnashead guessed truly," hissed Rustam. "Melcard's hiding a small army in here."

"A few guards do not constitute an army, Chalice," corrected Risada. "But he does seem to have an excess of men beyond those we have been permitted to see." Her nose wrinkled. "Do you smell something?"

"Two somethings actually," Rustam confirmed. "One I'd rather not investigate."

Risada gave him a withering look and set off towards the noisome odour. The stench rapidly became stronger and Rustam held a hand over his nose.

"Hisst!" An imperiously raised hand stopped him in his tracks. Risada motioned towards a closed door. Obediently Rustam approached, tried the handle. Not locked. At a nod of confirmation from the lady, he swung the door sharply open, but the chamber stood empty. Rustam could understand why.

The little room was bare of furniture or decoration, but revolting smears and stains daubed both floor and walls. Dim light entered by the same route the garbage exited: a fair sized hole in the wall.

Fastidiously trying not to touch the soiled brickwork, Rustam peered through the gap. They were about two lengths above a sluggishly moving waterway, its oily depths no more appealing than the room in which they stood.

"If it's all the same to you, my Lady, I'd rather find another way out."

"This time, Chalice, I concur."

They retraced their steps until the more appetising of the two smells became stronger and they followed it to another locked door. This one opened into a small pantry. The heat and delicious cooking aromas coming from beyond the interconnecting door indicated that their next few steps would take them into the mansion's kitchens.

They accomplished only two of those steps before the kitchen door swung open and a maroon jacketed steward swept in bearing a large silver tray. He barely had time to register the intruders before Risada's hand flashed out to touch his neck and he collapsed to the floor with a quiet sigh. Rustam instinctively caught the falling tray and placed it quietly to one side.

"Was that really necessary?" he asked as Risada reinserted a venomous needle into her waistband. "A dead body is a fairly good way to arouse suspicion."

"Give me some credit, dancer boy. This one will wake up in a few minutes with an almighty headache and no memory of us. Now put his jacket on and let's go."

Rustam struggled into the maroon jacket. It was rather short on his tall frame and the brass buttons strained across his chest, but it would serve for now. He followed Lady Risada through the door into the kitchen. She gave no one time to question her presence.

"Where is the meat chef?" she demanded imperiously. Stunned Rees-Charlay retainers pointed towards a short, red-faced woman sweating in front of a range of spits. The chubby face went blank with shock at the sight of a noblewoman in her domain and the woman stared stupefied as Risada bore down upon her. Ignored by all as just another of the extra fest stewards in his Fourth House colours, Rustam blended with the crowd and watched the lady's performance with professional admiration.

"Are you indentured or Guild contracted?"

The cook belatedly bobbed a curtsy. "Indentured, your Ladyship."

"Pity." Risada sounded genuinely regretful. "I am in need of someone with your skills with venison. How long before you can be released into another House's service?"

"Five years, my Lady."

"Ah well, I shall simply have to survive a while longer. Please, remember my offer when you are free to do so."

"I will, your Ladyship." The curtsey came again, and again. "Thank you, my Lady."

"Now will someone please show me the way out of here," Risada requested. "This heat is exhausting."

Melcard's staff practically fell over each other in their attempts to guide the noblewoman out of the furnace-like heat. None had any wish to try explaining to their master why one of his guests had been allowed to faint in his kitchen. Nor, goddess forbid, to have to answer to Doctor Hensar.

* * * * * * * * * * * * * * * * *

Maroon jacket secreted behind a settle in one of the long corridors, Rustam walked wordlessly with Risada back to the Royal Suite. For the sake of appearances, Lady Risada consented to rest her hand on Rustam's arm and his whole body tingled with awareness of the assassin's light touch. It had not been so long ago, he remembered, that he had lusted after that touch, but that had been before their formal introduction. Now it held different connotations to those he had imagined and his feelings were confused, but for the moment he pushed them away to concentrate on more important considerations.

His mind replayed the moment in the dungeon when his eyes had locked with those of the elf, and shock stabbed him in the guts.

An *elf*. Here, in the heart of Tyr-en.

Or in the depths, really. And he looked like he'd been there for a very long time.

But why? Did Melcard truly believe that the secret of eternal life flowed through the veins of the miserable creature in his dungeon? If he did, then either someone was perpetrating a huge hoax upon Melcard, or else Halnashead was wrong, and the elixir truly did work.

And how had he come into possession of a Shivan in the first place? Not a single elf had been reported in Tyr-en since the Shivan Wars ended some forty years earlier, although Rustam knew they were sometimes seen in the other four Kingdoms.

Forty years, he thought, shaking his head. *Long before I was born*!

Could elves really do the things that were told in the stories: call up a storm out of blue skies to soak and demoralise an enemy; stampede even the most highly trained war-horses; command the winds to rise in great funnels that could tear trees from the ground and pluck men from their mounts, casting their bodies across the landscape like so much scattered chaff?

They were even said to consort with Charin; to sacrifice to the goddess's evil twin.

Magic. The very thought of a creature that could use magic made Rustam uneasy. He tried to imagine what it must be like, living in one of the Kingdoms where magic was regulated solely by law. Like all Tyr-enese, he believed that outlawing the foul practice was far safer. No one should risk a repetition of the magical holocaust of four centuries ago that had forced humanity to flee its native land and brave the hostile ocean. Nearly two thirds of those who had set out had not survived the Crossing.

And wars aside, just imagine what havoc a player with magical skills could wreak in the game!

But if elves were truly capable of such feats, then why did this one remain imprisoned in Melcard's dungeon? The look in the creature's eyes had told of hope long abandoned and pain endured beyond imagining.

Rustam shivered at that memory. One way or another, he determined, this elf's suffering would be ended.

* * * * * * * * * * *

The guards outside the Royal Suite jumped to attention and Rustam vaguely noted their odd expressions at the sight of Lady Risada's hand on his arm, but he was too preoccupied to wonder what gossip that simple gesture might instigate.

Princess Annasala received them in the palatial sitting room of her suite and once the maid had withdrawn and closed the tall double doors, she offered them seats as far away as possible from both windows and door. At her signal the two minstrels retained for her enjoyment began a lively and long ballad, and proceeded to circle the room, one to either side of the group.

Annasala dragged over a high backed ornamental chair and perched on the very edge of the heavy brocade. She leaned forward and said in a low voice: "This is as secure as I can arrange. Now tell me, what did you discover?"

"You're not going to like it," Rustam warned her, matching her tone. "I don't like it at all." He bent down to flick away some dust—or flour—that marred the patent shine of his shoes, avoiding the princess's eyes.

"What? Rustam, what are you saying? Risada?"

Lady Risada glanced round at her name but scowled in a most unladylike manner and shook her head before standing up. She crossed the room to gaze out of the window, obviously deep in thought.

"Rusty, what is going on?" Annasala demanded.

He sighed and admitted: "We found the source of the elixir."

"And?"

Rustam plucked at a speck of lint that clung to his sleeve and took a deep, steadying breath before answering. "Sala, it's an elf. Elixir is blood drained from an elf that Melcard is holding in a dungeon below this mansion."

"What? But there hasn't been an elf in Tyr-en for more than forty years, not since—"

"Since the end of the Shivan Wars. I know. Melcard must have found him in one of the other Kingdoms. But Sala, think what the Wars were about."

The princess nodded, understanding bright in her clear grey eyes. "The Shivan secret for long life, which they wouldn't share with us. You're saying that the Fourth Family has the secret, and they've been keeping it from us for decades?"

"No," interjected Risada, rejoining them and sitting down, taking elaborate care to smooth even the tiniest wrinkle from the fabric of her multi-layered skirts before continuing. "The elixir doesn't work, and someone is going to great pains to disguise the truth, apparently from even Melcard himself."

"Then who?" asked Annasala. "Hensar? Or some other member of the Fourth?"

Risada shrugged. "I doubt we will find that out without further extensive investigations. Certainly whoever it is has succeeded in convincing Melcard—why else keep the elf if the concoction is a fake? But to my mind, the perpetrator's identity is less important than the fact that Melcard is the one accumulating the money and, from what Chalice and I have just seen, the manpower for an open offensive against the Royal House. Once that threat is neutralised we will have time to deal with the issue of who is really behind the scheme.

"So the question before us now is: what are we going to do about it?"

Like a terrier with its nose down a rat hole, observed Rustam. "I thought that was what you were here for," he said. "Can't you just slip back down into that dungeon during the ball tonight and slit the Shivan's throat? As far as Melcard is concerned, no more elf, no more elixir and ergo, no more money."

Risada and Annasala both frowned at him. "It's not that simple—" they began together then stopped, looking at each other.

"Go ahead, your Highness," invited Risada, settling back to regard Rustam.

"Rusty," began Sala, sounding less sure of herself.

"Go on," he prompted, worrying with his nails at the stubborn piece of lint on his sleeve. "I'm getting used to being the last one to know things."

Sala winced at his sarcastic tone. "We would have told you but there hasn't been time. A courier from father arrived earlier today with intelligence indicating that a highly placed Family has struck a bargain with certain of the Tylocian mountain clans." She looked from Rustam to Risada and back again. "I think we are now in a position to conclude which Family, don't you agree?"

Rustam nodded. "And I can guess the rest. Loan of fighting men in return for treasures. With a bit of rape and pillage on the side."

"Precisely," confirmed Risada. "But if you would be civil enough to listen to the princess without interrupting, there is more."

"More? Isn't that enough?"

Annasala glanced at Risada then back to Rustam, her brow drawn down with worry lines. "Rusty, the courier almost didn't get here. The clans have already begun to arrive and are forming a blockade to the north, between us and Darshan. We won't make it back with our information. We're on our own."

"How many men are we talking about?" Rustam asked grimly.

"Eight or nine hundred at least," Risada replied. "The Royal army is completely outnumbered."

"Even if Marten calls in all the reserves and the household guards of the Families known to be loyal? Oh damn!" Rustam interrupted himself. "There's been an increase in border raids from Tyloc, hasn't there? Those troops are weeks away from Darshan, even if a recall order reaches them. And how do we really know who's loyal? With enough money Melcard might have bought loyalty from any House, or be blackmailing them with the threat of withholding their supply of elixir. He could even be offering new positions in the hierarchy if he seizes the throne!"

"My, my; an intellectual gigolo. What a novelty!" sniped the Lady of Domn.

"Risada—" began Rustam hotly.

"*Lady* Risada to you, Chalice."

"Stop it! Both of you! I've had as much bickering as I can stand!" screeched Sala, leaping to her feet.

The musicians faltered to a stop. Rustam and Risada stared at Annasala in shocked silence which was shattered by the crash of the sitting room doors bursting inward. Rustam flung himself into a fighting crouch, knife at the ready as a soldier charged through brandishing a naked blade, but the face beneath the helm was that of the princess's bodyguard and Rustam straightened quickly, slipping his knife back into its hidden sheath. A glance at Risada caught her surreptitiously replacing a small emerald jewelled dagger into the fabric of her dress. The guard stopped in confusion, scanning the room for the threat that had caused his mistress's outburst.

Sala threw a sour look over her shoulder at Rustam and Risada before crossing the room to have a quiet word with the man. When he was gone and the doors firmly closed again, Annasala motioned for them to sit, and for the minstrels to resume. Retaking her seat, she regarded Rustam and Risada with her father's stern grey eyes.

"I apologise for my temper, but it's the survival of my House we're discussing, not to mention the damage a civil war could do to this Kingdom. We just don't have the time for your personal quarrels. Now please, do either of you have any ideas?"

Rustam looked from Annasala to Risada and back again. In Risada was all that men desired: beauty, grace, elegance. But in Sala, still little more than a girl, and without—yet—all those qualities, he saw something else. Something mature. He found he did not want to disappoint her.

"Let's start again," he suggested. "It's up to us to do what we can behind enemy lines, so to speak. Should we destroy the source of Melcard's wealth?"

Risada flicked her hand in a negative gesture. "The elf's survival has become irrelevant; it's already far too late to make an appreciable difference to Melcard's plans." She slumped slightly in her chair, as though a weight bore down on her shoulders. "I would rather not kill him unless it is deemed essential."

"Compassion from the assassin?" said Rustam cynically.

Risada frowned at him, apparently more puzzled than angry. "Does that surprise you, Chalice? Most of my tasks are more in the line of exterminating vermin. Slaughtering an already half-dead, defenceless elf is not a task I find palatable."

Rustam inclined his head, reconsidering. Perhaps she was not *entirely* composed of ice.

"So what about Melcard himself?" he suggested.

Sala shook her head. "I doubt that would work either. Melcard may be head of the Family, but the evidence points towards him being merely a figurehead, and there are several other strong characters that I'm sure would be only too willing to take his place."

"So what other solutions can we come up with? If we're too late to stop this at source, we have to find a way to help Marten fight back, and that means men. Trained fighters. Unless either of you has another suggestion?" Rustam looked hopefully at the two women.

"Reluctantly, I see no other solution," agreed Risada. Sala merely shook her head.

"Trained soldiers are what we need then," said Rustam. "So where do we get them?"

The ballad drew to a close and silence fell over the three like icy water from a cloudburst. The stark reality of civil war faced them and Rustam, whose whole life had been spent in one perilous situation after another, found the prospect terrifying.

How much more so was it for his companions? Despite their high placings in both society and the game, women of childbearing age were far too valuable to be risked in war. They would be forced to wait and see who triumphed, and who would decide their fates. For the first time Rustam found himself feeling sorry for a woman. Or for these two, at least, he amended.

As the minstrels started a new song Rustam stood and, like Risada earlier, wandered over to the windows to gaze out at the beautiful, tranquil gardens where the late sun was setting behind a stand of rhyll bushes, casting a golden glow on their perfect orange blooms. Freshly turned earth in nearby flowerbeds exuded a loamy smell rich with the promise of luxuriant growth. The prospect of war seemed illusory, unreal. Out on the lawns lords and their ladies drifted towards the mansion, on their leisurely way to prepare for the great ball later that evening.

Lords and ladies. An idea clicked into place in Rustam's brain. He spun back into the room.

"We can't be sure of our own people, so how about those of another Kingdom? Kishtan, for example. They have plenty of troops and just now, no major disturbances to occupy them."

"What makes you think we can trust Kishtan? Little love's been lost between our two Kingdoms over the years." Risada raised a delicately arched eyebrow.

Rustam shook his head. Just the response he'd expect from one of the hide-bound highborns. To his surprise, it was Sala who countered.

"It's not so impossible, Risada. Kishtan suffers raids from Tyloc too, but on a very small scale because they share such a short strip of adjoining land. If Tyloc were to gain a much greater hold in Tyr-enese land, they would increase that border enormously."

"I'm certain Melcard has no intention of granting Tyloc any holdings in Tyr-en," argued Risada.

"Since when did Tylocians need anyone's permission to hold land?" asked Rustam. "Once they've got a foothold, they'll cling onto it like a wolf to a bone. And remember, it's the Middle Mountains we're talking about. Those clans can live well anywhere in a mountain range, but you'll never find them."

"I suppose that's true," conceded Risada grudgingly. "But is that enough motivation for Kishtan to enter into alliance with us when it means certain bloodshed?"

"They have attempted alliance before, haven't they?" said Sala looking to Risada for confirmation.

"Marten's mother, you mean?"

Sala nodded. "My aunt was a Kishtanian noblewoman. Surely alliance was a major reason why she was married to the king?"

"You're suggesting we approach them on the grounds of blood ties? Even in view of the circumstances surrounding the queen's death?"

"Nothing was ever proven. And Marten is her son."

Silver blue eyes bored into Rustam's soul. *Save me,* they pleaded. *Take me out of this place...*

"We do have one other thing to offer them," Rustam said quietly. Both women looked at him in surprise.

"One thing I do remember from my admittedly inferior education is that elves were known to be passionate about each other's lives, related or not. I also recall that ten years ago King Graylin of Kishtan married a Shivan woman. So how grateful do you think Kishtan's queen would be for the rescue and return of one of her countrymen after so long in captivity?"

"You're forgetting two things, Chalice. We don't have the elf, and a Shivan is going to be the last person to trust Tyr-en."

Rustam smiled in triumph as he finally managed to pluck the irritating piece of lint free from his sleeve. "Agreed," he said. "We don't have the elf. Yet. But that shouldn't be too hard a task for the two greatest players in the Kingdom, should it? And if you have any alternative suggestions, I'm more than willing to entertain them."

"Rylond." Risada named the neighbouring Kingdom firmly. "They were only too willing to ally with us in the Shivan Wars."

"That bunch of merchants?" Sala said disparagingly. "They'd only be interested if there was the likelihood of a profit and besides, they still haven't recovered from the economic disaster of the last war."

"Hm." Risada capitulated reluctantly. "And I don't suppose those uncouth tent-dwellers of Ambl show any signs of developing a civilised structure to their so-called society." She looked at her two companions. "I believe I am forced to concur. Sala?"

"It seems the only viable option," said the princess.

Risada nodded once, gravely. "Then I suggest we must move swiftly. Rustam, tonight you will recover the elf from the dungeon while Princess Annasala and I keep our host occupied. It will then be up to you to get as far away as you can before his absence is discovered. We will arrange to delay any pursuit as long as possible."

Rustam snorted in disbelief. "You expect me to travel the mountains on my own? And to convince a king, on the word of a 'dancer boy' to bring his troops into Tyr-en? Which, as you so astutely pointed out, has not been the most trustworthy of Kingdoms in the past."

"I'm sorry, Risada, that won't do at all." Annasala stood and began pacing while she talked; a habit caught from her father. Rustam had seen that decisive look in his eyes too.

"What we will do is this: tonight at the ball you, Risada, will finally give in to the overtures of my handsome dancing Master—"

"I will do no such thing!"

"I'm sorry, Risada, but you will." Annasala stepped over to a small, ornate table and picked up a small velvet bag. She tipped the contents into her palm, held up her hand and regarded Risada over her father's gold and onyx signet ring. "You've prompted me often enough recently to remember my position. Now I'm afraid you must do the same."

Risada subsided, her expression rebellious.

Annasala continued. "I, poor scorned young princess, will bravely ignore the situation, consoling myself by gossiping about the new couple with every tongue-wagging lady I can interest."

"Be careful you aren't mobbed."

"Why Rustam dear, you do care! As I was saying, you will leave the ball together—a little early, mind—and be seen entering Lady Risada's rooms arm in arm. After that I will make a grand exit and the ball will have to finish as the guest of honour has abandoned it. This way there will be no ladies hanging around Rustam, and no men begging for your favours, Risada."

Risada surged to her feet, her cheeks flaming.

"Nobody will believe that I, a Lady of the Second House, would even contemplate a liaison with a...a—servant!"

"And why not?" Annasala asked. "All the other ladies have been only too happy to welcome him, and most think I have too. What makes you so different?"

Risada's mouth opened and closed as she struggled to find a suitable answer, before subsiding to her seat with a shrug. "Go on."

Sala acknowledged Risada's capitulation with a grave nod before resuming. "The two of you will recover the elf, and you will travel to Kishtan together. Risada, you will be our envoy to King Graylin, as Lady of the Second House and cousin to King Marten. Rustam will be your guard."

"I don't need him as a guard," muttered Risada.

"Lady Risada," said Rustam. "Have you ever tried crossing the mountains on your own?"

"I'm sure I could handle any difficulties I might meet."

"But who would guard your back when you sleep? And you'll be hauling a half dead elf with you for baggage. I can't say I'm thrilled at the prospect of travelling with you either, but it does make sense."

"Good. That's settled then," said Annasala. "When your absence is discovered in the morning—late, I'm sure, due to tonight's events—I shall throw a tantrum the likes of which you cannot imagine. I'm still young enough to be a Royal Brat when I feel like it. That should keep Melcard too busy to organise search parties."

"Sala," said Rustam. "How certain can we be of your safety after we leave?"

"I'll be fine," answered the princess. "What would Melcard dare do to me with members of every House in the Kingdom as witnesses? Even with the wealth he's accumulated, he can't hope to buy loyalty from every Family. He has to be hoping to win support from as many others as he can and that he has definitely not accomplished yet. If his political moves were more advanced I would worry, but not yet."

Risada rose from her chair, gathering her dignity about her like a voluminous cloak. "It's a clever plan, Sala, but what of my honour when I return? How can that ever be restored after running off with a servant? My position is what makes me so useful to your father."

"I appreciate that, Risada. I don't know. But consider this: if this mission fails, my father won't be there to need you at all."

* * * * * * * * * * * * * *

Doctor Hensar sealed the stopper of the tiny vial with hot wax and presented it to his lord.

"Are you certain this is wise?" he said. "Lady Risada is the King's cousin."

Lord Melcard's handsome face lit with a smile that failed to reach his eyes. "But Hensar, that's the best part of it: the irony! The King's own cousin contributing to his downfall. What could be more satisfying?"

"But my Lord—"

"Enough!" Melcard's expression lost its amusement. "One day you will question me once too often. I can always replace you, Hensar."

Oh, I doubt that, my Lord, thought the doctor. *I doubt that very much.*

But aloud, all he said was: "And what of Chalice? If what we suspect about him is true, we—you—could be risking all."

"Ah yes," mused Melcard, rubbing his temples thoughtfully. "Chalice. The meddlesome ladies-man. I suppose even the aristocratic Risada may not be above his charms."

His lips smiled again. "You know, Hensar, I do believe Master Rustam Chalice is going to have an accident tomorrow. A fatal one. See to it."

Lord Melcard spun on his heel and left Hensar's laboratory without waiting for the doctor's acknowledgement. Hensar bowed his head anyway. It was good policy to maintain such practices. He had not spent all these years establishing his position within Melcard's House only to throw it away with a careless oversight. And Melcard, damn his putrid hide to Charin's furnace, was such a petty stickler for protocol he could be easily offended.

Hensar returned to his work. Besides having no wish to end up on the wrong side of his own instruments of torture, he simply did not have the time for such foolishness. With the imminent arrival of the Tylocian clans his plans were too near fruition. No, he would just have to maintain the façade a while longer.

Putting on a pair of heavy gloves, he opened the cage at the end of his workbench and captured the hissing, scratching, biting creature within. Forcing its jaws open with one hand, he poured a sample of his latest test batch down the throat of the misshapen rodent, and then smacked it hard against the edge of the bench to break its hind legs. Satisfied that the damage was sufficient for his purposes, he flung the shrieking animal back into its cage and fastened the door, his nose wrinkling at the pungent smell of soiled straw.

He turned his attention to tidying the bench. It was frustrating having to work with animals, but lately it had become harder to secure human test subjects, and the last two had been so weak they had barely lasted from one solstice to the next.

Hopefully it would not be much longer now. He felt he was nearing the perfect formula for the real elixir of eternity; one that actually worked rather than producing the mere surface illusion of doing so.

He shook his head self-mockingly. Had he been content with less, he could have been the ultimate producer of ladies cosmetics. His formula made even the old seem radiant. The visible results were so impressive that Melcard himself was convinced he was daily growing younger.

Hensar, however, would never be satisfied with anything less than the reality of true eternal life.

In the meantime, the Bastard's grand plan drew ever nearer its completion. Had Arton vas Domn still been alive things might have been more complicated, but Hensar had dealt with that problem long ago. He ran his thumb along the roughened scar on the underside of his jaw.

How much neater the whole thing would have been had he been able to dispose of Arton's two brats at the same time, but—he shrugged to himself—perhaps it was better this way. Iain presented no particular problem; he could be dealt with at the appropriate time.

Risada, on the other hand, now held a pivotal position in his revised plans. Failing that, there was always Halnashead's daughter, but Princess Annasala looked frail compared to the Lady of Domn.

Hensar's fat pink tongue travelled around his moist lips and he absently rubbed his crystal pendant between thumb and forefinger as he contemplated what he could do to that perfect, smooth body. How fortunate that ladies' fashions demanded such a covering of skin. One could hide so very much beneath those concealing dresses.

A chorus of whines and whimpers rose from the cages stacked in the far corner of the cluttered room and, distracted from more pleasant contemplations, Hensar snatched a crucible from the bench and hurled it at the wicker containers. The occupants paused briefly before setting up such a ruckus that Hensar abandoned the laboratory in disgust. At least humans could be silenced with threats or promises.

Speaking of silencing, he had an accident to arrange. Rubbing his hands together in anticipation, Hensar turned the full might of his devious, sadistic mind to the details of his most recent assignment.

5. FLIGHT

Rees-Charlay's secret corridors were as deserted as before, most of Melcard's visible manpower fulfilling domestic duties at the fest. At this late hour the torches guttered in their sconces, and the slightly acrid smell of smoke hung in the still air.

Rustam glanced across at the blur of darkness on the opposite side of the passage. Even dressed in men's clothing the Lady of Domn was stunning. Perhaps even more so, amended Rustam, for her legs clad in black hose, with knee length boots of softest black leather were every bit as shapely as he had imagined. The honey blonde of her hair was subdued by a fine mesh net in strands of black dyed silk, topped by the sort of shapeless felt cap worn by stable lads. A curious mixture certainly, but the effect was striking.

As before, they reached the final junction of corridors prior to their goal without incident. Rustam repeated his ground level surveillance, and nodded confirmation to Risada—still only the one guard on the dungeon door. She motioned for him to proceed.

The maroon jacket, recovered earlier from its hiding place by one of Annasala's maids, fitted Rustam no better than before, and he hunched his shoulders forward to reduce some of the strain showing around the burnished buttons. At least the poor lighting was in his favour. Head high, he stepped around the corner and marched towards the single guard, his eyes firmly on the corridor ahead. Peripheral vision showed the soldier come alert, but Melcard's uniform gave him several lengths grace before he was challenged.

"Halt! What are you doing here?"

Rustam took three more steps before meeting the man's eyes, then another. And another. He pointed along the passage. "Just taking a short cut."

Another step.

"I know I'm not supposed to, but Doctor Hensar wants something very particular from the kitchens."

Step.

"He wants it immediately, and I'm not about to keep him waiting." Fixing his eyes firmly beyond the guard, Rustam strode past.

"Now wait a moment—"

His objective achieved, Rustam stopped and turned back to face the guard. "Do you want to explain to the doctor why it took so long to fetch this item for him?" he asked, and saw an answering flicker of fear in the man's eyes. "No, I thought not," he continued, aware of Risada's shadowy figure gliding silently towards the hapless guard's back.

"I'm truly sorry to put you in this position," he apologised as the man collapsed forward into his arms, "But I think you're going to have quite a lot of explaining to do."

Risada lowered a small tube from her lips and was reaching to retrieve the yellow feathered dart embedded in the back of the guard's neck, when the dungeon door opened from the inside. A second guard stood in the doorway, trencher in one hand, keys in the other. Rustam saw the tableau reflected in the man's startled eyes: himself, still supporting the unconscious body of the first guard, Risada spinning round, her hand a blur of motion.

The soldier's mouth had barely begun to shape the call that would have brought others running when, with a soft, gurgling sound, he slipped to the floor. The glittering hilt of a small dagger jutted from his throat. Silence ensued. When no further threats appeared, Risada went down on one knee beside the dying man. Gently, she brushed away the hands that fluttered feebly around the weapon. Her pale fingers closed around the emerald encrusted hilt.

"Be at peace," she whispered, and jerked the knife sideways. The body shuddered once then lay still. Risada withdrew her blade, and wiped it fastidiously on the maroon uniform which barely showed the spreading red stain, before slipping the dagger into a hidden sheath. She looked up at Rustam.

"Well don't just stand there; we need to get them out of sight."

"Just admiring your handiwork, my Lady."

"Perhaps we'll see some of yours before this night is out, Chalice. Or are your talents restricted to the bedchamber?"

Rustam refused to rise to the gibe. He was beginning to realise that this annoyed her even more. He watched as her jaw tightened, hardening the lines of her face until it formed the cold visage that must be the last sight of some of her victims. Rustam wondered how many faces the lady had. He had seen quite a number: the killer, the schemer, the concerned cousin, the lover. He wondered which one was really Risada if, indeed, any of them were. Did she know herself, after all this time? Certainly she was a consummate actress. Her performance at the ball had been so convincing even Rustam had nearly believed it. When they had kissed—passionately—before entering her suite, Rustam had found himself wanting her like he had never wanted a woman before. But her only comment after the doors closed had been a cold: "Go play with your horse, Chalice!"

Risada took the arms of the unconscious man and proceeded to drag him down the steps to the dungeon, leaving Rustam to follow with the corpse.

The dancer bent to pick up the keys and winced as he caught sight of the dead man's face in the torchlight. One side was disfigured by puckered scarring, probably a burn. Rustam shuddered. What would he do, should he suffer such misfortune? He knew without doubt that his looks were his livelihood. Without them, what Lady would look at him? Fashion was fickle, but good looks were a constant requirement.

With a muttered prayer to Chel, he hauled the body through the door. Blood seeped from the neck wound, but the dark stone floor showed no stains to betray them. Putting the keys in his pocket, Rustam pulled the door shut. The lock caught with a quiet snick, and he dragged the body down the spiralling stair.

Waiting impatiently at the bottom, Risada held out her hand for the keys. As she opened the barred metal gate, Rustam studied the incredible cell. Had it been built specifically for the Shivan, he wondered, and if so, how long ago? Even now, faded and dusty, it would be a comfortable prison.

"Come *on*, Chalice."

They dragged the two limp forms through the door and over to the bed where the elf lay quiescent.

Long, skeletal limbs disappeared into the rags of an old velvet tunic of indeterminate hue. One arm was swathed at the elbow with a thick bandage, giving the captive an oddly misshapen appearance. The pointed tips of two tall, backward sloping ears jutted from his head like the antennae of some improbable insect, the matted hair through which they protruded possibly blond, but the thickly caked layers of grease and dirt made it impossible to be certain.

Despite everything, Rustam could not help but stare in envy at the ethereal beauty of the still face; the smooth, angled cheekbones, the gently slanted eyes with their thick yellow lashes, the lips delicate yet firm, all the features as regular and flawless as if painted with loving care by a master doll maker. Perfect as an image of the goddess in repose.

But was he alive?

Concerned they might already be too late, Rustam licked a finger and held it before the slender nostrils. A weak breath reassured him only slightly.

"Do get a move on," snapped the Lady of Domn.

Wrinkling his nose at the rank smell of unwashed body and soiled bed linen, Rustam shifted the elf to the bottom of the huge bed, before hauling the unconscious guard into his place. With some cord produced from a concealed pocket, Risada bound the man's wrists and ankles, then wadded the blankets up around him so that a cursory glance would not reveal who lay there. While the door guard's absence was sure to raise the alarm, they could hope that the ostensible presence of the prisoner would lead to a hunt for the missing guard, rather than for them. They shoved the dead man under the bed as far back as he would fit.

Rustam lifted the Shivan effortlessly—despite his gangling height he weighed little more than a child—and, holding him gingerly in case any of the fragile-seeming bones might break, turned to leave. In the doorway, Risada squeezed past him. Where her body touched his, Rustam's flesh burned. His heart lurched with the surge of desire, and his fists clenched. The elf moaned, protesting.

Rustam drew a breath to curb his rioting emotions, and forced his muscles to relax. He was not used to working with a partner, and certainly not one as undeniably female as the Lady Risada Delgano vas Domn. He set his jaw and resolved to avoid physical contact with her for the duration of the mission.

Teeth clenched, he followed her up the stairs.

The corridor above was still empty and they made their way unchallenged almost as far as their goal—the noisome room with its exit into the offensive stream. Just one turning short, the measured tread of men on guard duty approached them. A quick glance revealed no hiding places. The one nearby door refused to open despite the rattling Risada gave it.

Two guards rounded the corner.

Risada swept off the shapeless hat and hairnet, her blonde hair spilling out like feathers from a split mattress.

"Could either of you gentlemen direct me to the Ball? I seem to have lost my way."

In the frozen moment of surprise Rustam shifted mental speed, and deposited his burden on the floor whilst palming the knife from his wrist sheath. He downed one guard with a slit throat before the man had time to clear his sword from its scabbard. Rustam spun to face the other but Risada was already easing the body to the ground, a poisoned needle just visible between her fingers.

As she straightened, Rustam hurled his dagger. Not meant for throwing, nevertheless it sped true to its mark. The disbelief on Risada's face vanished as the blade ruffled her hair in passing and embedded itself with a thunk in the chest of the man who had just opened the door at her back. Even as he clutched at the protruding hilt she whipped round and jabbed him with the needle. He collapsed with barely a sigh.

Risada turned to face Rustam, her breath coming a little too fast. "For a moment there I thought—"

"I know what you thought. It was written all over your face. Did you really think I would be that treacherous? I'm not a woman, you know."

Rustam turned his back on her and knelt down to check the elf. His whole body trembled with anger. *Women!* And it looked like he could be stuck with this one for weeks.

The Shivan lay curled in a ball, his face shielded from the candle light. He flinched when Rustam touched his shoulder, but at least he was alive.

A delicate hand appeared by Rustam's shoulder, proffering his recovered dagger. Wiped clean, he noticed.

"Your assistance, please, Chalice."

Risada's voice was subdued. Good. It was time somebody put a dent in her aristocratic arrogance.

Leaving the elf for the moment, Rustam made a quick assessment of the situation. The newly opened door revealed some sort of office. Risada extracted a key from the inside of the door and swung it shut, locked it and pocketed the key. Rustam concurred: an empty office was far less suspicious than one containing three bodies. In an unusual moment of accord, they dragged the dead men round the corner and into the disposal room. Apparently they had regained Chel's favour, as no more unexpected witnesses disturbed their clean up. When all three unfortunates had gone to their watery graves, Risada replaced the shapeless hat to disguise her bright hair whilst Rustam retrieved their burden.

And now, into the swill.

Rustam grimaced. This was his least favourite part of the escape plan. He put the elf down on the floor, swung his legs out over the sluggish, oily water and jumped. Mouth firmly shut and breath held in case, he was relieved though slightly jarred when his feet hit bottom sooner than expected. He was barely waist deep. One of the guards' bodies bobbed in the swell of his arrival, barely visible in the moonslight that seeped under the lee of the overhanging archway several lengths to his left.

One of Sala's agents had located the area earlier that day. The effluent stream emerged from beneath the mansion at the site of the stable middens, ideal to their purposes this night. A heavy mist roiled over the surface of the odorous stream, obscuring further vision, and Rustam could only pray that the remainder of their arrangements were in place.

A shadow moved above—Risada lowering the elf. He was light, but Rustam admitted a grudging respect for the lady's strength. He doubted many other women could have lifted the creature through the hole, let alone lowered it as far before letting go. The gangly legs splashed into the water, but Rustam caught and cradled the body with only the feet trailing beneath the surface.

Stinking droplets splattered his face and he spat a foul taste from his mouth. In the gloom beside him Risada staggered in liquid that came considerably higher up her torso than his. Grim faced, she kept her silence and once she found her balance, led towards the flickering, crepuscular light. As they emerged from the shelter of the building, moisture beaded their hair and ran down their faces. The smell of sewage mingled with the sweeter aroma of horse manure.

"Lady Risada?"

"Here," she confirmed in a sharp whisper. Hands reached out of the mist and helped them to struggle free from the slop and up the yielding surface of the midden. Sala's head groom and one of his lads led them across the cobbles to the stable buildings. The older retainer indicated where Rustam should put down his burden and pointed to a bundle. The man picked up a second pack, and handed it to Lady Risada with a bow.

Rustam peeled off his boots and emptied them out. "Ughh! I don't ever want to do that again."

Risada merely took her pack of clean, dry clothing and disappeared into an empty stable. Bitterly regretting the lack of opportunity for a bath, and beginning to shiver in the chill damp, Rustam did likewise. When he emerged—dry now though certainly not odour free—three horses and a pack pony stood ready saddled, their gently steaming breath just visible in the misty moonslight. Nightstalker whuffled a quiet greeting and he touched her nose briefly before hefting the elf into a sitting position on board the rather weedy looking bay mare standing beside his black.

"That's not goin' to work," muttered the groom as the elf toppled sideways. "You're goin' t'ave to tie 'im on."

Reluctantly, Rustam concurred. They wrapped the Shivan in a blanket and laid him face down over the saddle. Rustam apologised silently as the wretch groaned. The groom quickly lashed his hands and feet together beneath the confused mare's belly. Rustam mounted Nightstalker and bent over, catching hold of the bay's reins while Risada swung up onto her rangy grey gelding. The lad fastened the pack pony's lead to the bay's saddlebow and they were ready.

Risada led the way to the gate where the gatekeeper slumbered obliviously, thanks to the sleeping draught consumed earlier with his supper.

"Chel's blessing upon you," whispered the groom as he opened the gate. They rode through, their horses' shoes muffled by the fog and the sacks tied over their hooves. The gate swung closed behind them, and they were alone in the last hour of dim starlight while both moons slipped down the horizon to vanish behind the hazy blackness of the distant mountain peaks.

* * * * * * * * * *

The sun was high before they reached the foothills. The mist had been late to burn off, helping them avoid Melcard's regular patrols. They'd crossed the boundaries of four farms and seen no one. At this time of year, with harvests all in and autumn grain sown, there was little work to be done on the land. Rustam thanked Chel for her favour.

They'd endeavoured not to leave a trail but, squinting in the bright autumn sunlight, Rustam spotted several dust clouds that suggested search parties. One followed directly behind them.

The mare carrying the elf jogged a few steps, anxious about the odd arrangement of her rider. The Shivan moaned and Rustam reined the horses to a standstill.

"We mustn't stop," urged Risada.

"Lady, if we don't stop soon this will turn into an empty venture. He can't last long with this sort of abuse. Have you ever ridden in that position?"

"Well, no. But—"

"I have. And even when you're fit and healthy, it's hard to breath. I'm going to put him up in front of me. Nightstalker can cope."

Without waiting for her approval, Rustam jumped down.

"Chalice, we don't have the time! Get back on that horse."

Rustam already had the thongs untied, and carefully he slipped the elf off the jittery mare. The pack pony stood patiently to one side.

"Look, my Lady, I know you're in charge. Prince Halnashead made that quite clear. But I'm not prepared to sacrifice our best bargaining chip for the sake of a few minutes. We can move a lot faster when I'm done."

"You're impossible! What good is it my being in charge if you won't do as I say?"

The elf was easy to lift, even onto Nightstalker. The black mare obligingly kept her neck high so that Rustam could prop the limp body against her crest while he mounted behind. "Must be difficult for you, my Lady," he commiserated. "I don't suppose anyone's ever argued with you before. Here, you'll have to take these."

He held out the bay's reins, and Risada took them absently. Then she glanced down in surprise. "I can't lead these!" she protested. "What happens if we're attacked?"

"Then, my Lady, you drop them, just as I would have done if I were still leading them."

Risada made one more attempt to regain command. "Chalice, I do not lead spare horses or pack animals. I am a Lady of —"

"—the Second House of Tyr-en. Yes I know, believe me. But if we stay here very much longer you're going to be a dead lady."

Her jaw tightened until Rustam fancied he could hear her teeth grinding together, but she rode on, taking the bay mare and the pony with her. Rustam moved the elf's head to one side so he could see—goddess, the creature stank—and followed.

They made much better speed with the new arrangement. Nightstalker carried her double burden with ease and by midday they were well into the hills, the trailing dust clouds left far behind. Descending into a heavily wooded valley, they picked their way down the slope between straight trunks. High canopies filtered the light to a pale shade of emerald, and the resinous smell of pine rose from the ground as their horses hooves sank into the deep carpeting of fallen needles. They emerged into a clearing at the bottom where a few older, less regimented trees grew along the banks of a narrow stream, providing a welcome short break for both horses and riders.

Rustam laid the elf in the shade beneath an ancient spreading oak. His breathing was audible now, but that was no more reassuring. Now it rasped and bubbled like a drowning fisherman, and when Rustam touched his face, the skin burned.

He looked around for Risada and found her kneeling by the stream, scooping water in her cupped hands. She had removed the net and hat, and her pale golden hair tumbled down her back, kinked into waves by its confinement. Rustam's eyes fixed for a moment on the graceful arch of her throat.

He shook himself. "My Lady?" he called softly, aware that she was still furious with him.

She glanced up, frowned, and then rose to her feet. "Yes?"

Rustam pointed at the supine elf.

"What do you expect me to do about it?" she inquired icily.

Rustam shrugged. "I don't know. I just thought you might have some idea; he's hot as a baker's oven."

"What did you expect? He has very little chance of surviving this journey." The sunlight faded from the clearing and Risada glanced up at the clouds beginning to amass overhead. "Especially if winter decides to break early."

She knelt down beside the elf and touched his flushed cheek and forehead. "He has a fever—"

"That's what I said!"

"*If* you will let me finish? In my saddle-bags you will find a small twist of blue paper. No, the other side. Yes, that's it. Bring it over here with a canteen."

From the paper she took two pinches of powder and mixed them with a small amount of water in the canteen cup.

"Hold his mouth open."

Slowly Risada dribbled the potion into the elf's mouth, holding his jaw closed when he choked and gagged. Then, satisfied that he had swallowed enough, she rinsed the cup and stood up. "That should reduce the fever, always supposing he responds like a human. It's all I can do; I'm not an apothecary."

Rustam tightened the horses' girths while Risada filled the canteens. They had just remounted when thundering hooves pounded down the slope behind them and three riders burst into the clearing.

On the edge of his vision Rustam saw Risada drop the bay mare's reins, draw her dagger and raise a blowpipe to her lips in one fluid set of movements, while he struggled awkwardly to free his sword from the saddle scabbard beneath his left thigh.

Nightstalker pranced eagerly, destroying the tiny moment of concentration he needed to snap his mind into high speed. The elf bounced in front of him, blocking his view. He cursed and curbed the mare sharply. She half reared in protest.

The glint of a blade sliced towards him. Rustam threw himself sideways just as Nightstalker squealed and lashed out with her hind feet. Already off balance, Rustam slithered from the saddle pulling the elf with him, and they crashed heavily to the ground.

Hooves rose and fell finger distance from his face, trying to trample him, and they might have succeeded had his beloved black mare not lunged at the attacker's brown gelding with her teeth bared.

Rustam rolled away, finally managed to shift his time sense, regained his feet and darted in beside Nightstalker. He dragged his sword free with a satisfying rasp of metal on leather. The soldier, dressed in Melcard's maroon livery, guided his frightened gelding around the angry mare, and with a curdling battle cry attacked Rustam. His sword arced downward and Rustam ducked, twisted around as the horse passed him and sliced upward. A severed arm thudded to the ground at his feet.

Uttering a hysterical shriek, the soldier dropped his reins, and his horse lurched to a confused halt. The man sat frozen in shock, gazing without comprehension at his bleeding stump. Rustam sprinted forward, swerved around the spurting jet of bright blood—no point soiling yet another shirt—caught hold of his victim's sword-belt and dragged him from his saddle. One quick dagger thrust ended the man's worry.

Rustam turned to see Risada not faring so well. The blowpipe was nearly useless against fast moving armoured targets, and her dagger was too short to menace their swords. She was still mounted, but one rider was circling to get behind her.

Rustam vaulted into his saddle. Nightstalker grunted an objection at his rude arrival but bounded obediently forward. One soldier's back was towards him; the other saw him coming and cried out. The nearer one began to turn, pirouetting his horse on its haunches, but Rustam's charge brought him quickly within range and although the man managed to raise his sword awkwardly to parry Rustam's first blow, it flew from his grasp and the backswing sliced through his neck.

Turning to confront the last of their attackers, Rustam found only an empty saddle. The man lay spread-eagled on the grass, a tiny yellow feather adhering to his exposed throat.

Risada was already off her horse, kneeling beside the sprawled tangle of limbs that was the elf. As Rustam jumped down from Nightstalker's back to join her, she rose gracefully to her feet.

"Somehow I don't think falling on top of him has helped his chances of survival."

"I didn't have a lot of choice," hissed Rustam.

Risada looked back down at the prone figure and shook her head, her loose hair falling around her face, hiding it from view. "I realise that," she said. Was her voice softer? "And I owe you a debt of thanks for your assistance just now. It was gratifying to finally see your talents at work."

She knelt down beside the elf again and Rustam, unsure if that was a compliment or not, went to catch the bay mare and the pony. It was considerably darker now, and thunder grumbled in the distance.

After tying their own animals securely to a tree, Rustam turned his attention to their attacker's horses. The war trained mounts stood in a huddle, confused by the loss of their riders and suspicious of a stranger's scent. Crooning incessant nonsense, Rustam marched boldly up to them, ignoring the tossing heads and pinned back ears. He touched each horse on the shoulder, and their necks lowered, accepting him. He'd always had a way with horses.

He stripped off their tack and salvage a few useful items—a sword with its saddle scabbard for Risada, two daggers, a length of rope and a spare cloak to add to those already strapped to their packs—before chasing the animals back up the slope and into the trees.

He gathered his booty and carried it back to where Risada was making a closer inspection of one of the dead soldiers—the only one of the three to sport a beard. Her fingers parted the hair along the jaw line, and then she shook her head minutely and straightened up, pausing to survey the body strewn clearing. Her mournful expression struck Rustam and he stood silent, unwilling to intrude upon her moment of unguarded sorrow.

"What a waste," she said softly, and squeezed her eyes shut for a brief time. Then, with a toss of her fair locks, the emotion cleared from her face leaving Rustam to wonder if he had imagined it.

Risada beckoned him closer to inspect his salvage. Lifting the sword from his arms, she drew the blade and took an experimental swing. To Rustam's experienced eye it was on the heavy side for a woman, but it was all that was on offer. With a small nod she returned it to its scabbard and relieved Rustam of the shorter of the two daggers.

Wordlessly, they stowed the extra items and mounted up again. With his face pressed against the greasy, lank, stinking hair of the unconscious elf, Rustam followed the Lady of Domn's grey through the stream. They passed into the green twilight of the forested slope and began their climb up the opposite side of the valley, leaving the violated glade behind as the gloom deepened and the first drops of rain splashed into the stream.

6. SHEPHERDS HUT

Two days later, it was still raining. The horses slogged miserably along faint paths, twisting sideways to put their tails to the driving rain as they crested the exposed hill tops, then floundering through the thick mud that mired the depths of each valley.

After two damp, fireless nights nothing remained dry, and tempers were exceedingly short. Risada pulled her sodden cloak tighter around her shoulders. "Whose idea was it to cross the mountains at this time of year?"

"As I recall," said Rustam through chattering teeth, "it was a joint decision."

"Well it was stupid! If we don't find shelter tonight we won't make it any further."

"Believe me, my Lady, I agree with you. If you have any suggestions, I'm more than willing to take them."

Risada glared across at him, rain dripping off the end of her nose. "I thought you were the mountain-wise one. Isn't that what you're here for?"

Rustam scowled back. "You were the one who thought you could do this journey on your own."

Wiping her nose with a soggy sleeve, the Lady of Domn heaved a sigh. "Enough, Chalice. We're here together and I admit it'll probably take both of us to make it to the other side, but I'm cold, wet and filthy, and I have blisters where no lady should. If I don't get off this horse soon, I'll fall off it."

A stab of guilt jolted Rustam into searching the area for a likely camping spot. Risada was such a highly trained player, it had never occurred to him that she might not be fit. Riding fit, he amended. But why should she be? Ladies usually rode in a carriage, or at best went for a sedate hack around some estate or other. This flight into rugged mountain country was a far cry from that sort of gentle amble.

Peering ahead through the dismal grey streaks of rain, Rustam could see nothing that offered even the slightest hint of shelter.

"We should press on, my Lady; get beyond these foothills."

"Chalice—"

Rustam drew rein, forcing her to stop and look round at him. "My Lady, there is no shelter hereabouts. Our best chance is to find a cave and we won't find one here."

He watched in fascination as the Lady of Domn drew breath to argue, and then released it in a long sigh of miserable acceptance.

"Lead on Chalice. I trust you have been dutiful to Chel of late, we're going to need her favour."

They rode on until it became almost too dark to see, but Hesta, the larger of the two moons, rose early that night, and by her intermittent light shining between the now patchy clouds they spotted a shepherd's hut to the side of the trail as they breasted an open hill top. At this time of year it was deserted, but to their intense relief they found it to be dry, thoroughly stocked with firewood and possessed of its own well.

Rustam left Risada settling the elf on a bed of dried sweetwood, while he stabled the horses in the tiny lean-to. As he rubbed Nightstalker down with handfuls of hay, he voiced his concerns to her.

"Well, old girl, what do you make of her Ladyship? She's as prickly as a hedgepig and twice as venomous, yet she seemed really upset about killing those soldiers. On the other hand, I'll be amazed if we make it as far as Kishtan without slitting each other's throats. Why does she hate me so much? I don't recall ever doing anything to her. Believe me, if I had, I'd remember. She's not what you could call forgettable."

He shook his head, wishing that Nightstalker could answer. He badly needed to talk with someone. Before, in Darshan, there had always been Halnashead who, while never letting him forget there was a social gulf between them, nevertheless didn't make him feel like a mere servant. The prince was the nearest thing Rustam had to a friend.

Thought of Halnashead brought the prince's daughter to mind, and Rustam's stomach twisted into a knot of anxiety. Those guards should not have been after them so soon. Would Melcard dare kill a member of the Royal Family?

There were also things worse than death. Things such as those that Doctor Hensar was rumoured to do with prisoners who earned his special attention. Rustam shivered, but blamed it on his sodden clothing.

Nightstalker swung her head round and nudged him hard in the belly, nearly knocking him over. He gulped an involuntary breath of steamy air thick with the aroma of wet horse. Shaking himself, he pushed away his hideous contemplations and scratched the mare's forehead. "I haven't forgotten you. I'll just do the pony, and then I'll feed you all."

Soon the lean-to was full of the sounds of contented munching, each animal with a small ration of grain and a rack stuffed full of hay. The shepherd had left the place well stocked for next spring; the horses would not go short while they remained here. And after that? Rustam shrugged to himself and went inside the hut.

A blast of hot air assaulted his cold, damp face as he stepped through the door, bringing with it the rich fragrance of burning sweetwood mingled with an overpowering odour of wet and dirty clothes. Shadows flickered in the orange light of a roaring fire set in a rock edged pit near the centre of the further wall, and Rustam blinked eyes that suddenly streamed in the smoky atmosphere. He closed the door firmly against the weather and glanced blearily around their tiny refuge while he stripped off his cloak and the ruined blue velvet jacket beneath.

The elf was no more than a shallow mound of blankets on the single sweetwood lined pallet that stretched almost the length of the left hand wall. To Rustam's right was a crude wooden table and one chair, while in the corner nearest the fire was an edged box that probably doubled as a bed for either a dog or a sick sheep, but was decidedly too small for any of the fugitives. In the other corner were a stand of blackened pots and a cauldron hanging on chains from a tripod. A pile of buckets of varying capacities completed the domestic arrangements.

Risada glanced up from where she huddled beside the fire, her hair steaming gently as it dried. Rustam picked his way across the room, stepping over Risada's outer garments which were spread across the floor nearest the fire pit.

"The horses are all settled and happy," he reported. "How are we doing in here?"

"Fine," replied Risada sarcastically. "If you discount the condition of ourselves, our gear and our prisoner. I propose we stay here until we, and everything we possess, are good and dry."

"Do we have the time?"

"If we don't, you might as well kill him now." She gestured towards the mound of shaking blankets on the pallet. "You'd save him any more suffering."

"Isn't there anything you can do for him?"

"No more than I have; I'm not a healer."

"You're a woman."

"And that makes me an expert on sick elves?"

She glared up at him and Rustam was struck with a flash of insight: the lady felt as helpless as he did. If they didn't make it to Kishtan, or if they couldn't convince King Graylin to lend them aid in the shape of soldiers, the Royal House would almost certainly fall. And there lay their most valuable bargaining chip, dying before their eyes, and nothing they could do about it. Except wait and pray.

Rustam hunkered down across the fire from Risada. He felt the blood rise to his face as the heat finally began to penetrate the long damp chill of the journey.

"Can we try putting our differences aside?" he suggested, locking eye contact with the Lady of Domn through the heat haze and smoke. "For Halnashead and Annasala if nothing else. I don't know what I've done to offend you, but like I said before, we're going to have to rely on each other to make this journey and we can't afford to be at each other's throats all the time."

Risada inclined her head to one side. "That sounds fair enough, but will you do as I say instead of constantly making your own decisions? There can only be one leader on a venture such as this."

Rustam sighed inwardly, but if it made her happier, what in Charin's hell did it matter? "I will, my Lady, as long as it doesn't jeopardise our safety. Remember, I'm the mountain-wise one."

Her slight pause told of her annoyance at his qualification, but she nodded once, then rose to her knees and busied herself making tea from the kettle she had set upon the fire. Rustam accepted a cup gratefully, stood up and went over to gaze down at the elf.

The fine, boyish features were covered with a sheen of sweat, and the long fair hair was plastered to his face, yet the immaculate beauty for which the Shivan race was renowned still shone through.

There's every chance he'll die, thought Rustam. *And we don't even know his name.*

"If you don't remove some of those wet clothes soon, you'll end up like him," chided Risada.

"Since when did you care—?" began Rustam, and then stopped himself sharply.

"Practicality," she returned. "As you so succinctly pointed out, we need each other."

Rustam peeled off soaking layers until he wore just a simple loose shirt that clung damply like a second skin, and breeches. He inspected the grimy garments with distaste, but all the clean clothes in his saddle bags were wringing wet. He would have to wait until something dried enough to be fit to change into. He grimaced and crowded close to the fire, gratefully accepting the bowl of meaty-smelling broth Risada offered him.

She rose and took another bowl over to the elf. Rustam watched from the corner of his eye as the Lady of Domn spooned warm liquid into the Shivan's lax mouth, and stroked his throat gently until he swallowed. Using one corner of the blanket that swaddled him, she wiped the corner of his mouth like a mother feeding a sick child.

Rustam glanced away, embarrassed that he should picture Dart the assassin in such a tender role. But why not? She was a woman after all, and perhaps it was only Rustam himself that brought out the harsh side of her nature—for the goddess alone knew what reason.

To cover his moment of uncertainty, he dug into one of their packs and extracted some waybread. It was a trifle soggy but he found a spit in the corner behind the pot stand and impaled a couple of pieces, before suspending the metal rod across the fire with one end balanced on the chair and the other on the cauldron. By the time the bread was crisped enough to be palatable he was drowsy from the warmth and Risada had to nudge him awake to eat it.

She sat down across from him, watching. He studied her in turn, seeing how, even under these circumstances she ate daintily, fastidiously rinsing her fingers in a bowl of warm water between mouthfuls. Rustam glanced down at himself, ran his hands over the stubble on his chin and laughed self-mockingly.

"I thought I was the popinjay; now look at me."

"I am," she confirmed. Then later, when they were finished, she asked, "do you enjoy what you do, Chalice?"

"Do you?" he countered.

"The question is yours to answer first."

"Then will you answer also?"

"I might. It depends."

He shrugged, feeling warm and moderately comfortable at last. "It's not an easy question. There are aspects of my work I enjoy very much, and parts I detest."

"Yet you do it freely."

"Of course I do. Even you do Halnashead's bidding willingly, don't you?"

"How did you come to be a player, Chalice?"

Warning bells rang in Rustam's mind. She must know; she was probably Halnashead's closest associate. So why ask?

"My family has always served the Royal House," he began carefully. "My mother—"

"Ah yes," Risada interrupted. "Your mother. I knew your mother."

"Then that's more than I did," said Rustam sourly.

Risada looked startled. "But surely she trained you?"

"Not exactly. She had me trained, by the Master who trained her. I hardly ever saw her."

"And your father?"

"I never knew my father," said Rustam stiffly. It was not a subject he wanted to discuss, and certainly not with Risada.

"Never knew him? Or never knew who he was?"

So that was it. As a mere craft Master, Rustam was beneath her notice. But as a bastard, he was contemptible.

"You already know that answer," he said bitterly, "or you wouldn't be asking. Does it give you so much pleasure, being able to gloat over other people's misfortunes?"

"What do you know of misfortune?" Risada muttered so quietly Rustam was barely sure she had said it. Then her chin jerked up, and she stared straight across the fire at him. What he saw in her face made him recoil.

"Do you know why I do what I do?" she whispered, the stark intensity in her eyes holding Rustam captive like a snake mesmerising its victim. "I do it because I have to, because for me there was no choice. I watched my parents butchered, cut down by an assassin sent to make a final play against my Family. Only he failed. He didn't get me, or my baby brother, Iain."

Now her gaze turned inward and Rustam shuddered, trying not to imagine what she saw there. He knew the story—everybody did—but could not imagine what it must have been like, to witness such carnage at so tender an age. No wonder then, that her life had followed such a violent course.

An image of Annasala, strapped to a torturer's table, drifted across his mind's eye.

The fire hissed suddenly as a particularly heavy squall of rain found its way beneath the slanted slate protecting the smoke hole in the roof. Risada's eyes snapped back to Rustam's.

"No Family was ever accused of the crime. Somewhere out there, someone knows who was responsible and one day I shall find them. Then they will know what it is to have an assassin stalk their halls."

She turned abruptly away, wrapped herself in her nearly dry cloak and curled up in a ball with her back to the fire. Rustam sat a while longer staring into the dwindling flames before he too dragged his damp cloak around his shoulders and lay down to sleep as best he could.

* * * * * * * * * * * * **

Lord Melcard rested his elbows on the carved arms of his high backed chair, and massaged his temples with his fingertips. He held his rage in check by focussing on the punishments he would mete out once he had decided who was responsible.

"Tell me again," he instructed in dangerously quiet tones, "how one man and one noblewoman could break into my dungeon, spirit away a prisoner that no one was supposed to know of, ride undetected across my lands, and then kill three of my finest soldiers before vanishing into the mountains."

His cold eyes pinned the white faced guard captain to the spot.

"Am I surrounded by imbeciles?"

The last word was expelled at full volume and the tremors that shook the captain's body afforded Melcard at least some small measure of satisfaction. He was never quite going to attain Hensar's level of intimidation, and the thought rankled, but at least he was the Lord, and Hensar the underling.

"We—we believe they used magic, my Lord," blurted the desperate captain. Clearly he, too, had thought of the doctor in his mind.

"They're both Tyr-enese, you fool. Where could they have learned magic?"

But even as he said it, Melcard considered the idea. Although the use of magic had been outlawed in Tyr-en since the day of Landfall, there were undoubtedly still secret practitioners, as there were of any forbidden discipline or cult. As it was now obvious that Chalice was the Royal Family's fabled assassin—the proof had been found in his dungeon, after all—the magic wielder must be the

Lady Risada. What a gem of knowledge to have come his way!

Melcard felt the corners of his mouth twitch upward. He grimaced to hide his momentary lapse from the trembling guard captain.

"Return to your duties," he dismissed the man, eager to follow his thought path without interruption.

Lord Melcard allowed himself a brief, one-sided smile as his eyes followed the captain's rigid back retreating hastily towards the office door. The man was good at his job, and Melcard had no particular wish to replace him, but there was nothing like a little healthy fear to stop the servants becoming complacent.

Returning to the matter of Risada, Melcard finally allowed a gloating grin to spread across his entire face.

The Royal Family, using magic. The most heinous of all crimes in Tyr-en, employed secretly by the King's own uncle! How quickly the other Families would turn against Halnashead and his puppet King when this knowledge became public. Melcard twisted his hands together in delight. The most important thing for him now was to consider the correct timing and precise delivery of this precious nugget of intelligence.

At least three, possibly four of the major Houses were already firmly behind his plan to replace the Royal Family. He detested the word usurp. It had such an ugly ring and could hardly be applied here, when he was really saving the Kingdom from the excesses of such a debauched Family as Marten's. And with the advent of such damning news, he knew he would be able to count on more than half of the others.

Proof barely concerned him. It could always be manufactured, and that was an area in which Hensar was most resourceful. Melcard did not consider the doctor's alchemy to come under the heading of magic, and if the odious little man dabbled, well, Melcard could say with all honesty that he had never witnessed such. His spies kept a discreet watch—from a safe distance—but were under orders to report only should Hensar be observed in any activity not directly concerned with the good of the Rees-Charlay Family or estate.

Whilst Melcard considered the doctor to be a powerful and useful tool, he trusted Hensar no further than he could toss him.

And now it was time to inspect the other piece of unexpected good fortune to have come out of this same incident—a newly acquired asset that would fit perfectly into his plans with only minor modifications. Lord Melcard rose from his throne-like chair and headed for his dungeon.

* * * * * * * * * * * *

By morning the steady rain had thinned to a drizzle, and only the highest peaks were hidden by cloud. Rustam and Risada spent all of that day thoroughly airing the contents of their packs. When their clean clothes were finally dried, Rustam wasted no time changing. He dumped the soiled garments he had worn for the past three days into a bucket of hot water to soak.

Three days. Charin's breath! Had he really worn the same outfit for three whole days? He cast his mind back but could not recall the last time he had worn only one set for an entire day. Three or four were more usual.

Three whole days! He shook his head and left the clothes in the bucket.

The following morning the sun started to shine patchily. Rustam spent the day hunting, rediscovering his boyhood talents with a sling, and returned to the hut by mid afternoon with three rabbits and a small deer. They ate well that night, and laid out the rest of the meat to dry for the journey.

Neither of them mentioned the first night's conversation, and Risada remained distantly polite, busying herself with the need to constantly dribble water and strained broth down the elf's throat. On the third day in the hut she removed the filthy bandages from his arm and, holding the stained wadding between two fingertips, offered it to Rustam who accepted it at arm's length with a quizzical look.

"Burn it!" ordered Risada, and Rustam complied only too willingly: the stench was so appalling he was certain the wounds it had hidden must be gangrenous. But when he returned with the requested hot water and wash cloth, he could see nothing ill-humoured beyond an encrustation of dried blood.

Elixir of eternity! Rustam thought cynically as he studied the fevered elf. *It hasn't done him much good, has it?*

The scabs peeled away beneath Risada's gently ministrations, revealing a crazy patterning of criss-crossed and puckered scars upon scars that made even Rustam shudder. Hensar's work?

Probably.

By the fourth morning, the elf was showing signs of recovering from his fever although still no inclination to wake, and sometimes he cried out in his sleep; strange, eerie cries in an unknown tongue that had Rustam and Risada both reaching for their daggers.

Once, waking in the night, stiff from sleeping on the earth floor, Rustam sat up and saw the gently slanted eyes open, watching him. The silver-blue gaze cut to his heart like the point of a stiletto, and his cry of surprise strangled in a throat gone suddenly dry. He tore his eyes away and struggled out of his bedroll but by the time he made it to the pallet the elf had slipped back into unconsciousness.

The next morning, the fifth since finding their temporary haven, Rustam was grooming the now gleaming horses when he had the uncomfortable feeling of being watched. Casually he turned and scanned the scrub-covered hillside, but nothing revealed itself. He packed the brushes away and went around the back of the hut to where he had deposited the carcasses from the previous day's hunt.

Gone.

Not dragged away, but lifted and carried. Rustam hurried inside.

"We're leaving."

"Now? But one more day—"

"Now. We have company. No—" he raised a hand to stop Risada reaching for her weapons. "Not Melcard's men. Something else."

"What do you mean, *something*?"

"I don't know. It could be animals, but then again, maybe not."

"Rock trolls?"

"Could be."

"You start saddling up. I'll organise the packs."

By noon they were loaded and on their way, mounted as before with Nightstalker carrying both Rustam and the Shivan, Risada leading the bay mare and the heavily laden pony. Rustam hoped the shepherd would not be too put out to find most of his stores missing, particularly so much of the grain, but there was really no other choice; they had a long, hard journey ahead and there was no guarantee Chel would continue to smile favourably upon them.

Throughout the remainder of the day the feeling of being watched persisted, though neither Rustam nor Risada spotted their stalkers. Despite the threat, Rustam kept finding his eye drawn to the rider-less bay mare: she was definitely favouring her near foreleg.

That night they camped in the open, keeping the horses within the circle of firelight. An inspection of the mare's leg confirmed what Rustam had feared: heat and swelling around the fetlock. He took the last of the waybread—it was beginning to grow mould anyway—soaked it to make a poultice, and strapped it to the injured limb using a silk scarf purloined from Risada's saddle bags.

They stood watch for half the night each. The next day was just the same, only by evening they had reached the end of the foothills and the mountains proper loomed before them. By this time the mare was limping badly, the swelling extending up her leg as far as the knee. Rustam reapplied the poultice he had saved from the night before, but without much hope short of direct intervention from the goddess.

They set up camp beside a stream that ran with fresh cold water fed by the snow-capped peaks above. It splashed and bubbled its way over a miniature waterfall and into a small pool before running rapidly along a shallow course at the foot of the mountain, disappearing eventually into a distant forest-filled valley. A rough edged pebbly depression extended almost two horses lengths to either side of the streambed, and Rustam shuddered as he pictured the torrent that must rage along it in spring, when the first melt was under way. Not a site you would want to be caught camping on at the wrong time of year.

He tilted his head back, studying the route they would take in the morning. A rock strewn but easily negotiable slope led sharply upward away from their campsite, curving out of sight around the shoulder of the mountain looming above them. To either side, other peaks jutted like broken teeth into the crimson sunset. At least the violent colour promised better weather for a while.

"Chalice, a fire would be nice," prompted the Lady of Domn.

The twisted remains of a dried out tree provided firewood, and Rustam soon had a cheery blaze going to drive back the encroaching darkness.

Risada began boiling water in every watertight vessel they carried.

"What's all that for?" asked Rustam, genuinely puzzled. "Are you planning a bath?"

"As close as I can manage," Risada replied firmly. "This may be the last decent fire we have for some time, and I intend to make maximum use of it. Now go and see to the horses."

Rustam raised his eyebrows but obediently turned his back, and took his grooming brushes over to the animals. He was nearly finished when Risada shrieked. He ducked under the neck of her grey and sprinted around the fire to where she knelt beside the stream, staring into the water.

"What? What did you see?"

"There," she said faintly, pointing into the stream. "A face, in the water."

Rustam peered closely but all he could see were rocks and stones beneath the surface, not even weeds that could have moved enough to startle the lady.

But Risada isn't just any lady, he reminded himself. *She's Dart, the assassin, and she doesn't frighten easily.*

"My Lady, I don't see anything—"

"Of course you don't," she snapped. "It's not there anymore."

Rustam looked round at her and felt his eyes widen. She was still staring at the water, her face pale but composed, apparently oblivious to the fact that although she was clutching a towel across her breasts, she was naked to the waist.

"I'm sure there's a simple explanation," Rustam said carefully and put a comforting hand on her shoulder. Her violent reaction flung him backward, almost into the fire, and he lost all his breath as he slammed into the ground. He stared blearily up at the bare-cheasted siren that stood threateningly over him, dagger in hand.

"Don't you dare touch me, you bastard!" she hissed.

Rustam gazed up at her in astonishment—where did she hide that dagger?

"I intended no offence."

"Then remember your position, and keep your hands to yourself. I am easily offended."

"Can't say I'd noticed," Rustam muttered as he rolled over and regained his feet.

A groan behind him made his back crawl and he spun round, but it was only the elf shifting in his sleep. Or was it? Rustam squinted in the flickering light of the fire: was there someone standing over the Shivan?

A slender, wispy figure seemed to be hovering there, gazing down at the unconscious elf, but as Rustam took a step forward it wavered and dissipated into a column of mist.

"Did you see that?" he whispered, and took another step. The elf moaned and rolled over. Pale blue eyes gazed up at Rustam and this time there was no entreaty, no shock, merely curiosity.

"Risada, here!" he called urgently, neglecting to use her title. He knelt down beside the Shivan and took one of the fine-boned hands—so like a woman's—in his own.

"We're friends. We rescued you from the dungeon. Do you understand?"

With a rustle of fabric Risada knelt beside him. She had put on a blouse, noted Rustam.

"He's probably too weak to talk yet," she said.

"I understand. Thank you." The Shivan's voice whispered like a summer breeze, so faint Rustam had to strain to hear it.

"Who are you?" he asked.

"I am Elwaes," replied the elf. Then the canted eyes closed, and his head rolled to one side. Alarmed, Rustam checked his breathing but it was the even rise and fall of sleep, not the last sigh of death. He looked at Risada.

"At least we have a name now, to send with him to Chel if it comes to that."

"Hopefully he's past that now, unless this journey claims us all. And I have no intention of permitting that," Risada declared firmly.

7. ELWAES

"Take the first watch, Chalice. Wake me when Vana rises," ordered the Lady of Domn before settling herself near the fire. Rustam acknowledged her words with a vague nod, too wrapped in his own thoughts to answer.

He *had* seen something beside Elwaes. Something insubstantial, but there nonetheless. And by that reasoning, Risada had seen something also. A face, in the water. Was it the same creature?

More to the point, what was it? What did it want, and was it dangerous?

He debated telling Risada but decided she was already sufficiently on guard. Besides, he had no desire to attract any more of her caustic comments.

A noise to his left made him jump, but it was only a branch settling in the fire. He prowled the campsite, eyes roving the dark boundaries, but once again the night passed without incident and by daylight they were up and ready to move out. With one omission.

"Are you sure about this, Chalice?"

"I wish I weren't," Rustam said gloomily, "but we have no choice. I only wish it had happened earlier, back where someone might have found her."

The bay mare looked mournfully at him.

"Perhaps it would be kinder to put her out of her misery?" Risada suggested. "We could always make use of the extra meat."

Rustam's stomach turned at the idea, but he allowed nothing to show on his face. "No. Chel willing, as long as she finds enough to eat, she'll recover. It's only a sprain. Besides, how would we carry any more?"

Risada's brief nod evinced reluctant agreement. Dismissing the injured horse as though she'd ceased to exist, the Lady of Domn moved on to her next concern.

"So what route do we take?"

Rustam paused to consider. They had fled into the foothills without any immediate goal beyond reaching the mountains. Now they were here, and Rustam realised he had no real idea of where *here* was. The obvious trail leading upward from their campsite might go nowhere, but then again, it might. Careful not to reveal his concern to Risada and risk further sarcasm, he squinted at the more distant mountains.

"If I'm correct, we need to be heading towards those twin peaks over there." He pointed west.

"And if you're not?"

"Then we'll find another way. There are supposed to be dozens of passes through this range."

"*Supposed* to be?" echoed Risada in icy tones. "You were *supposed* to be the guide for this expedition."

"Guard, not guide," muttered Rustam behind his saddle flap as he tightened his girths. "My Lady," he said aloud, "I will do my best. I can do nothing more."

Risada tossed her head—her hair was loose and gleaming today after its wash—and jerked her grey gelding round to face the rock-strewn incline, dragging the reluctant pack pony along behind. Rustam winced and vowed to give the lady some lessons in horsemastership, if not in manners. He swung up behind Elwaes and nudged Nightstalker forward.

They splashed through the little stream, and jumped up the low bank. The broad, boulder strewn slope was carpeted with short grass that was more grey than green, but provided excellent springy going for the horses. Rustam scanned ahead with approval—too wide for an ambush and not enough cover to hide anything larger than a dog. *Or perhaps a small troll,* he thought and scowled, then dismissed the notion; why look for trouble before it appeared? It was bound to, sooner or later.

He glanced back down the slope. The bay mare grazed peacefully on the abandoned campsite, unconcerned by their departure. Rustam breathed a prayer to Chel, that she might not become someone else's meal.

Meanwhile, it was a beautiful morning. A lingering mist swirled restlessly around the horses' hooves, while the air, still fresh with early morning chill, smelled clean and bracing. Rustam took appreciative deep breaths and looked around at the spectacular landscape.

The Middle Mountains were widely spaced except in the centre of the range, and here on the edge they rose like massive sentinels to either side of the riders' path. The rising sun shone golden on the colourless land, contrasting the bright blue of the sky with the granite grey and the snowy white of the peaks. The stream they had camped beside ran chattering along a ravine to their left, the only noise in this hauntingly silent land aside from the muffled thud of their horses' hooves. Overhead a solitary eagle rode the thermals, hunting for breakfast.

I wonder what he sees, thought Rustam. *Are we really as alone as it seems, or do shadows move amongst the rocks?*

Just then Elwaes stirred and straightened a little in the saddle.

"Risada," called Rustam quietly. She looked back over her shoulder, a frown of annoyance on her aristocratic features, and Rustam realised he had done it again: *Lady* Risada. However, instead of a sharp reminder, she reined in and waited for Rustam to draw alongside.

"Well then, Sir Elf, how are we this morning?" she enquired.

"We are much improved," replied Elwaes, and Rustam could hear his smile. "I am in your debt," he added. His head moved a little as he looked around, and strands of long fair hair clung to Rustam's face, tickling his nose.

At least all that rain had washed the awful smell from it.

Rustam raised a hand and brushed the pale strands aside, then fingered his chin. Several days' stubble was thickening into a beard now and he wondered idly if it suited him. Some people said that women were more attracted to a man with a beard, but it looked like it was going to be some time before he would be in a position to test the theory. It certainly wouldn't work with Risada. If Annasala was correct, then the Lady of Domn only had one purpose in looking at bearded men—and she already knew that he bore no scar on his jaw.

His chest tightened at thought of the princess. He could only hope she had escaped the blockade forming between Rees-Charlay and Darshan. His training kept him from being distracted by situations beyond his ability to influence, but still, he was worried about his prince's daughter.

"Where are we going?" asked Elwaes suddenly.

"We are taking you to Kishtan, Master Elwaes," Risada replied firmly, daring him to query their choice. Rustam could sense the Shivan's bewilderment, and offered an explanation.

"King Graylin's queen is Shivan. We felt it best to take you to her, as we would not be welcome in Shiva itself. And besides, we have no idea how to get to your land."

Rustam received a small glare from Risada for his candour, but he was unrepentant. He had told Elwaes nothing of their mission, and the elf was bound to ask questions. Hopefully this would forestall many more awkward ones, at least for a while.

"I see," was all Elwaes said before his head started to drop sideways, and he relaxed back against Rustam in sleep. Rustam shifted him to a position more comfortable for them both. Although Nightstalker offered no objection to her double burden, Rustam worried about her, and hoped Elwaes would soon be strong enough to ride alone. Rustam did not mind walking.

He looked up to find Risada riding alongside, watching him.

"Take care what you say, Chalice. He might not take too kindly to being the main bargaining chip for an army."

"I would not dream of telling him, my Lady. It leaves a sour enough taste in my own mouth."

"Just remember what I've said," she commanded, then drew a slow breath as her face twisted with distaste. "Bear in mind also, that we have no idea what sort of magic this creature can command."

Her eyes flickered mistrustfully towards the elf, as if she expected to surprise him eavesdropping. Apparently satisfied with his quiescence for the moment, she turned away and rode on ahead. Rustam was left regarding her back, wondering how deeply the assassin's fear of magic burrowed into her soul, and how it might affect their mission.

They stopped for lunch where a small glade of stunted trees offered some shelter from the chill wind that had risen during the morning. Rustam built a fire despite the time of day, unsure how much longer they could expect to keep finding firewood. Risada took the kettle over to the stream and returned with an odd look on her face.

"Something wrong?" Rustam asked.

"I saw it again—the same face. Or not really a face this time, just the eyes." She shivered and locked gazes with Rustam. "What do you think it is?"

Rustam shrugged. "A spirit? Some magical creature? You know the further we go from Tyr-en the more likely we are to encounter magic."

"Mmm," Risada agreed, and bestowed a long, lingering look upon the sleeping elf before continuing. "I've heard it said that in Kishtan every second person is a magical practitioner. Ugh!" She shuddered. "Why does it have to be that barbaric Kingdom?"

Rustam laughed, a trifle harshly, and pointed at Elwaes.

"Barbaric? What do you suppose they'll think of us when they hear what Melcard has been doing to him for Chel alone knows how long?"

* * * * * * * * *

"Well?" snapped Lord Melcard Rees-Charlay as soon as Doctor Hensar had closed the door. "They've been gone ten days now. Ten whole days! And what have you done about it?"

Hensar bowed deeply, gritting his teeth against the infuriating whine in his master's voice. As he straightened he managed not to roll his eyes or sigh despite the exasperation he felt at being forced to work with such short-sighted greed. He viewed Melcard's private chamber with a jaundiced eye. The fool was so utterly convinced his plans would succeed he'd already had the room redecorated in the royal colours. Where once maroon and gold had lent the study an air of restrained grandeur, the purple and white stripes looked crass and gaudy.

Perhaps he was just trying to convince himself that it really would happen.

"My Lord, I can assure you—"

"I want no assurances. I want their bodies! And I want another elf. My personal supply of elixir will only last so long."

Hensar's fingers tightened around his crystal pendant. How easy it would be to dispose of the imbecile right now and finish this degrading charade. But the Bastard still had need of Rees-Charlay's resources. Hensar contented himself with images of Melcard's broken body strapped to his torture table.

"My Lord, it shall be so. Another elf will not be hard to secure, and I have associates who can reach even into the mountains and pluck the fugitives to their deaths wherever they are."

"Then why has it not happened yet, Hensar? Ten days you have had already."

"Even as we speak—"

Melcard held up a hand. "I will hear nothing of your plans, merely their results. Do not fail me again."

Hensar's jaw dropped. "Fail—?" he blurted before he could stop himself.

"Yes, Hensar, you have failed me." Melcard rose from his seat—an impressive throne-like chair atop a dais—and stepped down to circle Hensar like a wolf unsure of its prey.

As well you should be, thought the doctor darkly, struggling to keep his face impassive as he looked up to meet Melcard's eye.

"You failed," accused Melcard in clipped tones, "to suspect that the Lady Risada herself might be a player. Why should she not be? She is Halnashead's cousin and Halnashead controls royal security. Should it have been so hard to make the connection?"

It was as clearly before you, as me, Hensar thought angrily as Melcard favoured him with an accusatory scowl.

But in truth, Hensar was as livid with himself for the oversight as was his Lord. He should have dealt with the meddlesome whore when he had the chance, before she matured into the danger she now represented. Although the chances of her doing any real damage were very slight.

He bowed his head again. "My Lord, she will not reach the other side of the mountains. And even if she should, and she was to succeed in raising troops in Kishtan, she would be too late. You will already be upon the throne in Darshan."

As Hensar hoped, mention of the throne seized Melcard's thoughts. The Lord's eyes grew far away as he pictured himself seated in state, dispensing judgements and rulings to all the Families and reorganising the Kingdom to suit his aspirations.

Let him have his little fantasies—they would be swept away soon enough.

Melcard stepped back onto his dais and seated himself regally. "In that at least, Hensar, you see truly. I must direct my attention forward, and finalise my exact approach to Halnashead once Marten has been dealt with."

He rubbed his hands together, and drew his lips back into what passed for a smile on his passionless face. "Was it not a stroke of fortune that the Princess Annasala should fall ill and be unable to travel when our other guests took their leave? Of course, she had little choice in the matter, and that is one of your areas of expertise that continues to please me. Now go. I have much to consider."

Hensar bowed low and left the Lord to his empty scheming. Empty, because Hensar had no intention of allowing Melcard's plans to proceed that far. The fool actually envisaged using Annasala as leverage to force Halnashead into crowning him as the next King!

True, the King's gutless uncle had no desire to take the crown for himself, content to stay in the background and run his covert operations from the shadows behind the throne, but how Melcard could realistically expect Halnashead to lend visible support to a usurper—even in exchange for the life of his daughter? Hensar shook his head. Melcard was so naïve it defied belief. Despite a pathetic lack of ambition on Halnashead's part, the doctor had a healthy respect for the Prince's intellect and his network of players.

And little doubt he would sacrifice even his own kin to prevent the crown from passing beyond the grasp of his Family.

A sudden, gratifying tension in Hensar's groin accompanied thought of the helpless girl languishing in the cell beneath the mansion; the very cage that had until recently housed the elf that had been so central to his manipulations. How easy it had been to convince Melcard that the secret of eternal life ran though the miserable creature's veins; almost as easy to concoct a potion that produced the illusion of arrested ageing. Of course, in the ten years since they had begun marketing the elixir, a small number of customers had been inconvenient enough to die, but having been prepared for such eventualities it had taken little effort to blame the deaths on matters other than old age or illness.

Loss of the elf was a minor setback to Hensar's long term plans, but he doubted the Shivan would have lived much longer anyway. Once the Royal Bastard—Hensar scowled at the derogatory mix of terms—was securely installed upon the throne of Tyr-en there would be time enough to capture another and continue research into the true elixir of eternity.

And in the meantime, the cell's new occupant provided many fresh possibilities. The tension became an almost painful ache as Hensar eagerly anticipated the time he would spend in the dungeon, persuading the stubbornly defiant princess to accept her new destiny. She had already proven she was not the frail flower he had first thought her to be.

Guards snapped to attention at his passage, backs rigid with fear lest they draw his unwelcome notice, for all Rees-Charlay's staff knew who chose those to be punished, and who carried out those punishments. Even the strongest amongst them flinched from the brilliant shards of rainbow light that preceded the doctor along the corridor as late afternoon sunlight struck to the heart of the crystal pendant rolling gently back and forth across his barrel chest. Had anyone dared lower their eyes to his face they would have seen the slight smile upon his lips as he allowed himself to savour the effect his mere presence had upon them.

It felt good to be feared.

* * * * * * * * * *

Afternoon in the mountains passed in the same manner as the morning, with the horses plodding steadily uphill. When Rustam looked back down the slope he found it impossible to gauge how far they had travelled. Apart from the gradual increase in size and frequency of boulders, the land looked the same ahead as it did behind. He estimated they should have covered perhaps twelve leagues, maybe more, yet they seemed to be no further past the peak that rose to their right than they had been at midmorning. He tried not to let the enormity of the distances daunt him, but it was hard.

Elwaes drifted in and out of sleep, but remained silent. Rustam wondered what was going on inside the elf's head, and although he was relieved that Elwaes was recovering he shared Risada's unspoken concern—had they been safer when the Shivan was sick? They didn't know the nature of his magical skills, but the fact that he had them was not in dispute.

To add to Rustam's unease, the sensation of being watched was stronger than ever. Once, he thought he saw something dark and hairy dart from behind one rock to another, but when he rode over to investigate he found nothing.

Risada turned her horse to face him. "Are you quite finished sightseeing?" she demanded.

"Just doing my job, or would you rather I ignored the possibility of ambush?"

"Please, no. Chel forbid I should keep you from your duties. After all, we only have the safety of the Kingdom to secure. What do a few delays matter?"

Rustam gritted his teeth. "Risada—*Lady* Risada—we have to make it to Kishtan first. Alive. If you want to press on and ignore the possibility of attack, go ahead. But my first loyalty is to Halnashead, and I will do everything I can to reach Kishtan safely. Hopefully with all three of us, but getting Elwaes there has priority over even your safety."

Risada looked murderous. "I should have known. Like mother, like son. Well know this, Master Chalice: I have no intention of being the victim of one of Halnashead's little schemes like my parents were. If my father had had his mind on the game instead of on your mother he'd be alive today and I wouldn't be traipsing over some goddess-forsaken mountain range with you and an elf for company!"

She spun her mount around to continue, but the grey snorted and pranced nervously sideways.

Rustam studied the surrounding rubble. Plenty of hiding places. "I think we should be moving, your Ladyship."

"I would if I could Chalice," she snapped, "but this stupid animal refuses to go."

She drummed her heels ineffectually against the horse's flanks.

"It's no wonder, really," observed Rustam. "Where did you learn to ride?"

"Enough, Chalice—look!"

Rustam followed her pointing finger and this time there was no mistake. Something dark and hairy, about the size of a large dog but with oddly jointed limbs, scuttled across an open stretch of ground between boulders. Rustam glanced over his shoulder. There were others behind. Even Nightstalker began to shift uneasily from hoof to hoof.

"We're in trouble," he muttered. In front of him Elwaes stirred. "Stay still," ordered Rustam. He felt the elf tense.

"Ride!" whispered Elwaes. "It is our only hope."

Rustam opened his mouth with a sharp retort, but stifled it as more and more dark shapes rose from behind the rocks. Now that he could see them clearly, Rustam shuddered. The trolls were vaguely human in shape, but covered in thickly matted clumps of dark hair, with overlong arms that seemed to have too many joints, and protruding, slavering snouts lined with rows of sharp teeth. They exchanged strange, warbling cries that made Rustam's skin crawl.

As they edged closer, Rustam realised why the horses were so upset—at this distance even his nose could detect the pungent stench.

The largest troll, almost half the size again of the others, and the only one wearing any form of adornment—a chunk of rough crystal dangling from a leather thong around its neck—shambled closer until Risada's mount reared and plunged in panic, almost unseating her. She dropped the pack pony's lead rope and drew her blowpipe.

"No!" cried Elwaes hoarsely. "There are too many!"

"Risada, no!" yelled Rustam, infected by the Shivan's panic.

A tiny speck of yellow attached itself to the approaching troll's chest, beside the glittering pendant. The creature howled indignantly and fell over. The others paused, and Risada bestowed a mocking smile upon Rustam.

"You were saying?"

"Look at it, my Lady. *Look!*"

The troll felled by Risada's dart was sitting up again, peering short-sightedly at the yellow feather. With a snarl it plucked it out and threw it to the ground. Risada turned pale.

"But that's impossible! No one can survive that poison."

"No man, perhaps," Elwaes corrected quietly. "My Lady, we must ride for our lives and now, whilst they are still unsure of us."

Rustam leaned over and gathered up the pony's lead; it had pressed close to Nightstalker for comfort. Rustam nudged his mare forward, up the slope where there were no boulders directly in their path to conceal a troll. Nightstalker snorted, but complied. Risada's gelding merely stood where it was, tossing its head, nostrils flared and eyes white-rimmed. Muttering, the trolls began to edge closer.

Then an unearthly sound, a high-pitched singsong that was so rapid and yet at the same time languid that Rustam could distinguish neither tempo nor source, drifted from somewhere in front of him, back towards Risada and her panic-frozen mount. Rustam looked round and watched almost in a dream as slowly, so slowly, the grey's eyes calmed and his ears flickered back and forth, trying to locate the elusive melody.

It's the elf. It's Elwaes!

Realisation jolted Rustam out of the semi-tranced state into which he had fallen, and he focused fully on the still tableau behind him. The trolls stood or crouched, their eyes half closed and their weapons—stone knives and flints—dangling from their limp hands. Risada's eyes were glazed but her horse looked calm, and when Rustam squeezed Nightstalker with his legs she walked slowly forward and the grey followed.

They were almost out of the ring of trolls when the song faltered, then died. Elwaes fell back limply against Rustam.

"Damn!"

The spell broken, the trolls surged forward with angry howls, almost catching the horses as they sprang into a gallop. Something dark clutched at Rustam's leg and he kicked out hard. The creature shrieked as it fell away and then they were fleeing at high speed, swerving and jumping to avoid the rocks littering the slope. At one point Rustam nearly lost the pony's lead as it jumped one way and

Nightstalker the other. He swayed dangerously in the saddle but hung on grimly. They could not afford to lose all their tools and food.

The sharp air whipped tears from his eyes, and when he glanced back his vision was so blurred all he could see was the vague outline of horse and rider several lengths behind. He faced forward again and concentrated on putting as much distance behind him as he could without risking a fall on the treacherous going.

Finally Rustam was forced to slow to a trot. Nightstalker was blowing heavily and the poor pony was tripping and stumbling, threatening to tear Rustam's arm out of its socket every time it jerked the lead rope. He looked back to see Risada cantering up on her labouring grey.

Rustam eased his grip on Elwaes. The elf still slumped limply in the saddle, and Rustam was relieved to feel the shallow rise and fall of his chest.

Risada drew alongside them. Rustam glanced across at her and was transfixed by her glare.

"You might have waited for me."

Rustam blinked in disbelief. "What help could I have given you, my Lady? I didn't have so much as a spare hand. What did you want me to do—swing my sword with my teeth?"

"Don't get sarcastic with me, Chalice. You were prepared to leave me back there, just so you could get your precious elf to safety."

"He saved both our lives, in case you hadn't noticed."

"I'm willing to admit he helped, but I'm sure we could have fought our way out of that rabble."

"At what cost, your Ladyship? We could have lost Elwaes, not to mention the pony, and if you think we can make it over the mountains without the supplies he's carrying, think again."

And you were supposed to be leading him, Rustam added silently to himself, though he said nothing aloud. Things were bad enough between them as it was. What was the matter with the woman? Anyone would think she didn't want this mission to succeed.

Sudden ugly suspicions surfaced in Rustam's mind. Risada was presumed to be utterly loyal to the crown, but she had already admitted her mistrust of Halnashead. Suppose, just suppose, even she could be bought. The implications were horrifying. What might she have been offered: jewels, land? She already had those in abundance. Position? But the Second House was as high as any noble could aspire to, unless—*Queen* Risada? It had a fair ring to it. Marriage to Melcard? This vibrant young woman wedded to a murderous, soul-dead man like Melcard?

But why not? Dart was as at home with murder as the traitor. What better—and safer—alliance could Melcard make for himself?

But why go through with this charade of a mission to Kishtan? Risada could have slit his throat and disposed of the elf the first night out from Rees-Charlay, then made her way back in secret so as not to arouse Sala's suspicions. No, there had to be something Risada wanted in Kishtan. He would have to watch her very carefully from now on.

8. SPRITE

"Risada, stop! If we go any further tonight, one of us will break a leg."

Several lengths ahead of Nightstalker, Risada's grey glimmered ghostly in the moonlight. It stopped abruptly and stood, head drooping with fatigue, too tired even to protest the jab in the mouth it had received from its rider. Risada's face was a pale blur as she twisted around in the saddle.

"Chalice," she said, her tone so cold it might have turned him to ice had he been closer. "If I have to remind you once more, I may consider finishing this journey alone. You will use my title now, and every time you address me."

Rustam felt his patience corroding. In court circles and social gatherings he would not have thought twice about such a thing. He had been raised knowing his place. But out here, far from any urbane company, did it really matter?

Besides, within the framework of the game, Rustam considered Charmer to be of equal standing with Dart.

"Lady Risada, the time it takes for me to say that could be the difference between your life and a knife in the back."

"Chalice, I've guarded my own back since I was six years old. You *will* use my title and you will remember your place." She peered around. "We'll camp over there, on the lee side of that boulder."

"Yes Ma'am," muttered Rustam, and slid awkwardly from Nightstalker's back, bringing the limp Shivan with him. He propped Elwaes against the boulder before leading the tired horses over to the stream. The temperature had dropped sharply and Rustam shivered. The horses waded part way in to drink, their legs and noses disappearing into the mist that rose from the water.

The pony blew gently through his nostrils, swirling the mist into a rising column. He snorted and stepped back, but the column continued to rise until it broke away from the surface and drifted towards Rustam.

"*Charin's breath*! What are you?" He felt no fear and was alarmed by its absence. Whatever this being was, it wanted him unconcerned. Was this its means of catching prey?

Slowly a form grew clearer within the column, and soon Rustam was staring at the slender figure of a young woman, his gaze ensnared by two smoky grey eyes set in a delicately pretty face. Her long hair writhed and twisted around her, hiding most of her body from view, but clearly she was naked aside from that adornment.

"Who are you?"

She smiled at him; a bright, impish smile. Then she vanished.

"Damn, damn, *damn*! What is it?"

"Muttering to yourself, Chalice?"

Rustam glanced round sharply. He had been so enthralled by the wraith he had not heard Risada approach.

I don't suppose I'd hear her anyway, if she didn't want me to.

"Not exactly, my Lady. I just met our travelling companion."

Risada glanced at the water. "The face?"

"Actually, no. She had a body this time. Rather a good one."

There was easily enough moonlight to see Risada's scowl. "I think we should move on," she declared. "Away from this stream."

"We can't. We need the water and besides, there's no other pass between these two mountains."

"I don't like it."

"Neither do I, but I'd say we've no choice. Wouldn't you?"

"So what do you suggest, Chalice? We wait here to be murdered by whatever that thing is, or we go back to the trolls and surrender?"

"I suggest we get what sleep we can, and make an early start. We must be quite a way ahead of that troll pack even if they're still following us and, whatever it is, I don't think it's dangerous."

"That's your solution?"

"If you have another, I'd be happy to hear it."

"No." This time Risada smiled, but even in the gloom Rustam could see that it touched no more than her lips. ""You're my guide in the mountains, remember. But remember too, if anything goes wrong it'll be your problem to deal with."

* * * * * * * * * * * * *

Rustam forced his aching knees to straighten as he pried his cold-stiffened body up from the boulder where he'd sat out the last hour of his watch. In the faintest glimmer of first light, he cast an eye over his sleeping companions. Elwaes slumbered on peacefully. Beyond him, Risada stirred inside her bedroll.

Rustam looked up and his stomach clenched.

"Damn!"

"What?" Flinging her blankets off, Risada sprang up, dagger in hand. Rustam pointed to where the horses picked at the short tufts of grass within reach of their picket line.

The pony and most of the packs were gone.

Warily, Risada moved towards the horses. Rustam regarded her with suspicion. Was this her first move? He'd made it only too plain that they could not continue without the supplies. Had she risen silently during that last hour, so stealthily that even his sharp senses had not alerted him, and disposed of the pony?

He crunched his way across the frosty ground to join her. It would have been difficult for anyone to move quietly on such ground, but obviously someone had. Risada bent over to inspect the area.

"It's too hard—there are no marks at all. What were you doing, Chalice, sleeping on watch?"

"Whoever did it was a damn sight closer to you than they were to me," Rustam pointed out as he moved around the horses, and squatted down to study the frozen ground.

Damn it all to Charin's hell—I should have heard something!

"Here," he said after a moment, and pointed.

"Where? I don't see anything."

"Look here: the ice is scuffed off this tuft of grass. And again there. If we're lucky and they don't take to the rocks we should be able to follow them."

"Who are *they*, Chalice? Did you see who took it?"

Rustam bridled at her accusatory tone. As if he was the traitor!

"No, I didn't. I'd guess at more trolls. These mountains must be infested with them. If the pony had simply strayed, the packs would still be here, and animals would have torn them open without bothering to drag them away."

"Bandits?" Risada suggested.

Rustam considered. "I doubt it. They would have taken the horses too, and probably cut our throats."

"So why didn't the trolls?"

"Because," said Elwaes's voice weakly from behind, "There were too few of them to risk attacking us."

Risada turned to face the elf, her eyes narrowed with suspicion. "And how can you be so sure? Unless you had something to do with it."

"Because I know the mountains, and the ways of rock trolls." The Shivan's voice was faint, and it tremored as he shook with cold.

With stiff fingers, Rustam fumbled open one of his saddle bags—those at least they had used as pillows—and drew out a woollen jerkin. He handed it to Elwaes.

"My thanks, friend. Again, I am indebted to you."

"I believe we have some thanks of our own to offer," said Rustam with a meaningful look at Risada.

She regarded him haughtily for a moment, and then turned to the elf. "Indeed Master Elwaes, Chalice is correct. Our gratitude for our deliverance from the troll pack yesterday. Please, tell us how you lulled them so."

Elwaes smiled and the dull grey morning was touched golden by the radiance of his beauty. Even Risada's frosty demeanour seemed a little thawed.

"It is my gift, to talk with animals. And trolls are not much brighter than the average wolf."

"Talk with them, or command them?" asked Risada, and Rustam could hear the intense interest in her voice.

Probably thinking how much safer it would be to use animals as tools of assassination. How could you accuse a snake of loyalty to one Family or another?

The elf shook his head. "I command no man or animal. I may suggest, but the choice to listen must be theirs."

"The trolls didn't seem to have a choice."

"They chose to listen this once. They may not do so again."

"Which leads us back to our current dilemma," Rustam reminded them. "We can't go on without supplies, but there's an angry mob of trolls somewhere behind us. Any suggestions?"

"Chalice," said Risada in an oddly strangled tone. "Behind you."

Rustam turned slowly. Hovering not two horses lengths away was the misty woman from the stream. In daylight, her features were less defined, more a suggestion of human form, but the eyes were the same.

"What does it want?" hissed Risada, and Rustam was jarred by the undercurrent of naked fear in her voice. Fear from Dart, who had killed men with nothing more than her bare hands or her dagger. Dart, who only last night had confidently faced down a whole pack of trolls with nothing more than a blow pipe.

But this was *magic*.

Like all Tyr-enese, Rustam distrusted magic, but he did not suffer from the blind terror that afflicted many.

Risada's reaction suggested that she did.

And this creature was certainly magical. It drifted towards them, and out of the corner of his eye Rustam saw Risada draw her dagger. He stepped aside, wondering silently how you fought a creature with no corporeal form, but instead of continuing on towards Risada, the shadowy figure turned and followed him. He backed away and dropped into a fighting stance.

A strange buzz came from near the boulder, and Rustam risked a quick glance. To his chagrin he saw that it was Elwaes with his head thrown back, laughing. Indignantly Rustam straightened and glared at the elf.

"What's so funny? What is she?"

Elwaes coughed, drew a deep breath and wiped his eyes before answering. "She's a sprite—a water elemental. And she's taken a fancy to you, my friend."

"I might have known!" grated Risada in disgust. "No matter where he goes there's bound to be a woman involved."

"I didn't ask for this," Rustam protested as the sprite drifted closer. He flinched slightly as a vaguely-seen hand reached out to touch him on the shoulder, but the sensation was the delicate touch of a feather, or a warm breeze on bare skin; not at all unpleasant.

The hand drifted down his chest, his waist. Lower.

"Excuse me!"

He jumped back, face burning with embarrassment, but the sprite moved relentlessly with him, more and more of her misty body flowing around him, caressing his skin, moving through his clothes as if they did not exist.

"Can't you call her off?" he pleaded with Elwaes, but the elf shook his head.

"Elementals do as they please."

Rustam shuddered as the sprite enveloped him. His pulse raced, and his skin tingling with hypersensitivity. His knees gave way and he crashed to the ground.

Everything ceased to exist outside of the familiar rhythm, the gasps of pleasure, the swelling heat. He lost all sense of reality, of time and place. And of his bemused audience. He heard himself cry out, as though listening to a stranger far away, as violent orgasm clutched him with intensity far beyond anything he'd experienced before. Again and again it swept him until his mind and body were saturated with sensation and he passed out.

* * * * * * * * * * *

Gradually, Rustam became aware of his surroundings. He was stretched out on the frozen ground, breathing quick, shallow gasps of icy air, and shuddering uncontrollably, though not with cold.

He groaned and rolled over, opened his eyes—he didn't recall shutting them—to find Risada leaning against the boulder, regarding him with a malicious humour. Elwaes seemed to be asleep again, and the sprite had vanished.

"Well, Chalice, that was some performance," observed the Lady of Domn. Rustam winced. She was hardly likely to let him forget this episode in a hurry. For now though, she seemed content to let him fret without prompting as, with a toss of her head, she turned away and began packing what little remained of their supplies.

Rustam sat up, still breathing hard, and tried to sort out exactly what *had* happened. His face flamed with embarrassment, but beyond that—he put a hand inside his shirt and checked his skin. Quite dry. He had expected the sprite's touch to leave him damp, but she'd taken all her moisture with her when she left, even taken his sweat. His breath caught as a humiliating suspicion crossed his mind and he put a hand down, checked his crotch. Also dry.

She was thorough, he'd give her that.

Still shaking, Rustam stood up and tottered over to Nightstalker. He buried his face in her mane for a moment, trying to put the world back to normality. He doubted it could be done, but at least the sweet smell of horse gave him something familiar to cling to.

"Are you going to saddle it, Chalice, or make love to it?"

Rustam scowled into the mare's mane then arranged his face into what he hoped was a bland expression. "Have you decided which way we're going then?" he asked, pleased to find his voice under control.

"Onward," said Risada firmly. "There's no gain in going back, and we still might catch up with whoever has our supplies. If you're quite finished dallying?"

Heat rushed to Rustam's face, and he opened his mouth to retort but Risada suddenly swore and jumped sideways, knocking him off his feet. Scrambling up, he looked wildly around for the threat, and then sucked in a sharp breath. He put a hand on Nightstalker's neck to steady himself.

The sprite was back, hovering above Elwaes and their packed saddle-bags. She reached down to touch the elf. He stirred and opened his eyes, smiling up at the elemental.

"I'm no good to you. I haven't the strength."

The sprite drifted upward, turning around until she faced Rustam. His knees shook and he clung to Nightstalker's neck.

Not again. Please Chel, not again. Not yet.

Then, to his disbelief, the sprite winked at him.

Elwaes began to chuckle.

"You find this really amusing, don't you?" snapped Rustam.

"Friend, she likes you."

"Honoured, I'm sure—"

"Indeed you should be. In some Kingdoms the man who has loved an elemental is the envy of all. Friend—"

"Rustam. The name's Rustam."

"Friend Rustam, she wants us to go with her."

"She wants him, you mean!" interjected Risada.

"My Lady," said Elwaes, somehow managing to bow in courtly fashion despite being seated on a frosty mountainside. "It is not for Rustam's company alone that she desires this: she knows where they will take your pony."

"Hmmph," grunted Risada. "How can we trust such a creature?"

Elwaes shrugged. "One cannot trust an elemental, my Lady. They are self-indulgent creatures. But I sense no deception in her at this time. Friend Rustam has pleased her. She simply wishes to please him in return."

Rustam felt, rather than saw, Risada roll her eyes upward.

Smoky vague hair trailing behind her, the sprite turned and drifted back towards her stream. She hovered there, and Rustam could sense her impatience. With a sigh he bent over and heaved his saddle off the ground. He placed it carefully on the mare's back and fastened the girths. One of the buckles slipped from between his shaking fingers and snapped the nail of his index finger.

Rustam yelped and stuffed the digit in his mouth. He sucked it for a moment before inspecting the ragged break. He smiled ruefully to himself and wagged his head. What a start to the day. How much worse could it get?

* * * * * * * * * *

By midday the odd party had rounded the shoulder of the mountain and the way ahead had narrowed to a deep canyon between two rock faces. The stream chattered along a central groove, rattling over a bed of loose shale. Rustam glanced up uneasily at the walls on either side—a perfect place for an ambush. And yet, other than the sprite drifting along near the water, almost invisible in the brighter light of full day, they were apparently alone.

Risada had been silent since leaving the site of Rustam's degrading experience, though he suspected she was merely saving up her more choice comments for future jibes. He was confused by her decision to go on with the journey—there must be something of import to her and her co-conspirators in Kishtan and it was imperative now that he find out what. Unless he was wrong about the whole thing and she really was following Sala's plan. His head spun with possibilities and implications, but above all loomed one major puzzle that had nothing to do with loyalties and kingdoms, and probably affected no one but himself.

He could understand Risada despising him for what he was—a bastard who didn't know the identity of his father—and he understood her desire to keep a formal distance between them.

But what made it so personal?

Risada had mentioned his mother. She apparently blamed Soria Chalice for the death of her parents, but there was something more, something deeper. Could her hatred truly be transferred so absolutely to Soria's son, when he had not even been born at that time? Rustam's mind gnawed away at the puzzle but found no solution.

In front of him, Risada drew rein and halted. "Time to break for a rest," she declared.

Obediently Rustam dismounted and assisted Elwaes down, half supporting, half carrying him to a flat stretch of rock beside the stream. The Shivan immediately curled up and went to sleep.

"He's so weak," observed Rustam as he loosened the horses' girths and gathered up their reins to lead them to the water.

"Elves have a reputation for incredible healing abilities; I doubt a human would have survived so long in Melcard's tender care. Ah, look Chalice: your *inamorata* is back."

Rustam's head jerked round and he found himself eye to eye with the sprite. Indeed her eyes were the only parts of her that were really visible at this time of day.

He jumped back, colliding with the chest of Risada's grey which knocked him forward and straight through the elemental. He blinked in surprise and tried to swing round, but the thirsty horses dragged him the last few steps to the water, and when he looked back again the sprite had vanished.

"What's the matter Chalice? Surely a man of your capacity is ready for a repeat performance?"

"I prefer a little more privacy than was available last time," Rustam replied stiffly.

"Somehow I doubt such concerns are a priority with your amorous friend, and I get the distinct impression that she's not finished with you yet," said Risada with a nasty little smile.

Rustam gritted his teeth and busied himself with picketing the horses amongst the sparse patches of tough grass that sprang up between the rocks. Nightstalker lipped a few coarse blades distastefully and looked at Rustam with an aggrieved expression.

"I know, old girl. I'm sorry," he sympathised, stroking her smoothly muscled neck. "I doubt we'll be doing much better than you before long."

He turned around to find Risada staring at him, the spiteful smile still firmly in place.

"I'd often wondered why you spent so much time with the horses, Chalice, but then it occurred to me what comfort a mare might provide for you in the absence of a woman."

"That's enough!" bellowed Rustam, his temper thoroughly over stretched. He lunged at her, so intent on shaking the smug expression from her face he did not even bother to alter his time sense. And failed utterly to recall the speed of her highly developed reflexes.

He found a poisoned needle weaving threateningly before his face and the sharp point of a dagger pricked his side.

"Always thinking with your muscles, eh Chalice? How typical of a man! Try laying a hand on me and you may find yourself separated from it."

Trembling with anger and frustration, Rustam backed carefully away.

"Just remember who's in charge Chalice. Make such a stupid mistake again and you won't live to regret it."

The weapons disappeared and Risada waved a hand at the horses. "Do something useful and fetch the food over here."

Rustam allowed himself a brief, vindictive smile. "I'm sorry, my Lady, there's nothing for lunch today."

"What are you talking about, Chalice? I packed it myself."

"Sorry Lady Risada. We've lost most of our supplies and what little we have left must be rationed; we've no idea when we'll find any more."

The stunned expression on Risada's face went a surprisingly long way towards soothing Rustam's frayed temper.

* * * * * * * * * * *

The city of Darshan basked in the heat of a glorious autumn day. Dench considered the slight figure gliding along the colonnaded walkway beside him. Swathed in sepia mourning robes from crown to toe, she must have been sweltering, but she uttered no complaint. She had, in fact, said nothing aside from requesting an audience with Prince Halnashead at his earliest convenience, and had waited silently until his scheduled meetings were concluded. A stoic character, or perhaps one so encompassed by her grief that personal comfort no longer held any meaning.

The sweet smell of freshly cut grass announced their arrival at Prince Halnashead's private garden. Dench halted beside the gated entrance set into the tall hedge. With a bow and a sweep of his hand he indicated the carved benches in the centre of the lawn, placed beneath the shade of a creeper-encrusted wicker dome. Scarlet and russet foliage glowed in the sunlight, like a living pyre.

Prince Halnashead rose to greet his guest. "Betha, my dear, you have my heartfelt condolences. Herschel was a good man."

"My thanks, your Highness, but that is not why I am here."

Dench watched impassively as Prince Halnashead took Lady Betha Fontmaness's gloved hand and raised it to his lips. Her features were indistinct behind the iridescent fabric of her veil, but her voice betrayed anxiety more than sorrow. Dench knew well that his prince would have marked the anomaly, yet his demeanour remained unchanged.

"Whatever the reason, my dear, you are most welcome. I have sent for tea. Please, join me and we can discuss whatever it is that weighs so heavily on your mind at a time such as this."

Betha hesitated, half turning to glance obliquely towards Dench. Halnashead nodded slightly and the guard withdrew to a discreet position. He was still within safe distance of his prince, able to hear how the conversation progressed, yet screened from the Lady's sight by the pyramidal hedge. He could be at Halnashead's side within two seconds, and the prince obviously judged himself to be safe enough with Lady Betha for that interval.

Dench was not so comfortable with that assumption. Poison might be administered in a fraction of that time, and the Lady's voluminous robes could conceal almost anything short of a sword.

This was not by any means the first time the prince had put himself at risk—he did so almost daily in these increasingly unsettled times—and Dench simply had to accept it. That did not mean he was happy about it. His position with the chief of Tyr-enese security was just as he wanted it, and he would do anything within his power to sustain it.

The Lady Betha's voice was faint, muffled no doubt by her mourning veil, and Dench had to breathe very quietly to catch her words.

"Denia simply could not wait to tell me all about it."

Even through both the veil and the hedge, Dench could not mistake the disgust in Betha's tone.

"But it simply cannot be true," Betha protested. "Lady Risada would never run off with a Craft Master. She's far too devoted to her brother."

It was equally clear to the listening guard that it was not Risada who was the object of Betha's concern.

"My dear," Halnashead's comforting bass carried clearly in the still air. "I have no doubt you are correct, but try to remember, Rees-Charlay is close to the mountains. Who knows to what influences those unfortunate young people may have been subjected. The Tylocian invaders had already descended and may have brought magic wielders with them. Perhaps they were lured away in the enemy's bid to gain information. It is surely only by the goddess's blessing that so many escaped their clutches."

"Well, I suppose it's possible." Doubt crept in. "But, why Rustam? What possible information could a dancing master provide them with that Lady Risada could not?"

Dench could almost hear Halnashead's shrug. "Dear Lady, I have not the faintest notion. But please tell me, did Denia speak of my daughter at all?"

Shocked silence greeted the prince's question. Even the songbirds flitting amidst the shrubbery fell quiet, the rustling skirts of a maid delivering the tea tray the only intrusion. After the maid's departure, Betha's next words were so faint they were almost inaudible.

"You mean, Princess Annasala hasn't returned either?"

Halnashead's tone sharpened. "Either? Tell me, my dear, who else hasn't returned from Rees-Charlay?"

Betha sounded even less sure of herself. "Well, that's really why I came to see you. I thought you should know. Over the past eight days, since Herschel died, I have been entertained by a number of important ladies. Whilst Fontmaness is only a minor House, Herschel had kin links to a number of the major families and they have always been kind to us."

She hesitated. After a brief pause during which Dench could picture the prince taking Betha's hands in his, the deeply reassuring tones of his master encouraged, "Please, go on, my dear."

"Oh, I don't know. I could be imagining things."

"What sort of things?"

Betha hesitated once more, and then plunged on. "I only ever saw the Ladies of each House. Whilst it is true they were the ones to invite me, I would at the very least have expected their Lords to present their condolences to me in person. One or even two, perhaps I could understand—there's always estate business that takes husbands away from home. But not all of them." There was a gulp of air, as if Betha was trying to suck in courage, then it all came out in a rush.

"That's when I noticed they were all Houses who are overtly loyal to the Crown. The only two I visited whose husbands had returned from the Rees-Charlay fest are sometimes scathing—begging your pardon, Highness—of either your or King Marten's government. They're usually very careful how they couch their criticism, but there was something different this time, something more blatant. Perhaps *confident* is a better word? As if they already knew the outcome of this Tylocian uprising, and they supported it.

"Your Highness, I believe the others are being held hostage against their Ladies' silence and good behaviour. I thought Denia looked rather strained, and whilst she is known for her gossiping, she prattled beyond even her usual abilities. I felt she was trying to tell me something without actually speaking it, and the more I thought about it, the more convinced I became that I should bring this to your attention."

Her voice quavered, losing the conviction of a moment earlier. "You probably know all this already." There was the rustle of heavy silk; no doubt Betha rising. "I've wasted your time, Highness. I—"

"Betha, child. Sit down. You were absolutely correct to come to me. Your loyalty is much appreciated at a time when such a commodity is a precious gift. Sit. I insist. Now, tell me. Was my daughter mentioned?"

"Well, yes. Denia always has plenty to say on the subject of others, and she was of the opinion, oh I really shouldn't be saying this to you."

"Go on, child. It may be important."

"If you're certain? Oh well, Denia thinks that Princess Annasala was sulking. Lord Melcard said she was ill and that's why she couldn't leave with everyone else. In fact several people had seen her faint earlier and be carried back to her rooms. But Denia said that Annasala had been in a terrible temper in the morning when she found Lady Risada and Rustam gone during the night. Denia thinks she wasn't really sick, just having such a tantrum she worked herself into a state of exhaustion.

"And why should she be sulking?" Halnashead sounded like he knew the probable answer.

"Because of Rustam, my prince. He really is the most gorgeous man in Chel's domain—and Denia thinks Annasala was furious that he should run off with her cousin instead of staying with her. Denia mentioned also that Rustam considered the princess still to be a child, which did not sit well with her Highness. Oh, I really shouldn't be telling you this."

Halnashead's reply held a grim smile. "Betha, my dear, you can always talk to me. Your father was a loyal servant and I trust you will continue to bring any such concerns directly to me, hmm?"

"Your Highness is too kind to someone as unimportant as me, but if you really mean that, there was something else Denia said."

"Yes?"

"She told me there was a rumour going around that your bastard brother was with the Tylocians, and he was behind this uprising. Could that be true? I thought he was just a myth."

"That, I cannot answer, dear child. Such rumours have been rife since before my birth, yet no conclusive evidence has ever come to light. Now, I really must get on. Your candour is much appreciated, and my silence on your words assured."

Betha murmured her thanks and Dench stepped back away from his eavesdropping post. When his master and guest stepped through the garden gate he was awaiting them at attention.

"Ah, good man," said the prince. "I need you to run some errands. Betha, my dear, if you will excuse us?"

"Highness." The Lady Betha dropped a small curtsy before walking away.

Halnashead faced Dench, deep frown lines etched between his eyes. "How is it that a girl who is not even a player should be the one to bring me such momentous news? Where are all my agents?

Not one of them has delivered even a hint of this. It can't be so well hidden if Betha noticed it, which leads me to a disturbing conclusion: someone is intercepting them. How many are missing? How much information has failed to reach me? Ah, goddess; I'm crippled without them."

Dench waited patiently, knowing no answer was expected of him. Halnashead began to pace up and down the stone flags, pausing every so often to tug at the waistband of his leggings. Finally he tightened his belt. "Damned leather must have stretched," he muttered as he reached a decision and halted. "I want to see all my players who are within a day's travel of Darshan. Use as many messengers as you need, but discreetly, Dench. I don't want to alert anyone to our problem."

"Of course, Highness."

One side of Halnashead's mouth quirked up. "Perhaps I should recruit the Lady Betha. I'd always had the impression she was a little vacuous, but she had a far tighter grasp on the politics of the situation than I would have dreamt."

"Indeed, Sir." Dench agreed. "Who would have thought it?"

9. TROLLS

The canyon continued to narrow until they were forced into single file, with barely enough room for the horses to walk without stepping in the stream. The incline gradually steepened as the walls drew in, and Rustam began to worry that they might be headed towards a dead end.

The sprite continuing ahead of them was the only indication that the pony had passed this way and, despite Elwaes's reassurances, Rustam did not trust the elemental. There was also no sign of any sort of growth in this rocky defile, and he fretted about the horses. What would they eat tonight? The pony had carried the remaining grain and, strong though they were, the two animals could not be expected to carry their riders for much longer without something to eat.

"Elwaes, are you awake?' Rustam asked.

"I am.'

"Would you feel capable of riding alone for a while?'

"Surely.'

The elf twisted around in the saddle to look back at Rustam. "You worry about her strength?'

"Yes,' Rustam replied, knowing instinctively that Elwaes shared his compassion for Nightstalker. There was something in the way the Shivan touched the mare, the soft words he murmured to her that warmed Rustam to Elwaes in a way nothing else could have.

"She is strong, you know,' the elf reassured him. "But your concern is laudable; I shall do my best.'

Rustam slipped down the mare's side, landing with a slight splash in the stream. Ahead of them, Risada glanced round.

"Whatever are you doing, Chalice?'

"No horse should have to carry double up a hill like this.'

The Lady of Domn looked at Elwaes swaying along on top of the tall mare. "Just make sure he doesn't fall off,' she ordered shortly, although Rustam thought he detected a hint of real concern in her tone.

Rustam found a faint trail on the opposite side of the narrow stream, room enough to walk as long as he placed his feet in front of each other, and close enough that he could just touch Nightstalker's neck if he stretched a little. He would be able to catch Elwaes should the elf fall asleep and slide off. Always supposing he slid in Rustam's direction.

"Is the Lady always so brusque?' Elwaes enquired in his quiet voice.

"I'm afraid she is. At least, she is when I'm around.'

"Ah. There is something between you.'

Rustam glanced sharply up at the elf. "Nothing of that sort,' he snapped, then apologised. "I'm sorry; it's complicated.'

He was surprised to hear Elwaes sigh. "Isn't it always, with you Tyr-enese?'

"What do you mean?'

"This game of yours. Nothing is ever quite what it seems, isn't that so?'

Rustam paused, concentrated for a moment on negotiating a particularly awkward pile of rubble in his path, and tried to tease out the thread of an idea triggered by Elwaes's observation.

Nothing is ever quite what it seems.

How true. And how illuminating. The thought snapped sharply into focus. Risada's attitude, her hatred and disdain, so blatant in everything she said and did. *But was it real?* What did it hide?

It must be a play of which he was wholly ignorant, and so far Risada had done an exemplary job of manipulating him like a novice. That would have to change.

He looked to Elwaes. "You speak truth, my friend. Tell me, how long were you in Melcard"s dungeon?'

A shadow dimmed the Shivan"s beauty, and again Rustam was struck by his youthfulness. Rustam fingered his own beard. It was really quite established now, yet the elf showed no sign of any growth on cheeks or chin. Somehow though, he was certain Elwaes was no youngster.

"I doubt I could tell you, even if I knew,' Elwaes replied, and glanced away, but not before Rustam caught sight of such hatred on the Shivan"s face it made him shudder. Not for anything would he want to be the object of such loathing.

"How so?' he asked cautiously, but when Elwaes looked back, his face was serenely peaceful, and Rustam wondered if he"d imagined the malice of a moment earlier.

"Because, friend Rustam, we do not measure time as you do. In Shiva there is no night, so we are not accustomed to counting days.' He shrugged. "I probably wouldn"t have thought to do so even if my cell had had a window.'

"No night? How do you decide when to sleep?' Rustam struggled to imagine a land of perpetual daylight. Elwaes smiled gently.

"In health, we do not sleep. We dream a lot—visions, you would call them—and we meditate. Your need for sleep has always puzzled me. For a people who are so concerned with the passage of time, surely it is wasteful?'

Rustam smiled in turn. "I"m sure it is, but we can"t do without. Not totally, anyway,' he added, remembering many nights when sleep had been far from possible. The corners of his mouth twitched upward; some of those memories were delicious.

The light began to fail early that evening, and with no sign of the gorge coming to an end. Despite the dangers of traversing such rocky terrain in the dark they continued for some time after nightfall, their way lit only by the pallid glow of Vana, the smaller of the two moons.

Rustam, mounted behind Elwaes again, called a halt after his mare stumbled badly for the second time. "It's no good, we need to stop.'

"For once I agree with you, Chalice.' There was a splash as the Lady of Domn's feet landed in the stream. "This is ridiculous!' she railed. "How in Chel's name are we going to camp in a place like this?'

"I'm sure we'll find a way,' said Rustam. "At least we have something to eat, which is more than the horses do.'

He helped Elwaes down. The elf was limp again and Rustam thought about their earlier conversation, wondering how much longer Elwaes would continue to sleep like this. He lowered the gangly Shivan to the ground and leaned him over until his head and shoulders were propped against the wall of the canyon.

Turning to unsaddle Nightstalker, Rustam found instead that he was face to face with the sprite. She moved closer and reached out a wispy hand to stroke his hair, then began to trace a line down his spine.

"Not again!' he groaned.

"I do believe she's looking for her reward Chalice. Go ahead. I'll see to the horses.'

Rustam's mouth fell open in surprise at Risada's offer, but all that escaped him was a gasp as the sprite touched him again, deeper, and in a spot he had no idea could be that sensitive.

This time he kept control over his knees long enough to reach a slightly wider place on the trail behind the horses, though not at any great distance. Certainly not beyond earshot. He tried to keep from crying out, but the sprite was more demanding than before. She played with him for longer, sometimes drawing away until he thought—hoped— she might leave, before flowing back to engulf him and send a riot of uncontrolled sensations coursing through his body. Guilt mingled with intense pleasure, fuelling the confusion that wrestled within him.

Should he really be enjoying this?

He writhed on the rocky track, barely aware of the sharp stones beneath him, panting and gasping and eventually begging. His last coherent thought was that surely he'd reached the point where his senses must begin to numb, when she pushed him over the edge.

His body convulsed. Colours sparked through his brain like shooting stars and a violent scream ripped his throat. Fire sizzled along his nerves, searing pain and bliss in equal measure. Darkness swallowed him.

Awareness returned slowly, and with it all the pains of lacerated and bruised muscles. He was lying on his side curled in a tight ball, twitching. He winced as an involuntary spasm jerked his head forward, and a stone gouged his cheek. Gradually he managed to unfold himself, limb by limb.

He could feel Risada's eyes burning into his back.

What twisted pleasure did she get from watching these bizarre events? Rustam paused in mid thought. How to classify it? Mating? Rape? Or something previously unknown?

Despite misgivings, Rustam acknowledged that he wasn't an entirely unwilling participant—it was a mind-blowing experience.

Perhaps that was it—Risada was jealous!

He began to laugh but stopped, his throat too sore.

Risada, jealous of anything to do with Rustam Chalice? Now that *would* be bizarre.

Rustam forced himself up, and tottered over to check the horses. Risada had removed their tack but her grooming left a lot to be desired; sticky sweat patches caked the saddle and girth areas. Perfect if you wanted to contend with saddle sores and girth galls the following day.

Rustam fetched the brushes and methodically worked his way from head to tail on both animals until their coats felt smooth and silky beneath his fingers. The exercise eased a few kinks from his sore muscles, and allowed his brain to idle for a while before having to face Risada. When he eventually did pick his way over the rocks to where their gear lay stacked, she said nothing, retreating again into the cold silence she seemed to use to isolate herself from him. Heaving a quiet sigh, Rustam checked that Elwaes was warmly wrapped in his bedroll—quite a feat, considering the length of the Shivan's limbs—before crawling into his own and trying to find a comfortable position against the canyon wall.

He slept fitfully that night, and when he did he had nightmares about something foggy wrapping itself around him and invading his mind. He jerked awake in the faint glow of pre-dawn and shivered. Stretching carefully, he winced as stiff, sore muscles protested the movement.

"I think we should move on,' said Risada from behind him. He twisted round painfully and found her sitting on the pile of tack, watching him and Elwaes. He blinked in surprise. Had she sat there all night? She should have woken him to stand his watch hours ago. He could not decide whether he was grateful for the extra sleep, or annoyed with her for making herself unnecessarily tired. In terrain such as this, their safety could be compromised by a simple lack of concentration. The only one to seem at all rested was Elwaes, who stirred at the sound of Risada's voice and, after a bone-cracking stretch that thrust the ends of his elongated limbs outside his blankets, sat up and looked brightly around.

They saddled the horses wordlessly and mounted up, riding out as the first shafts of dawn light shone between the clouds. By midmorning they reached the end of the gorge, so steep in its final fifty lengths they were forced to dismount and scramble ahead of the horses, tugging on their reins and dodging their hooves as the animals jumped and scrabbled their way to the top.

Pausing to catch his breath, Rustam leaned against his horse. Every bit of him ached, even his throat as he sucked in air. He prayed that after last night, the sprite would be done with him. Even such amazing sex could not be worth this discomfort.

A broad plateau stretched out of sight ahead of them, bordered on either side by forbidding grey granite cliffs up which nothing but a mountain goat would be likely to climb.

At least that limited the options for the troll pack with their captive pony.

Their guiding stream meandered along the centre of the plateau, and both banks grew a coarse grass that Nightstalker and the grey attacked with enthusiasm.

Elwaes slumped to the ground whilst Rustam and Risada cast around for evidence of their quarry's passage. A shape on the ground caught Rustam's eye and he hunkered down to get a closer look, tracing his finger around the indentation in the gritty soil. "At least we know we're still going in the right direction—the pony came along here.'

"Where?' demanded Risada, striding over to look. Rustam couldn't help but admire her long legs and the provocative sway of her hips.

"Here,' he said, pointing. "That print's too small for either of the horses.'

Risada peered down. "You see truly, Chalice. What I don't understand is why they haven't butchered and eaten it yet.'

Rustam looked to Elwaes, spreading his hands in question. It was something he had wondered too.

Elwaes grimaced. "Rock trolls like their meat very fresh—preferably still alive. It may be that they have a lair somewhere ahead, and are taking it back to share with a family group.'

"We might not be too far behind,' Risada said. "Let's move.'

"We've no way of knowing,' Rustam pointed out quietly. The look Risada gave him was as poisonous as one of her assassin's tools. Rustam shrugged.

"We're moving.'

* * * * * * * * * * * *

The plateau looked deceptively flat, but proved to be criss-crossed by huge cracks, some so deep and broad they were forced to detour rather than risk jumping and, while they continued to use the stream as a guide, they were on occasion forced to splash along in ankle deep water.

The sun shone fitfully, bringing a glorious autumn brightness to the bleak landscape long enough to warm the travellers through and entice them to remove a layer or two of clothing. Then the clouds would close in and the temperature would plummet. After Rustam had stripped and redressed for the sixth time his temper was nearing boiling point. He felt the need to scream, or beat something to a pulp.

Suddenly Elwaes shifted in front of him.

"Rustam?'

"I see them.'

He had caught sight of them in the same moment—a band of trolls rising from their hiding place in the depths of one of the great crevasses. He glanced over his shoulder. Another group had materialised at their backs.

"Master Elwaes, perhaps now would be a good time to perform your magic,' suggested Risada, slowing until she rode beside them. Both horses began to jig, agitated by the sight and smell of the trolls.

"I can try, but I doubt they will listen.'

"How can you tell?' Rustam asked.

"Just a feeling.'

Rustam felt Elwaes draw a deep breath, and unearthly song filtered across the plateau. To Rustam the song seemed almost tangible, as though he could reach out and touch it, feel its textures and melodies, see it wafting on the air currents and insinuating itself into waiting troll ears.

The creatures paused, listening. Rustam hardly dared breathe in case he upset Elwaes's concentration, yet at the same time he wanted to join in, to sing with the elf. He almost felt that he could—

The leading troll roared, and the spell broke. The shaggy creatures started jumping up and down, hooting and screeching angrily, and Rustam's eye was drawn to a small spark of glittering light on the leader's chest. Almost buried in the depths of the thick pelt lay what looked like a chunk of crystal.

An irritatingly vague memory tickled at the back of Rustam's mind—something to do with a crystal. He knew he had seen the like somewhere else, but where?

"I'm sorry,' said Elwaes.

"It's not your fault,' Risada reassured him, and Rustam almost smiled at the hint of relief in her voice. Despite the danger, the Lady of Domn was clearly thankful that the situation would be resolved by steel, rather than magic.

"It appears we must fight our way out this time, Chalice.'

"Indeed it does, my Lady. Are you as good with a sword as you are with your darts?'

"We'll soon find out, won't we?'

Rustam drew his sword. It made a satisfying rasp as it cleared the leather saddle scabbard, as though pleased to be freed from its constraints. In front, Elwaes murmured something.

"What was that?' asked Rustam suspiciously.

"Nothing,' Elwaes answered, a little too quickly. "I don't suppose you have another blade?'

"You can handle one? I don't have another sword but here, take this.' He slipped his long dagger from his boot, flipped it and handed it hilt first to the Shivan.

The circle of hideous creatures drew closer. Risada swung her sword experimentally and the nearer trolls jumped back a few steps before venturing tentatively forward again.

"Seem a trifle nervous, don't they?'

She sounded almost cheerful.

A sudden squall of rain descended from nowhere—sharp, driving rain mixed with sleet. Rustam threw up a hand to shield his face, but not a drop touched his skin.

Trolls yelped and screeched, running to and fro aimlessly as ice bit into their hides. Some ran towards the encircled riders and Rustam and Risada cut them down with ease, barely needing to exert themselves.

"What in Chel's name is going on?' Risada demanded, frowning at the furious weather that raged scant lengths away but never touched them. An idea nagged for Rustam's attention, and comprehension dawned.

"It's the sprite! Elwaes, you called her, didn't you?'

In front of him the Shivan shrugged bony shoulders. "I called. I wasn't certain she would answer.'

"Well she has. And for once, I'm pleased to see her!'

"Only for once?' gibed Risada.

Rustam rolled his eyes. "Let's get clear of this rabble, yes?'

Nightstalker tossed her head and minced reluctantly forward, her eyes showing white around the rims as she regarded the maddened trolls. Ahead, one of the ugly brutes stumbled into their haven of still, dry air, and chunks of ice flew from its shaggy pelt as it shook violently and roared its anger. Several of its compatriots blundered towards the cry. Abruptly, two thirds of the circle plunged into gloom, the rain transmuting into thick fog.

The cacophony of howls redoubled, joined by the clash of troll fighting troll in the sudden gloom.

"Well, that evens the odds somewhat,' Risada said as she eyed the remaining seven trolls milling nervously in the arc left clear by the sprite. "Shall we?'

"Delighted, my Lady,' Rustam concurred, anxious to be away from the noxious creatures. He wrinkled his nose. Even the drenching had done nothing to abate the awful smell.

"'Ware!' cried Elwaes. Rustam blinked his mind into high speed, and raised his sword as the nearest troll roared and lunged. The blade arced gracefully down through a beam of sunlight, flashing silver like some divine bolt of lightning before slicing easily into flesh and decapitating his assailant.

It felt good to kill something.

Dazzled by the after-image, Rustam's backswing missed the next one which ducked and grabbed at his boot, trying to pull him from his saddle. Nightstalker squealed indignantly and cow-kicked, smashing the troll's leg with her hoof. The creature fell away screaming.

"Your left!' Rustam yelled at Risada in warning.

"Rust—'

Elwaes's shout came almost too late, and Rustam cursed himself for a fool as a prodigious leap gained an attacking troll the dual advantages of height and surprise. Despite his expanded time sense, Rustam barely managed to raise his sword, spitting the creature like a hog for the roast and fouling his blade.

Sharp talons punctured Rustam's left thigh, tearing a howl of pain from his still raw throat. Struggling to free his sword, he smashed his elbow into the gruesome face, but it was Elwaes who struck the creature in the side, burying the long bladed knife between its ribs. It fell back, purple blood bubbling between its fangs.

Rustam looked around for another adversary but there were none left standing. Risada scanned the battlefield. "Let's get out of here,' she said grimly and put her heels to her grey. The gelding jumped forwards and raced through the gap, while the remaining trolls continued to fumble about in the persistent fog.

Rustam raised a hand in salute to the sprite, and then followed Risada at the gallop.

10. FRIENDS OR ENEMIES?

"Ow! That hurts!"

"Lie still, and don't be so pathetic, Chalice. There's no way of knowing what that troll had its claws into last."

Risada gave a sharp tug, and the remainder of the leg of Rustam's breeches ripped away.

"That was an expensive pair of breeches!" he complained through gritted teeth.

"I'm sure Halnashead will provide you with all the breeches you want, if we succeed. Now lie *still*!"

Rustam looked away, caught Elwaes studying him, and made a face which turned into another yelp of protest as Risada probed one of the holes in his leg.

"As I thought—it's festering already."

"I could have told you that without you poking your nails into it." Rustam's leg throbbed in confirmation.

"Where are *you* going?" Risada asked suddenly. Rustam twisted around to see Elwaes wandering off towards some rocky ground further along the stream bank where they had paused to rest the horses. The trolls were many leagues behind them now, and Rustam was not sure the sprite would have released them yet anyway. She liked to play with her victims.

Elwaes failed to answer, and Risada began to rise but Rustam caught her by the wrist and held tight. "Leave him be. He saved us again, in case you hadn't noticed, and I should think he wants some privacy for a change; it's the first time he's been strong enough to get very far from us. What do you think he's going to do, run away?"

"Remove your hand, Chalice," Risada hissed, "unless you want to lose it."

Rustam released her, and lay back with a sigh. "Don't you ever get tired of making threats? Or is it the only form of conversation you know?"

"It seems to be the only sort you respect. And I hardly think the kind you're used to is appropriate outside the bedchamber."

She stood up and flounced over to her horse, began digging through a saddle bag. Rustam reconsidered—flounced was not really the correct verb. It would be hard for anyone to flounce wearing those figure hugging breeches and bulky jerkin, but that was how she moved and it made for interesting watching, particularly from his prone viewpoint.

Goddess, he thought in frustration, *what a gorgeous woman. Why must she be so obnoxious?*

A pair of thin legs walked past his face and Rustam glanced up, startled, his wrist knife slipping instinctively into his fingers.

"Don't do that!" he snapped at Elwaes.

"Pardon me? Do what?"

"Creep up on people like that. You can get killed that way." He slid the dagger back into its sheath.

"Apologies, friend Rustam. I had no intention of creeping and, I might suggest, your thoughts were elsewhere at the time."

Rustam scowled, unable to dispute the Shivan's observation.

"What's that?" he asked suspiciously, eyeing the greenish mess in Elwaes's hand. The elf smiled.

"Rhak moss. It makes an excellent poultice."

At that moment, Risada returned with a length of cloth. She raised her eyebrows as Elwaes proceeded to slather the gooey moss onto Rustam's wounds, but wordlessly handed him the cloth which he bound tightly around the whole mess. Rustam stood up and tentatively put some weight on the injured leg. It did feel a touch better, cooler at least. He hobbled over to Nightstalker and began rummaging through his saddle bags for a new pair of breeches.

"Can we ride on now?" Risada asked with a touch of impatience as he fastened his belt.

"Lead on, your Ladyship."

For the remainder of the day they followed the stream along the plateau, keeping a wary eye out for further ambushes. The towering peaks to either side drew a little closer, but still there was no end to the broken ground staggering endlessly away in front of them. Mosses and short tufts of coarse grass were the only vegetation and they saw no signs of either animals or trolls, other than the occasional pony sized hoof print in the softer soil of the stream bank. As night fell, Risada reluctantly agreed to make camp where they were, rather than fumble on in the dark and risk falling into a crevasse.

"I don't think we should risk a fire," she said. "If they're following us it'll act as a beacon."

"I agree," said Rustam, unsaddling Nightstalker. "How about that?" he muttered to Elwaes who was removing the mare's bridle. "We actually agreed on something."

"Don't expect it to last," snapped Risada from behind her grey, and then added, "I have very sharp hearing, Chalice."

"Matches your tongue then, doesn't it?" he murmured beneath his breath.

This time she didn't hear.

* * * * * * * * * * *

Doctor Hensar could feel his face contorting into a scowl that would have fit better on Lord Melcard during one of his temper storms. He resisted the impulse to rant at the distorted image in the shallow bowl of water over which he bent. Long ago, he had learned the futility of venting his anger upon a medium which could not transmit pain. Besides which, shouting produced too many ripples and that was guaranteed to give him a headache should he need to communicate for any length of time.

Instead, he stroked the chunk of crystal in his palm until it lit with an inner glow. He smiled in satisfaction as he watched the image of the troll flinch in response to the answering glitter in the heart of the pendant it wore.

"And why are they not yet dead?" he asked, rubbing harder as the crystal warmed to his touch.

"S..st..strife," the creature stammered, trying to form words with a set of teeth and a palate not designed for such intricacies.

"Strife?" repeated the doctor. "I'll give you strife!"

"N..n..no! Spite!"

Under other circumstances, the look of panic on the troll's face would have amused Hensar. Now he frowned in annoyed confusion. Spite? What was the moronic creature trying to—?

Then he had it. Not spite. *Sprite*!

Foiled by an elemental. That had to be the elf's doing. Somehow Halnashead's spies must have forced him to work for them.

Quite frankly, Hensar was surprised the elf was still alive, but perhaps that was all to the good. Trolls were extremely partial to elf meat, and that would serve as extra incentive to the rest of the pack. For despite all the things Hensar had taught the stinking beasts, the one thing he found impossible to instil in them was a sense of gratitude. All they really understood was pain. And, apart from the trembling one upon whom he gazed now, that was hard to inflict at such a distance.

Not that their dim-witted brains—if one could truly call something so simplistic as that little knot of cells, a brain—would necessarily associate the punishment with him, even if he could. Gaining control over this pack and educating them until they became useful had been one of Hensar's longest and, sometimes, most rewarding projects. There were quite a number of potentially troublesome persons from his dubious past who were no longer extant thanks to his moronic minions. But the effort entailed in maintaining his mastery over them at such a distance—that was almost as tiresome as all the fawning and flattery needed to keep Melcard oblivious to his plans.

Hensar squeezed his pendant until the rough edges cut into his palm. Blood streaked the stone's surface and he watched impassively as the troll fell to its knees, clutching at a pain inside its chest that it could neither comprehend nor combat.

When it had toppled over and lain writhing on the cave floor long enough for Hensar to start losing interest, he stopped. Fastidiously, he wiped the crystal clean with a white linen handkerchief before returning his attention to the image in the water bowl. Despite the thick covering of hair, the troll appeared several shades paler.

"Now, you know what you must do?"

Frantically the creature nodded its head in a parody of human behaviour.

"Y..yes, M..master. Kill humans and elf. Eat them too?"

"Oh, yes. Most certainly." Hensar allowed himself a small smile. "Eat whatever you like."

* * * * * * * * *

Both moons set early that night and Rustam lay quietly in the dark, staring up at the stars. His leg throbbed gently, but with decidedly less heat.

Risada had wandered off somewhere, and the only sound was the gentle grinding of teeth as the horses picked at the tough grass. The sprite had not shown up, for which Rustam was immensely grateful.

"Why does the lady treat you so brusquely?"

The question came so unexpectedly out of the dark that Rustam was half way to his feet, knife in hand, before he remembered he was not alone.

"Shh!" he admonished. "She might hear you."

"No, she cannot," replied the elf. "She's over by the stream and the water masks our voices."

"How can you be so certain?"

"Because I am Shivan and my senses tell me so."

"They're that acute? What an asset that would be in the game."

"So thought those who tried to force us into service in the days leading up to the first War. But we knew nothing of stealth or duplicity, only what we learned from your people, and by then it was too late. Your people and mine—we are not compatible."

"Does that have to be true? We seem to be getting along well enough."

"We're existing together because we have to, but you two Tyr-enese don't even get along with each other."

"That's a personal matter, but it doesn't have to affect how you and I relate to each other, does it?"

"Truly said, friend Rustam."

"My friends call me Rusty."

"Then I shall too."

Elwaes paused, seemed to struggle for a moment as if he wanted to say something more, and yet didn't want to at the same time. In the quiet, Rustam studied the Shivan's shadowy features, the glimmer of starlight on the angled planes of his face, the shimmer of his long, pale hair. Rustam had never found himself attracted to another man, yet there was something compelling in the almost feminine allure of this displaced elf.

"It won't work," Elwaes said suddenly. "I know why you're taking me to Kishtan but I warn you, you will be disappointed."

"How can you be so sure?" asked Rustam warily. Was the elf digging for information, or had he worked it out?

A sad smile was evident in Elwaes's voice as he replied. "Because I understand the depths of the hatred between our peoples, and you yourself have told me that the Kishtanian Queen is Shivan. Rusty, if you are truly my friend please don't try to play your game with me."

"I'm sorry," Rustam answered faintly, ashamed for a reason he struggled to comprehend. It was his duty as Halnashead's player to see this scheme through to the end.

So why did he feel so guilty.

* * * * * * * * * * * *

The morning dawned clear and cold. Rustam splashed icy water on his face and shivered. He dug out the last of his spare shirts and put one on over the other three he wore already, handing Elwaes the remaining one. He noticed Risada putting on extra layers too, but she seemed to have some still left in her saddle bags. They were too small for him, but would surely fit Elwaes.

"My Lady, could you spare a blouse for our Shivan friend?"

She looked blankly at him a moment, and then smiled. Rustam could not help but compare her beauty to that of Elwaes. Hers was the cultured elegance of the sophisticated highborn; his, the wild fairness of nature. Rustam could not choose between the two.

"Of course. Please Elwaes, have this one. It wouldn't do for you to freeze to death because of my thoughtlessness."

She drew out a deep purple silk blouse and held it for Elwaes to put on, then turned him about and fastened the buttons. She giggled suddenly, sounding like a little girl. "I haven't done this since Iain was a small boy."

"Iain?" Elwaes queried.

"Iain Merschenko vas Domn, Lord of the Second House. My brother."

"Lady." Elwaes bowed. "I was not aware I was in such exalted company. Rescued by the King's grand niece, no less, though I admit I have no recollection of you having a brother."

Rustam and Risada exchanged glances.

"Elwaes, who was King when you were captured?"

Elwaes appeared confused by the question. "King Belcastas. Why, does he no longer rule?"

"My friend, I think you were in that dungeon a lot longer than we guessed. Belcastas was killed in a border skirmish some twenty three years ago, probably by his own men, and no one was sorry to see him go. His son Saimund reigned for thirteen years before he fell from the roof garden at the top of his tower, and his brother Prince Halnashead was regent until Saimund's son, Marten, reached his majority last Solstice."

"Twenty three years? Do you count that a long time?" asked Elwaes.

"Does it not seem so to you, Sir Elf?" Risada sounded unconvinced that anyone could discount that amount of time—almost as long as she had been alive—as inconsequential, but the Shivan merely shrugged. "I never really have understood your human reckoning of time."

Risada raised her eyebrows but said nothing more, turning away to finish tightening her girths.

"Do you miss him, this brother of yours?" Elwaes asked.

"I've never been away from him for so long," she answered without looking round. Her voice had an odd quaver to it.

"He's a grown man—" Rustam began.

Risada spun round and glared at him. "That's not the point! I brought him up—he's everything I have and I'm everything he has. We've never needed anyone but each other. There are plenty of people in Domn willing to give him advice to their own advantage and he's not experienced enough to sift the good from the bad. He needs me."

Poor sod, thought Rustam. *Stuck with a woman who thinks he can't do without her.* The urge to support a fellow male against meddlesome women made Rustam reckless. "He's twenty years old, for Chel's sake, and Lord of his own House. Is that why it took so long for the Domn guardians to declare him ready for Lordship? Because you make all his decisions for him?"

The blood drained from Risada's face until her skin was paler than her hair. Rustam wondered belatedly if he hadn't pushed her too far this time, but she drew a deep breath, turned and mounted her horse. Looking down on him she curled her lip in her best aristocratic sneer.

"I wouldn't expect a bastard like you to understand anything about family loyalty. Your mother certainly never did."

She swung the grey around and kicked it hard in the ribs. With a startled grunt the gelding leapt into canter and left Rustam and Elwaes struggling to mount Nightstalker as she jigged around them in a tight circle, upset at being left behind.

They rode for the entire day in a silence as cold and deadly as the blizzards that would soon smother the mountains. Not once did Risada look around to check that they were following, and the only indication they had that she was aware of her surroundings was the route she chose, skirting the worst of the cracks and jumping others. Rustam and Elwaes took turns to walk for brief periods though neither could go very far. Rustam's limp worsened as the day wore on, and Elwaes's complexion took on a yellowish tinge.

Risada called for no midday break, and when they stopped that evening she ate her rations and marched away along the stream bank. Rustam rolled his eyes skyward.

"She's not going to forgive me this time, is she?"

"You do seem to have a talent for annoying her," Elwaes observed as he snuggled into his bedroll for warmth.

Rustam followed suit and settled down beside the elf. He was suddenly struck by the realisation that he no longer noticed the smell of unwashed bodies. Had he grown so accustomed to the odour that he was no longer aware of it? He shuddered at such an appalling notion.

"You've never answered my question," said the elf.

Question? What question? Rustam frowned. "I'm sorry Elwaes, I can't have been listening."

"Why does the lady treat you so brusquely?"

"It was yesterday you asked me that!"

"Yesterday, tomorrow, now. What's the difference? You still haven't answered."

Rustam opened his mouth, intending to tell the Shivan to mind his own business, but paused. Didn't Elwaes deserve better? Twice the Shivan had saved their lives, yet their only motive in saving his, had been to use him for their own ends. That made Rustam uncomfortable. Yesterday they'd spoken of putting aside the mutual hatred and mistrust of their peoples, and that was a beginning Rustam intended to build upon. He could not have explained why Elwaes's friendship had become important to him, he only knew it had.

He sighed again. "It's a matter of status. If it was just the normal social divide it wouldn't be so bad. But, you see, I'm a bastard. Fraternising with me could be harmful to Risada's reputation if that should ever become common knowledge. Not that she'd be the only one—I've had relationships with a lot of highly placed

Ladies—but Risada actually has to pretend that we eloped."

Rustam wasn't sure what he expected, but Elwaes's total lack of response surprised him. As the silence stretched into the starry night he breathed out his tension, unaware until then how tightly coiled the subject made him.

I've done it now. He's probably from some high caste Shivan family and he shouldn't be associating with me either.

Disgruntled, Rustam fidgeted into a more comfortable position and closed his eyes. Maybe if he went to sleep it would all be different in the morning. It had never worked before, but there was always a first time.

He was starting to drift when Elwaes asked, "Rusty, forgive my ignorance, but what is a bastard?"

Rustam was lost for words. Was the elf making some subtle taunt? He propped himself up on his elbows and peered into the dark, trying to make out the Shivan's face.

"Are you serious?"

"Is it an affliction I should know of?"

"Well, put it this way—I've never met anyone who didn't. Elwaes, surely you're joking?"

"Rusty, I am your friend, and this does not sound like a subject for humour."

Rustam wagged his head in amazement. "Perhaps your people have another word for it. It means I'm the son of an unmarried woman."

Copper red ringlets waved enticingly just out of reach. The tinkle of her bright laughter. How dare *she!*

"Ah—I begin to see. Humans attach great significance to marriage, don't they?"

"Don't elves?"

"Not in the same way. As well as I can tell, human marriage means that the woman becomes the property of the man."

"That's not true," began Rustam, but he had never really thought of it from that perspective. Never thought about it at all, if he was honest. "Well, perhaps, in a way. But please, go on. What does marriage mean to your people?"

"Elves rarely marry. Only if they meet their soul-mate, and even then, not always. We hold little store by ceremony. If two people love, why should they not have a child? Is that how your parents felt?"

Was it? Why did you never try to tell me?

The world seemed to pause, and a shiver ran up Rustam's spine. He could almost hear the answer.

Savagely he shook his head, dismissing his fantasies. "I have no idea," he answered bitterly. "That's the worst of it. I have no idea who my father was."

He could hear Elwaes struggling to understand his shame. "That can happen in Shiva also, but such a child is considered fortunate. He may have two, or even three possible fathers all of whom will want to help raise him."

Rustam's mind swam at the thought. "That's not the way it works here, and I don't even have any possibles."

"Did you never ask your mother?"

"Elwaes, at the age of four I tried to ask her. That's when she abandoned me."

"Abandoned?" Elwaes sounded scandalised. "How can any mother abandon a child? Even the elven women who were forced to bear children to humans would not have dreamed of abandoning their children."

Rustam's mind swam. "Forced? With men? When and why?"

"I can't tell you when, or if it is still happening. As to why, it's all to do with this accursed game of yours. Others thought, as did you, about the acuity of our senses, and they decided that if we could not be coerced into performing for them, then they would breed children who could. It seems we are compatible in that respect."

Rustam's throat tightened, echoing the loathing in Elwaes's voice. At the same time, his player's mind went into high speed, searching memory for any reference to such an abhorrent experiment. Why had he never heard of it, and did Halnashead know? Could this be yet another secret weapon of Melcard's? That seemed likely, and Rustam wondered how old these children would be by now, if any of them were already in service.

"Rusty, are not your children as precious to you as they are to us?"

Bringing his mind back from speculation he could not hope to pursue at this time, Rustam nodded grimly into the dark. "Indeed they are, my friend. Since we landed on this continent our numbers have slowly but steadily declined. We must have been here nearly a hundred years before it really became apparent. It took us that long to get any truly settled structure to our society and during that time groups were constantly splitting away from Tyr-en and crossing the mountains to form the other four Kingdoms, so our numbers were constantly falling.

"But now—whether our ancestors were damaged by the magic wars that forced the Crossing, or there is something inimical to us on this continent, or even that we are cursed by Charin for whatever reason, our numbers fall year by year. Pregnancies are harder to bring to term and every child is counted as precious—except for those born to unmarried women. That, at least, does not change.

"And, I suppose, abandoned is the wrong word for what my mother did to me. She did, at least, ensure I was cared for."

Bile rose to his throat as he recalled his excitement that day. The promised treat; and his first painful lesson in how untrustworthy women could be.

"She took me to visit the old Master who had taught her to dance. She left me there."

Why was his voice trembling like that? Angry, he shook his head.

"I never saw her again."

Something light touched Rustam on the shoulder and he flinched, but it was only Elwaes's hand. A comforting warmth seeped from it into Rustam's cold core, and he shook as it took away some of the chill.

"Rusty, my friend," Elwaes murmured, "I grieve with you for your loss. And for hers."

"She didn't care!" spat Rustam, shrugging off the comforting touch. "If she'd cared at all she wouldn't have kept the pregnancy."

He knew he was being ungrateful but he couldn't help himself. This had been a part of him for too long to let it go now.

"Elwaes, I'm sorry. This isn't something I've thought about in a long time."

"Perhaps it's time you did."

"Nothing can change it. For all I know she's been dead and buried for years. And that's how I intend my memories of her to stay."

11. MAGIC

Five days after losing the pony they ran out of food.

An icy wind had risen during the night blowing stray flakes of snow from the surrounding peaks, and the travellers huddled inside as many layers of clothing as they possessed. For the first time it occurred to Rustam that even if they made it to the other side and successfully negotiated for troops, they might be too late in the season to make it back again. He shivered and licked his cracked and chapped lips before blotting them irritably with his sleeve.

The horses plodded dispiritedly along the seemingly endless plateau. The further they went the less hospitable the land became. The constant backtracking and detours to skirt the larger crevasses prolonged the journey, and stretched already frayed tempers to breaking point.

Rustam's mind was so numbed by the constant rattle of water along the stream bed, and the wind moaning through the high peaks that it took him some while to realise another sound had joined those. He looked around in confusion until he located Elwaes as the source. The elf was singing.

Risada glanced over her shoulder, face set in annoyance. But as he watched, Rustam saw the frown relax into a gentle smile that softened her features. Beneath the dirt and the wind-chafed skin he was able for the first time to see the natural beauty underlying the cultured and carefully presented persona of the Lady of Domn. He glanced down at himself in dismay: the filthy tattered clothing, hands that would give his manicurist heart failure, the beard.

Would any of his former lovers recognise him now?

He looked up at Elwaes swaying along on the tall black mare, and wondered why the elf looked cleaner than the rest of them. With his fair hair streaming in the wind and his face upturned as he sang he looked wild and fey, an unreal figure in a nightmare landscape.

Rustam stumbled on the uneven ground and gritted his teeth. The inflammation in his injured leg might be gone, but there were still several large holes in his thigh. He returned his gaze to the ground and listened hard, trying to capture the elusive song that had no familiar melody, nor words that he could identify, yet felt like something he could almost remember.

Finally in frustration, he broke in. "Elwaes, what is that? I can't quite place it..."

His voice trailed off in confusion at the elf's astounded expression.

"Forgive me, friend Rusty. You *heard* me?"

"Well of course I did. So did Risada."

"Ah, but the Lady forgot in the same instant."

"*What?*"

Rustam jogged forward until he was level with the grey. Risada's eyes were open but vacant. He waved a hand in front of her. No reaction, yet she sat the horse as though she were awake.

He stopped and waited until Nightstalker came alongside. His body shook with fear and anger. Why had he trusted the creature? Elves were magical, and all magic was evil, wasn't it? His fingers curled around the hilt of the wrist dagger he slipped into his palm.

"What in Charin's hell have you done to her?" he demanded. "We saved your life, remember?"

"Rusty, please—"

"Don't you '*Rusty*' me! You're using *magic* on us!"

Elwaes spread his arms wide. "All I've tried to do is to give the Lady some of the rest she so badly needs. You too, if you'll let me."

"No way! Leave me out of your unnatural schemes."

Elwaes sighed as though the accusation was a familiar one. He looked down on Rustam with a pitying expression. "Is that really what you think of me? Unnatural?"

"You? No. It's what you do. This—magic."

Elwaes shrugged. "To me it's as natural as, say, day and night are to you." He cocked his head to one side. "And that's not really how you feel about it, is it Rusty? It's how you *think* you should feel; how you've been told to feel. But how do you *really* feel?"

Rustam looked away, looked at anything but Elwaes. Heat flared through him. He slipped the dagger back into its sheath, nicking his thumb in the process. He stuck the bleeding digit in his mouth and sucked.

Ridiculous.

Yet it made some crazy sense. What Elwaes said was true. He didn't fear magic like other Tyr-enese. Like Risada. Actually, he was rather fascinated by the idea.

But how to say so?

Elwaes saved him the bother. The elf chuckled and Rustam's head snapped up.

"I should have known sooner," said the Shivan, smiling down at him.

"What? What should you have known?"

"Rusty, do you always perceive time in the same manner as your countrymen?"

Rustam blinked. Now what was the elf babbling about?

"Of course I...do. *Oh!*"

The world around him seemed to recede. He shook his head.

It couldn't be true. But when had he heard of another Tyr-enese who could view a fight in slow motion, or find the time to duck to keep from getting bloody when everybody else was concentrating on simply staying alive?

He'd always assumed it was just a family trait, albeit a very useful one. But now?

"You see, my friend, you have the talent. What a conundrum for a magic-shy Tyr-enese."

"No, you're wrong. You must be!"

But the words were hollow. Conflicting feelings chased each other around inside his head leaving him dizzy. Terror, delight, disbelief, mixed and mingled to produce an intoxicating blend of emotions. He looked to Elwaes to save him.

"You know I'm not," the elf said gently. "When the sprite chose you I should have suspected, but I thought she was just amusing herself. When she came back, then I should have been sure."

"But why? What does it mean?"

"Elementals are drawn to those who carry the power. They feed off it."

Rustam blinked hard and rubbed his temples. "Are you trying to tell me that she was using me for something other than, well—that? She was drawing energy from me? I couldn't understand why I felt so drained, but... "

"Precisely. She came to me too, but I didn't have the strength to spare. Yours was there for the taking."

"So she took it. Giving me no choice."

"Rusty, remember she paid her debts, which is more than many elementals would do."

Rustam shuddered. "I know. But the thought of it..."

He fell silent, pondering the implications. He must keep this from Risada or she might consider him a risk to the mission—to Tyr-en itself—and eliminate him. Could he rely on Elwaes to keep silent?

And what was he going to do with this knowledge? To fear it or ignore it would be foolish. What a tool it could be! But it could also make him the most feared player in the game, and thus the most hunted.

One step at a time.

"Elwaes, you have to help me understand it. Are there other things I can do?" He paused, and then added, "But for both our lives don't let Risada know!"

"I can try, my friend, though I am no tutor and my own abilities are limited. Learning to control what you have is the first step, but I suspect your talent is closely aligned with my own, which should make things simpler."

"And Risada? She has the true Tyr-enese terror of magic. If she even suspects you or me of using it—well." Rustam spread his hands.

"I won't say anything, but Rusty I'm curious—"

"I'd noticed."

Elwaes laughed, and Rustam relaxed inside, only then realising that he had been expecting the same sort of barbed reply Risada would have made. What a relief to enjoy someone's company again.

"I'm curious about the Lady. Surely this is not the sort of mission for a woman, even if her nobility is essential to your cause?"

Rustam pursed his lips. How much should he tell the elf? Technically, he was under Risada's orders, and those included not informing Elwaes about the details of their mission. But Elwaes's question did not ask *directly* about the mission, so an answer wouldn't *strictly* violate those orders.

He stared at Risada's back, the relaxed slump of her shoulders as she swayed with her horse's walk. How quickly she could turn into the perfect killer. He looked back up at Elwaes.

"Risada sorts out problems for the Royal Family."

Elwaes nodded. "I suspected as much. Her task, no doubt, was to remove me as a threat."

"You have a fair grasp of our politics."

"Tyr-en doesn't change. Tell me, why didn't she just kill me and end it there?"

"Because it was no longer that simple. Melcard has what he needs to go ahead with his rebellion even without you." Rustam looked away, studied the ground around his feet.

"And she saw the means to gain help from Kishtan, using me as a gift to placate their Queen?" asked Elwaes. Rustam nodded, keeping his lips tight together. He felt rather than saw Elwaes lean down and peer at him

"Is that all? Or was there something more?"

Rustam sighed, and then nodded. "It galls me to admit it, but to be fair to Risada, the gift idea was mine, not hers, and she didn't want to kill you anyway."

"Ahhh," breathed Elwaes and Rustam looked up in alarm, expecting to see the elf expiring. Instead, he fixed Rustam with an intense gaze.

"Rusty, the Lady carries a great deal of anger—and pain—inside her, yet I believe she is truly a gentle soul."

"Hah! You wouldn't think so if you'd been at the wrong end of her temper as often as I have."

"Perhaps not, but I urge you, try to make your peace. Such division will not impress the Court in Kishtan, or its Shivan Queen."

"Why should that be important to you?"

Elwaes's delicate features twisted into such a mask of hatred that Rustam took an involuntary step away from him. The elf moaned, and covered his face with his hands, dropping Nightstalker's reins. The mare tossed her head and rolled her eyes, sensing something amiss. Rustam reached a hand out to stroke her neck and murmur reassurances, not quite daring to look up at Elwaes. He never wanted to see such a tortured expression again.

"What's the matter? What have you said to him?"

Rustam glanced up in surprise. Risada had turned around and was staring back at them, the spell broken.

"I—"

"It's not Rustam's fault, Lady Risada," Elwaes broke in. "I was recalling Melcard's dungeon."

"Oh." Risada raised an arched eyebrow and swung the grey forward again, but not before favouring Rustam with a glare that said she didn't believe a word of it.

Elwaes leaned down, spoke only for Rustam's ears in a tone laden with death. "I will have my revenge on Melcard, and Hensar too. They will pay for what they did to me."

An icy gust embraced Rustam, making him shiver.

* * * * * * * * * * *

Lord Melcard frowned through the bars at sight of the girl bound to the chair.

"Hensar, why is her Highness restrained in this unseemly manner?"

"My Lord, it is for your protection," said the doctor. "Princess Annasala has turned out to be rather more aggressive than one might have anticipated from one of her gentle upbringing. And I fear she holds you accountable for her current predicament."

The object of Melcard's scrutiny scowled. "When my father sends his army to rescue me, you will discover the full extent to which I hold you responsible," she promised.

Melcard shook his head, and motioned for the doctor to open the cage door. He stepped inside and glanced around. While the elf had been in residence, Melcard had failed to notice how dingy and decayed the once comfortable furnishings had become. Now, with the vibrant personality of the captive princess fairly bouncing off the walls, he saw for the first time how very long his schemes had been in the making.

As well, then, that they were nearing completion.

He smiled apologetically at his prisoner. "My dear, I regret to inform you that there will be no rescue. I now command troops far in excess of those at your father's disposal, and very shortly they will secure both the palace in Darshan and those of your family who are sensible enough to surrender to me."

Annasala's expression remained disappointingly defiant. "You're very sure of yourself, traitor."

Melcard bridled. "I am no traitor! History will celebrate me as the liberator of my Kingdom, dethroner of a corrupt and tyrannical family that should have been removed from power generations ago. Your uncle—"

"Is long dead!" spat Annasala. "And Marten has none of his qualities. He's a gentle, compassionate ruler—"

"Who has yet to grow into his true family inheritance," Melcard interrupted in turn. "And I intend that he should never have the opportunity to do so."

"You'd kill Marten?" The first chip in Annasala's composure lent the slightest quaver to her voice. "But he's barely more than a boy."

"Unavoidable, I'm afraid, your Highness. There cannot be two claimants to the same throne."

"Two?" The princess laughed, a hysterical edge to the tone. "You honestly expect the other Families to accept you as their next King?"

"My dear, I admit there could be some resistance if I were to attempt to crown myself, but if your father could be persuaded..."

"Ah, *now* I see why I'm still alive. But you can't honestly believe my father would agree to crown you, even to save my life."

"To save your life, dear Annasala?" Melcard feigned puzzlement, drawing out the moment to drain it of every last drop of pleasure. "Why, no one has threatened your safety, have they?" He frowned theatrically at the stout doctor. "Hensar, you haven't frightened the poor child, have you? I entrusted her comfort to you—I do hope you have done nothing to abuse her of our hospitable intent."

He returned his attention to the princess, "I have only your wellbeing at heart, dearest Annasala. You don't mind if I call you Annasala, do you? It is so much more acceptable these days for a husband to call his wife by name."

He fell silent, the swelling heat of his enjoyment bringing an unaccustomed smile to his face.

The princess's face was another matter. Disbelief turned to horror and back again as she comprehended. The girl was intelligent—she must have inherited that from her father—and, he was sure, devious. But at that moment, Melcard held all the important tiles in the stack and she was powerless.

The bonus that completed Melcard's day was the stunned expression on Hensar's face. Never before could Melcard recall catching the doctor by surprise, and this made up for all the real and imagined slights that Hensar had subjected him to over the years they had been together. Surely Hensar could not have imagined him so naïve as to think Halnashead would not sacrifice his daughter to keep the throne securely within his Family. Now *that* was an unvoiced slight that would not be forgotten.

Halnashead would sacrifice his daughter, certainly. But if Melcard became his son-by-marriage? Surely then, the prince would take the offered compromise and save Annasala by crowning her husband—a move that would merely ally the Royal Family with the Fourth.

"Well, my dear," he beamed. "I must be away. There are many preparations to be made with both a wedding and a coronation to organise. If you have need of anything, just ask Doctor Hensar."

"You can't honestly believe this will work." Annasala's defiance was faint now, mere words with which to comfort herself.

"Why yes, my dear, I do." Melcard leaned forward to kiss his bride to be, unsurprised when she turned her head away. He frowned at the purple bruising that marred her cheek.

"Really, Hensar, you must be more careful. I don't want her visibly marked."

"I apologise, my Lord. As I've said, her highness has been more troublesome than I'd anticipated. It won't happen again."

Melcard addressed the princess firmly. "Annasala, please restrain yourself. It is not my intention that you suffer, merely that you learn how important it is to be obedient to my will."

For the second time, disbelief spread across his captive's face. "You expect me to believe you? After you've turned *him* loose on me? I don't suppose you would care to lift my skirts and view his handiwork?'

Melcard feigned shock. "Before our wedding night? What a scandalous suggestion. I thought you more genteelly raised than that."

He stepped from the cage, unmoved by Annasala's visible terror; the doctor had strict instructions about how far he was allowed to indulge himself. It was essential the girl be cowed, but Melcard did not want her damaged beyond usefulness. He still needed an heir, after all. He determined to visit his prospective wife every two or three days to see how her attitude adjustment was coming along.

And to keep the doctor in check, at least to some degree.

* * * * * * * * * * * *

Towards mid-afternoon the plateau came to an abrupt end, falling off into a sheer cliff face so tall that Rustam felt dizzy looking down. Sunlight gleamed on a huge lake far below, its shore dotted with trees miniaturised by the distance. An eagle circled level with their feet then dived abruptly, down and down until it was a mere speck lost in the glare off the water.

"So what do you suggest we do now?" Risada demanded.

Rustam shrugged. "Look for hoof prints I guess. The pony didn't go that way, that's for sure."

"How perceptive of you Chalice."

Rustam ignored the gibe. Elwaes was the second person to tell him he should try to understand why Risada was so spiteful, and he was trying. It just wasn't easy.

The ground was very hard, and it took almost until dark to find any sign that the pony had passed this way. Eventually, some way back from the cliff's edge, Rustam found a place where the moss was scuffed off the rocks at the base of the mountain on the left of the plateau, close beside a water cascade where their guiding stream descended from the heights over a mass of jumbled rocks.

A faint trail led upward, paralleling the rapids and disappeared out of sight amongst the rubble. Definitely the route taken by the trolls with their captive. Rustam called the others over. Risada eyed the trail dubiously. "We can't try that tonight," she declared. "We'll camp here and start at first light. Oh and Chalice, I think there's something you should know. Your friend is back."

Rustam's head jerked round. Sure enough, hovering over the bubbling water was the sprite. Rustam scowled.

"What? Not pleased to see her?"

Unwilling to answer, afraid of what he might give away, Rustam turned to Elwaes who nodded.

"Don't worry about the horses, I'll see to them."

Rustam strode briskly to the upward trail. He scrambled the first few lengths, then found the going easier than he had expected. The path wound around rocks and boulders but was worn quite smooth, and he wondered briefly what had made it.

He flinched from a light touch on his shoulder and shrugged it off. When he looked back, the sprite's face held a comic look of surprise as though she couldn't believe what he'd just done.

"I know about you now. I can't stop you but believe me, if I could, I would."

A brief flash of annoyance—had he imagined it?—turned into the impish smile he remembered from before. But there was something else too. Cunning, perhaps? It was difficult to tell on a face formed of mist.

"Come on then, let's get it over with."

He held out his arms and she flowed into them, enfolding him. He couldn't help but respond. His skin crawled where she touched him—which was almost everywhere—caught between revulsion and arousal. He sucked in a lungful of mist and coughed, choking on vapour. Did she mean to smother him?

Next moment, he drew a breath of clean, sharp mountain air—and as quickly lost it in a gasp of erotic delight. His knees buckled and he collapsed to the ground.

The path was hard but smooth under his back, and he moaned, writhing in the elemental's embrace. Contradictory impulses rioted along his nerves. Agony. Rapture. Everything in between and in combination.

Rustam was vaguely aware of his limbs thrashing, dimly noticed the pain as his hand smashed onto unyielding stone, as he rolled over and bashed his face on rock but it was all sensation, all adding to the heat of his arousal.

The sprite thrust down onto him hard, again and again. His breath came in ragged gasps but it didn't matter, nothing mattered except concentrating on the core of molten fire building within. Something slashed his arm and the metallic tang of blood tainted the air, but the pain was ecstasy and the fire erupted, engulfing him in exquisite torture.

* * * * * * * * * * *

Rustam lay on his back, gazing up at the starry sky. He blinked, trying to clear the haze from his eyes before he realised that the sprite hovered above him, distorting his vision.

He moved carefully, wincing at the pain in his arm, his hand, the dull ache in his head. He felt drained, and knew it was not just from exertion. He glared up at the sprite. She stared impassively back.

Rustam struggled to his feet, stiff and sore as if he'd been in a fight. Something nagged at him, something he couldn't quite place, like an itch just out of reach.

Shaking his head with care, hoping to clear the ringing in his ears, he felt his way back along the dark trail. The last few lengths he sat down and slid, not trusting his legs. He could feel the sprite close behind him.

"Why don't you go away," he hissed. "You got what you wanted."

He staggered the last distance to the camp, grateful when Elwaes caught him by the shoulders and lowered him to his bedroll. The elf gently peeled the layers of shirts away from Rustam's bleeding arm, shook his head but said nothing. He tore one of the sleeves into strips and used it to bind the wound.

Rustam was beginning to think he'd escaped Risada's sharp tongue for the evening when a light step heralded her approach. She bent over him, scrutinising his face in the light of the rising moons.

"What happened to you? Had a lovers' quarrel?"

She straightened to leave. For a second her lithe figure was silhouetted against the star-sprinkled sky and Rustam's breath caught in his throat. All at once he identified the feeling that had bothered him on his way back to the camp.

Lust.

Unquenched, all consuming, insanely intense lust.

He looked around wildly until he found the sprite hovering behind Elwaes, the glint of starshine showing through her vague form. He stared at her in horror.

"What have you done to me?"

His voice was so hoarse he hardly recognised it.

* * * * * * * * * *

"What did she do to me?" he asked Elwaes in the morning as they saddled the horses. The elf looked uncomfortable.

"I don't know, but my guess is you upset her."

"Oh, great. Ouch!"

The girth he had been fastening slipped through his fingers and he stared at the blackened bruising that spanned the back of his hand and spread down over his knuckles. He looked at Elwaes in dismay.

"How does the rest of me look?"

"Much the same, except your face. That's purple."

"I don't believe this. I doubt I could hold a sword today, even if my life depended on it."

"It may well," cut in Risada's voice. She appeared from the other side of the animals. "My, my, that must have been some tiff. Or did you enjoy it, Chalice? I know some people's tastes run to that sort of thing, but it looks like you got carried away. Do try to remember how serious this mission is."

Rustam clenched his fists—he found he could, despite the pain—certain that otherwise he would strangle her there and then. He said nothing, just glared at her and for the first time something showed in his face that made her take an involuntary step back.

"Well then, let's be on our way," she snapped, covering the tiny moment of fear. She swung up onto the grey and Rustam's eyes followed her every move, his breath a little shallow, his heart beating a touch too fast. He pictured himself dragging her out of her saddle, throwing her to the ground...

"Rusty. Wake up."

Elwaes was tugging at his sleeve. "Sorry," Rustam muttered and shook his head to clear the images.

"You ride first, my friend," offered Elwaes. "I don't think you're up to walking."

"Thanks," Rustam whispered, and clambered awkwardly onto Nightstalker while Elwaes held the mare still. He sat hunched over in the saddle, panting and trembling. What was the matter with him? Angrily he shook his head again, trying to banish the unwanted impulses but all he succeeded in doing was to aggravate the headache that already plagued him.

He glared at the stream, expecting to see the sprite hovering there, mocking his discomfort, but there was no sign of the elemental. Bright sunlight glinted off the water made him squint.

Risada led off. No one mentioned the fact that they had not eaten since yesterday morning. Their hopes now rested on finding the pony and their supplies, if the trolls hadn't already eaten or discarded the contents of the packs.

The trail led sharply upward but, as Rustam had noted the night before, it was smooth and easy to follow. It wound around various outcroppings, vaguely following the course of the frothing rapids that bounced and bubbled their way down the cliff side. At one point it crossed the water course and they dismounted and led the horses over the slippery rocks, the water churning around their ankles and soaking their boots. On the far side the path angled away from the water and narrowed to a ledge leading beneath a huge outcropping. Risada's grey balked at the prospect.

"Let me lead," Rustam suggested.

"Be my guest." Risada waved him forward and he squeezed past her on the narrow path. For a brief moment they were face to face, close enough to feel the heat of each other's breath. Rustam hesitated, overtaken by a violent urge to crush her against him and kiss her hard. The moment passed, but not before Rustam had seen the defensive look in her eyes.

Nightstalker surged forward, unhappy about passing the grey in such a confined space, and propelled Rustam forward until his feet were on the ledge. He stopped briefly, stroked the mare's neck to calm her nerves, and whispered inane comments into her ear. Gently, she rubbed her face on his shoulder and he smiled to himself. You could always trust a horse.

Rustam walked carefully forward, confident that Nightstalker would follow. He concentrated on the path in front; it was up to the others to make sure that Risada's horse followed.

The ledge was not as narrow as it had first looked, but the promontory above leaned steeply outward forcing them, particularly the tall black mare, to walk very close to the edge of the precipice. Rustam risked a glance downward: loose shale in a scree some fifteen horses' lengths across and more than that down to a jumble of sharp boulders at its base. Anything that went over there was not coming up again.

"Stop, stop!" Risada screamed.

Rustam tried to turn around but Nightstalker bounded forward in alarm, almost knocking him down. Hooves scrabbled frantically behind them, and Rustam caught a glimpse of the grey with its hind legs over the edge, starting to slide.

"Hold on!" he yelled but Nightstalker was so panicked he had to grip her bridle tight to stop her from bolting. All he could do was watch as Risada and Elwaes hung onto the reins of the terrified horse as it struggled to regain its footing.

"Pull, Elwaes, pull!" Rustam shouted. His heart hammered in his chest as he watched helplessly.

For one heart stopping instant, Risada, Elwaes and the grey teetered on the edge and Rustam thought they were all going over, when the grey's hind legs suddenly found purchase, and with one almighty push he bounded upward onto the relative safety of the ledge. Elwaes and Risada fell backward, landing in a heap in front of the shaking, sweating horse.

"Are you hurt?" Rustam called anxiously.

Risada glared at him. "You might have helped."

Rustam opened his mouth but nothing came out. He watched as Elwaes helped the Lady of Domn to her feet. The elf said something to her that was too quiet for Rustam to hear. Her shoulders slumped and she waved to Rustam to continue, but avoided meeting his eyes. He shrugged, both puzzled and angry. *Charin's breath!* What did she want of him? Always, she expected the impossible and wasn't even appreciative when he achieved it. Sooner or later he was going to make her grateful, one way or another.

Nightstalker blew through her nose at him, and he patted her, gently tugged on the reins to urge her into motion. Voices rang out behind and he looked back again. The grey was refusing to move.

I don't believe this!

He brought Nightstalker to a standstill again, but before he could go back to help Risada surrendered the grey's reins to Elwaes. The elf murmured into the horse's ear in his singsong voice, and the animal bowed its head and shuffled blindly forward. Rustam ached to learn that ability, to be that close to Nightstalker. He led the black mare on again.

Shortly after, the trail rounded the bluff and widened out. At a spot where it became broad enough for them all to gather together, they paused for a rest.

Rustam studied the dishevelled group. Both horses stood with their heads drooping, sweating from their exertions and the heat of the sun. Elwaes sat in a heap on the ground with his head on his knees. Risada perched on a boulder, staring into the distance, her skin pale beneath the dirt except for the dark rings framing her eyes. Rustam's breath caught in his throat: *Chel and Charin, he wanted her!*

He took half a step towards her. Stopped.

What am I doing?

He covered his face with his hands. What was happening to him? *Asking to get yourself killed, that's what*, he told himself savagely.

"Let's move," he said. "We're not getting any closer to that pony sitting around here."

To his amazement nobody argued. Risada even failed to comment on his audacity at giving her an order. Ungracefully, she clambered back onto the grey, and Rustam boosted Elwaes up onto Nightstalker.

"Don't fall asleep, you hear me? I won't be there to catch you if you do."

Elwaes smiled wearily. "I shall do my best," he promised, but he was struggling to keep his eyes open.

Risada led the way and within a few lengths the ledge turned sharply downhill but remained a more comfortable width, broad enough for the horses to walk without getting too close to the edge. The cliff-side above them to their left was a cluttered jumble of rocks and boulders, but climbed less steeply away from them than before, while the fall off to their right skittered dizzily downward towards the blue lake far, far below.

Rustam walked between the two horses, fixated on the sway of Risada's hips as her horse awkwardly negotiated the descent. It was only when she halted and looked back with a puzzled frown that he realised something was wrong.

He glanced up. An area of mountainside directly above them, approximately the size of a large ballroom, was devoid of rocks, but pockmarked with holes about half a horse's length in diameter. From the dark depths rose a malodorous stench, and as he watched with mounting foreboding something large, pale and insectoid moved in the mouth of one of the burrows.

"What—?"

"Rustam, get up behind me," ordered Elwaes. "Quickly."

"What are they?" Risada asked, the pitch of her voice higher than normal.

"Tunnel creepers. We have to get out of here. Now!"

12. TUNNEL CREEPERS

Rustam squeezed past Nightstalker, and scrambled up behind Elwaes. He had no idea what tunnel creepers were, but the fear in the elf's voice was all too apparent.

"Go Risada, go!"

The grey leapt forward, kicking loose stones from beneath its feet to clatter away down the mountainside, adding to the horses' rising panic. Sickly pale, bloated creatures swarmed out of the holes, and Rustam gagged on the mephitic stench that preceded them. Risada's mount spooked sideways and jumped half a length up the left bank to reveal the pallid, segmented body of a creeper blocking the path ahead.

The nightmarish thing, which stood as high as the gelding's chest, shifted its weight rapidly between its six legs, threatening great speed although the huge body merely quivered up and down with the multiple joints clicking loudly. Tiny eyes glittered from behind its mouth-parts, vanishing as ragged fronds waved under its pincers. Those pincers with their wickedly serrated edges and pointed tips held Rustam's horrified gaze, and he felt his empty stomach constrict even further: the monster's exoskeleton looked as tough as armour, probably impervious to steel, except perhaps at the joints. Not that he had any desire to get close enough to test the theory.

The grey's feet scrabbled on the uneven surface and one hind hoof went down a hole.

With an almost human scream of terror the horse catapulted up and forward, landing on the trail beyond the creeper. Nightstalker snorted and reared, bringing her forefeet pounding down on the monster. Rustam heard its body casing crack and it emitted a high pitched wail as it disappeared beneath the mare. He yelled encouragement to her as they fled down the steep track, but more of the enormous insects erupted from their burrows and swarmed towards them.

Rustam drew his sword, his injured hand forgotten in the adrenaline rush. He knew it was hopeless long before the blade cleared the scabbard. Even with his speeded time sense and disregarding the creepers' armoured hides, there were just too many of them.

"How do we fight them?" he yelled at Elwaes above the roar of wind and clattering hooves. Their headlong flight ended abruptly as the grey sat back on its haunches and skidded to a stop. The trail ahead was invisible, obscured by a seething mass of invertebrates.

"We don't," answered Elwaes and the defeat in his voice made Rustam furious.

"Then we'll die fighting. Yahhh!"

He swung his blade at the nearest creature, aiming at the juncture of legs and body, and proved his hypothesis by removing a couple of limbs and a pincer. The creeper fell to the ground, but another stepped on top of it and used the extra height to lunge at the riders. Rustam swayed sideways to avoid the outstretched pincer and succeeded in felling that one too, but they were surrounded and he glimpsed Risada hacking with her sword, trying to keep the pincers at bay.

Elwaes had his head thrown back and was screeching in some unintelligible, harsh language that hurt Rustam's ears. He hoped whatever the elf was calling would come quickly because they weren't going to last long.

Nightstalker stamped and kicked as the creepers tried to take her legs from under her. Rustam clung to his saddle as she bucked and lunged. A chilling scream wrenched his eyes forward in time to see the grey go down and Risada vanish under a mass of sickly white bodies.

—Risada!"

His cry was lost in a clamour of hoarse shrieks as blackness descended from the sky. Rustam covered his head, and talons raked his already injured arm as a flock of huge birds dived into the swarm and began pecking and tearing at the giant insects. In waves of disordered panic, the creepers retreated. The birds created mayhem in the midst of the rout, ripping off legs and pincers with razor sharp beaks, not killing but maiming as many as possible.

The noise was incredible. The creepers chittered frantically as they dived for the sanctuary of their tunnels, but there were far too many of them exposed on the mountainside to fit down the holes at once, and many were knocked to the ground by their fellows in the battle to reach safety. The gigantic avians screeched and cawed, and Rustam yelled at the top of his voice.

—Risada! Where are you?"

The path in front cleared of creepers, and the grey gelding, liberally streaked with blood, scrambled unsteadily to its feet.

Of Risada there was no sign.

—Chalice, help me! *Rustam...*"

The terrified wail drew Rustam's gaze just as Elwaes's arm shot out to point. Only Risada's head and arms were still visible above ground, and they vanished quickly as she was dragged feet first into a burrow.

Rustam flung himself off Nightstalker and landed running, scrabbling up the steep mountainside, dodging beaks and talons that struck indiscriminately around him.

"Risada!" he called, and he could just hear her despairing cry as he plunged into the burrow on his hands and knees.

"Rustam, help me!"

The reeking air became heavier and more pungent the deeper he went. Light began to fail but now he could see her, struggling and writhing in the grip of two creepers, hampering their progress. Something struck him from behind and Rustam twisted round in the confined space, thrusting his sword into the creeper that had entered the tunnel at his back. It shrilled as the blade embedded itself just below its mouth, and retreated up the tunnel, taking the sword with it.

"Damn!"

Rustam slipped a dagger into his hand and crawled after Risada. A bend in the tunnel blocked much of the remaining light but she was there, hanging onto a protruding lump of rock and kicking at the pincer gripping her boot. Only one creeper was beyond her now and Rustam hurled his dagger, was rewarded with a hiss and an ear-splitting wail as the blade struck a faceted eye that glinted in the near blackness. The injured monster relinquished its grip, and scuttled backwards into the dark.

"Come on," he urged and grabbed Risada's hand, half dragging her behind him as he scrambled back along the tunnel towards breathable air and daylight.

They emerged on a mountainside reminiscent of a battlefield. Dismembered bodies littered the ground and the huge black birds scavenged amongst the carnage, like messengers of Charin clothed in flesh and feathers.

Rustam hauled Risada to her feet and wrapped his arms around her. Then, flushed with the triumph of the rescue, he kissed her. She tasted of earth and sweat, but her lips were still sweet.

Her fists pummelled his sides.

"Take your filthy hands off me!"

Rustam's arms dropped obediently away, but Risada's actual words barely registered, her angry voice coming as though from a great distance.

The world around Rustam receded. He no longer stood on the blood-bathed mountainside. Instead, he existed in a tiny patch of still, silent darkness, alone but for a pair of glowing silver eyes that hung before him like two colossal stars against a backcloth of eternal night. A deep voice laughed mockingly.

"Where am I?" whispered Rustam, struggling to look around but unable to move. "Why am I here?" he demanded, ashamed of how his voice shook. "Who are you?"

The hollow laughter boomed again, hurting his ears.

"I am your conscience," hissed a terrible voice, and a disembodied, luminous hand reached towards him. He tried to twist away, but his body was immobilised by some magical force, and the glowing fingers caressed his face, tracing a path of fire from his temple to his jaw. The taste of blood filled his mouth and a stench of burning flesh assailed his nostrils.

Rustam Chalice screamed in agony.

Searing pain blotted out his awareness, and when he came back to himself he was standing at the mouth of the creeper burrow with Risada tugging at his sleeve. He swayed, almost falling.

–Come *on*, Chalice."

–Wha" ?"

He looked dazedly around. His otherworldly experience had transpired outside the normal flow of time. The massive birds still fed voraciously all around him, and a dead creeper lay at his feet with his sword protruding from its body. He bent over dizzily and grasped the hilt with trembling fingers, dragged the blade free before staggering after Risada. He pressed his bruised hand against the torment of his face.

Elwaes stood in the middle of the path holding the reins of both horses. The animals stamped and snorted, anxious to be away from the smell of blood and death.

"Please hurry," pleaded Elwaes. "Carocs are not to be trusted" they could easily turn on us." He glanced nervously over his shoulder at the huge avians.

"Is he in any fit state to be ridden?" Rustam asked, eyeing the blood streaked grey. His words came out curiously slurred.

"It's not as bad as it looks," Elwaes assured him, and held the horse while Risada swung into the saddle.

"We must ride double for a while, Rusty. We need to get away from here."

Infected by Elwaes's anxiety, the horses jogged quickly down the trail. As they rounded a bend both animals balked and side-stepped around a pale, crumpled shape on the ground. Wispy bits of what looked like hair covered the vaguely body-shaped husk.

"Ugh! What was that?" asked Risada.

"That was a troll," Elwaes replied grimly. "After the tunnel creepers finished with it."

* * * * * * * * * * *

They rode until darkness forced them to stop. The trail continued steeply downhill but was interrupted at intervals by broad, flat ledges, one of which they chose to serve as a camp.

The horses stood listlessly while Rustam poured what water they carried into a pan, his hands shaking so badly he spilled probably a third, and offered them a few sips each before placing the remainder aside for later. It was too dark to investigate the animals' injuries, but they were mercifully still sound; anything else would have to be dealt with in the morning when they reached the lake below.

Rustam ached all over. His face was a strange mixture of pain and numbness, but the terrifying memory of that *somewhere else* was fading, and he began to wonder if he had imagined the strange voice and that awful hand. He found it hard to believe they were all still alive.

In the faint gleam of starlight he could see Risada sitting on a boulder. She had been withdrawn since seeing what remained of the troll. Silence from Risada was not unusual, but this was a strained, unnatural quiet.

And Elwaes; there was definitely something wrong with the elf. He had been listless throughout the ride, and not even willing to help Rustam care for the horses. Now he was leaning back against the cliff wall with his eyes closed, and even in this faint light his skin looked sallow.

How much energy did it take to make those summoning spells? And without food he had no means to replenish his reserves. All that on top of the fact that he was nowhere near recovered from his years of incarceration.

What chance do we have of surviving this journey? Rustam asked himself miserably as he eased his sore body into his bedroll, past caring about sentry duty. His last conscious thought was of a pair of disembodied silver eyes dancing to sardonic laughter.

* * * * * * * * *

Sunlight shone through Rustam's eyelids and he turned his head away with a groan, burying his face into blankets that reeked of horse. Short hairs caught in the weave tickled the right side of his face although the other seemed oddly numb.

Reluctantly, he peeled away the layers of wool between himself and another day. Before leaving the cosy cocoon he stretched his limbs in a series of slow exercises designed to minimise the pain of stiff, bruised muscles, but every fibre of his body screamed abuse at him for daring to suggest that he move at all, let alone with any efficiency.

Resigned to another day of misery, Rustam crawled out of the bedroll and went to offer the horses the rest of the water. While they sucked greedily on what little remained, Rustam looked them over. Nightstalker seemed none the worse for her ordeal, but the grey was a very sorry looking sight. Covered in raw welts, he was shifting uncomfortably from one hind leg to the other, both limbs swollen from hoof to hock.

"Damn i' all t' Charin's hell!"

Why do I sound drunk?

"What's the matter now?" asked Risada in a weary tone. She stepped round behind her grey, her attention on its legs before turning to Rustam.

The Lady of Domn flinched back against her horse. Her eyes widened as she stared at Rustam's face.

"What *happened* to you?"

"Wha" ? Wha's wrong?"

Rustam's hands flew to his face, but even before they touched the sagging skin of his left cheek he knew what he would find. He'd seen it before, on an old man whose speech slurred just as his did now. One side normal, the other hanging limp, dragging the mouth and the eye down in a perpetual frown.

"No," he denied. "*NO!*"

His voice echoed back from the cliffs, mocking him.

Elwaes appeared then, tottering with one hand to the rocks for support. His pitying look was more than Rustam could bear.

"Help me Elwaes, please," he pleaded. "Use your magic."

Risada's horrified recoil barely registered.

Elwaes shook his head, eyes downcast. "Rusty, I have no healing powers. If there was anything I could do" "

His voice caught and he turned away. Rustam had the uneasy feeling the elf was weeping.

Exhausted, wounded, and demoralised, still there was nothing they could do but go on. They saddled the horses and mounted up, Rustam riding behind Elwaes to hold the exhausted Shivan in place. Fortunately the grey was still able to bear Risada's slight weight, and as he walked the swellings began to reduce.

The sun was bright and warm, a glorious autumn day. Rustam squinted at the lake below. Cupped in a picturesque bowl between five jagged peaks, the brilliant blue water shimmered serenely in the sunshine. Random up-thrusts of granite interrupted the surrounding verdant growth and, as they descended, several patches of darker green resolved into small copses. A dense evergreen forest edged the far lake shore, while jumbled boulders littered the nearer, evidence of a rock slide.

Rustam's head ached. His eyes wandered away from the tranquil scene below, straying back to Risada. Why was it that even under these circumstances he kept recalling how good it had felt to hold her in his arms, to crush her lips against his? What crazy desire drove him to want the one woman in Tyr-en who despised him?

But" his shrunken stomach turned over queasily and his hand strayed up to finger his sagging skin beneath the shaggy, unkempt beard" what woman would want him now? His looks had always been his fortune.

No longer.

Elwaes shifted in front of him, muttering incomprehensibly.

–Elwaes?"

Rustam tapped his arm. The elf's head lolled back onto Rustam's shoulder. His face was flushed and the almond eyes were half open, but without focus. A moan escaped his lips. Had he not been wedged between Rustam and the high pommel of the saddle he would have fallen.

"Risada," called Rustam, angry at the inebriated way his words slurred. She glanced round, her expression weary. She even failed to chastise him for not using her title.

"It's Elwaes. He's ill."

She shrugged. "Nothing we can do here. Just hold onto him until we get down there."

Speechless with frustration, knowing that her words were true, nonetheless Rustam was infuriated by her perfunctory dismissal of the situation. Pressure built inside his chest and he ground his teeth to keep from voicing his rage.

They reached the lakeshore somewhere around midday, dismounted beside one of the copses and laid Elwaes in the shade of the branches. He muttered and groaned, tossing from side to side in the grip of a raging fever.

"Fetch some water, please," said Risada, holding out a canteen. Rustam took it wordlessly, the politeness of her request doing little to mollify his anger, but for Elwaes's sake he trudged down to the lake, some fifteen lengths away.

He knelt and dipped the leather bottle into the sparkling clear water. A semicircle of concentric ripples spread out, glittering with rainbow coruscations. He winced as the brilliance stabbed his eyes, renewing the pounding in his head which only served to amplify his other pains. His dry throat constricted in a spasm of coughing and he raised the canteen and drank greedily, regretting it almost immediately as the leathery taste made him gag.

Weary beyond all experience, Rustam forced himself back to his feet and returned to the others. Risada accepted the canteen and, after a well-considered couple of small sips to ease her own immediate thirst, mixed some of the potion she had administered to Elwaes before. Luckily it had been in her own saddle-bags and not in the pony's packs, and she dribbled some down the elf's throat in one of the rare still moments between his restless thrashings. She glanced up at Rustam from two bruised and swollen-looking eyes. If he hadn't known better, he might have thought she'd been crying.

"We can't go on," she said. "Even if we catch up with them we're in no condition to fight. We should stay here until we're stronger and then decide what to do. There must be fish in this lake and the water's bound to attract game. What do you think?"

"You're in charge," said Rustam tightly.

Risada's shoulders drooped. Then she squared them and rose to her feet.

"As you say. Untack the horses then, and do something about building a fire." She gazed beyond Rustam, to the shining waters of the lake. "I'm going to take a swim."

Rustam blinked. "A swim?"

"Yes, Master Chalice, a swim. In case you hadn't noticed, we're all filthy and we stink to Chel's domain. The sun's hot enough it might as well be a summer day, and I intend to take advantage of it even if you don't. Oh, and don't get any funny ideas" you can have your turn when I'm finished."

"A swim," muttered Rustam as he untacked Nightstalker. "She's going to take a swim. See to the horses, Chalice. Make a fire, Chalice. Catch our supper. How about build a castle while I'm at it? *Charin's breath!*"

Bridles off, the horses fell on the lush grass. Not much danger of them straying far, thought Rustam as he looked them over. The exercise had reduced the grey's legs to a normal size and his other injuries, while sore and unsightly, were all superficial. Nightstalker was miraculously unscathed. Both animals were lean as hounds, but not as bad as they might have been, all things considered.

Rustam gathered up the tack and slung a bridle over his shoulder. He swore as it twisted the makeshift bandage on his arm, tearing the scab beneath. As he lugged the gear awkwardly to where Elwaes lay beneath the trees, he could feel blood seeping through the silk. He gritted his teeth against further outburst for fear of disturbing the elf who slept now, quiet but for the occasional moan. Rustam dumped the tack in a heap and tiptoed away.

He made his way between the boulders lining the lakeshore, meaning to wash the blood from his arm and shirt. He had no intention of spying on Risada, and only realised when he stumbled across her clothes that he had followed her tracks. By then he was too close to resist a peek, and he trod softly down to the edge of the lake.

Her smooth white body flashed through the water, twisting and turning like some fantastic fish cavorting for pleasure. A narrow brown belt hugged her waist, accentuating the slenderness of her figure above the swell of her hips. Emerald and steel glinted as she rose and dived again" even naked she could not bear to be parted from all her weapons.

Rustam's breath caught, twin bands of rage and desire tightening around his chest, constricting, throttling him. He turned, and stumbled blindly away.

How *dare* she? It was obscene that she should be enjoying herself like that, alone, in the water. Something snapped inside him.

If it was pleasure she wanted, he would oblige.

Her clothes lay neatly folded on top of a small flat rock. A jumble of head-high boulders surrounded the clearing and would have shielded it from sight had Rustam not blundered into it. Now he dropped to his knees and searched her garments methodically, removing all the needles, blowpipes, darts and daggers until he had a small, deadly arsenal which he hid in a hollow to one side of a larger rock. Meticulously, he refolded her clothes, positioned himself out of sight, then settled back to wait.

She was humming to herself as she came up from the lake, and Rustam heard the splatter of water as she shook the drops from her hair. He heard her sigh" no doubt at the prospect of climbing back into filthy clothes" then silence, quickly followed by a furious howl.

─*Chalice!* You meddlesome cur" what do you think you're playing at?"

She stood nude, holding a blouse in one hand, some underwear in the other. He slipped silently up behind her. She sensed him, half turned, but he was already too close and he pinned her left arm, knocked the half-drawn dagger out of her fingers and clamped his right hand around her long neck.

She struggled, flailing at him with her free fist. He tightened his grip on her throat until she scrabbled at his hand, her jaggedly broken nails gouging his already bruised flesh.

Rustam was beyond pain. All the fears and frustrations of the journey, the anger, the hurt and humiliations, melded together in an overwhelming desire to vent his rage upon her. He felt himself stiffen with lust, pressed himself against her and savoured her terror.

Thought she was superior to him, did she? She was just like every other woman in his life" use him then discard him the moment he was inconvenient. Well he would show her who did the using now. He would throw her face first to the ground and mount her like an animal, thrust himself into her again and again until"

He became conscious of a strange sound and, with dawning awareness, realised it was himself, growling.

What was happening to him? How could he have sunk so low? Ever since the sprite"

His vision cleared. Sure enough, the elemental was there, hovering over them, her misty features leering in eager anticipation.

Revulsion swept though Rustam and bile shot up into his mouth. He flung Risada aside as though she might contaminate him too. She fell heavily and lay on her side, gasping for breath.

Rustam glared at the sprite. "I won't do it! Go find yourself another victim, you'll get nothing more from me."

For a brief moment the sprite's grey eyes brightened to a glittering, glaring silver that bored into Rustam's soul. Then with a hiss of fury she spun round on herself and evaporated.

Rustam sat down hard. He pressed the heels of his hands against his eyelids until he saw stars, in an effort to blot out the images of what he had nearly done.

When eventually he dropped his hands and blinked to clear his blurry vision, he found Risada beside him, curled in a shivering ball. He put a hand tentatively on her shoulder. She flinched.

"Risada, *Lady* Risada, forgive me. It wasn't, I never meant to..."

She pushed herself up and slightly away from him. She hugged her knees to her chest, peering sideways at him from behind a veil of tangled wet hair.

"I know." She croaked, and then coughed. "I saw it. That *creature*!"

To Rustam's utter astonishment, she burst into tears.

Rustam's breath caught in his throat, and he did the only thing he could think of: he put his arms around her. She leaned into him and buried her face against his shoulder. Her sobs were eerily silent and as he held her, Rustam struggled to make sense of events.

Clearly the sprite had manipulated him with one goal in mind. How much energy would they have generated if he'd gone through with it? More than she could drain from him alone, that was certain.

And those terrible silver eyes...

With a shudder, he fingered the numb folds of skin beneath his unkempt beard. How many more concealed dangers awaited them between here and Kishtan?

He dropped his hand to Risada's head and began stroking her damp hair.

Questions and worries chased each other through his head until he was distracted by something trickling down his shoulder. His shirt was soaked where Risada lay against him.

Just then, she moved a little. Tear tracks streaked her face. Without thinking, Rustam wiped a stray droplet from her chin. To his amazement, she didn't pull away. Instead, she closed her eyes and relaxed against him.

Rustam didn't know how, but he wanted to put things right. Gently, he stroked away the tension creases in her forehead and traced a fingertip down her cheek, smudging the harsh lines where her tears had run through the caked dust from her fall. He ran his hands lightly down her throat, wincing inside as they passed over the bruises he'd made, and began to massage her shoulders. She arched her neck back in pleasure. Then:

―No!"

She stiffened and drew away.

―I'm sorry," said Rustam, shaking his head. The moment was lost, but it was different this time. The aggression was gone from her voice, replaced by, what? Regret?

Rustam sat back in confusion as Risada rose unsteadily to her feet and started to draw on her clothes. Why regret? Out here, they were alone. No one else need ever know. So what held her back? Was it his disfigured face, or"

The answer flashed into his mind with such clarity that he gasped. So simple, yet it explained everything.

Everything.

―You think I'm your *brother*! That's it, isn't it? It's so obvious, why didn't I see it before?"

The Lady of Domn stopped dressing and looked down at him, expression heavy with defeat. He didn't miss the slight wince as she focused on his damaged face.

—I hoped that if I kept you enough off balance, you never would."

So that was why she'd been so unreasonably foul. All the petty, spiteful, hurtful comments finally made some sort of warped sense.

Risada shook her head. —As soon as you were born, I knew you were my father's. I prayed daily to Chel that you would never know, or that your mother might tell you otherwise."

—But why? What would it matter? I'll always be a bastard no matter how august a father I might claim."

—Put that brain of yours to work! It's why we continue to search for the Royal Bastard, even though we're not sure he really exists. If it came to it, there would always be some who would support his claim with their own eye to advancement under a new king. The same would be true for you. There are those who would back you if you made a play for the Lordship of Domn."

—But Iain" "

The anguish on her face made Rustam pause. He reviewed his memories of the Lord of Domn, all the little oddities he had noticed in recent times. Small things, nothing too obvious until you added them together. The simplistic conversations, the apathy about Family matters, the childish glee at party tricks and entertainers. His lack of interest in women.

Rustam stared at Risada in dismay. She glanced quickly away, hiding her face. Her voice, when she spoke, was brittle.

—So now you understand. They tell me it's nobody's fault, but I can't help feeling it was something I did. Or something I didn't do. I raised him, you see. After our parents were murdered I couldn't trust anyone. You do see that, don't you?"

She faced him with a helpless, pleading look, and Rustam dared wonder if he was finally seeing the real Risada. Careful not to shatter the fragile mood, he said: —I understand some children are born that way, and there's nothing anyone can do. At least if they never grow up they never know that they're different."

Risada twisted her hands together, and Rustam suspected she wasn't really seeing him. Or the rocks, or the pile of clothing she still hadn't finished donning.

—But it's no good for Iain. He's Lord of the Second Family..."

Her voice trailed off and she stared for a long while at her white knuckles. When she raised her face next, she was fully focused on Rustam, though something haunted lurked in the depths of her brilliant blue eyes.

—That's why I have to keep you at a distance. If we ever make it back to Tyr-en, I can't afford to risk letting you live."

There was an edge to her voice which told Rustam one thing for certain: she might regret doing it, but do it she would, to protect the myth of Iain's competence. If Rustam had ever had any doubts about the nature of women, Risada had just dispelled them.

And, more disturbingly, Rustam found himself resenting the implication that he should surrender his life to preserve the political stability of Tyr-en. While he had always considered himself willing to die in Halnashead's service" for the good of the kingdom" this felt like a step too far. Would he, should Halnashead ask it of him? Would the prince do that?

The shrill neigh of an angry horse startled them both.

—My weapons?" demanded Risada. Rustam barely paused to point out the rock that hid them before he took off running. He burst out of the jumble of boulders and skidded to a halt, stepping sharply backward to avoid a flying hoof.

Three trolls hung off the mane and neck of Risada's grey, trying to drag it towards the cliffs, while another of the hairy monsters danced around waving its arms under Nightstalker's nose, dodging her bared teeth and screeching at a fifth which was swinging round on the end of the infuriated mare's tail.

Rustam yelled in outrage and threw himself into the fracas. Short blades slid smoothly into each hand, though he almost dropped one as his bruised hand fisted sluggishly. As the nearest troll sailed past clinging onto Nightstalker's tail, he grabbed it and slit its throat. He threw it aside, ducking to avoid a hoof that snapped past his face, grazing his cheek.

The glint of sunlight off steel announced Risada's arrival and one of the trolls fell from the grey's neck, clutching at a dagger embedded in its back. The others screeched their alarm and abandoned the horses, fleeing towards the cliff.

The grey bolted to the water's edge and stopped there with his head and tail raised high, snorting his alarm. With one last contemptuous kick at a fallen troll, Nightstalker followed. Panting hard, Risada pointed towards the horses.

"That was stupid, diving in like that. You might have been killed."

After a careful look around to ensure no other nasty surprises awaited them, Rustam knelt to retrieve Risada's dagger from the troll carcass. He wiped it as clean as he could on the creature's matted hair and handed the hilt to her with a glare.

"Then I would have saved you the trouble, wouldn't I?" His speech slurred worse with his anger, but he knew she understood.

"Chalice" Rustam" the politics aren't of my choosing, but you must see my dilemma. You may not even want to challenge Iain" "

"Damn true, I don't."

"But others may do it in your name, whether you like it or not."

"Why now? Why not" ah, of course! The Domn guardians. How many of them know of Iain's condition?"

They started walking after the horses.

"All of them, of course," said Risada with a scowl that, for once, was not aimed at him. "They had to assess his competence to rule."

So they've thrown him into deep water to see if he'll float or drown. And without you there to guide him."

Precisely. If there are no crises he might cope, but with this rebellion..."

Anything might happen."

She nodded unhappily.

And how many of them either know or suspect about me?" Rustam asked.

They can all count as well as I," she replied with a miserable shrug. Aching inside for her, Rustam put a comforting hand on her shoulder. At first she stiffened, and then she relaxed and patted it.

You have your moments, Chalice. Sometimes it's hard not to like you. Oh, and Rustam" "She pointed back to the lake shore. That never happened. You understand?"

They caught the horses and led them towards the camp, but even before they arrived Rustam knew something was wrong. He dropped the handful of forelock he had been using to lead Nightstalker, and sprinted forward.

Elwaes? Elwaes, answer me!"

The camp was a shambles. Tack thrown around, saddle-bags emptied and scattered, bedrolls ripped to pieces.

Of the Shivan there was no sign.

13. TROLL DEN

"Now what?"

Risada kicked the empty blankets where the Shivan had lain.

"I'm out of ideas," Rustam admitted. He laced his hands behind his neck, staring at the ground. "There aren't even any tracks. Damn it all to Charin's hell, we should never have left him alone."

"It's too late for recriminations. Come on man, think!"

Rustam wandered the camp, scanning for tracks he knew he wouldn't find. The ground was too firm for imprints of creatures as lightweight as the trolls, and Elwaes had no doubt proven an easy burden for several of them to carry. He sighed. "We'll have to backtrack to the end of the rock path and see if we can pick up the pony's tracks again."

"Rustam."

He glanced up, surprised by her use of his given name. She was staring at the cliffs and he turned, scanning the craggy rock face.

"What is it? What do you see?"

"Can trolls make fire?"

"I've no idea. Why?"

She pointed. A narrow plume of smoke rose from near the base of the cliff, barely visible as it drifted up the rock face but just discernible to the keen eyed. The mobile side of Rustam's mouth stretched into a predatory smile.

"Apparently they can, but without enough sense to hide it. Shall we pay them a visit, my Lady?"

"By all means, Master Chalice."

* * * * * * * *

They left the horses catching up on some much needed grazing time, and covered the short distance on foot.

By the time they reached the source of the smoke, the sun had fallen from view behind the mountains and the broad valley was filling with a dusk that seemed to rise from the ground. They crept the last stretch, but instead of the camp they expected to find they were confronted by a hole in the ground from which the thin, steady column issued.

"A chimney?" whispered Risada.

"Looks like it. Now all we have to do is find the front door."

They separated and searched one to either side, but it was nearly full dark before Risada hissed at Rustam and beckoned him over, waving at him to keep low. He slunk to her side, darting from boulder to boulder in the shadow of the overhanging cliff. Risada crouched behind a jutting lump of rock, and Rustam eased himself down beside her. She said nothing, pointing.

He peered past and saw a blur of movement, black against the dark cliff. His nose told him what his eyes could not: trolls, coming towards them. He put a hand on Risada's shoulder and squeezed to let her know he had seen.

Just short of where Rustam and Risada hid, the trolls turned towards the cliff. They were dragging something that snarled and spat, and Rustam shuddered as the night was rent by a blood curdling yowl. After a brief scuffle, the trolls and their now silent captive vanished into the deeper gloom beneath the overhang.

They waited, but no more trolls appeared. Finally they ventured forward until they found the narrow slit in the rock between two protruding boulders. Nerves tingling, they entered the mountain.

Forced to hug the walls and feel their way, they followed the troll stench. The rock beneath their feet was worn smooth, and it slowly dawned on Rustam that it was not a cave they had entered at all, but a curving, sloping tunnel leading downward, into the bowels of the mountain.

Every small sound, from their tentative steps to each carefully controlled breath, sounded loud enough to alert an army. Expecting at any moment to be discovered, Rustam wondered if Risada was any more confident than he. This skulking in the dark was definitely more her field of expertise. The only time *he* skulked was getting into and out of a lady's bedchamber. Even then he was only at risk from the odd guard, or an enraged husband. Not an entire pack of bloodthirsty trolls.

Step by painful step, they crept down the tunnel. The air grew fouler, and sweat trickled down Rustam's back. His chest tightened, ribs aching. When the first hint of ruddy light flickered across his vision, he held out a hand to see the shadow before he was convinced his eyes were not deceiving him. Smoke tickled his throat and he swallowed to keep from coughing.

They edged forward, certain that at any moment they must encounter a denizen of this stinking underground, but nothing challenged them. The light strengthened until the tunnel emptied out onto a ledge overlooking a vast cavern dominated by a central fire pit.

Rustam counted around sixty trolls. Youngsters, smaller and less hirsute, cavorted amongst the females attending the cook fire. The females, easily distinguishable by the double rows of teats poking from their hairy bellies, were stripping unidentifiable carcasses. The larger males sat around in groups, rolling chunks of what looked like bone in parody of a tile game, snarling and swatting any youngster who ventured too close. The parallels with a human trader camp were chilling, but no traders ever smelled so bad.

"I thought Elwaes said they weren't very intelligent," whispered Risada.

"I would have agreed with him, but now I've seen this I don't know what to think."

Rustam studied the camp again and found the troll he sought. Sitting immobile near the fire, the one who had led both the earlier attacks stared into the flames. The chunk of rough crystal hanging from the thong around its neck glittered in the light, and Rustam noted how the other trolls avoided the tiny rainbow shards that cut the surrounding air.

Risada nudged him and pointed. In front of them, the path became a series of zigzagging shelves leading down to the cavern floor, but the horizontal ledge on which they stood also continued to their right, about one and a half lengths above the cavern floor. With a quick nod of agreement Rustam followed Risada along it.

They trod carefully, aware that the smallest dislodged stone might bring the pack swarming after them. The ledge was rough and uneven, littered with loose rocks and debris, and the fitful quality of the light strained Rustam's eyes as he scanned the ground carefully before placing each step. At intervals, the ledge dwindled almost to nothing, forcing them to squeeze along a narrow shelf with their backs tight against the damp rock wall.

When they were about a quarter of the way round the perimeter of the cavern, they paused for breath.

"I don't see any sign of Elwaes or the pony," whispered Rustam, struggling to form clear words.

"Neither do I, but what do you think *that* is." Risada pointed and Rustam squinted past her. A short distance ahead the ledge appeared to end where a deep niche cut into the cavern wall.

"Let's take a look."

Rustam had a strong suspicion about what they would find, and he wasn't disappointed. The ledge went a short way around the corner into the recess and the two of them lay down on their bellies to study the little group of captives below.

The pony looked considerably slimmer than the last time they had seen it, but it stood contentedly munching on a pile of half rotten apples, occasionally switching its tail and stamping a foot with a hollow thud on the rock floor. Their packs lay heaped behind it, the contents strewn haphazardly around.

Elwaes was less content. His hands and feet were lashed together and he tossed restlessly, murmuring in delirium. The trolls had hacked off his long flaxen hair and his tall ears looked obscenely naked for the loss.

Rustam assumed that the third prisoner was the one they had seen carried in earlier. The man laid awkwardly, hands bound behind him and with his wrists and ankles tied together by a short rope. His swarthy skin glistened as though oiled, and he had a short fuzz of dark hair on his head, his chest and his loins. Other than that, he was naked.

"Where do you suppose they found him?" mused the Lady of Domn.

"I've no idea, but any captive of theirs is likely to help us get out of here. I'll lower you down."

Risada delved into a pocket and drew out the shapeless cap she had worn in Melcard's dungeons. She twisted her hair up and secured it with a clip, then put the hat on, leaving only her face and hands visible in the dim, flickering light.

Rustam smiled. It was the first time he had really appreciated how satisfying it could be to work with another professional.

Risada squirmed around until her feet were over the edge, searching for purchase. Rustam gripped her wrists, wincing as he closed his swollen fingers, and for a moment their faces were so close her sweet breath warmed his cheek.

"Chel go with you," he murmured. Risada blinked in surprise but said nothing as she backed slowly away.

Rustam shuffled forward on his belly as she slipped lower. He clenched his teeth against the pain in his hand, and winced as he noticed how unevenly his jaws closed. How long could this affliction last? He refused to even contemplate that it might be permanent.

He dragged his attention back to the matter at hand. When he was nearly at full stretch, with as much of his upper body as he dared hanging out over the edge, he squeezed his fingertips against Risada's wrists to let her know they had reached the limit.

"Let go," she whispered, and pushed away from the wall as he released her. She landed lightly on her feet on the cavern floor some two lengths below, her soft soled boots making no sound. She dropped to a crouch and they both froze, waiting to see if any trolls had marked the movement, but it seemed they had regained Chel's favour.

After a dozen deep breaths during which she held motionless, Risada ran lightly to the front edge of the recess. Hidden behind a jutting buttress of rock, she had a good view of the cavern. Without looking around, she beckoned Rustam to follow her down.

He shook his trembling arms in an attempt to restore some co-ordination to his overstrained muscles. *Not that she's heavy*, he thought, guilty as if he'd said as much to her face, but he'd pushed his body beyond its limits once too often this trip.

Maybe more than once.

Taking a deep breath, he prepared to do the impossible yet again. Turning around, he slithered over the edge feet first, finding a foothold here, a handhold there until he was spread-eagled against the rock wall.

He was about to jump when Risada's sharply whispered: "Stay!" locked his muscles tight. He clung where he was, face to the stone, forced to ignore the agony in his arms and hand to become one with the rock.

In his peripheral vision, he watched a small troll dash past Risada into the alcove. The juvenile man-eater skidded to a halt beside the dark prisoner and glanced over its shoulder, as though worried it might have been noticed. Rustam could just make out the huddled shape of Risada beside the entrance, face turned to the wall to hide her pale skin.

The young troll missed her entirely. It turned back to the bound stranger and leant over him, slavering. Great gobs of drool fell from its toothy snout onto bare skin. With a gnarled paw it tried to remove something that hung around the man's neck.

The captive rolled over with a snarl. The young troll jumped back and, jabbering unintelligibly, fled the niche.

The naked man lay now with his face toward the wall and Rustam found himself the object of scrutiny for two piercingly bright green eyes. He let go the wall and jumped down the rest of the way, landing beside the tightly roped captive. They regarded one another in silence until Risada spoke.

"Any ideas on how we get out of here again?"

Rustam glanced round at her and laughed quietly. "I thought you were the one who always planned your escape routes before going in."

Risada's face blanked for a moment, and he awaited her sarcasm. Then her lips curved into a wry grin. "You have me there. But I usually have the leisure to study all possibilities before I go in. Improvisation is not my style."

The stranger's head turned, following the conversation. Risada glanced down at him and shuddered as the glowing emerald eyes settled upon her. For a moment she froze like prey before a snake, and then jerked her head up.

"I have a sssuggestion," offered the stranger in a deep, guttural voice. His accent was new to Rustam, with a strange sibilance.

Risada turned away, ignoring him.

"What?" asked Rustam as he knelt down and drew his knife to sever the bonds.

"Rustam!" snapped Risada. "Here."

He hesitated, then shrugged and went to join her. She drew him into the farthest corner of the recess, behind the pony. "We can't trust him; we know absolutely nothing about him."

"Are you suggesting we leave him here?" Rustam's words slurred almost incoherently with indignation and he forced himself to calmness, continuing as clearly as he could. "Goddess knows what the trolls want with him but it won't be pleasant, you can be sure of that."

"But if we let him loose he might betray us to save himself."

"There's only one way to find out."

Rustam left her in the corner.

"Chalice!"

His knife sliced through the ropes and the powerful stranger rolled to his feet in one graceful, fluid movement. Rustam stood warily, dagger at the ready, but all he received was a deep bow.

"Friend. My lifeblood iss yoursss." The voice resonated from somewhere deep inside the barrel chest, and carried with it a strong, musky odour.

"Who are you?" Rustam demanded, acutely aware that his ruined face was being studied in minute detail.

"You may call me Shamnac. More can wait until we are out of this sstinking pit."

Rustam nodded once. "Agreed. But how?"

"Surely, Chalice, that is my decision?" Risada stepped around the pony, something concealed in her hand. Shamnac turned towards her, and she stopped as though she'd walked into an invisible wall.

"Lady, you have no need of your weapon with me."

"Ah, but how do I know that?"

"You cannot tell truth? Then you musst be human."

"What—?"

"Ssss. They will come soon. See to the elf. The vermin are mine."

The stranger slipped out of the alcove and vanished. Almost immediately a chilling yowl reverberated around the cavern walls, followed by a moment of utter silence before pandemonium broke loose. Trolls fled in all directions, shrieking and jittering, cannoning into each other and falling down.

Risada looked pointedly at Rustam "What did I tell you? Now how are we supposed to get out?"

Sheltered from the panic outside, it was some while before they noticed that the number of trolls was diminishing. Rustam spotted some entering a tunnel on the far side of the cavern. The awful howl came again, and they caught a brief glimpse of something black and sinuous, close to the ground, which whipped through a retreating group of trolls leaving torn off limbs and bloody bodies in its wake.

"What was that?" Risada sounded shaken.

"I don't know, but let's get out of here while they're busy."

Together they bundled the scattered supplies back into the packs and flung them onto the startled pony. Rustam hefted the unconscious Shivan up amongst the bags and prayed to Chel to keep him there. Taking hold of one side the bridle each, they dragged the reluctant pony out of the niche and ran for the exit.

* * * * * * * * *

"I'm certain we didn't come this way." Risada's voice whispered around the tunnel walls.

As Rustam turned his head towards the sound of her voice, he realised he could just see her. He reached a finger out to the damp rock wall and scraped off a faintly shining layer of phosphorescent moss. A pungent odour made his eyes water.

"We didn't, I'm sure of it, but I could have sworn there were no side turnings."

"Well apparently there were and we didn't notice. Can we turn the pony around?"

Rustam pushed the pony as close to one wall as possible, and then bent the animal's neck round and pulled steadily while Risada pushed on the other end. For a moment it stuck across the tunnel, shoulders jammed against one side, haunches against the other. Then with a rush it pulled free and stood there snorting and tossing its head in protest, but facing back the way they had come. Rustam steadied the elf.

"Come on, we need to keep moving."

Rustam patted the pony to reassure it and urged it into walk, following Risada's faint outline. The tunnel darkened as they left the eerily glowing walls behind, and the only sounds were the chink of the pony's shoes and the laboured breathing of the unconscious elf.

* * * * * * * * *

"We should have been outside by now."

"I know," said Rustam, and stopped abruptly as he bumped into Risada.

"We'll have to backtrack again, but more carefully this time."

"We can't. This tunnel's too narrow to turn the pony."

"Well we can't keep on going—we could get lost."

"Risada, we *are* lost. There's no way we should have missed the exit last time but we did, and if we can't turn the pony round the only option is forward."

"We could leave it here."

Rustam shuddered. "After all the trouble we went to, to get it back?" he argued rationally. "Let's at least see where this leads before we make any drastic decisions."

Don't worry, he thought at the pony as they set off again. *I won't leave you here, though there's someone else I might if she keeps making suggestions like that.*

A musty smell tickled Rustam's nose and he muffled a sneeze. He blinked twice and realised he could see again. Sure enough, the same spongy growth appeared in patches on the rock wall and overhead, sufficient to see Risada's outline.

Which suddenly vanished.

Rustam yanked the pony to a halt. He scanned the empty tunnel where Risada had been just seconds earlier. Rocks rattled in the distance, as though falling a long, long way down.

"Rustam?"

Her hollow whisper reverberated somewhere close by. Rustam's belly knotted and he narrowed his eyes, squinting into the gloom. Instinct dropped him to his hands and knees and he felt his way forward, palms flat to the path until his fingers found the tips of hers where she clung to the lip of a vertical shaft. Rustam wormed forward until he could see the upturned white blur of her face. Her feet scrabbled for a hold and kicked more stones loose. They clattered away, falling, echoes bouncing around until it was impossible to tell which was echo and which, stone striking stone.

In the gloom, they stared at each other.

Rustam knew they were thinking the same thing: if she were to fall now, here inside this mountain, no one would ever know that he might have saved her. No one would be able to blame him, and he would be free from the threat she posed. Free from a life of constantly looking over his shoulder, free to challenge Iain if he chose.

He moved back from the edge and stood up.

Was that a muffled sob, or just the pony chewing his bit? Rustam put his hands against the animal's chest and pushed gently, urging it backward along the passage. When it was far enough back for safety, he left it and retraced his steps.

Lying down on the cold stone, Rustam reached over the lip of the shaft and took a tight hold on Risada's wrists, flinching at the sharp pain in his injured hand. He began edging backward.

Stones cascaded as Risada struggled to gain purchase, the noise deafening after the quiet darkness. Rustam hissed as Risada's hand slipped and her fingers dug into his bruises, but her face appeared over the edge and she slithered forward like a snake, tearing her wrists free from his grasp and scuttling past him as though in fear that he might change his mind and push her back over.

Rustam crawled back from the edge before curling up to sit in an exhausted heap, propped against the damp wall. He hugged his knees to his chest and watched Risada watching him, their faces no more than arm's length apart. Her lips moved but her voice was so small he strained to hear it.

"When you backed off I thought..."

"Yes, well. So did I."

"So why—?"

The pony snorted in panic and jumped forward.

"What—?"

As one, they scrambled to their feet and Rustam grabbed the pony's bridle, yanking savagely on the rein to stop it from running headlong into the pit and taking Elwaes with it. In the same movement he slipped a dagger into his other hand.

Behind the trembling pony were two luminous green eyes.

Rustam could have sworn they were at no more than waist height when he first saw them, but then Shamnac stepped into the light, still naked but now sporting a number of dark gashes across his shoulders and arms. Little rivulets of blood decorated his torso with gory patterns.

"How did you come here?" he asked.

"How did you find us?" demanded Risada in a tone that struggled to be imperious, but shook too much to succeed.

Shamnac regarded her in disbelief. "A jest, ssurely? Making that much noise you expect not to be found?"

"Can you get us out of here?" Rustam asked.

Shamnac cocked his head on one side, and then smiled—a brief flash of very white, very sharp teeth. He slipped past them and walked towards the open shaft.

"*Stop!*"

But Risada's hoarse yell bounced around an empty passage.

"Follow me," whispered Shamnac from the darkness ahead.

Rustam grasped the pony's bridle and led it tentatively forward, one hand to the tunnel wall and testing every step with his toe before putting his full weight onto the foot. Just before the abyss, the wall under his hand vanished.

"There's another side turning here," he breathed incredulously.

"Are you certain? I'm sure it wasn't there earlier."

He eased the pony around the bend. Ahead, he could see a glow at the end of the tunnel and Shamnac's powerful figure silhouetted against it.

"There's something very wrong with these tunnels," he muttered.

Fresh air caressed his face and the pony surged eagerly forward, bursting out of the cave mouth into a bright moons-lit night. It dragged Rustam through several lengths of rough scrub before slowing.

"I guess you're as glad to be out of there as I am," he said, patting the sweating animal. He glanced back to see Risada emerging as if from solid rock. Curious, he looped the pony's reins around the skeleton of a dead tree and stepped back past Risada. He ran his hands along the unbroken rock face.

"It's not here; there's no opening."

"I know," said Risada with a shiver. "I felt it close behind me. It's Charin's work, this goddess-be-damned *magic*."

Rustam freed the pony and adjusted Elwaes to a more comfortable position. They trudged down to the lakeshore, finding their horses dozing contentedly beside the stand of trees where the whole episode had begun.

"I'll take first watch," Rustam offered.

"There iss no need," said Shamnac's deep voice from the shadows. He stepped out from behind a tree, eyeing the weapons that had appeared in Rustam and Risada's hands with apparent amusement.

"You have returned to me the freedom I forfeited through my arrogance. As long as you remain in thiss valley, I shall guard your ssleep. It will be my penanccce."

And he was gone. Rustam could not recall blinking, but one moment a naked man was standing in front of him, and then he wasn't.

"I don't think I can take much more tonight," he groaned.

"Well I don't trust him."

"As you please, my Lady. I'm going to sleep."

He bundled the unconscious elf with blankets, dragged together the scattered remnants of his bedroll, climbed into it and closed his eyes. The last thing he heard was the distant yowl of a hunting wildcat.

14. SHAMNAC

"How did we get down here?"

Rustam opened bleary eyes, and propped himself up onto one elbow. Elwaes was sitting up, regarding the lake in surprise.

"You don't remember?"

The elf looked round at him and flinched slightly as his eyes slid across Rustam's face. He shook his head. "No. I have some hazy recollections, but they must have been bad dreams.

"Such as?"

"Trolls. I thought I was being carried away by trolls."

"That was no dream my friend, but it had its good side—we found the pony and most of our supplies. At least, the bits they had no use for."

He would have said more, but Elwaes's distressed expression stopped him. He sat up, keeping his bedroll clutched tightly around his shoulders.

A fine mist hovered over the lake, chilling the early morning air. Risada had obviously been busy for some while: a small fire smouldered in a shallow pit and the contents of several packs lay strewn across her vacant bedding. There was no sign of the Lady of Domn, but their cooking pans lay beside the fire, barring the kettle.

Covertly, Rustam studied Elwaes's pale, drawn face, but the Shivan seemed to have recovered composure and Rustam decided to ask the question that had puzzled him since the previous night. "I thought trolls always killed their victims, yet they took you alive. What did they want with you?"

Elwaes shuddered before answering. "The same thing they wanted with your pony. They consider elf meat a delicacy, but only when exceedingly fresh, preferably still alive."

Rustam felt his face slacken, the undamaged side sagging to match the other. The sudden tightness in his chest made it hard to breath, but he was spared from having to comment by Risada's arrival. She put the filled kettle onto the fire.

"So you're back with us, Master Elwaes."

"Only by Chel's grace, it seems. I am again in your debt."

"Does that mean we're equal now," asked Rustam. "Or are you still one up on us?"

Elwaes and Risada both looked blankly at him.

"Never mind," he muttered.

"Please forgive Chalice, Master Elwaes. His thoughts are sometimes rather obtuse."

She turned back to the fire but not before stabbing a warning glare at Rustam: Lady Risada wanted the Shivan in their debt, not the other way around.

Breakfast tasted wonderful despite consisting of hard travel biscuits and stale waybread. The tea, at least, was fresh and tasted as good as a well matured wine to palates that had survived on nothing but water for three days.

When they were finished, Risada gathered up a change of clothes and headed for the lake. She paused briefly and glanced back at Rustam. "I'm going to swim. I trust you will stay here this time."

He nodded, turning away to hide the flush that rose to his cheeks. When she was gone, he busied himself sorting out their supplies and tried to calculate how many days the salvaged food might last. To his relief the bags of grain were still intact, so the horses would not go short for some while. But of their own provisions only biscuits, stale bread, salt and herbs remained. Apparently trolls maintained their carnivorous tendencies, however their other habits may have changed.

Something nagged at Rustam, a feeling that persisted until his head suddenly jerked up in recognition. He was being watched.

But it was only Elwaes who lay there, regarding him with a faint frown on his delicate features.

"What?" Rustam demanded. That stare unnerved him.

"You and Lady Risada. Something has passed between you."

"It has," Rustam confirmed. "But I don't really think she would care for me to discuss it with anyone else."

The elf smiled, and Rustam was relieved to see some colour seeping into his sallow complexion. He looked quite different with his tall ears sweeping up in clear view from the sides of his head, the short ragged tufts that remained of his blond hair doing nothing to hide them. Before, he might have passed as human. Not so now.

Rustam sank down beside him. "Elwaes, how well do you know these mountains?"

"Well enough. Something puzzles you?"

"Last night after we escaped, we took a wrong turning and ended up in a maze of tunnels. This may sound stupid, but each time we retraced our steps, they'd change."

"Ah, I see. And what were you thinking, just before you entered this labyrinth?"

Rustam shrugged. "I don't know. Pleased to be getting out of there, I suppose. Anxious about being followed." He stopped in confusion. "Why? What does it matter what I was thinking?"

"Friend Rusty, there are parts of these mountains affiliated more strongly to one power than another. I think it unlikely that trolls would find a welcome home in a region claimed by Chel."

"Charin, you mean? Now wait a moment, don't go all mystic on me. You can't tell me the rocks are in league with Charin—that's ridiculous!"

"Is it? Tell me more about these tunnels and how you escaped them."

Rustam frowned, irritated for a reason he could not pinpoint. "I'm sure we just lost our way. We turned round once and tried to get back to where we'd gone wrong, but we missed it again and then Risada fell over the edge of this pit. I had to pull her out."

"And?" Elwaes prompted.

"Shamnac turned up. I don't suppose you remember him?"

Elwaes's face closed. "Tell me about him."

"He was a prisoner of the trolls too. We found you both with the pony. It's odd now I think about it: he was tied up in a very peculiar way."

"Hands behind his back with his ankles linked to his wrists?"

"You do remember."

Elwaes shook his head. "Not at all, but the name *Shamnac* suggests a particular type of creature, and that is precisely how to bind one."

"What are you saying Elwaes—what is he?"

"What colour were his eyes?"

His eyes. Rustam couldn't forget those eyes glowing in the dark. At waist height.

"What colour?" Elwaes demanded urgently.

"Green. A vivid emerald green."

"Ah. Chel still guards you then."

The tension drained visibly from Elwaes and with it, his strength. His eyes began to close.

"What are you talking about? Elwaes, don't you dare fall asleep on me now!"

Rustam put a hand on the elf's shoulder and shook him gently. With an effort the Shivan raised his head. "I'm so tired," he moaned. "What were we talking about?"

"Shamnac. And tunnels that appear in solid rock then close behind you."

Elwaes stared past him, and for a second Rustam thought the elf had gone into a trance, but a warning shiver ran down his spine and he sprang to his feet, twisting round.

Crouched beneath one of the sheltering trees was one of the biggest wildcats Rustam had ever seen. Not that he'd seen a live one this close before, nor ever wished to. From the end of its bewhiskered muzzle to the tip of its sinuous tail it was easily the length of a horse, possibly more. It stood waist high and the muscles rippling beneath the sleek black coat warned of enormous strength. Around its neck hung some sort of talisman on a leather thong. The mouth opened in a silent snarl, the broad head cocked to one side.

"Eyes that colour?" asked Elwaes calmly.

Rustam would have answered, but the emerald gaze trapped him so completely he missed the first signs of transformation. It was only when the cat's eyes began to change shape that he blinked and took in the scene unfolding before him.

The creature's outline blurred, the ebony of its coat fading to a paler tone and taking on the texture of skin. The limbs elongated, joints changed shape, the trunk shortened, and it rose to an upright stance. The facial features refined into human form and the black pupils became round instead of slitted.

Shamnac stood there, his glossy black hair and green eyes—and the talisman around his neck—the only signs that linked him to the cat he'd been a moment earlier. He smiled and Rustam amended that thought: his teeth were as sharp.

"What are you?"

The catman looked past him to the Shivan. "You have yet to tell him?"

"I was trying to think of a way to break it gently. These people come from a land where your kind is unknown."

Shamnac's eyebrows lifted. "Ssstrange, but that explainss much. The woman ssat guard all night desspite my pledge."

"She—"

"Excuse me please," Rustam interrupted, words slurring with annoyance. "I'm still waiting Elwaes. What *is* he?"

"A werecat. No, don't look at me like that—you asked."

"I don't think I can take any more," Rustam groaned, and sat down hard. "First you tell me those tunnels appeared in solid rock at Charin's bidding, and now I find I'm acquainted with a werecat. What about a werewolf? When do we get to meet one of those?"

"Never, I hope," said Elwaes. "Nasty creatures; bad tempered."

"Would you like me to change back?" Shamnac offered.

"No thank you! Once is enough." Rustam lay back on the ground, propped himself on his elbows and looked Shamnac over from head to toe. He shook his head again.

"I know what I saw and *I* don't want to believe it. Risada would have a fit!" He looked from Shamnac to Elwaes and back again. "We can't tell her."

"Rusty my friend, I agree. Shamnac, might we prevail upon you not to transform in front of the Lady? She is Tyr-enese."

"Ah, I undersstand. And you are not?" The emerald eyes fastened on Rustam.

"I am, but, well... Elwaes, you explain."

The Shivan looked amused and nodded. "Rustam is a talented Tyr-enese; one of a rare breed, and even rarer because he knows what he is, even if he has only come into this knowledge recently."

"Sso that is how you entered the *Charinsbahl*," said Shamnac.

"The what?" Rustam looked helplessly at Elwaes.

"It's what I was trying to tell you earlier Rusty. Those tunnels could only have been *Charinsbahl*—a region so closely linked with Charin's power that even the rocks respond to evil thoughts. That's why I asked what you were thinking before you entered them.

Deborah Jay

"What are you talking about? Evil thoughts, what a load of—why are you looking at me like that?"

"Rusty, you may find magic hard to believe, but to us it's a part of normal life. The only way you could have entered *Charinsbahl* tunnels was by having something evil in your mind. It may have been nothing you really intended, but the idea would have been sufficient. It's well past time we began your lessons in control, before you endanger yourself more."

"But I don't recall—" Rustam began in protest.

"I think you do," Shamnac said softly.

Rustam looked to Elwaes for support. "What would he know about it? We've only just met."

Elwaes sighed. "It's hard to remember how little you people know of life outside your kingdom. Are all Tyr-enese so closed-minded? No." He held up a hand. "There's no need to answer that. Rusty, all werecats have the talent of truthsaying, so it's not worth trying to argue, or even to deceive yourself. Shamnac would know."

"But I truly don't remember. Unless—oh goddess! Was I really...?"

He looked first at Shamnac, then at Elwaes. "I—I think I was preoccupied with what happened down by the—but she asked me not to talk about it. It's, oh what the hell! I was thinking about losing Risada somewhere along the way, but I didn't really mean it."

Rustam stood up and walked to the edge of the copse, looking back towards the cliff. Goddess, how could he even have entertained the idea? Risada might be able to stomach killing in cold blood—it went with her job—but he found the concept repulsive. Even though he knew she was determined to keep her Family pure at any cost, even that of his own life, he did not believe he was capable of murdering her.

But did I make that pit open beneath her feet?

In view of what Elwaes had just said, there seemed little doubt. Rustam began to wish he'd never left Tyr-en. How much simpler life had been back there, without magic.

"The elf iss sick," said a quiet voice from right beside him. For a split second, Rustam stopped breathing. No one had ever managed to get this close to him unnoticed. Was it just the werecat, or were his own senses failing?

He drew a deep, deliberate breath—and then sneezed. This close, the werecat's musky scent irritated his sinuses. Through gritted teeth, he said, "We know that, but we don't know what to do for him. Do you?"

Shamnac regarded Elwaes, who had fallen asleep again. The werecat shook his head. "I have met few of Chel'ss favoured. Rarely do they enter our territory."

"Yet Elwaes seems to know a good deal about your people."

"They live long, the Shivan."

Rustam's eyes slid past Shamnac and scanned the forbidding mountain range beyond. "Shamnac, where *is* Shiva, really?"

Folklore insisted that the elven land could only be reached through one of their magical Gates, but it had to be located *somewhere* within this range.

The werecat made a rumbling noise that was almost a purr. "You will not find Her land with your eyes. It doess not exisst where you can see it."

The knowledge-hungry mind of a player sharpened Rustam's attention. "What do you mean?"

This time Shamnac laughed out loud. "Human, Shiva iss a *magical* land. It is the home of the goddesss; it is everywhere and nowhere. It lies within these mountainss, but is not *of* the mountains. Thosse who live there may enter from one of your kingdomss and arrive in another, without ever having touched the rocks of thiss territory."

"But how—?"

He bit off his question as Risada re-entered the camp. She saw Shamnac and raised an eyebrow. "So you're still around."

"A vow I made and it iss not my nature to renege on a promisse." The werecat's voice was low, almost a snarl.

Risada inclined her head. "I respect that in a man. If, in fact, you are a man."

But she didn't seem to expect a response. She sat down on her bedroll and proceeded to pull all her clothes out of the saddle-bags. "I'm going to wash everything," she declared. "I hope I never have to wear such filthy clothes again! Rustam, does your modesty require that I wait until you've had your swim, or shall I just keep my eyes averted?"

She turned to look at Rustam, but stopped before her eyes reached him. Her expression was carefully neutral as she regarded Shamnac's nakedness. "Do you never wear clothing, Master Shamnac, or do you reserve it only for colder days?"

Shamnac smiled, white teeth glistening in the bright sunlight that had burned away the early mist while they talked.

"Lady, I have never covered mysself. What purpose would it sserve?"

For once Risada seemed at a loss for words. She shrugged and peeled her eyes from him, sorting the pile of clothes in her lap. Rustam grinned, picturing the effect of the werecat's transformation on a set of clothing.

"I think I'll take my swim now," he said. "Please yourself, my Lady; I'm used to nudity around women."

He picked up a cleaner set of clothes—those he had worn topmost—and marched away from Risada's studied silence.

It felt wonderful to peel off the filthy, smelly garments. Even better to slide into the bitingly cold, clear water of the lake. He swam out toward the middle, stroking fast to generate some heat, then dived down, coming up spluttering and gasping but refreshed and invigorated in a way he had not felt for a long while. Even his cuts and bruises ached less.

He turned and made his way back towards the shore with a more leisurely breaststroke. Risada was there, dunking her clothes and wringing them through. Rustam wondered if she had ever done such menial tasks before. He strode from the water, shaking droplets from his hair as he came and towelled himself down with some of his dirty garments, reflecting that he most assuredly had, though not in a long while. He could certainly manage to do so again, though he would be in serious need of a good tailor before he might be seen in polite company once more.

Thought of his old life in Tyr-en jolted his conscience. What had transpired in their treason-threatened kingdom during the time they'd wasted chasing the troll pack? He dismissed his speculations before they were fully formed, determined instead to concentrate on completing the task they had set out to do as quickly as possible. He dragged his clothes on, shivering slightly in the chill breeze that was starting to blow over the lake, and paused long enough to wring his dirtier clothes—which accounted for most of them—through before laying them on sun-warmed boulders to dry.

He walked briskly back to the camp to find Risada had preceded him and was busy making lunch. Without preamble, he stated: "We should be on our way." Risada looked up at him and raised her eyebrows. "I agree," she said with a weary smile. "But not before we've eaten. And not before our clothes are dried. We'll leave first thing tomorrow morning."

Rustam plumped down, irrationally annoyed that Risada had agreed so readily, even more irritated that she was correct. They needed rest, dry clothes and well fed mounts. He sighed, eyes roving their camp for something productive to do.

"Fish."

"Huh?" He stared at Risada in confusion.

"Go fishing, Chalice. We need some food to take with us, and you're cluttering up the camp. Go. Be useful."

"Yes ma'am," he obeyed with a bow, but her words no longer held the sting they had in the past. He was glad of something to do and as he sauntered down to the lakeside his walk recovered some of its old swagger.

*   *   *   *   *   *   *   *   *   *

In the end, they had both fish and meat to pack for the journey. Shamnac arrived in the firelight not long after dark, true to his word in human form, bringing with him the still warm carcass of a mountain goat, which he made short work of butchering and dividing into joints. They roasted one haunch over the fire and salted the rest before wrapping it in leaves and packing it in the saddle bags. Rustam was careful to spread the food amongst the packs this time, so that should one be lost they would not starve again.

They feasted greedily on roast goat almost before it was cooked, and Rustam noticed that where they stripped the browner meat, Shamnac surreptitiously tore red. Rustam shuddered, recalling the black whirlwind that had swept through the troll camp, all teeth and claws, and thanked Chel that the werecat was on their side.

Following a full night's sleep—Risada at last consenting to trust Shamnac's oath—they all felt fitter and ready to proceed. Elwaes looked brighter though still somewhat pale as he directed Rustam in the gathering of a variety of fruits, berries and fungi that grew amidst the trees and rocks of the jewel-green haven, and by midmorning they were ready to leave.

Shamnac guided them to a winding path on the far side of the valley. It vanished steeply upward into the rocks but, he assured them, led to a low pass between the two peaks towards which they had originally been heading. As he took his leave of them the werecat bowed low, the bending of his spine more sinuous than that of a true human.

If Risada noticed, she said nothing.

"Russtam. Lady. My debt to you iss not in full repaid." He lifted the leather thong from around his neck and slipped it over his head. "Take thiss token, the ssymbol of my *pahn*." He paused, groping for words to explain, and then looked beseechingly to Elwaes.

"Tribe, I think is the nearest translation," suggested the elf. Shamnac cocked his head on one side, considering.

"Not entirely accurate, but it will do. Pleasse, take it and keep it ssafe against need. It iss the only gift that I can ssend with you."

"And a handsome gift it is," Risada said graciously, and stretched out her hand to accept the talisman. Rustam could now see that what swung on the narrow strip of hide was a tooled leather medallion, but in his mind's eye he saw instead a glittering crystal pendant, and a brightly lit corridor within the mansion of Rees-Charlay.

"That's it!" he breathed.

The Lady of Domn regarded him askance. "Pardon me? To what precisely are you referring?"

"The pendant—the one the troll wears! It's the one Hensar was wearing at the fest, or damn near identical." He turned to Elwaes. "Could he be using it somehow to control the trolls—is that possible? I don't know enough about magic."

The Shivan's reply was drowned out by Risada's oath and Rustam blinked in surprise. He had no idea that a Lady of noble birth would know such language. He glanced at her, expecting to see fear and loathing, but instead her face was livid with fury. Not directed at him, he noted with relief.

"Melcard!" she spat. "Not only is he intent upon seizing the throne, but he's using magic to do it! I should have killed him when I had the chance."

"We didn't know, then," Rustam reminded her. "Elwaes? Is it possible?"

"It is." The elf sounded dubious. "But I fail to understand how a Tyr-enese could have come into possession of such knowledge, or such power. Unless..."

"Unless what?" demanded Risada and Rustam together.

Elwaes wagged his head. "I suppose it may be, and I was too distracted to consider the possibility." He focussed on his companions. "Do you know anything of Hensar's background?"

Risada gestured in the negative, and raised her eyebrows at Rustam.

"Not a thing," he confirmed. "Why? Do you think he might not be Tyr-enese?"

The elf shrugged. "He may or may not be, but he may be more besides."

"Elwaes, please stop talking in riddles," said Risada.

"My apologies." Elwaes bowed slightly.

How did the elf manage to look so urbane, standing on a rough mountain trail, dressed in rags and with his cropped hair sticking up in wild spikes? Rustam fingered his shaggy beard irritably.

"What I mean is, while Hensar may indeed be Tyr-enese by birth, and by some of his parentage, I would judge him—simply from his stature, mind—to also bear dwarfish blood."

"Dwarves?" Risada's disbelief was plain to see. "Are you trying to tell me that humans and those...those filthy cave dwelling *animals* can *interbreed*?" She raked her hands through her long hair. "Is there no end to the depths of depravity I must learn about on this journey?"

Shamnac frowned at her. "Dwarves are not animals. Intelligent as human, elf or—." He didn't finish his sentence, much to Rustam's relief, but he did turn his intense gaze upon the Shivan. "Educate them, you musst, or they will bring trouble upon themselves."

"I shall do my best."

Risada's face closed. She obviously had no more knowledge of the inter-species breeding programme than Rustam had before Elwaes enlightened him to its existence, and Rustam thought it best to leave it that way.

The Lady hung Shamnac's gift around her neck and tucked the talisman inside her many layers of clothing. Her eyes travelled one final time over the naked man.

"Fare you well, Master Shamnac. Meeting you has been an—interesting—experience."

"May She guide your hunt," said Shamnac in what sounded like a ritual phrase. Then he was gone.

"Our hunt?" Risada repeated. "Whatever did he mean?"

"His people are hunters, my Lady," said Elwaes. "He merely invoked the goddess's blessing on our journey."

"Then let's be on our way, and hope his words have some effect. Chel knows, we could use an easier trail than we've followed thus far."

By nightfall, the winding path had emptied out onto a broad track rutted by wagon wheels and hoof prints. They camped there and in the morning followed the trade route between the peaks, and on into Kishtan. For the next eleven days they rode as fast as they were safely able to go. No living thing threatened them and they met no other travellers, but as they traversed the higher passes, winter snapped at their heels.

* * * * * * * * * *

Hensar could feel his patience corroding. "So why did you not kill the elf immediately?" he demanded. The troll's image in the water cringed.

"Elf meat g...good. F...fresh."

Of course. While the pack had learned to enjoy a variety of foods cooked on the fire Hensar had gifted them, there were still certain items they considered delicacies only when raw. Or alive.

Understanding, however, did little to ameliorate his temper.

"And the pony? The same, I suppose," he answered himself. "It might have worked well, drawing them all to where they could be disposed of together, but it didn't, did it? You lost them!"

By the look of utter panic on the troll's face, Hensar could tell how clearly his fury blazed within his eyes. The creature had every reason to cower, for the doctor's patience was ended.

"You have failed me," he stated simply, and closed one hand around his pendant, stroking the facets with a concentrated gentleness until an answering vibration sang within the crystal.

His fingers gathered speed, just barely touching the warming surface of the stone, gaze fixed upon the image of the panicking troll as it tried desperately to remove the twin pendant from around its neck. Clawed fingers tore at intricate knots which refused to part beneath the clumsy assault, and now the corners of Hensar's mouth lifted in amusement as he watched the troll pack hurriedly vacate the area around their erstwhile leader.

Beneath Hensar's caressing fingers, the throbbing tone of the crystal rose to a whine, then a howl that would leave him partially deaf for days to come. He regretted not taking the time to cover his ears, but the blood pulsing through his head added a tympanic counterpoint, and his annoyance was quickly forgotten in the rush of heat that originated in his groin and rose like a fountain of lava through his guts and on upward, finally bursting from the crown of his head in a cascade of exquisite pain.

In the cavern, the matching pendant exploded, shattering into myriad slivers of white hot crystal. A hundred tiny darts embedded themselves in the flesh of the unfortunate troll leader and one other who had been too slow to leave. Incandescent flames burst into life, searing hair, skin, eyes. Hundreds of leagues away Hensar's nose twitched in anticipation of the stench he could only imagine. Shallow breaths caught raggedly in his throat as he watched his victim throw itself screaming to the floor to roll in the dust, but the unnatural fire was not to be cheated and it crawled relentlessly across the crisping skin of the writhing figure.

Hensar wiped sweaty palms across his shirt front, and struggled to regain control of his breathing as the charred lump of flesh—two, actually, the other just visible within the limited range of his scrying bowl—twitched less often, and then became still. The doctor shrugged tense shoulders and waved one hand across the water's surface to dispel the image. The fingers of the other absently stroked the chunk of crystal that hung cold and inert against his chest.

What a waste, he thought with rekindling annoyance. Now that the heady thrill of the kill was over, he faced the tedious slog of rebuilding decades of painstaking work. And such perfectly matched crystals were hard to come by. That particular pair had taken him more than two years to locate.

The old, familiar ache of long term frustration settled back into its accustomed place in the pit of his stomach, and he scowled at his reflection in the water. How much longer would it be before the Bastard sat upon the throne? On that day, all Tyr-en would cower before Hensar's skills as the troll had done. The grand plan had been many years in the making and he had learned to curb his impatience, but with the end nearly in sight it became harder by the day.

He needed something to distract him.

Slicking his hair with the last of the sweat on his palms, he exited his tower room and headed downwards, to the dungeon.

15. CHILDREN OF CHEL

'Open up! Please, in Chel-s-name give us shelter!"

The bitter wind swept Rustam-s-words away. He pounded on the heavy wooden gate with a hand so frozen he could barely feel it, his eyelashes so clogged with ice and snow he almost missed the tiny spy hole opening.

'In the name of the goddess, let us in!" he yelled against the shriek of the storm, but the little shutter slammed shut and he was left staring at featureless wood.

He glanced round at the others, barely more than vague outlines in the driving whiteness. If they didn-t-get inside, they would be dead by nightfall. The roaring of the gale intensified, and he raised a snow encrusted arm to hammer once more on the barrier.

His arm fell through empty air.

The gateway stood open. It took Rustam-s-disorientated mind a moment to realise that the rumbling sound had not been the wind, but the huge gate rolling aside on ice-encrusted runners.

Several dark figures robed and hooded against the blizzard rushed out to grasp the horses—bridles. An arm appeared round Rustam-s-waist though he could not feel it, and he was guided into a large square cloistered courtyard. The gate squealed shut at his back. Risada and Elwaes were helped down and the horses led away.

'Where" ?" began Rustam, taking half a step after his beloved mare before his foot slipped on the packed snow and he crashed to one knee. A steaming cloud of breath whooshed out of his lungs and he discovered he was not yet too frozen to feel pain.

' Come," shouted the figure at his side, the voice thin against the howling gale. ' They will be well cared for."

Against his instincts, he allowed himself to be helped to his feet and led after Risada and her guide. Another robed figure followed them carefully across the ice, carrying the meagre weight of the elf.

A thick wooden door opened a crack to receive them, and they stepped over the threshold into gloriously warm air, rich with the scent of burning sweetwood. Melting snow ran down Rustam s face and he wiped it with the soggy sleeve of his cloak.

' Here, let me help you with that," offered the voice by his side, and for the first time Rustam noticed that his guide was tiny. She shed her outer clothing to reveal the simple grey robes of a daughter of Chel. White hair coiled neatly atop her head and the lines that creased her chiselled features told of much laughter.

Rustam took quick inventory of their refuge. To either side stretched a long hall filled with trestle tables and benches. Overhead, vines and ivy thick with white and red berries looped the rough wooden beams and trailed down the walls. The stone floor was strewn with a thick layer of straw.

The door through which they had entered was now hidden behind a heavy grey curtain, and beside it hung a devotional lamp, its red flame glowing steadily. Little piles of snow heaped on the floor around them, not yet thawing.

Rustam realised that despite being indoors, it was not as warm as he had first believed. He shivered as the daughter peeled his stiffened cloak from his shoulders and shook it free of snow. Risada was likewise assisted by a woman. The man carrying Elwaes slid the elf s hood back to reveal the still white face and the tall ears sticking out of the tufts of hacked hair. The son of Chel turned a surprised and questioning look towards the woman by Rustam s side, received a brief nod in reply and hurried away with his burden into the flickering torchlight at the distant end of the huge refectory.

'Our friend?" Rustam's distorted and frozen mouth struggled to form the words, but the diminutive woman had no trouble understanding his concern.

'Rest easy, my brother. Your companion is in greater need than you. He will be well cared for, but for the moment you must remain here."

'Why?" Risada demanded. 'Are we not welcome? In our own Kingdom the children of Chel assist all who come in need."

'As do we, young sister. It is for your health, I say this. Warming your bodies too fast may cause more damage than has already been done."

Risada bowed her head, her arrogance shadowed with shame. 'I apologise, sister; I spoke without thought."

The wizened old woman smiled gently. 'It is surely by the grace of the goddess that you are in any condition to speak at all, child. We thought the high passes closed these many days, and expected no more travellers before spring."

Risada turned openly frightened eyes to Rustam and he knew her thought. If the higher passes were blocked already, how much longer could they rely on the lower routes remaining open?

But the Lady of Domn's voice betrayed none of her fears.

'Sister, our journey was delayed by trolls and we were later arriving here than planned. It is urgent that we continue with all speed" we have important business with King Graylin. How long before it is safe for us to move on?"

'Goddess be praised you reached us at all," said the old woman. 'As to continuing, who but Chel can say? In the meanwhile, please accept our hospitality. You are most welcome...?"

Risada flashed a warning glance at Rustam. 'Rista of Domn, oh wise one. And this is my brother, Rustam."

'We are pleased to be of service, Rista of Domn. We receive few travellers from the Kingdom of Tyr-en."

She appeared to be on the verge of adding something, but changed her mind.

'I am Honora, eldest daughter of this House, and if there is anything you require, please feel free to ask me or any of my siblings."

They followed her to the far end of the hall where they were met by other grey robes bearing platters of steaming food and drink. Rustam-s-stomach started to churn in anticipation as delicious aromas wafted beneath his nose.

A large curtained portal divided the refectory from the next room and beyond the heavy drapes came the excited, piping tones of small children. Honora smiled. 'You have arrived amidst the celebration of a birth; perhaps it is a good omen for your mission."

So saying, she bowed her head and slipped away, barely disturbing the drapes as she passed between them. Once assured there was nothing further they could do for the immediate comfort of their guests, all but one of the others departed. As they left, Rustam caught a glimpse beyond the curtains of roaring fires and a seething mass of children surrounded by watchful adults all clothed in the same grey.

The young man who lingered near the table cleared his throat, apparently ill at ease. Risada raised an eyebrow. 'All our needs have been met," she said bluntly. 'Is there something you wanted?"

The youth shifted uncomfortably. 'I, well that is we" some of us" "

'Yes?"

'We were wondering if the war had begun yet."

Risada drew a deep breath. 'War?" she prompted, putting as much confusion in her voice as she could muster.

'Well, yes." The young man sounded even less sure of himself now, and Rustam noticed his clenched his fists. Probably worried that Honora would return and find him asking questions. She did not strike Rustam as the sort to approve of gossip.

He half turned as though to leave, then gathered his courage and turned back again. ' We've heard that a great number of Tylocian clans have moved down out of the mountains into your Kingdom and that must mean war, surely? I mean, that's why you're here, isn't it?"

' Is it?" replied Risada, managing to sound completely surprised. ' You obviously know a lot more than I: this is the first I've heard of it. Rustam, did you hear anything?"

' No," he confirmed with a shake of his head, and then turned an anxious look upon the son of Chel. ' Please, tell us anything you know. Perhaps Honora would like to send word to your King; we could deliver such a message when we visit Court."

' Then you're not...?" The clenching fists flew up to cover the man's mouth. ' Forgive me, I shouldn't have bothered you. Please, do not concern yourselves, I'm sure we must have heard wrongly. There's no need to disturb the Eldest with what is almost certainly just a rumour."

The drapes settled back into place following his hasty departure.

' I don't believe this," grated Risada.

' Believe what?" said Rustam, reaching for a cup of mulled wine and warming his fingers around it.

' That we can come so far, through so much, only to be defeated by the weather!" Risada tore angrily at a roasted breast of fowl.

' It might not be as bad as you think," Rustam began, and then hurried on as Risada swallowed her mouthful and drew breath to contradict him. ' Although the lowest passes are far longer than the route we took, they should stay clear for some while yet. And anyway, if the weather is as bad on the other side of the mountains, Melcard won't be able to move his forces either."

' Hmm," Risada agreed reluctantly. ' It's possible, I suppose. But if it's not?"

'We have no way of knowing. All we can do is continue. And pray. Perhaps Honora says truly: that our mission is favoured by Chel." He sipped the hot spiced wine and it slid warmingly down his throat, leaving an aromatic aftertaste. The fumes heated his face and wafted up his nasal passages, clearing his sinuses.

'Now you're beginning to sound mystical," Risada complained around a chunk of hot fruit. 'I would rather rely on my own resources."

'If I were you," Rustam cautioned, 'I would be careful about dismissing anything mystical or magical here. This isn't Tyr-en."

'No, indeed it's not." Risada shivered and looked around at the rough but sturdily constructed building. 'The sooner we get this over with, the sooner we can get back to civilisation. Oh, and Rustam, be careful what you say around these people. They may be considered holy by some, but I don't trust their morals; there's no telling who they could be associated with in this barbaric Kingdom."

* * * * * * * * * *

Soon after the noise beyond the curtains died down, Honora returned to her guests and invited them through the portal into the adjoining room. This, too, was a huge hall with fireplaces set into each of the long walls. The debris of a celebration littered the floor, and older boys and girls moved purposefully amongst the heaps of straw and overturned chairs, putting the room to rights. The blazing log fires dispelled any remaining chill in Rustam's bones, but also made him embarrassingly aware of the ripeness of his over worn clothing.

Goddess, what must I look like? It was so long since they'd been in the company of others he had almost succeeded in forgetting his appearance. He ran a hand through his lank, greasy hair and fingered the shaggy beard that he hoped partially disguised his lop-sided face. He turned to their hostess and spoke as clearly as he could. 'Honora, that meal was nectar to the starving, but I fear we are a less than pleasing sight. Do you have bathing facilities?"

The old daughter smiled again. 'But of course, brother." Then she frowned and peered at him closely. 'But perhaps we should attend to your injuries first."

The right side of Rustam's lips curved upward in the wry half smile that was all he could manage these days. How foolish to imagine he might disguise such a hideous disfigurement from anyone. Then Honora's words repeated inside his head and his body stiffened.

'You have a healer here? A real healer?"

'Certainly. There are many in need of her services following passage through the mountains. That is one of the reasons our House was built here."

A healer! Rustam drew deep breaths to calm the fluttering in his belly.

Not one of those herbal potion pushers that passed for healers in Tyr-en" a real, sorcery-trained healer with magic at her fingertips. He knew he should be revolted by the very idea, but he was less and less inclined to be slavishly bound by his Kingdom's traditional rejection of the arcane.

This magic might restore his looks!

Risada was led away to bathe, and a young man barely past adolescence guided Rustam to the infirmary. They passed dormitories full of squealing children, a room of cots where two daughters with expansive bosoms fed and attended several infants, and curtained doorways behind which lovers grappled and moaned, making no effort to conceal their activities. Despite his wealth of carnal experience, Rustam felt his cheeks reddening. He sneaked a look at the youth walking by his side. The boy seemed unaffected.

He might be deaf, Rustam considered, but then he realised the answer was simpler: this was a House of Chel. To the children of Chel there was nothing more sacred than the act of love, nothing more joyous than the making of a new life. Small wonder Risada thought them amoral: this was a whole community of bastards!

Perhaps this would be a better vocation than the game, mused Rustam. Then he glanced at the coarse home spun grey robe of his companion and shuddered.

Perhaps not.

The infirmary opened off the right hand side of the corridor. It was a long, narrow hall lined with beds, some surrounded by curtains for privacy, but few occupied. A number of work benches took up the space at the farthest end, their tops littered with the ingredients and utensils of an apothecary, and in the end wall a fire blazed merrily in its hearth with a bubbling cauldron suspended above it on chains. A strong aroma of herbs and spices pervaded the room, mixed with the sharp taint of some unidentifiable substance. Rustam felt a momentary jolt of panic at the proximity of magic, then grasped tightly to the promise of having his face restored. He marched purposefully towards the tall grey-robed figure crouched beside the fire.

'Ah, brother? Brother wait!' Another grey robe' a stout, matronly woman' waved an arm in agitation and hurried from a bedside to intercept him. 'I-m sorry, but you-ll-have to wait your turn.'

She pointed to a row of chairs, three of them occupied, and indicated that Rustam should take the first empty seat' the one farthest from the healer. Rustam plonked down with a small sigh and fingered the flabby folds of skin on the left hand side of his face.

It's not getting any worse, he told himself. *Waiting a bit longer can't do any harm.*

He wished he could sound more convincing.

A small, mousy daughter was beckoned forward to consult with the greying, slender apothecary and Rustam allowed his training to distract him from his condition, taking careful inventory of his fellow patients. The son now at the head of the line looked to be in need of a good tonic to bring some colour to his waxen skin. And a fair dose of hair restorer.

The young man beside Rustam was far more intriguing. The swarthy skin and aquiline features framed by thick black ringlets and beard marked him for a mountain man" a Tylocian. The heavily bandaged hand, many cuts, bruises and half healed wounds that spread across every visible portion of his skin did nothing to disguise his origins.

So what was a Tylocian doing in Kishtan at this particular time? Coincidence? Rustam held a jaundiced view of coincidences.

His knowledge of the insular Tylocian people was sparse. They were not much given to interacting with other Kingdoms, except in the lightning swift raids for which they were so well renowned.

Their only other well known trait was the ease with which they could be bought. For Rustam the questions were: did this beaten young whelp have any information worth purchasing, and if so, what would be his price?

'Have you been here long?" Rustam opened, unprepared for the violent flinch that his words elicited.

From behind a hand raised to ward off blows, the Tylocian growled: 'What do you care?"

Rustam shrugged, and spread his hands in what he hoped was an unthreatening gesture. 'Just making polite conversation. I-ve only recently arrived, and I-ve never been inside a House of Chel before."

Dark eyes regarded him with suspicion, but the warding hand lowered. 'You-re Tyr-enese," he accused.

'I am, and you-re Tylocian. What of it?"

The stranger laughed bitterly. 'I've no reason to trust anyone in the Five Kingdoms, least of all a meddlesome Tyr-enese."

'I'm sorry for that," said Rustam with another shrug. 'I'm just a traveller passing through, like you."

'Who says I'm passing through? What have you heard about me?"

'Nothing, but you're not wearing a grey robe so I assumed" "

'Assumptions can be dangerous," warned the youth and despite himself, Rustam laughed.

'And you would know a lot about danger? You're barely old enough to have seen much of life, let alone danger."

'Do not mock me! What would you know of my life?"

The mousy daughter swept past Rustam clutching a phial of amber liquid and the balding son rose for his turn at the apothecary's side. Rustam spread his hands again. 'Not enough to judge you by, obviously. Why don't you tell me?"

'Why should I?"

'Because neither of us has anything better to do."

The Tylocian appraised Rustam, from his badly scuffed boots, up his soiled and tattered breeches and ruined velvet doublet, so stained its original colour was hard to distinguish, to his straggly beard and disfigured face. Rustam stared back, resisting the urge to wince as the dark eyes studied his distorted features.

Then a quick, impish smile touched the lad's lips.

'You first."

Rustam let out his breath, only realising then that he had been holding it. Perhaps this Tylocian was more cunning than his apparent youth suggested. The mountain clans were known to plot and scheme against one another" on a minor scale compared to the complexities of the Tyr-enese game, but perhaps they were learning. Or, more insidiously, being taught. He shrugged with studied indifference.

'My companions and I had a run in with a persistent pack of trolls. I received a blow to my head and this was the result."

The lad raised a bushy eyebrow. 'Then you fared well; rock trolls are not known for their intelligence, to know when to retreat. Your party must consist of many skilled warriors."

Fishing for information, Rustam surmised. Again he shrugged. 'We coped. Now, tell me how you received your injuries: whoever did that to you was very thorough."

'What makes you think someone did this to me?"

Rustam merely cocked his head to one side and stayed silent. Eventually the young man glanced away with a twisted smile.

'I suppose if youd been sent to finish the job we wouldnt be sitting here, discussing it. And besides, I cant imagine my father stooping low enough to hire a Tyr-enese."

'Indeed," said Rustam neutrally.

'Im a twin," the lad confessed.

'Ah," Rustam acknowledged the admission with a nod of understanding. 'A younger twin? You have an older sister?"

Now the youngster dropped his head forward and his shoulders shook. Rustam sat impassively, waiting for the emotion to pass. Perhaps the boys presence here really was coincidence. Of all Five Kingdoms, the Tylocians were the most superstitious and under the circumstances it was a minor miracle that the lad had survived to maturity at all: twins were rare and ill favoured, particularly a male with an older female sibling. If the girl was indeed dead, as the boys reaction suggested, the Tylocians would believe that Charin had scored a victory over his twin sister Chel, and to kill the boy who represented that evil would be their only recourse. Miracle indeed that he still lived.

'I know what youre thinking," the youth snarled from behind his shielding ringlets, 'But it truly was an accident."

'I have no doubt," Rustam replied. 'My people are not as chained by foolish beliefs as yours."

'Pah! Your people s beliefs are as flexible as their morals!"

The two of them glared at each other for a moment.

'You have a very poor opinion of Tyr-en, don t you?" asked Rustam, mildly amused once the first flush of anger passed. The Tylocian gave a short, sharp nod.

'I ve seen nothing to make me feel otherwise. Even now you people are disrupting our alliances" "

Yes! Rustam thought in triumph. *Here it comes, and not a coin spent!*

' " buying aid from enemies and allies alike, upsetting the order of things such that once your little war is over we ll have one of our own to sort it all out again. And you wonder I feel as I do?"

So that s how Melcard plans to keep them out of Tyr-en once he's in power. They'll be too busy re-establishing their own internal power structure to trouble him while he's consolidating, and after that they'll be too weakened to threaten him for years to come. Neat. Very neat.

'I can offer no excuses I m afraid." Rustam shrugged. 'I have no knowledge of what you speak of, but I can assure you, we re not all the same."

The boy laughed hollowly. 'You ll forgive me if I don t believe you. From my mother I inherited a small measure of the sight, and if you re a simple traveller, then I must be the son of a rock troll."

'Really? Then you re the best looking troll I ve seen yet."

The lad gaped at him, and then burst into great, side-splitting guffaws reminiscent of Prince Halnashead. Reminded of home and duty, Rustam s mind flew back over the mountains, wishing he could see what was transpiring on the other side of that huge barrier. Had the fighting begun yet? Did the prince believe them dead, or had Annasala managed to evade the Tylocian blockade and return with news of their desperate plan? Did they even now await the help Rustam and Risada sought?

The Tylocian beside him wiped streaming eyes. 'Tyr-enese you might be, but I believe I like you! You have nothing to do with those who seek to disrupt my kinsmen, you" " He paused and his gaze turned inward, apparently searching for something inside himself. He must have found it, for his eyes lit with a bright gleam. 'You oppose them!"

Rustam frowned. How could this stranger know that, unless he was more involved than circumstances suggested. 'How" ?" he began, but stopped as the lad-s- expression turned swiftly to annoyance.

'I told you: I have the gift. Now what else do you need to know? For the sake of my kinsmen I will help you as far as I am able. I can never return home, but aid them I shall."

'Are you exiled then? I thought..."

Pain clouded the dark eyes as the dark head nodded. 'You thought truly: my sentence was" is" death. I was rescued. By a gemeye."

Rustam sighed silently again, but this time in exasperation. Was there really any point in listening to the ramblings of an obviously deranged mind? The gemeyes were a tale told to small children" magical guardians who could appear out of thin air and rescue those beset by evil.

Not that he hadn-t-appreciated the tales when he was younger. The gemeyes had always been stunningly beautiful individuals, clothed in little more than the gems that gave them their name.

The Tylocian wagged his head. 'You Tyr-enese! You believe in nothing you cannot see. Well I-m not mad, and I do have some information that might assist you. Do you want it or not?"

* * * * * * * * * *

The apothecary looked haggard, with deep frown lines etching her face. Rustam had grown accustomed to Elwaes, but this woman was a stranger and his ingrained Tyr-enese mistrust of magic screamed at him to run away.

Reining in the urge, he ran his fingers through his lank hair and cleared his throat, enduring the woman's meticulous scrutiny of his face with increasing impatience. He flexed his shoulders and tugged at the ragged hem of his doublet, shifting weight from foot to foot. Finally he could bear it no longer.

'Well? Can you cure me or not?"

'I am unsure," she replied in a voice unexpectedly robust from one with such a scrawny frame. 'There is something odd about this injury. Tell me how you came by it."

'I'm not really sure," said Rustam. *Would she think him hysterical or insane if he started babbling about giant hands and ghostly voices?* 'It's all rather muddled; we were being attacked by tunnel creepers at the time. Or perhaps it happened before, when I hit my head while tangling with the sprite." He shook his head. 'Sound crazy, don't I?"

The careworn face lit with an affable smile. 'Only to a Tyr-enese." The smile faded. 'But you are something of a puzzle. I sense" a power. Something that shouldn't be here, something..." She broke off and the frown marks deepened until Rustam could see them for what they were: lines of concentration, not of ill temper as he'd first assumed.

'I suppose there's only one way to find out," she said. 'May I touch you?"

'By all means," Rustam invited. 'It doesn't hurt" it doesn't even *feel* any more."

He took a couple of deep breaths to compose himself before closing his eyes, unwilling to trust his reactions to the sight of an approaching hand. He waited, every muscle in his body tense.

The apothecary's warm breath whispered across his cheek. Then she screamed.

Rocking back, reaching for his knives, Rustam's eyes flew open to see the woman crash backward into a bench of bottles and crocks, strewing herbs and broken pottery across the floor.

'What ?"

A grey robe" the same one who had intercepted Rustam when he entered the infirmary" barged past him. He slipped his knives away.

'Sister! What happened?" demanded the stout one as she helped the shaking healer to extricate herself from the shambles.

'It's nothing, sister," whispered the apothecary in a faint echo of her fine voice. 'Really, I'm fine."

She lifted her head and fixed Rustam with a haunted gaze. His heart lurched downward.

'I can do nothing for you," she said. 'You bear the mark of Charin's touch. Your fate is in the hands of the goddess."

She waved him away and stooped to clear the mess beneath the bench. Numb, Rustam stayed frozen to the spot until the stout daughter gave him a nudge. He trudged down the long aisle between the beds.

What did she mean" the mark of Charin's touch?

A swift anger overlaid his puzzlement. Simply put, it meant that the charlatan could not heal him. He would just have to find someone who could.

Rustam Chalice refused to be condemned to ugliness for the rest of his life.

He paused just beyond the curtain separating the brightly lit infirmary from the dark corridor, waiting for his eyes to adjust. Voices approached from behind him: the apothecary and the stout one.

' What a waste!" the healer proclaimed, her voice restored almost to its former strength. ' He must have been such a bonny lad" before."

Rustam fled down the corridor.

16. MELCARD

'So he confirmed their numbers at about nine hundred.—

Risada favoured Rustam with a less than enthusiastic air. 'And you gained all this information from one disaffected Tylocian youth? How can you be so certain of his accuracy, much less his motivation for telling you?—

Rustam glanced the length of the refectory, past fifteen tables occupied by the cheerful, noisy children of Chel to the lone youth seated at the far end. He handled his food clumsily, using his unbandaged left hand, and chewed awkwardly, no doubt around the gaps where his teeth used to be.

Rustam returned his attention to Risada, glad for the chattering and giggling of the children seated alongside them. Covert conferences were so much easier when masked by the babble" particularly now, when he found it so hard to speak quietly yet still be understood.

'The lad's knowledge of his Kingdom's political structure, and of the families involved in Melcard's little scheme, seemed quite sound to me. And the estimates could only ever be vague. The actual numbers the clan chiefs chose to send probably changed by the day according to their own internal situations. I doubt anybody made an accurate count. As to motive? I don't know. But I believe him.—

Risada frowned, an expression she seemed to wear daily more often. 'So now we know approximately how many, but we still have no idea of Melcard's planned schedule. We *must* continue on to

King Graylin's court.—

A pair of small hands reached past Rustam's nose and plucked his barely touched plate from the table.

'Hold on!—he protested. 'I haven't finished with that yet.—

The whole table went quiet. The child with the plate in her hands froze, her tiny dark eyes fixed in terror on Rustam's face. She dropped the plate with a clatter and shoved it back towards him.

'S..s..sorry,—she stammered. 'Please sir, I didn't mean nothing.—

Rustam felt awkward with children at the best of times, but he had never intentionally frightened one. He reached out to pat the little girl on the shoulder, intending to reassure her.

She shrieked and evaded his hand, dashing to hide behind several of her older siblings. A red haired boy of about ten summers glared at Rustam and announced loudly into the intense silence that followed the girl's scream: 'Don't be frighted, Flissy; old troll face weren't goin"t"hurt you.—

Flissy threw Rustam a wide eyed stare that said she didn't believe a word of it, then fled the refectory, her little leather-soled slippers slapping loudly on the stone flags. A brief, embarrassed hush ensued before the general buzz of conversation restarted jerkily.

The other children at Rustam's table followed Flissy in haste as Honora strode up the long hallway towards them. By the time she arrived, Rustam and Risada were the only ones still seated amidst the debris of abandoned crockery.

The elder bowed her head. 'Please accept my apologies for the ill manners of our offspring; it will be attended to.—

Rustam shook his head and listened to his voice calmly assure Honora that no offence was taken, while inside his skull his mind whirred noisily and the refectory receded into blackness. Panic squeezed his heart and his stomach knotted. He cringed, recalling the searing touch of that awful hand on his face"

'Rustam?—

The voice was strange, yet familiar at the same time.

' Rustam!—

Something touched him, but mercifully no pain followed.

' Rustam, speak to me. Are you ill?—

He blinked and glanced down. Risada's long fingers gripped his arm.

' I" —

He wiggled his stiff jaw and wiped the sagging corner of his mouth where saliva dribbled onto his chin. Risada bent to inspect his face, close enough that he could smell the wine on her breath and the floral scent of her freshly washed hair.

Heat rose to his cheeks as he recalled how he"d frightened the children.

' Do I really look like a troll?—

Risada stared blankly, then threw her head back and laughed like a serving wench.

' What did I say?—Rustam demanded.

' Oh Rustam; if only you could hear yourself! Is that all you"re worried about?—

' It may not seem important to you,—he bridled. ' But it"s my livelihood we"re talking about.—

Risada wiped a tear from her cheek and took a deep breath. ' I apologise. Of course it"s important to you. It"s just, well, considering the seriousness of the situation I" . No.—She shook her head. ' It was cruel of me to laugh. Please forgive my manners: they were no better than those of the children earlier. At least if your vanity is still intact, I know you"re not seriously unwell.—

' Now you sound like Halnashea" .—He cut the name off, glancing guiltily around, but Honora was nowhere to be seen. In fact, there was no one in the refectory besides themselves. Rustam looked at Risada in confusion.

' What happened" how long was I out for?—

'Out? You weren't out anywhere. You've been sitting here staring into space for over half an hour.—

'Half an hour?—Rustam gaped. It had felt like no more than a couple of minutes. But then the last time, on the mountainside, had seemed an eternity yet transpired in the blink of an eye. Elwaes's question rang through his mind: *do you always perceive time as others do?* Obviously not. A cold shiver ran down his spine. Beside him, Risada rose to her feet.

'We must leave this place. Honora says Elwaes is not truly fit to ride, but we dare not delay longer. If there is no more snow overnight we'll leave at first light. Oh, and Honora insists on sending an escort.—

'All this was discussed just now? I must really have been out of it.—

Risada's light touch on his shoulder made him glance up in surprise, her words even more so.

'Rustam, considering what you've been through, I'm amazed you're as sane as you are. It's this Kingdom.—And now it was her turn to shiver, 'It's doing something to us.—

Food, warmth and rest had restored a great deal of the Lady's stunning appearance, but to Rustam the strain showed in the tightness around her eyes and the set of her jaw.

Of one thing, however, he was certain" whatever effect this journey was visiting upon her life, it was quite unlike the marks it was scoring into his.

* * * * * * * * *

Lord Melcard sank to his throne-like chair and put his head in his hands.

'You're certain it was an accident?—he asked for the second time, dismayed by the emotion his voice betrayed. He had thought himself above such weakness, had rigorously schooled himself not to care for anyone, not even kin.

Not since Mellisand.

No! He refused to go there. Chel had seen fit to take his dear, sweet, beautiful wife and infant son unto herself, thereby teaching him the most important lesson of his youth: that love was a weakness the noble classes could not afford.

At first he had tried hard to deny the harsh lesson, but gradually had come to see it for the divine revelation that it was. Since then he had learned to suppress all such unwanted emotions, and had done his best to educate others: his family, all the women that had fallen for his handsome charm" even the king" in the lesson of the goddess.

He had, he believed, been diligent in his attempts to educate Marten, but the boy was already beyond redemption. *Perhaps,* Melcard considered, *this is the goddess's way of reprimanding me for my failure.*

He raised his face to look upon the bringer of bad tidings. Doctor Hensar stared impassively back.

' Tell me how it happened.—

Hensar bowed slightly and Melcard frowned, distracted by the nagging notion that something was missing. Then he had it" Hensar"s pendant. The doctor's barrel chest displayed plain unadorned black. Melcard praised Chel for that small gift. Those sharp flickers of light as the thing moved had always given him terrible headaches.

' ...then the carriage turned over, but although they were thrown from it they fell directly into the path of those behind. Your sister and her youngest were killed immediately, your older nephew, Melvan, died later that day.—

' And no one knows what caused the animals to stampede?—

' No, my Lord. It is a mystery to all who were there.—

I doubt that, thought Melcard. *The real question should be, who made it happen?*

His guts clenched. Could it have been an agent of Halnashead's? Had the prince discovered he was holding Annasala and engineered this blow to Rees-Charlay in retribution?

Following the recent death of his cousin Mendel, and in the absence of an heir of his own body, Melvan had been Melcard's choice of successor. Since coming of age the lad had shown himself to be much in accord with his uncle's views, and had developed the single-mindedness that was necessary to any prospective ruler, whether of House or Kingdom.

But Halnashead should *not* have discovered his daughter's fate. Melcard had precautions in place. Even if such news had somehow made it as far as Darshan, the prince would never have received the message.

A disturbing thought occurred to Melcard.

'Have the guard alert for any sign of my cousin, Druldar. Inform me immediately of his presence should he try to approach Rees-Charlay.'

'Yes, my Lord,' said Hensar. Melcard did not need to elaborate" they both knew that with this latest tragedy, Druldar was the only other living Fourth Family male. And he had always been one to exploit any opportunity that came his way. Or, indeed, to manufacture one.

'Now,' said Melcard, squaring his shoulders. 'Do you have any news of that other matter? The one involving the mountains.'

Hensar hesitated just long enough to confirm Melcard's suspicions that the situation was still unresolved. Very aware of his fragile hold on his feelings at that time, Melcard raised his hand to forestall an answer which would be certain to raise his ire.

'I expect a result soon, Hensar,' he warned.

'Yes, my Lord,—acknowledged Hensar with a bow, but to Melcard's heightened sensitivity, the doctor's demeanour lacked the subservience of an underling. Melcard wondered if, in the freedom he had granted to the undoubtedly useful tool that was Hensar, he had created something he could no longer control. On top of the day's other distressing news, it was an unwelcome thought.

'Have you any other news?—probed Melcard.

This time Hensar did not hesitate. 'The rumour? Yes, my Lord. Several of the Tylocians confirm they have indeed seen a man claiming to be the missing son of King Belcastas.—

Melcard scowled. 'Even if it were true, he would still be a bastard, with no legal claim to the throne.—

'It may not be quite as simple as that, my Lord.—

'How so?—snapped Melcard.

'Well, my Lord,—began Hensar, sounding as though he were about to explain something very simple to a moron. Melcard found he was grinding his teeth together and stopped quickly. There was nothing as guaranteed to give him a headache. Nothing, that is, apart from that blessedly missing pendant of Hensar's.

'I hesitate to question my Lord's plans,—

'As well you might,—growled Melcard. To his annoyance, Hensar did not appear overly concerned by his own presumption.

'What of Chel's Casket?—said the doctor. 'Even when you succeed in eliminating all the legitimate members of the Royal Family, *you* will never be able to open it. Unless the goddess can be persuaded to change her mind, that box will only open for one of royal blood, and whilst you do not possess such, *he* does. The Families have always accepted the ability to open that casket as a sign of Chel's favour.—

The headache Melcard thought he had escaped gripped his skull. Why did this pretender have to crawl out from under a rock now? And why did Hensar's expression display that tiny hint of smugness. Did he know more than he was telling? Was he likely to change allegiance or, worse still, had he already done so? Melcard put his fingers to his pounding temples.

'That thing is an anachronistic relic of our blighted history and should have been tipped over the railings into the deepest portion of the sea. It has nothing to do with Chel's favour. Once Marten and Halnashead are dead, its hold on our Kingdom will be broken and the Families will see it for what it truly is" an object of foulest magic.—

He scowled. 'And should the worst come to the worst, it will open for my wife. Now go,—he dismissed the doctor, unwilling to look upon the small but deadly man any longer. His eyes followed the retreating back almost involuntarily, fascinated by Hensar's rolling gait, and the insolent set of his broad shoulders.

Just as soon as was practical, he determined, something would have to be done about Hensar.

Lord Melcard sighed and closed his aching eyes, massaging his temples in an effort to relieve the pain that was now firmly lodged there. This rumour" true or not" of the long absent Royal Bastard was not yet a major problem, but it was a potential complication he could have done without. And, to his fury, the tales were escalating as only rumours may. Latest whispers suggested that the Bastard was the source of elixir!

Whilst Melcard had gone to great lengths over the years to protect the truth, he was not about to allow some upstart to steal the credit for his House's product.

That Hensar was the only one who knew the precise ingredients of the final potion was a fact that had escaped neither Lord nor servant.

* * * * * * * * *

In an endlessly white landscape, the loosely packed snow swirled around the horses" fetlocks and despite the thick layer of cooking fat smeared across the undersides of their hooves, it balled up inside their shoes to form ice-stilts that caused them to trip and stumble unpredictably.

Rustam swayed sharply sideways to avoid a hoof-shaped chunk of ice that flew out of Risada"s grey"s foot and whizzed past his left ear. A yelp from behind told him that Elwaes had not been so quick. Looking round, he saw the Shivan brushing ice and snow from the front of his thick grey cloak.

Then it was Nightstalker"s turn to flounder and Rustam suddenly found himself clinging to her neck with his face buried in her silky mane. He righted himself quickly from the undignified position, and patted his mare reassuringly on her sleek black neck as she pranced in annoyance. In five days of enforced rest with nothing to do but eat, the horses had recovered from their trek across the mountains with remarkable ease, regaining a vigour their riders could only envy.

Studying the others in their party it was obvious to Rustam that the small wiry mountain ponies ridden by their escort handled the conditions with greater ease than his and Risada"s tall, rangy mounts, but no matter how hard he tried he could not picture himself on a pony. Sneaking another glance behind at Elwaes, Rustam smiled at the absurd picture the tall elf cut, sitting astride a pony so small his feet nearly dragged in the snow.

Their own pony puffed along beside Nightstalker, content to carry his restocked packs, serenely untouched by any of the bizarre things that had happened during their passage through the mountains.

Risada reined her grey in until she was alongside Rustam.

'I don"t trust these people. How do we know they"re taking us the correct route?—

Even to Rustam's suspicious mind she was beginning to sound paranoid. 'Why wouldn't they?—he countered.

She eyed him sceptically. 'If a couple of Kishtanians appeared out of nowhere in Tyr-en, complete with an obviously sick elf as a captive and demanded to see the King, would *you* take them to him?—

'I see your point. I might take them to Halnashead, but I'd certainly try to find out what it was they wanted first.—

'Precisely. So why haven't they asked us?—

Rustam shrugged. 'Maybe because they're children of Chel, Risada, and they don't consider it their business.—

'Yet they insisted on an escort.—She glared at the backs of the three brothers riding ahead of them.

'They may be holy people, but they're still Kishtanians. I'm not surprised they don't want to let a pair of Tyr-enese wander around their Kingdom unaccompanied. And besides, they're the only ones who can find the road.—Rustam swept a dramatic arm at the vast empty expanse of featureless whiteness.

Risada sighed in frustration. 'Rustam, do you know how irritating you can be? You're always so damned reasonable!—

* * * * * * * * * * *

For the next ten days they trekked steadily across the Kingdom of Kishtan. By the end of the first day they had dropped below the snow line and entered a land of rolling hills and deep, wooded valleys. Small villages dotted their route, located in the open areas between the woods. Their escort explained that, despite the relative peace of the Kingdom, forest-dwelling bandits were an ongoing irritation only kept in check by regular troop patrols.

'Barbarians,—muttered Risada, and Rustam could see her calculating how this might affect their request for the loan of fighting men.

At night, they stayed in taverns when the villages were large enough to support such facilities or in barns when they weren't. Rustam and Risada slept lightly and in turns, unsettled by the idea of free dwellers" in Tyr-en such villagers would have been beholden to a noble House or a Guild. Ultimately, each province in Kishtan was ruled by a Duke answerable to King Graylin, but that lofty government seemed so far removed that Rustam struggled to see how Kishtanian law might be upheld.

Perhaps they had come seeking aid from the wrong Kingdom after all.

Added to that worry, Rustam fretted over the continuing deterioration of his clothes; no one would take them seriously at court if they arrived looking like hobos. Chel's children had washed and mended their soiled outfits, but all they could offer as replacements were the coarse grey robes and pants of their order. Frankly, Rustam would rather be seen naked. After all, nudity hadn't looked so bad on Shamnac and whatever else Rustam had lost in terms of looks, he was still proud of his figure.

Finally they drew near to the Kishtanian capital, Teshondra, the city by the lake. Nightfall found them entering the outskirts by way of an ornate gate with only a token company of guards who made no move to question them. Their guides led them through a maze of narrow cobbled streets down to the water front. The clatter of the horses" hooves blended with the rattle of handcarts as market vendors trundled their stocks home for the night, and the sharp slap of halyards striking masts. All manner of fishing vessels bobbed gently on the swell raised by the growing northerly wind that brought with it the fresh tang of pine forest and the bite that promised snow was not far behind them.

'We have a lodging house here,—volunteered one of the sons, a garrulous individual who had hardly paused for breath the entire journey. He led the way beneath a wooden arch into a stone flagged courtyard and dismounted. 'We'll stay the night here and send to Court in the morning to see if an audience can be arranged.—

For once, Rustam willingly surrendered Nightstalker's reins to a stranger. If these people were as good with horses as those at the foot of the mountain pass, he knew he would be leaving her in good hands.

The House of Chel in Teshondra was neither as large nor as populated as that other, but the travellers were made to feel as welcome. Rich cooking smells wafted from the kitchens promising a hearty supper, and they were delighted to be offered bathing facilities to wash away the grime of the trail before the meal was served.

Risada was led away to a guest bathing room, while Rustam and Elwaes were asked to share the communal tub used by the men of the House. Accepting graciously, Rustam considered the arrangement opportune. He'd had no chance to be alone with the Shivan since the mountains and was eager to ask some questions he had no wish for Risada to hear.

Resembling half a giant beer barrel, the bath was big enough for five, maybe six at a push. After stripping off clothes not fit to be worn by even the lowliest peasant, Rustam climbed in. The fresh scent of rose oil filled his lungs as the divinely hot water embraced his filthy body.

Opposite him, Elwaes already lay half submerged with his eyes closed, head inclined backward over the edge and both arms stretched out, hands resting on the rim.

It was the first time Rustam had seen the elf fully naked, and he was shocked by the gaunt, skeletal appearance of what should have been a slender, elegant figure. The white tracery of scars caused by Doctor Hensar's blade criss-crossed both arms around the elbow joints, but now Rustam could see that the Shivan's injuries had been far more extensive. His entire torso was lined with the fine marks of long healed torture, and Rustam would have laid odds that his back displayed more of the same.

Mind swept clean of his planned questions, Rustam blurted, 'Did Melcard do all that too?—

The Shivan's lanky body jerked, as though reliving the touch of the knives. His chest rose and fell once, twice, as he relaxed his spasmed muscles before answering.

'Melcard, yes. By his pet demon, Hensar.—

'But why? And when?—Rustam found it impossible to tear his gaze from the horrific blemishes.

Elwaes cracked an eye open " an eye full of rage and revenge.

'*Before*,—he hissed in a tone that chilled Rustam to his core. 'Before Melcard determined to use my blood for his vile scheme, they questioned me.—

Rustam nodded understanding. 'The secret of long life.—

'There *is* no secret, damn them all to Charin's hell! They tortured me for something that exists only inside their twisted minds.—

The Shivan's fury was almost palpable, and Rustam found himself clutching at the tub's brass-bound rim. His heart thundered, all his flight instincts kicking in at once. He was halfway to his feet when screams erupted from beyond the wall, accompanied by the thud of pounding hooves. A board behind the tub splintered, and Rustam flung himself over the edge onto the floor, dodging chunks of timber whizzing past.

He crouched behind the tub. The din of human and equine voices made it clear they were next to the stables, and it sounded as if a full scale stampede was imminent. Even the sturdy wooden tub would be no protection if a horse broke through.

'Elwaes! Get out of there!—He grabbed the still semi-submerged elf by one bony shoulder and shook him.

'What" —

Elwaes thrashed wildly before reason cleared his eyes. Hearing the racket in the adjacent stables, as if for the first time, his face blanched even paler than usual. He gulped a quick breath and began to sing, his voice surprisingly strong considering his physical weakness, and gradually the commotion beyond the wall quieted.

Rustam put a grateful hand on the elf's arm. 'Well done, my friend, It's fortunate you were to hand" —

He broke off as the Shivan gripped his hand with feverish strength. Elwaes shook his head and tears flew sparkling from his face.

'*I caused that!*—

Rustam felt the blood drain from his cheeks. 'How?—he began, and then stopped. Stupid question. 'Why?—

Elwaes glanced away and his flesh turned icy. Realising how cold he was too, Rustam climbed back into the tub.

'It wasn't your fault,—he said. 'It was me, making you think about, well, you know.—

'That's not the point. *I lost control!*—

'Happens to everyone, once in a while. Goddess knows you've had enough provocation.—

Elwaes's face turned grim. 'Rusty, you don't understand. I can't *afford* to. No one who commands magic can. Think of the damage I might have caused!—

Rustam's mind spun. 'But what happens if you're ill? Or provoked beyond restraint?—

'If I'm ill, I'll take an herb to dampen my powers. Provoked? That's no excuse. No cause exists that could justify such a lapse. As soon as we are finished here I will seek an apothecary and obtain some hestane; I cannot risk putting others in danger again.—

Rustam studied his friend. Was he really that ill? Undernourished certainly, and no doubt bruised in both mind and spirit, but the self-control he was describing sounded a mite too virtuous for even the most stout hearted. It was not something Rustam had any desire to aspire to.

But did he have a choice?

'Elwaes, what about someone who has no idea how to use his powers?—

'Oh goddess! Rusty, what have you done?—

Rustam shook his head. 'Nothing. At least, I don't think so. It's just" well, I've had these unsettling experiences.—

And he poured out the tale of the giant hand, and the later, less eventful incident. Elwaes regarded him with such understanding in his pale blue eyes that Rustam did not feel as foolish as he had anticipated. He wished he'd talked to the elf earlier although when he thought back, the opportunity had never really presented itself.

When he concluded, Elwaes nodded. 'So that is the truth of it. I suspected, but could not be certain. Rustam, you may be the only living Tyr-enese to have actually met with Charin.—

Rustam tensed, drawing a sharp breath. 'Of all people, I didn't expect you to mock me. I thought you were my friend.—

Elwaes's eyebrows drew down and he tilted his head. Then his face cleared.

'Ah, you think I jest at your expense. Believe me friend Rusty, I meant no such disrespect. Perhaps there are some things you are not yet ready to accept, but you are most assuredly overdue for some lessons. We must delay no longer.—

'I agree, but will you be able to help me if you take this" hestin?—

'Hestane,—Elwaes corrected. 'Yes. I have no need of magic to teach you basic control techniques. We'll begin this evening.—

17. AURAS

The blood splatters on the walls of the torture chamber jumped and shifted in the torch light. The stink of fear and death lingered in the air, powerful reminders of the purpose of the room, if the dark table with its straps and fittings were not enough.

Hensar had chosen the venue for this meeting with great care.

Sweat trickled down the guard captain's face, dampening the stiff collar of his maroon uniform. Hensar marked the passage of the droplets with satisfaction. Fear was the world's most useful tool, with the added advantage that it gave the user such sublime pleasure.

He lifted a hand, gratified by the flinch that simple movement elicited.

"Is it done?" asked Hensar.

"It is."

The doctor scowled. The words *'My Lord'* were missing from the guard's answer and, whilst it was still prudent to be circumspect, the continuing omission rankled. *Patience*, he admonished himself. *So many years in the planning, and this, the first step towards completion. I need wait only a little longer.*

"You have done well," he said in unaccustomed praise and watched the guard's relieved sigh with amusement. How quickly he could change that for terror. But, for now, he needed absolute loyalty; something that Melcard failed to inspire no matter how hard he tried. One of the many reasons Hensar had chosen to cultivate this particular Lord.

And it was that Lord's fate to which he must now attend. The first piece of the final plan was in place. Tylocian hostages had been taken and secreted in a location only he knew. The mountain clans were close knit and highly superstitious—such an easy combination to manipulate for one of Hensar's devious persuasion and arcane skills.

The Bastard required unquestioning obedience of the clan leaders, and that was now assured. Melcard would find out too late that it was not he, but his rival who controlled their allies.

Hensar casually put a hand on the table and stroked one of the cold metal wrist bands. The guard captain's eyes could not help but follow the motion. The man swallowed convulsively.

"And the others?"

"In place...sir. At least three in each strategic location, and five in his Lordship's personal guard."

"And I thought that personal guard were chosen specifically for their unswerving loyalty to their Lord," Hensar mused, running a fingertip the length of the gore stained table.

"They are, sir...doctor. But they also know who wields the real power in Rees-Charlay."

"Yes," said Hensar in satisfaction. He placed both palms flat onto the wood and leaned forward, feeling the pain and horror, the many lives that had seeped into the grain and lingered yet, testimony to his art.

He wondered briefly, when this was all over, would he miss it? Once the coming change in his circumstances was complete, he doubted he would have the freedom for such time-consuming diversions.

"You may go," he dismissed the guard captain.

He lingered after the man had left, turning to the darkest corner where even torch light failed to reach.

"You can come out now."

A slight figure, clad all in black, drifted out of the gloom. It seemed to glide noiselessly over the stone flags, halting just on the edge of the flickering light. There was the merest hint of a face beneath the ebony hood, just enough to suggest human features, but to Hensar the man's lithe height gave away more about his elven ancestry than any sight of his countenance could have done. Such a pity that Halnashead had put a stop to the cross-species breeding programme, just when it was beginning to bear fruit; this second generation had proven almost indistinguishable from humans in appearance, but oh, so successful as operatives within the game.

One more reason the old order had to change.

"Well?" Hensar demanded. "Did you see or hear anything you felt might merit a report; anything that could in any way be construed as threatening to the Fourth Family?"

"I did not," confirmed Melcard's spy. "I shall continue to watch you, as my Lord has instructed, but I have seen nothing as yet which would impel me to disturb him from either his rest or his work."

The spy inclined his head to the doctor before drifting from the chamber with nothing more than the soft whisper of cloth to mark his passage. Hensar followed, and then paused and turned for one last, affectionate glance over the central table and the neat racks of instruments, for so long a major part of his life. How many lives had ended here, to further his research, to satisfy Melcard, and to silence threats? How much passion and dedication had he spent in here, building the foundations of the great plan?

Now all those years of plotting, all the humiliations, all the debasing subservience were at an end. His eyes swept the chamber one last time. It had served its purpose.

Doctor Hensar closed and locked the door.

* * * * * * * * * *

"Now focus. Control the speed of your heart. Slow it with your breathing."

Elwaes's voice wound itself into and around Rustam's awareness. The outside world had ceased to exist. All that was real was the wood-scented air filling his lungs and the thumping muscle within his chest that struggled to break free from its constraints. With a last violent lurch against his rib cage, the rebellious organ conceded. A gentle shushing sound filled his inner hearing as the blood flowing through his veins slowed. A feeling of utter serenity washed his body free of its last lingering tensions.

Rustam had been tutored by the best in Tyr-en, and he knew many diverse exercises to induce physical relaxation. But nothing he had previously achieved could compare to what Elwaes had taught him this morning: a total blending of self with surroundings, with the air that hissed quietly across his ears and caressed his skin, with the flowing energy currents of the living world that permeated everything and seemed almost tangible.

With the very essence of the goddess.

His mind drifted, tugged gently at its mortal moorings and sent him floating free, drifting upward like a bubble in still water. Below him, two motionless and oddly glowing figures sat cross-legged on rugs on the wood-tiled floor of the sparsely furnished guest room he shared with Elwaes. Rustam gazed down at his body which sat in the space between the table and the bunk beds, facing the door and the elf who sat upon a second rug borrowed from the hallway outside. In the knowledge that he could never be comfortable with his back to a door, Rustam found it astonishing that Elwaes could be so oblivious to the possible dangers, but the Shivan was, if anything, more relaxed even than his pupil.

Rustam regarded the lambent shell he had temporarily vacated. It was surrounded by a cocoon of fluid colours, dominated by bands of sulphurous yellow. A counterpoint of sharp green peeked through, the whole overlaid near the head by muddy browns.

He studied Elwaes's aura for comparison, and was enthralled by the purity of the soft blues and golds, somehow still clean and strong despite the overlay of brownish-grey mist that sheathed him almost to the top of his head, where all was lost in a brilliant white circle of radiance.

A third figure entered the room. This one pulsed with an angry scarlet tinge, streaked with indigo bars of barely suppressed anxiety and impatience. Risada's sardonic tones intruded upon the quietude of the moment.

"What *precisely* are you two doing?"

With one deep breath, Rustam's awareness snapped back into normal time and place. Contrary to his expectations, his mood remained tranquil, undisturbed by what he had seen, and by Risada's untimely interruption. He glanced across at his teacher's serene countenance, and curved the good side of his mouth upward in self-mockery. What an incongruous picture they made—the ragged Shivan tutoring the dishevelled Tyr-enese.

Not that Risada must ever be allowed to know what truly passed between them.

"Elwaes was teaching me a Shivan meditation technique."

Risada raised a freshly plucked eyebrow. "Indeed? I hadn't realised your tastes ran to such esoterics." She proffered a large bundle clutched between her crooked arms and her chin. "What I have to offer is far more mundane, but closer to your usual preferences."

Clothes! The sight of fresh, clean garments shot Rustam to his feet as fast as if he had sat on a nest of biting spiders. He unloaded Risada's arms in one scoop, deposited the bundle on a table and began to strip it apart, shaking out first a pair of leggings, then a tunic of unfamiliar design. A puzzled frown lowered his brows and he glanced questioningly round at the Lady of Domn, only to feel his eyes widen as he saw what her burden had concealed.

The gown she wore was of deepest red—a strong, dominant colour that would be considered too strident for a woman to wear in Tyr-enese court circles. After the initial shock, Rustam decided that the shade set off Risada's fair complexion to great advantage. His eyes lingered on the curve of her throat and the little hollow at its base, framed by the leather thong bearing Shamnac's gift. The talisman itself was tucked inside the low scooped neck line that was edged in satin ribbon.

And the shape! It took a moment for his mind to adjust to the flowing lines. Cut on the bias, the fabric clung to Risada's figure before sweeping over her hips into a full flared skirt which trailed behind her on the floor. None of the masses of underskirts and petticoats that produced the voluminous contours of a Tyr-enese gown.

Rustam ran a finger around his ragged collar. *Goddess, my thanks for revealing our relationship in time' I could have been in real danger of trying for a serious relationship with an assassin who's promised to kill me.*

"Mmm." Risada eyed the looking glass hanging behind the table and turned sideways on to it, smoothing her palms over her waist. "It takes a little getting used to, doesn't it? But it is the latest vogue in this Kingdom, or so I am led to believe."

Rustam took a deep breath. "Where did you get them?"

"While you've been sitting here—breathing—I've been busy. Our hosts might not be interested in wearing anything aside from sackcloth, but they have many benefactors, some of whom were only too willing to earn an extra intercession to Chel in return for a new outfit or two. Try them on. I fear the fit won't be as perfect as you're accustomed to, but you'll just have to make do."

"My Lady, to be rid of these rags I'd wear almost anything. Except the sackcloth."

To his amazed delight, Risada laughed. "I agree completely. Anything but that. Oh, and Rustam—" She pointed at his chin and nodded. "I approve."

Rustam ran a finger along his jaw, naked now that he had dispensed with the beard. One of the brothers had offered to trim it, but in deference to Risada's discomfort with bearded men, he had decided to dispose of it entirely. Clearly a good choice.

While Risada sorted garments that she thought might suit Elwaes, Rustam drew on a dark, high necked under tunic and a pair of grey and black striped leggings. He tried a pair of soft leather boots but found them too tight and reluctantly replaced them with his own scuffed but comfortable ones. A long, slim cut over-tunic in rich purple velvet completed the ensemble and Rustam surveyed his image critically in the looking glass.

Everything below the neck. He still could not bring himself to look at his damaged face.

Used to the short cropped doublets and hose of Tyr-enese high society, he was initially disappointed. The long tunic covered his tight buttock muscles—a feature of which he was inordinately proud. But as he turned this way and that in front of the glass, he began to appreciate the aesthetic qualities of the outfit. The stripes accentuated the lean length of his legs, and the tunic lent an overall slenderness that was really quite becoming. He added a metal chain belt that dipped into a vee over his flat stomach and trailed a golden tassel to swing provocatively as he moved.

He began to feel more like his old self.

Shrugging his shoulders, he checked the fit of the sleeves, but they were roomy enough not to impede the daggers strapped inside his forearms. Satisfied, he looked round to find Elwaes gone and Risada watching him with an indulgent smile on her lips. He wondered briefly how often she had watched her brother Iain—his half brother, if her assumption was true—in just such a manner. He grinned back at her. "I might very well believe we *are* related, if dressing tastes and good figures run in the family."

Intended as a compliment, Rustam quickly realised he had overstepped the mark. Risada's face closed down to the cold mask of old. She regarded him stonily.

"We are to be presented to the Kishtanian court at two hours past noon. I expect you to be ready to depart one hour before then."

And she swept out of the door, only just whisking the unfamiliar trailing hem of her gown clear as it closed behind her.

Rustam rolled his eyes skyward. *Never learn, do I?*

Not since his youth had a woman made him feel so gauche, but then he'd rarely been in the company of a woman who didn't want him for the pleasure his body could offer. He gritted his uneven teeth and turned, forcing himself to look at the glass; to study the ruined face above that perfect body.

It was every bit as hideous as he had imagined. Even the undamaged side was distorted, pulled sideways by the sagging weight of limp skin that hung from his skull in a parody of extreme old age. The left eye was red rimmed, the lower lid gapping to expose inflamed membranes. Moisture gathered in the well, dripping over the rim to trickle down the florid cheek. His lips drooped asymmetrically, gums and teeth showing through the gap and a gob of spittle ran down his chin even as he watched.

What woman would want him now?

An intense surge of anger destroyed any lingering tranquillity. What had he ever done to deserve such punishment? Granted, he had always been proud of his looks, always relied on them to get what he wanted, but was that so wrong? All the information he gleaned was used for the good of Tyr-en, not for his own self-aggrandisement. How was he supposed to pursue that career now?

He scowled at his distorted image and turned away just as the door opened. Elwaes entered, and Rustam gladly allowed the elf's cringe-worthy appearance to distract him from contemplating a future stuck with that awful face.

The mossy shade of green that Risada had chosen suited Elwaes's pale colouring, but none of the garments fitted his lanky frame. Sleeves and leggings both finished far short of their intended positions, leaving his bony wrists and ankles on view, and the close cut of the leggings turned his already thin limbs into sticks. He ran long fingers ineffectually through his shaggy blond hair and gave a lop-sided grin. "At least I won't be mistaken for one of your countrymen."

"Would that bother you so much?" said Rustam, twisting the tassel of his belt between his fingers.

The elf tilted his head and regarded Rustam in silence for a moment. Then his lips curved into a sad smile. "Rusty, you have become a good friend but you are still a product of your kingdom."

Stung, Rustam's mouth snapped open to deliver a sharp retort, when the Shivan asked: "Tell me, what did you see?"

Off balance, Rustam's mind took a moment to relate the question to his earlier lesson. He frowned, recalling.

"Colours," he said. "I saw colours. There were two figures: you and me. You were all blue and gold, with a hazy cloud of brownish-grey hanging around you. I was yellow and green." He stopped and grimaced. "They were poor shades—the colours of an infected wound. What do they mean?"

Elwaes's eyebrows lifted. "You saw far more than I anticipated. But you saw truly." He shrugged in apology. "Yellow is the colour of deception; green that of jealousy. The aura of a person reveals their inner nature and cannot be counterfeited."

Rustam winced and turned back to the glass. Was his face now a reflection of his true self? Had the handsome, boyish face been just a façade—one he had built to hide the anger and hurt that had shaped his young life?

Abandoned by his mother, a bastard with no knowledge of his father's identity, he had used his looks and athletic physique to great advantage. But for whom? For Halnashead, for the good of the kingdom certainly, but perhaps without conscious intent he had used it also for himself, to hide from his true nature, to clothe putrescence in surface beauty because no one was going to look deeply enough to discover how rotten he was inside. Until now.

Was this his unstated crime?

A shiver ran through him and he clamped a firm hold on his emotions. He was *not* going to fall apart now. He had come too far and survived too much to give in now to self pity and the words of a Shivan whose motives did not hold the interests of Tyr-en paramount.

"I'm sorry, I can't accept that," he said, planting his fists on his hips. "Deception is part of my job. As for jealousy—what man doesn't wish for better? Even a king may desire another life, free from the responsibilities of the crown. That doesn't make him evil."

"Rusty," Elwaes interrupted Rustam's indignant tirade. "I never suggested you were evil."

"No? Well that's how it came over. Devious and jealous: my two main attributes!"

The elf wagged his head. "You're reacting as a Tyr-enese," he accused, and when Rustam opened his mouth to protest that that was exactly what he was, Elwaes held up a hand to forestall him.

"Your kingdom clings to its order as though change would bring about destruction. Do you not yet see how this stagnates your culture? Of all Five Kingdoms of men, only Tyr-en has refused to embrace this new land for its differences as well as the similarities it holds to your old continent. You have tried to impose your traditional regimes where they're not needed, and refused to adapt to a land that is far more hospitable than that which spawned you.

"But this doesn't mean that you as an individual cannot change. You are your own man, Rusty, despite your allegiances, and if one dares to change, others may follow."

Rustam sighed and shook his head. "I really don't understand what you're trying to say. We keep to the old ways because they work. What's wrong with that?"

Now it was Elwaes's turn to sigh. "Have you learned so little from our exchanges, or from what you have seen of Kishtan thus far?" He put a hand on Rustam's shoulder. "Never mind, my friend, there is plenty more yet for you to see. I just ask that you will keep my words in your mind as you look upon a kingdom other than your own."

"I'll certainly try," Rustam promised. He'd figure out later what exactly it was that he'd agreed to. The elf's ideas were unsettling in an indefinable way, as though someone was testing Rustam's loyalty to his kingdom. He glanced aside at Elwaes, mistrustful of the Shivan for the first time since the early days of their journey. Certainly the Shivan had every reason to hate the Tyr-enese, and to try to take some form of revenge, but perhaps his reasons were darker than simple hatred.

A vivid memory of Elwaes's terrifying expression when he recalled his imprisonment slid across Rustam's mind. Ice crept up his spine. Perhaps the old stories were true after all, and elves were indeed the servants of Charin as many Tyr-enese believed. His left hand twitched upward, toward the sagging folds of skin that bore the mark of Charin—if the healer's words were to be believed. Maybe Elwaes had had something to do with that, too.

Rustam determined to watch him closely from now on.

He was suddenly eager for company other than that of the elf. "I suppose we'd better go thank our hosts for our deliverance from those rags that used to be our clothes," he said. Elwaes inclined his head in mute accord, but caught Rustam's arm as he reached for the door.

"Yes?" said Rustam, reclaiming his arm a touch too quickly. Elwaes appeared puzzled, but Rustam quickly realised his reaction was not the cause.

"Rusty, are you certain there is no Shivan blood in your family?"

Rustam felt his jaw drop. *Shivan blood?* What a ridiculous idea.

But then again, why not? He knew of no other Tyr-enese with his odd perception of time. His tall elegant frame and—formerly—fine features could almost aspire to the ethereal beauty of the elves. And he seemed to be taking to magic like one born to it, as no Tyr-enese should.

But where did that leave him, considering his misgivings of scant moments earlier? He shook his head in denial. "I don't see how. Although I don't know my parentage for certain, it seems likely that I share a father with Risada."

"Ah!" Elwaes breathed. "So that is behind the change in your relationship. And yet," he added, "I cannot help but feel that some form of blood tie exists between us. Else...no." He shook his head and his ragged locks flapped around his face. "It must be pure fancy, or perhaps merely a whim to be with my own kind once more."

Rustam patted him awkwardly on the shoulder. "I'm sure it won't be long before you're home."

"Are you?" Elwaes demanded, anger replacing wistfulness. "Are you not forgetting why you brought me here? I'm a bargaining chip for an army, nothing more."

"No!" Rustam denied. "It may have started out that way, but the time and the dangers we've shared together have changed all that. You've saved our lives several times over."

"As did you, mine. Rusty, you may feel differently now, but what of Lady Risada? To her, the only thing of import is her mission, as she believes it should be to you also."

"But—"

Knuckles rapped on the door. In truth, Rustam was grateful for the interruption, both his mind and emotions in an unsettling flux. After all the years of putting Tyr-en and his master Halnashead ahead of his own considerations, how had his unquestioning devotion become so inexplicably muddled? Perhaps this was the true danger of associating with elves—a confusion of the heart and a misdirecting of priorities. Were they deliberately subversive, or was it just a part of their nature to make one question what had always seemed so clear cut?

Silent and brooding, Rustam followed the son of Chel who had come to lead them to the refectory for the noon meal, uncomfortable with the feeling that the elf walking close behind him could see clear through his outer flesh to read the doubts that troubled his soul.

* * * * * * * * * * * *

"Sir. Madam." The stranger bowed. "My name is Javed Yorth, equerry to the Court of King Graylin."

Clad in fine silks of a strong yellow hue unseen in Tyr-en, Javed Yorth looked distinctly out of place in the House of Chel's rustic entrance hall. Of similar cut to the outfit Rustam wore, Yorth's silks were undoubtedly not intended for wear out of doors, if the splashes of dirt now marring his leggings and soft soled slippers were any indication. The equerry bowed again and Rustam almost choked on a strong masculine perfume. Even the man's breath, when he spoke, was laden with the smell of unfamiliar spices.

Risada hurriedly raised a scented square of lace to cover an undignified sneeze.

"I am charged," intoned Yorth in a nasal voice, "to convey King Graylin's sincerest apologies for the lack of an official reception. It appears the messenger bearing news of your intended visit has gone astray somewhere between your kingdom and ours. My ignorance is likewise unforgivable, but I would be eternally grateful should you choose to enlighten me. Whom do I have the honour to be presenting to his Majesty?"

Rustam watched in mild amusement as Risada bit off a sharp retort. She was not accustomed to being unrecognised. Indeed, it was probably a unique experience for her to introduce herself to anyone, especially a servant. She drew a deep breath through the lace square then raised her chin imperiously.

"Please reassure King Graylin that apologies are unnecessary. No messenger was dispatched prior to our departure—an omission I shall explain to his Majesty in person. I am the Lady Risada Delgano vas Domn, of the Second House of Tyr-en, cousin to his Majesty King Marten of Tyr-en. Here are my credentials."

She drew a small scroll from a pocket hidden deep within the capacious sleeve of her gown and handed it to the equerry. Rustam made out Halnashead's seal on the parchment as it exchanged hands.

Risada indicated Rustam with a dismissive wave of her hand. "This is my personal assistant, Master Rustam Chalice."

"Lady Risada. Master Chalice." Yorth swept a deeper, more appropriate bow now that he knew to whom he was speaking, and Rustam could see the mind racing behind the startled eyes as the equerry sorted the implications of the unannounced, almost clandestine arrival of one of Tyr-en's most important nobles. After a quick glance at Rustam's damaged face, the man averted his gaze before returning his attention to Risada.

"And the remainder of your retinue?" Yorth enquired.

"There is but one more, and he is presently indisposed, though I trust he will be recovered soon," Risada replied smoothly, as if it was an everyday occurrence for noble ladies to travel into foreign lands without a full retinue of servants and guards.

Yorth blinked several times and tugged at one earlobe, clearly perplexed. Risada seized control of the situation, stepping close and lowering her voice.

"Master Yorth, the matter upon which I must speak with your king is both urgent and highly delicate, and I am not at liberty to discuss it with anyone but his Majesty. The security of both our kingdoms may be at stake and anything, or anyone, who delays that meeting may permit an already precarious situation to develop into one that could have grave consequences for us all. Do I make myself clear?"

Rustam almost chuckled as Yorth's mouth opened and closed wordlessly. Risada had disclosed nothing, while making it very plain that should anything ill come of it—whatever *it* was—Yorth himself would almost certainly be to blame.

Tugging at his tunic collar, he cleared his throat and swept another deep bow. "Perfectly, my Lady. Allow me to escort you to the palace with all haste, where I am certain I can introduce you to someone more capable of meeting your needs than I."

Risada smiled, and Rustam could see her beginning to enjoy herself for the first time since they had entered Kishtan. Court politics and court officials were something Lady Risada understood, no matter what kingdom they were in.

"But Master Yorth, we have no need of anyone else. You are in a position to introduce us to King Graylin and it is my wish that you do so. Please, conduct us to him with all haste."

Yorth drew a deep breath, and inclined his head in bemused capitulation.

"My Lady, I am yours to command."

"Then lead on, Master Yorth."

"My Lady," murmured Rustam close to her ear. "Elwaes?"

Risada matched his tone. "I have made arrangements for him to remain here until I send for him. I wish to assess King Graylin's disposition towards Tyr-en before I play the final tile in our stack."

Rustam bowed his head. Restored to the position of servant, he found to his dismay that he was uncomfortable with something that used to feel natural. He toyed with his belt tassel, and worried about what else might have changed inside him that he hadn't yet realised.

Outside, a troop of mounted soldiers overwhelmed the tiny courtyard. In their midst stood a richly decorated coach drawn by four black horses. The golden lion blazoned on the door of the carriage was repeated throughout the harness and the scarlet uniforms of the assembled escort. But it was not Graylin's gilded crest which drew Rustam's eye and distracted him from his concerns: it was the extraordinary bright, shining silver of the horses' bits.

Risada led the way to the coach, horses backing neatly out of her way with a minimum of fuss and clatter of hooves on cobbles to form an aisle, while the trailing hem of her gown acquired a smattering of the marks that marred Yorth's yellow silk. The equerry handed her up the steps into the yellow draped interior while Rustam paused by one silky black nose and raised a hand to allow the animal to sniff his skin.

He studied the flawless gleam of the horse's bit—not a sign of rust. He had never seen such a metal. Was this magic at work?

18. KISHTAN

"You appear distracted, Master Chalice. Is anything the matter?" enquired Javed Yorth.

Rustam blinked and focused on the equerry. The carriage jolted over the cobbled streets. The clatter of their escort's hooves drowned out most of the background noise, but the sharp chink of halyards had long since been replaced by the cries of market vendors as they moved away from the lake shore and into the city centre. Rustam wished he could see beyond the yellow drapes screening the windows, yet the bitter draughts that insinuated themselves around the edges of the doors argued for maintaining the cosy, cocoon-like interior undisturbed.

"Bits," said Rustam. The equerry looked confused, an expression that seemed rarely to have left his face since Risada took control. "Your horses' bits," Rustam clarified, but Yorth seemed none the wiser. "The metal is new to me," Rustam tried again, aware that he had captured Risada's interest as well.

"Ah!" Yorth's face brightened. "It is a new process, not yet in wide use but one which has great potential. The metal is stronger, far less brittle and it neither tarnishes nor corrodes. The process is a secret as yet, I fear, as the trade implications are prodigious."

"Indeed they must be," Risada agreed. "And would I be correct in thinking you have developed new dyes also?" She indicated the brilliant yellow silk of Yorth's garments and the matching hangings that turned the interior of the coach into the heart of an unopened marshflower.

"Why yes, my Lady. This is the latest shade—not available to just anyone, of course."

Of course, echoed Rustam inside his head, sickened to realise that the strutting peacock seated opposite was probably the Kishtanian version of himself. *Am I really that shallow? Probably.*

Raised voices penetrated the coach's interior and without warning Rustam was flung from his seat, landing in Javed Yorth's arms as the vehicle lurched to a stop. Risada managed to maintain her seat by dint of clinging to some of the draperies, and as Rustam disentangled himself from the flustered equerry, he spied the glint of emerald and steel in the Lady's hand. His own dagger slid smoothly from its hidden sheath into his palm, and he wished fervently that etiquette for this royal audience had not required him to leave his sword behind—while relations between their two kingdoms were far from hostile, they were also a long march from cordial.

Risada twitched the curtains aside and peered obliquely out of the window. Looking over her shoulder, Rustam coughed and wiped his eyes, which streamed in the sudden rush of cold air. He was, however, grateful for the influx of fresh—if somewhat horse-smelling—atmosphere that freshened the heavily spiced and perfumed miasma clinging to both Yorth and his carriage.

Risada ordered the nearest soldier: "Find out what's happening."

The dagger vanished from her hand—*where did she keep it?*' and Rustam glanced at Yorth to ensure he hadn't seen it, but the equerry was too involved with straightening his disarrayed clothing to have noticed such a tiny weapon. Risada raised an eyebrow in question and Rustam gave the barest shake of his head. A sick feeling quivered in the pit of his stomach. To bring such deadly tools into the presence of the Kishtanian king might seal not only their own fates, but could be enough to bring the two kingdoms to the brink of a conflict they had so far avoided, even during the political turmoil of the Shivan Wars.

Yet neither Tyr-enese was willing to venture into the Kishtanian court totally stripped of protection.

With the barest hint of a grim smile, Risada settled back to her seat, smoothing the close-fitting fabric of her gown beneath her to prevent it creasing. Rustam had a sudden memory of her attired as she had been for all those interminable Grand Balls, swathed in the voluminous skirts required by Tyr-enese convention. How much simpler this Kishtanian style, and how much more flattering.

Rustam found himself beginning to warm to the idea of a kingdom not held rigidly by the concepts and traditions —not to mention the fashions—that had endured in Tyr-en since the time of the Crossing.

"My Lady."

A soldier's torso appeared beside the window. Rustam jerked guiltily, vexed that his attention had been so easily distracted from a potentially dangerous situation, and alarmed that he might be succumbing to some of the outrageous notions tendered earlier by the elf.

"Speak!" commanded the Lady of Domn as Yorth opened his mouth.

"The road is blocked, my Lady. By a trader's wagon."

"Well, make him move it!" Risada ordered in exasperation, although her relief at the simple explanation was evident to Rustam in the minute relaxation of her shoulders.

"I'm afraid the axle is broken," the soldier explained, stiffly uncomfortable. "His load of fruit is in danger of falling and being spoiled. We will have to wait until the wagon is unloaded before it can be moved."

"I beg your pardon?" Risada was outraged. "A common tradesman is going to make *us* wait?"

"My Lady!" The trooper snapped a salute. "I will go and see what can be done to hasten proceedings."

And he was gone before Risada could say anything further. Denied an easy target to vent her pent up emotions upon, she turned on the equerry who had just barely regained his composure after his entanglement with Rustam.

"*Do* something, Master Yorth!" she demanded. "You are equerry to the King and I am a foreign ambassador. Instruct your escort to remove the obstacle, and I want an apology from whichever Guild this peasant is beholden to."

"Guild?" repeated Yorth, bewildered. "My Lady, there is no trader's guild in this city, and all who use the streets are entitled to the same common courtesies as each other. My position at court does nothing to affect that."

"You mean this man if a *free* trader?" Risada's tone betrayed her horror and disgust at the idea. "Then, to whom is he answerable?"

"Why, to Kishtanian law, of course." Yorth's confusion deepened, and then cleared. "But forgive me, my Lady, I forget that your kingdom has no concept of individual rights as do we of Kishtan." His voice took on a hint of superiority. "We progressed beyond the need for such a rigid control over our citizenry nearly one hundred years ago. Each of our five Dukes governs their own regions under the auspices of King's Law—we have no need for Guilds or serfdom."

"Perhaps that is why you have such a problem with thieves and bandits," Risada commented tartly, and Rustam's mouth twitched as Yorth shook himself like a bird with ruffled plumage.

"That is an inconvenience we are addressing, Lady Risada. But as this is hardly the place to be discussing politics, I shall go and see what may be done to hasten our journey."

So saying, Yorth wrenched open the carriage door and stepped out. A sharp cry and a dull thud announced his somewhat unseemly meeting with the cobbled street as, in his haste to exit the coach, he had neglected to request the steps be folded out. A minor flurry of activity surrounded his prone form as troopers dismounted to assist him to his feet, and brush down the now thoroughly soiled court garb.

Rustam and Risada looked at each other, struggling to keep straight faces.

"Well," said Risada, letting the single word stretch out with a sustained exhalation. "That was a perfect example of the lack of civilisation in this goddess-forsaken country, wouldn't you agree, Rustam?"

"Quite," concurred Rustam, warmed by the comradely tone of her words. At the same time, he wondered what it would be like to live in a kingdom where one had the freedom to think and act for entirely selfish reasons. Before crossing the mountains he'd have expected anarchy but, aside from a few malcontents, it seemed to work. His gaze drifted past the vibrant yellow drapes to where their escort's mounts stamped and tossed their heads, the cold autumnal sun glinting off the burnished silver of their bits.

In fact, it seemed to work very well. When did one ever hear of a Tyr-enese displaying the originality required to develop something new?

* * * * * * * * * *

The diminutive embassy from Tyr-en entered King Graylin's Hall of Audiences via the smallest of six doors arranged at intervals along a huge arcing wall. Javed Yorth paused inside the door just long enough for his charges to be impressed by the magnificence of the structure before leading them onward. Rustam could almost forgive the dishevelled equerry that small conceit; the Hall was truly imposing.

The floor space of the quadrant shape was subdivided into coloured segments, one for each of the ruling Dukes, plus one tiny sliver of white marble along which he and Risada now trod. Rustam's eyes swivelled from side to side as they walked, noting the distribution of petitioners and court officials, each keeping strictly to their own colour coded sectors.

The saffron area to their left was the busiest, with upwards of fifty people milling near the point of the segment adjacent to the raised dais. The deep emerald space beyond was inhabited only by ten or so officials and a priest of Chel, startling against the rainbow hues of the floor in his silver-embroidered white robes. An empty expanse of violet furthest from them was marred only by one bored looking scribe seated upon a stool on the lowest of the dais's five broad steps.

The remaining ducal colours lay to Rustam's right; a deep ruby and a sombre shade of midnight blue, populated by a smattering of courtiers and scribes, all of whom appeared to be concluding their business for the day.

Two high-backed and heavily carved wooden thrones dominated the dais, one of them occupied. King Graylin of Kishtan was a man in his older years, his grey hair and beard streaked with white, but his striking blue eyes as they surveyed the Tyr-enese were as sharp as any youth's. Beneath his elaborate court robes Rustam's practised eye picked out the lines of a stocky yet powerful physique—the body of a soldier not yet gone soft with age.

Rustam's gaze was drawn to the screen behind the throne, hung with the Kishtanian flag—a rearing black horse against an ice blue background. He smiled as he thought how like Nightstalker it looked, and then stiffened, detecting the tiniest whisper of motion in the shadows beside the screen. It was almost lost amongst the vibrant background of huge historical tapestries draping the rear wall, but someone lurked there and Rustam knew it was only by chance he had spotted the movement.

"My Lady," he murmured into the cloud of her fragrant hair. "There is someone behind the screen." A slight twitch of her shoulders acknowledged his words and Rustam returned to his position one step behind her.

Reaching the bottom of the steps, Javed Yorth paused for a brief word with the scribe stationed there. Rustam searched the shadows but found nothing more than a deeper patch of darkness. Fear spiked through him as he remembered that this was not Tyr-en. Magic was an everyday tool in Kishtan, and whoever lurked there was probably blocking his sight. Rustam's fingers twitched, longing for the cool familiarity of a dagger hilt against his palm, but he restrained himself. He doubted that the guards stationed along the second step would stop to ask against whom he intended to use the weapon.

Yorth turned from his conversation with the scribe. "My Lady." He bowed deeply. "If you would please wait here until I have announced you to the king, you may then approach to the fourth step, your servant to the third. His Majesty acknowledges the importance of your visit by agreeing to receive you ahead of other petitioners."

The equerry bowed, and ascended the steps to the throne. As his nasal tones recited the list of Risada's titles, Rustam glanced to his left, at the disgruntled faces of those being displaced in the order of things, and was shocked to note that amongst the sumptuously robed courtiers and officials were a number of plain clothed peasants. Did the king of Kishtan actually speak with commoners? Yet the bizarre notion seemed somehow in keeping with this strange kingdom.

Then Risada was moving and Rustam found that three full strides were required between each step up. Comfortable level space upon which to fight, he noted automatically. He halted on the third step while Risada continued, and his senses sharpened as the distance between them widened. At this juncture the Lady of Domn was probably Tyr-en's only hope for deliverance from Melcard's treason, and Rustam felt very nervous having her beyond the protective reach of his dagger.

"My Lady of Tyr-en, be welcome."

King Graylin rose to his feet, revealing a thickly padded cushion on the seat of the wooden throne. Well, the monarch *was* old, and apparently spent lengthy stretches sitting there, listening to petitions—no doubt a great deal more than did Tyr-enese rulers, if he received commoners as well as nobles.

Risada bowed low and Rustam's breath caught as the red fabric stretched across her posterior, scant distance in front of his face. As she straightened, he drew a steadying lungful of air and shuffled a few steps to his left until her profile rather than her rear filled his vision. A tiny claw of guilt hooked itself into his innards—surely he should not feel this way about his sister? But, dammit, he was still struggling to come to terms with that revelation.

One side of Graylin's mouth quirked up, and he waved an open hand over the empty throne beside him. "Lady Risada," he said in a deeply rich, apologetic tone. "I am prepared to hear and consider your words. But, as you can see, my queen refuses to acknowledge your presence at all, and has counselled me against any dealings with your kingdom. I am sure you are aware that my wife is a princess of Shiva."

Rustam saw the slight stiffening of Risada's shoulders at much the same moment as his heart dropped into his stomach. A Shivan princess! While fully aware that Queen Keril was elven, somehow the minor detail of her lineage had been overlooked. Mentally, Rustam berated himself for missing such a vital piece of information—or was it just a telling example of how little attention Tyr-en paid to its neighbouring kingdoms, that their intelligence was so flawed.

They had escaped Melcard, crossed the mountains, braved trolls and nightmare creatures, survived not only each other's company but the onset of winter as well. But to what purpose? To discover that the Kishtanian queen whom they sought to win to their cause was not just any elf, but daughter of the Shivan king whom Tyr-en had assassinated during the final battle of the Wars! What terrible deed had earned them such disfavour with the goddess?

Rustam blinked, realised he had missed Risada's reply, and raised a hand to rub at his numb cheek. He wondered if whatever had scarred his face had damaged his mind also, for his usually reliable concentration seemed to be another casualty of this goddess-forsaken mission.

"—what else may I say to convince you, Majesty?" Risada said, and Rustam winced at the note of desperation.

"This situation may have no immediate consequences for your kingdom, but have no doubt—they will come."

King Graylin settled back to his throne, leaned his chin into his left palm and stroked his beard. Even from behind, Rustam could see the anguish that tore at Risada—the tautness across her shoulders, the rigidity in her arms as she no doubt clenched her fists across her flat stomach. An answering tension stabbed upward through Rustam's neck into the base of his skull and he forced himself to relax, flexing his muscles minutely to restore their efficiency.

Not that they should be in any danger here, in public, in the presence of the king. But Rustam no longer trusted his knowledge of Kishtanian society. The glaring omission of the queen's true parentage might be only a minor example of the gaps he now suspected riddled the Tyr-enese information net.

Suppose the queen had influenced her husband to the point of taking on the Shivan hatred of anything—or anyone—Tyr-enese?

Rustam's spine crawled at the thought of all those guards at his back.

And into that heart stopping moment of doubt, slipped the lurker behind the throne.

One second the space beside the king was empty. The next, a tall dark figure stood there, his mouth close beside Graylin's ear. The king's eyebrows lifted slightly at the whispered words.

Rustam frowned. There was something vaguely familiar about the secretive advisor. Even now the man did not turn to reveal his face to the outlanders, but Rustam knew beyond doubt that he kept watch upon them from behind his heavy fall of glossy black hair.

"Well, Lady Risada." Graylin sounded mildly amused. "It seems you have an unexpected advocate." His eyes flickered towards the motionless figure at his side.

Risada inclined her head towards the stranger. "You have me at a disadvantage, sir, but my deepest gratitude for your support."

She bowed again.

Several things happened all at once. As Risada inclined forward, so Shamnac's talisman slipped from concealment between her breasts, swinging forward on its leather thong like a fortune-teller's pendulum. The dark advisor moved so swiftly from his monarch's side that he ensnared Risada's wrists before she had a chance to react to his approach, and Rustam flung himself across the intervening space to bring his dagger point beneath the stranger's chin, scant moments before they were all surrounded by a ring of drawn swords.

"Stay!" Graylin barked, and the guards took a reluctant step back. The man holding Risada's wrists seemed oblivious to Rustam's knife at his throat, intent instead upon the swaying talisman.

"Where did you get thisss?" he demanded in a sibilant whisper heavy with the promise of death. It belatedly occurred to Rustam that the man had done something he himself had never achieved: caught Risada unawares.

Not easily intimidated, Risada stared icily past her captor to the king's throne. "Is this how you treat foreign ambassadors in Kishtan?" she demanded.

"Chelmod," ordered Graylin quietly. "Release the Lady."

With a growl that rumbled from deep within his chest, the advisor freed Risada's wrists and, almost as an afterthought, batted Rustam's dagger aside with a casual strength that jarred Rustam's arm all the way to his shoulder. The dark head turned towards him and for the first time Rustam had a clear view of the man's strong, smooth face, dominated by a pair of glaring emerald eyes.

Werecat~~s~~ eyes.

"I will ask you again, Lady: where did you get thiss?" It was almost a snarl.

"If it is any of your business," Risada said frostily, "It was a gift."

The werecat looked perplexed. "The symbol of a *pahn* is not a thing to gift to outlanders, yet you speak the truth. How sso?"

Rustam could feel Risada's confusion. He recalled that she had no knowledge of the truthsaying gift, so he intervened.

"The one who gifted the talisman was in debt to us for his life. We freed him from the captivity of a troll pack."

The slitted green eyes widened and the advisor exchanged a startled glance with his ruler, a glance which stretched into a silent exchange redolent with hidden meaning and shared history.

At length, King Graylin rose to his feet. "Lady Risada, we will meet with you as you ask," he said. "And I shall endeavour to persuade my wife of your sincerity. You have certainly convinced me."

* * * * * * * * *

Hesta, the larger of the twin moons, had set early that night over Darshan, capital city of Tyr-en. Now her smaller sister, Vana, rode low in the sky, her pallid light casting deep shadows across the shrub-filled palace gardens. The last lingering scents of autumn flowers hung in the still, cool air, corrupted by the metallic taint of blood.

Dench stood at his accustomed post, beside the private entrance to Prince Halnashead's apartments. He stared at the back of his hand, turning it this way and that in the jaundiced moonlight. Was that a bloodstain? Unable to decide, he scrubbed at it with his other sleeve, belatedly noticing the dampness of the fabric and remembered that he had already used the dark cloth to wipe the slim blade of his stiletto.

Curse Chel and her warped sense of humour!

He peered into the darkness beneath the bushes, at the darker patch of shadow that lay motionless there, and swore again. He would have to do something about that smell before the watch next passed his position.

He cast about for an answer. Then he had it. The gardens were being prepared for the onset of winter, and several nearby borders were redolent with the rich smell of fresh mulch. With a last glance to check that he was still alone, Dench hurried on tip toe across the damp grass, hoping that his footprints would vanish in the morning with the dew. He scooped up a double handful of the moist compost and proceeded to spread it over and around the still warm body. Several trips later he had succeeded in his goal and the garden's fragrance was restored.

Dench straightened his aching back and wiped his dirty hands on his tunic. He studied the concealing bushes, checking that nothing would catch the eye of the patrolling guards—no glimmer of buckle or sword, no pale patch of skin. Nothing. He was safe for the moment.

He tucked the message tube that had sealed the courier's fate into a pocket. It was too dark to read, but Halnashead's most trusted servant had a fairly shrewd idea of the contents, and of their importance to the prince's defence plans.

What he didn't know was how this messenger had managed to evade the Bastard's troops and the roving Tylocian cut-throats. The man must have been very, very good at his job.

Shame for him then, that at the last, believing himself to be in friendly territory, he had let down his defences. The expression on his face when Dench's blade had slipped between his ribs had been one of such complete disbelief, the traitor guard had almost felt compelled to explain his motives. But death had closed his grip so fast no words had been needed.

Regret overtook Dench. Not that he had killed the messenger, but that it had happened here, within the palace grounds. Never in all the years he had been playing this double game had he been forced into such a clumsy solution, and he strongly resented the complications it forced upon him.

As the lanterns of the regular patrol bobbed round the corner and towards him Dench raised a hand in greeting, but his mind was already running ahead. When the watch was gone he would have to be swift in accomplishing his next task—that of moving the body to a safer location. He needed a breathing space in which to think upon the most suitable—and least traceable—method of final disposal.

19. SILVER LIGHT

Risada fumed all night at the delay, alternately pacing the vine-draped hall, then standing in the open doorway to stare morosely out at the heavy rain beating into the puddles in the courtyard. The red gleam of the devotional lamp beside her shoulder refracted across the flooded cobblestones to form a ceaselessly shifting mosaic, like some direful foretelling of blood soon to be spilled.

Sometime in the early hours Rustam left her to her vigil and retired. They had been offered accommodations within the palace but Risada had declined, not yet ready to allow them sight of Elwaes. Rustam was not certain how the lady planned to use their 'gift', or if she had even made a decision yet.

As he traipsed back to the room he shared with the elf, Rustam reflected uneasily upon the way that the events of this mission seemed to be dovetailing together—almost as if someone or something was using them as pieces in a giant puzzle, slotting them into their appropriate positions in a pattern too vast for him to see.

Rustam scowled. It was one thing to call yourself a player in a game over which you had some measure of control; quite another to be an unwitting pawn in someone else's obscure machinations.

He paused outside the door and took a couple of deep breaths, cleansing his mind of disquieting thoughts, aware by now that even his vague sense of anxiety could be enough to disturb the sensitive elf. Only when he had achieved the calmness he sought did he slip into the room and ease the door shut behind him. He turned—and stopped, frozen with shock.

A faint aureole of silver light danced around the Shivan's head, shimmering in his pale hair and highlighting the gauntness of his delicate face.

Guts twisting with fear, Rustam forced himself to step closer. But even as his rigid muscles creaked into action, the light faded away until he was left wondering if he had imagined the whole thing.

He shook his head, and his stomach slowly unknotted. Despite all the strange experiences and endless doubts that plagued him nowadays, Rustam remained certain of one thing: his senses were still as keen as ever. What seemed to have changed was his perception of those senses, and once he overcame the brief, paralysing moment of panic, he reasoned that what he had just seen was not illusion, but evidence that the acuity of his vision was changing, enabling him to see far more truly than before.

What the light meant, however, was another matter entirely.

Storing it away as yet another thing to ask Elwaes when time permitted, Rustam lowered his somewhat shaken self onto the hard board that passed for a bed, closed his eyes and tried to sleep.

The haunted restlessness he achieved gave him little relief, for his dreams were filled with silver shadows and gigantic hands reaching out to caress his face with fire. He woke breathless and drenched in cold sweat in the early light of an overcast grey dawn.

Leaving the sleeping elf undisturbed, he shrugged on a thick velvet cloak and made his way down to the refectory. A mug of marshflower tea was thrust into his chilled fingers by an elderly son of Chel and he sipped it gratefully, savouring the feeling as the hot liquid trickled slowly through his icy guts. Still shivering from his dreams, he chose a bench in the inglenook beside the banked log fire and by the time he felt able to face the world again, Risada had joined him, taking the seat opposite. As the refectory slowly began to fill with the grey robed children of Chel, and the air became heavy with the salty smell of cured meat, they continued to sit together in a silence that spoke to Rustam more clearly of their shared concerns than any words could have done.

Eventually Risada stirred and lifted her face. Even the dullness of the rain-washed morning did little to disguise the dark rings framing her blue eyes, or the half suppressed dread that lurked behind them. Rustam felt the blood rise to his cheeks, and glanced away embarrassed—surely he should not be seeing such blatant emotion in the eyes of Dart, the Royal assassin.

Then a cold flush extinguished the heat beneath his skin. Could this be another aspect of his burgeoning magical abilities, to see into the hearts of others without their consent?

Goddess! What must others see in him?

He focused on Risada's small hand where it lay in her lap, the grime of their journey ground into the pattern of her skin well beyond the ability of any mere washing to remove. Her once beautiful nails were raggedly torn, and two were edged with half healed scabs where hangnails had torn away. On impulse Rustam reached over, placed his palm across the slender fingers and, when she neither struck him nor threatened him, he found the courage to look into her eyes.

"I'm sure Iain will be fine," he murmured.

Her eyes rounded in surprise. "Actually, I was thinking of Marten," she confessed. "He's so young to be King, yet he shows so much promise. If we should fail..."

"We won't! They cannot deny what we say. Even Graylin's own truthsayer vouches for us."

Risada snatched her hand from under his. "*Truthsayer*? You mean you knew there was magic involved and you didn't think to enlighten me?"

Rustam glanced away, nettled that such a lovely and intelligent woman could be so stubbornly prejudiced. His eyes focussed on the early morning bustle of the refectory yet little registered other than the approach of a short, stout daughter bearing a steaming platter of food in each beefy hand. His stomach growled in emphasis of his irritation.

"Does it really do any harm when it aids our cause?" he demanded of Risada.

The Lady of Domn frowned, and he could see her mulling over the idea. She gave absent thanks for the plate of food that was thrust into her hands and when the woman was gone she reached her decision with a short, sharp toss of her head. "No, it doesn't. It's up to us to use any tools available to complete the task before us. But be warned, Rustam—magic will not be tolerated when we return to Tyr-en, no matter how useful. And it seems to me that you are embracing the concept with rather too much ease. I believe you have been too long in Elwaes's company."

She sounded worried, as if Rustam's future was of concern to her. *Did her warning mean she had recanted her decision to kill him upon their return home?*

Risada paused in thought a moment, and then continued.

"No matter. That part of our mission is almost over. Please ask Elwaes to join us today." A spasm of anxiety marred her face for a brief instant.

"And Rustam—"

"My Lady?"

"Do your best to convince him that his support of our cause could help save many lives, not all of them Tyr-enese."

She glanced down at the plate of food on her lap and began pushing a piece of meat around with her fork. Rustam smiled tightly. "I see. You want me to appeal to his Shivan reverence for life in all forms, regardless of what's been done to him?"

"No!" Risada dropped the fork with a clatter. Her gaze locked with Rustam's and he recoiled, startled by the intensity in her eyes. "Because of it. Such a hideous perversion should never be permitted to recur."

Rustam raised his eyebrows in genuine surprise. Risada stared defiantly back, and then shook her head slowly from side to side. "Does it amaze you so much that I should care? I still have some feelings, despite what you think of me."

Rustam put a strip of salted meat in his mouth and chewed thoughtfully before replying. "I don't really know what you expect me to think," he said. "Aside from your brother, I thought the only thing you cared about was the preservation of Tyr-en."

Risada frowned. "That is what we're here for, isn't it? But that doesn't preclude our solution being of benefit to others. Who knows how grateful they could be in the future?"

Rustam slammed his fork down on his plate with such force that several strips of meat bounced into the air, before dropping into the fire and sizzling in a merry counterpoint to the crackling logs.

"I knew it!" he exclaimed as he watched the remainder of his breakfast incinerate itself. "There had to be a motive in there somewhere! Altruism would be a hard character trait to reconcile with the rest of your personality."

"That's not fair!" Risada protested. "This is duty we're talking about. Of course it would be wonderful to benefit others if we can, but the survival of Tyr-en must come first—and that doesn't mean just now. We need to secure our future too."

She studied him with a worried expression. "Rustam, I shouldn't need to tell you this. Is something the matter with you?"

Rustam lifted his shoulders in a slight shrug. "I really don't know," he began, on the verge of confessing the turmoil of doubts and confusions that had plagued him of late. But on the edge of his vision he saw her slender fingers clutching the table knife, and his mind flashed with the image of another knife in that hand—a short, deadly blade with an emerald encrusted hilt—and he stopped himself. He shrugged again. "I'm sorry."

"Never mind," said Risada in soothing tones, and to complete Rustam's profound sense of confusion, she placed her hand on top of his and gave it a friendly squeeze. "I'm sure that once we're away from this Kingdom and its insidiously subversive magic, everything will get back to normal for you." She favoured him with a sympathetic smile, then rose to her feet and gazed down at him. "Now be a good player," she commanded. "Go have that word with Elwaes."

And she swept away along the aisle, leaving Rustam staring speechless after her.

* * * * * * * * * * *

King Graylin received them in a room that appeared to Rustam uncannily like Halnashead's study. The sombre deep red of the walls was offset by the fantastically carved ceiling decorated in white with accents of gold, and the room smelled strongly of warm leather and ondal oil, with an overlying hint of the rich spices that seemed to cling to everything Kishtanian. Numerous chairs and small tables littered the floor space, while the room was dominated by a huge wooden desk positioned prominently before a tapestry of gigantic proportions.

As they entered, Graylin rose from his seat behind the desk and Rustam found that even the king's strong presence was overshadowed by the dark scene depicted so vividly upon the wall hanging. Unlike its Tyr-enese counterpart, the illustrations so painstakingly stitched onto this canvas portrayed the last days before the mass exodus of the Crossing. Indiscriminate death bled freely in scarlet silk against a background of orange fire and charcoal rubble as the two warring sides unleashed the ultimate in their arcane arsenals.

Even Risada's attention was captured by the horrors so graphically displayed and Graylin, apparently used to such a reaction, waited until they had stared their fill before moving around the desk and leading them to a group of chairs near the centre of the room. The king sat, inviting them to join him.

Elwaes sat down heavily in the nearest chair and Rustam worriedly searched the Shivan's waxen face, trying to pry out of the closed expression some hint of the familiarity he had been convinced existed between them.

Until this morning.

From the moment Rustam had arrived back in their room dutifully prepared to carry out Risada's orders, he had known something had changed. Whatever it was, and if it was connected in any way to the silver glow he had seen during the night, the elf was not saying, but the rapport that had been there was gone.

As if it had been merely a figment of Rustam's imagination.

Elwaes seemed more alien now than he had even in that first eye contact in Melcard's dungeon. Then, he had seemed strange but pitiful, little more than a helpless victim of the more brutal side of the Tyr-enese game.

Now? Rustam struggled to identify the change. Now, he seemed aloof. Not arrogant, exactly, but somehow distanced. As if his existence had moved onto another plane, one that shared mere points of coincidence with the physical world.

And Rustam was filled with the aching emptiness of a loss he could not define.

Risada moved between them and Rustam automatically held her chair while she seated herself and took elaborate care to smooth all the wrinkles from the clinging fabric of her dark green gown. While she performed this ritual, Rustam took the opportunity to study the room until he found Graylin's advisor. The werecat stood motionless, hidden in the shadows cast by the heavy window drapes. Even at that distance there was no disguising the curiosity that gleamed in his emerald eyes as he studied the silent elf. Graylin's face too, betrayed a host of unvoiced questions, suppressed for the moment by the niceties of political and social form.

"My wife will join us shortly," the king informed them. "She insisted on personally overseeing our daughter's first lesson in arcane control. She was a teacher for so long herself she has trouble believing anyone else can do it correctly."

Beside Rustam, Risada shifted uneasily and threw a quick glance to her left, towards the tapestry.

"Perhaps you wonder, Lady Risada, why we keep a reminder of such horror, and yet permit the practice of magic to continue."

"The thought had crossed my mind," Risada said.

Graylin stood and re-crossed the room to his desk. He placed his hands onto the polished wood and leaned there, studying the terrible scenes with an air of intense concentration, as though searching for something lost in the wreckage of a devastated continent. Finally, without turning from his contemplation, he said: "We do so because magic is no more or less a tool than fire. It is not the tool that is the danger, but those who wield it. And that," he turned to face them again, "is why we permit its use, though only under the strictest of controls. Forgive me if I offend you, but to pretend magic does not exist is sheerest folly, as I have no doubt your kingdom will one day realise. I trust that revelation will not be in such barbarous terms as you see here."

"Your Majesty, we don't put our heads under water," Risada replied. "We do not ignore the existence of magic. We simply prohibit its use."

At that moment the study doors crashed together with a resounding thud that startled even Chelmod from immobility. Rustam's mouth twitched into its lopsided smile as out of the corner of his eye he saw the werecat shake himself, lick one palm and smooth it over his disarrayed hair.

A new voice entered the conversation. "And do you honestly believe you are successful in doing so?" asked Queen Keril, her voice laced with derision.

Rustam and Risada rose hurriedly to greet Graylin's consort. Rustam knew it could be no other from the moment he set eyes upon the woman's tall, slender frame, for although the soft clouds of pale blonde hair cascading around her shoulders hid the tell-tale backswept ears, there was no disguising the delicate bone structure of her exquisite face.

The ice blue of her gown echoed the eyes that regarded them with open hostility as they made obeisance. A fractional inclination of her head provided them with the barest acknowledgement that was all the pride Kishtan's elven queen was willing to sacrifice to propriety. However, her decorum deserted her as she stepped close enough to see the yet seated third member of their party.

"*Elwaes*?" The queen's voice rose. "Is it really you?"

"Keril?" Elwaes shot to his feet, his wan face animated with such joy that Rustam was awed by his fierce beauty. The two elves stared at each other for a brief moment before falling into an embrace that excluded all others. Even the king looked surprised by his wife's actions, and Rustam concluded that Queen Keril was not normally given to such demonstrative behaviour. In fact, he mused, her sylph-like body looked almost too frail to encompass such verve.

Finally the queen returned her attention to the others and, keeping a possessive arm around Elwaes's shoulders, she demanded of her husband: "Why didn't you tell me?"

Graylin spread his hands wide. "Had I known, I would have summoned you immediately, but there was no mention of a Shivan yesterday." He turned to the Tyr-enese. "Perhaps you would care to explain, Lady Risada."

But even as Risada opened her mouth, Elwaes cut in. "My apologies, your Majesty, the fault was mine. My health, as you can perhaps see, is not at its best. I was in need of an apothecary's services yesterday, and was unfit to be presented to your court."

Risada exchanged an astonished glance with Rustam who shrugged his shoulders minutely. Elwaes was full of surprises today.

King Graylin leaned forward, polite concern on his face. "My dear fellow, you have no need to apologise. I trust you are feeling better now?"

"Of course he's not," snapped Queen Keril, her temper at odds with her manner as she gently pushed Elwaes back down to his chair. "Graylin, you've seen enough elves by now to know that not even the eldest amongst us look as pale as this. Chelmod, a word."

The werecat glided silently to his mistress's side. While she gave him quietly voiced instructions, Rustam exchanged another glance with Risada. He knew they were thinking the same thing: just who was the real ruler of this kingdom?

He studied the king's face as the monarch silently watched his wife. There, Rustam found at least part of the answer: Graylin was hopelessly in love with his beautiful, independent Shivan wife.

And who could blame him, Rustam asked himself. She was truly lovely. Strong and full of fire, yet so ethereal he almost expected her to dissolve into mist and blow away on the breeze like the sprite.

Like the sprite.

Warning tremors crawled up Rustam's spine. Queen Keril was an elf, and that meant magic. Just how much of the king's infatuation was real, and how much controlled by his consort? They could be putting Tyr-en into even graver danger by revealing the kingdom's current weakness to a far deadlier enemy than that it already faced. Who knew how many elves still existed in their hidden realm, or how many held positions of influence in the human world the way this Shivan woman did?

Perhaps the army they sought to bring to Tyr-en's aid would turn into an invading force once Melcard was defeated.

He could almost feel the concurrent passage of thoughts through Risada's mind, so he was not surprised when she moved to take control of the situation.

"Your Majesty," she began, deliberately ignoring the queen who was just dispatching Chelmod about his errand. "I apologise most sincerely if I appear impatient, but our situation cannot tolerate delay. We need your decision."

"And, Lady Risada, you shall have it soon," King Graylin assured her, clearly not willing to be rushed. After all, Risada was asking for the loan of fifteen hundred men—over half of Kishtan's royal guard—and while the kingdom was presently at peace, no one could predict when trouble might erupt.

Graylin turned to his wife. "Keril, my dear, tell us how it is that you know Master—?"

"Elwaes," supplied the queen as she put a hand on the shoulder of the one so named, and smiled such a bittersweet smile that Rustam's throat tightened in response.

Goddess, but these Shivans were achingly beautiful.

"Forgive me, husband, but you know how little store my people set by protocol."

"I should do by now," sighed the king.

Keril smiled again and this time it was all for Graylin—a look of such adoration that Rustam was forced to revise his earlier suspicions. In his profession, he saw all manner of brilliantly executed deceptions by the accomplished actresses most unfaithful wives became. This, in his reluctant opinion, had all the marks of real love.

"Devim," began the queen, putting a comforting hand on her countryman's shoulder, "was Elwaes's brother."

"Oh, Keril, my love."

The depth of compassion in the king's voice so commanded Rustam's attention that he nearly missed Elwaes's reaction. Pale and ill though he looked, the elf who had survived so much had never seemed aged. Now his shoulders sagged and his face crumpled, leaving him looking like a wizened old man.

"Was...?" he whispered.

Queen Keril knelt before him, tears shining in her pale blue eyes. "I'm sorry, Elwaes, Devim is dead." She bowed her head and the blonde veil of her hair swung forward to hide her face. Rustam strained to hear her words.

"He died saving my life, that I might deliver *Rhesmett* safely back into Shiva."

"Then, it is done?"

Elwaes's question was awed, though whether inspired by the action or the subject, Rustam could not be certain. What he did know, was they were talking of a legend, of *Rhesmett*, a sword—a *Shiva* blade—said to be imbued with the spirit of its wielder such that it had taken on a life of its own. A sword no one chose to face unless they wished for certain death.

A weapon that had almost changed the outcome of the final battle of the Shivan Wars until the traitor planted by the Tyr-enese within Shiva had stolen the sword from their king and slipped a dagger between the monarch's ribs.

King Rhe. Keril's father.

Rustam and Risada exchanged a hopeless glance. It seemed that whatever they did, no matter their motivation or their belief in the justness of their cause, *something* was out to stop them.

An argent glow lit Elwaes's eyes and he clutched the queen's hand so abruptly she started.

"Keril, you must help these people."

"But—" she began, and then paused and looked closely into the other elf's face. After a moment of intense silence, she bowed her head. "It is the will of the goddess," she said, and looked round at the king. "Husband, you have my blessing for this venture."

"Well then, Lady Risada, it seems you have your answer," said Graylin. "Preparations will begin immediately."

Rustam bowed a fraction of a second after Risada, his mind frozen in shock. As he straightened, he schooled his features to calm acceptance. A sidelong glance showed Risada doing the same.

What the hell just happened?

Queen Keril remained on her knees before Elwaes, eyes locked as though nothing beyond them mattered. Rustam's memory fled back to his first encounter with Elwaes's gaze, in Melcard's odorous dungeon. His stomach lurched as he relived how his surroundings had receded to leave the Shivan's silver blue eyes the only point of reality in a world turned the black of non-existence.

That same silver hue shone from the elf's eyes now as then—the same as those of the monster who had maimed Rustam.

The eyes of the demon Charin.

* * * * * * * * * *

Rustam was relieved to escape the king's study without being subjected to Elwaes's attention. The gentle elf he had grown to consider a friend was gone. Had been gone since last night if his guess was not mistaken.

And now they were committed to accepting the offer of help *he* had endorsed.

"I must say, Rustam, I am impressed."

Startled out of reverie, it took Rustam a moment to comprehend Risada's words and when he had, he shook his head in denial. "That was none of my doing. I spoke with him as you asked, but he barely heard a word I said, much less acknowledged them."

"Nevertheless, he secured Kishtan's aid for us when nothing we might have said would have held any weight."

"But—" began Rustam, then stopped. How could he explain his suspicions to Risada? He had never shared with her his experience on the mountainside, in the entrance to the creeper burrow, much less the words of the healer. How was he now to convince her, on the dubious evidence of subtle fluctuations in Elwaes's eye colour, that the elf's assistance should be rejected, when it was giving them the very thing they had travelled all this way to secure?

He canted a glance at Risada and knew he had lost the argument before even making it. Her gaze was leagues away, on the far side of the Middle Mountains, back in Tyr-en. She would be planning how best to bring her newly acquired troops to Marten's aid, and perhaps anticipating her return to her own family's estates and to the side of her brother, Iain.

How ironic, thought Rustam in defeat. *For the first time since I have known her, Risada trusts something. She believes this is truly the answer to all our problems.*

And I? I would have trusted Elwaes with my life.

How much simpler life was back in Tyr-en, where his only concern was avoiding the undesirable attentions of other players and jealous husbands. At least there you could be sure of trusting no one except the master you served.

The doors of the palace swung open to permit them egress and the two Tyr-enese descended the steps to the waiting carriage, their cloaks gripped tightly against the thick, wet snow that splattered against the cobbles with the sound of over-ripe fruit striking the ground.

20. DESPERATION

After two days of steadily laying snow, the two Tyr-enese stood again in King Graylin's well heated study. Risada's expression, however, reflected none of the warmth of the huge log fire. Anguish and betrayal sat openly on her face—genuine, intense emotions that Rustam would have been shocked to see back in Tyr-en, before their journey. He knew the time they had spent together had scored great changes into his life, and wondered briefly if those changes were as easily visible upon him as they were on the face of the Lady of Domn.

"What do you mean, we can't return to our Kingdom?" demanded Risada. "You have no right to hold us here. And you pledged your troops—"

"Lady Risada!" the king broke into her angry tirade. "You misunderstand. And you presume a great deal to speak to us so."

"But you gave your word!"

"And my word is still good. This is none of my doing—it is the weather that has closed the passes, not I. You simply *cannot* reach Tyr-en."

Rustam moved out of Risada's way as she began to pace the length of the hearth. Her measured steps took him back to simpler times when he had watched Halnashead pace his way through so many problems. Invariably the solutions generated had been startlingly brilliant.

And what solutions do you find now, my prince? Rustam wondered in sinking despair. *No matter how wily the schemes you might concoct, nothing can save you against a force the size of Melcard's. At least, nothing short of this army which we cannot bring to your aid until too late.*

Risada halted. "Surely it will thaw?" she asked of Graylin, a raw edge to her voice. "It's too soon in the season for this to be permanent."

"That may be so," agreed the king gently, "but winter has come early this year. It would be the act of a desperate or a foolish man to risk the lives of so many on what is, at best, a slender hope."

"But we *are* desperate!"

"Lady Risada, I am sorry. My people would never support such an undertaking, nor would I be the king they deserve, should I order them to a mission with so little chance of success, not to mention survival."

Risada lifted her pale, tightly drawn face to Graylin's, her eyes filled with disdain. "So," she observed bitterly. "It is you who are ruled by your people, not them by you." So saying, she turned her back on the king and grated: "Kishtan truly is an uncivilised kingdom."

Rustam's breath stopped in his throat. Even in defeat he would not have expected Risada to resort to petty insults unless she was deliberately trying to goad the king into action. It was certainly one of her tactics that Rustam knew intimately.

Surely Graylin could not let such affront go unpunished? From where he stood, Rustam could see the glowing green of Chelmod's eyes in the shadows beside the window drapes, fixed keenly upon the monarch who could unleash his deadly speed. Rustam doubted even Risada, with all her assassin's skills, would find herself a match for an angry werecat.

With a sinking feeling of inevitability, Rustam twitched his hidden daggers loose from their wrist sheaths. He had no wish to die, and particularly not for the sake of a comment apparently born of frustration. But Risada was Halnashead's cousin, and Rustam's own sister if she had the truth of it, and if this was to be the way of it, who was he to argue with the vagaries of the goddess?

Strange though—he had always considered himself favoured of Chel.

Perhaps he had presumed upon that favour too much. He drew a breath in preparation of shifting his time sense—

Graylin gave the tiniest shake of his head. He'd had no need to meet the werecat's eyes, and in that one tiny movement he completely defused the tension in the room. He gazed with pity upon Risada's stiff back.

"My Lady of Tyr-en, do you truly believe it uncivilised to put the needs of the people ahead of those of the monarch? Here in Kishtan we would consider it barbaric to do anything but."

Risada's shoulders slumped in defeat. "We think so differently. It's hard to believe we all spring from the same origin."

King Graylin shook his head. "All we have done in Kishtan is to move forward from the starting point, while you try to preserve it unchanged."

"We see no need to tamper with an order that we know to work."

The Lady of Domn turned to face the king. "I did not come here to debate politics with you, your Majesty. If you cannot help us, I must seek those who can. On behalf of King Marten, I thank you for the time you have so graciously given."

She inclined her head to Graylin and turned towards the door, making precisely three steps in that direction before it swung open and Queen Keril entered, accompanied by Elwaes.

Though still pale, Rustam nevertheless thought their former travelling companion looked healthier than at any time during their acquaintance. His eyes were their old blue, and the clothes helped—similar in shade to those selected for him by Risada, these were of the correct proportion for his lanky frame, making him appear less alien. No doubt they belonged to another elf. He looked so normal that Rustam began to question all his doubts of three days before.

"Leaving already?" enquired the queen with an acerbic bite to her tone.

"There seems little point remaining," Risada replied evenly. "I have failed in my task here, and although I see no alternatives at present, I cannot just give up and watch my kingdom fall to a self-serving murderous sadist."

Queen Keril searched Risada's face, and then glanced aside at Elwaes before bowing her head slightly in apology. "Forgive me, Lady Risada, if I seem to judge you harshly. Being Shivan, I find no sympathy for Tyr-en within my heart. Yet you demonstrate a loyalty and compassion for your kingdom that I am forced to admire."

A wordless silence stretched uneasily while Risada and the elven queen regarded each other. Finally the Lady of Domn glanced down. "Your Majesty is too kind," she said in a neutral tone.

"Kindness has little to do with honesty, my dear. And vice-versa. Perhaps one day you will be blessed with an understanding of this."

Risada's face hardened. "The only blessing I want now is one that will free this land of winter and allow me to take the troops I was promised to save my kingdom."

"That, I am afraid, seems unlikely."

In the awkward silence that followed, a bright, shining idea stabbed Rustam through the heart. A wild idea.

A crazy idea.

He turned to Elwaes, put a wary hand on the elf's arm and drew him aside, searching his pale blue eyes for any hint of metallic gleam.

"Rusty, I am truly sorry," said Elwaes, his guileless gaze as clear and open as an empty sky.

"Sorry enough to help us?" Rustam asked, his heart pounding.

Was he insane?

Perhaps. But they were out of options and, given Elwaes's support, this offered a slim chance for success. Although the friendship they had formed during the journey seemed little more than a memory now, and Rustam knew he would never completely trust the elf again he felt that, as long as their goals continued to coincide, he was willing to work with the Shivan. He would just keep a close watch on the colour of his eyes.

Now, those eyes looked back at him in confusion. Rustam said nothing more, merely observed as the elf's expression changed from bewilderment to shocked comprehension, then disbelief.

"Rusty, do you know what you are asking?"

"Yes, Rustam," broke in another voice. "Do enlighten us."

Risada and their hosts were studying him intently. Rustam was not even sure which of them had spoken. He drew a steadying breath.

"We need to return to Tyr-en, together with the troops you have so kindly offered." He bowed his head to Graylin. "We need to do it now, yet the mountains are impassable until spring. Which leaves us with one alternative."

He studied three blank faces.

"If we cannot go over the mountains, then we must go through them."

Risada's brow furrowed, but after a moment's startlement, Kishtan's rulers glanced askance at each other. *They* understood what he was proposing.

Queen Keril shook her head. "Absolutely not. Even if it were possible, my people would never sanction such an invasion. And certainly not to aid Tyr-en."

"Not an invasion, your Majesty," Rustam argued. "Merely a brief inconvenience."

The queen's face took on an obstinate cast, and Rustam searched his mind for any arguments he might use. In the end, his only recourse was to turn to Elwaes.

"If ever our friendship truly existed, then for the sake of it, please, help me now. Even if you won't do it for us, then for yourself. You want revenge, and if we leave it until spring, Melcard will be out of reach of anything short of war."

Rustam glanced at the faces around him: Graylin neutral, Keril opposed, Elwaes torn between his loyalty to his people and his desire for vengeance.

And Risada's eyes gazing back at him from the depths of two dark pits of horror as she comprehended exactly what he was suggesting.

Shiva.

The elves' magical homeland that existed within the mountains, yet at the same time somewhere else altogether. Rustam proposed to enter Shiva through one of the Gates on this side of the mountains, and exit from another on the Tyr-enese side. Always supposing that such a one still existed. Neither elf had said it did not, so hope remained.

Voice strained with anguish as he reached his decision, Elwaes asked of the queen, "Could it be done?"

She regarded him with sad eyes, clearly understanding his choice. "I honestly do not know. But even if it were possible, the council would never endorse such a plan."

"Then I must convince them otherwise."

There was a moment of quiet, and Rustam was aware of a rapport between the Shivans, something passing between them without the need for words. He realised with a tiny jolt that he was jealous of that closeness. What must it be like to know someone so well that you could tell their innermost thoughts and feelings without having to resort to the clumsiness of speech? He could only imagine, and hope that one day there would be someone like that for him.

Queen Keril faced her husband. "It seems I shall be going away for a while."

"Keril!" Elwaes raised a hand in negation. "There's no need for you to come—this is not your mission."

The queen's lips curved wistfully. "Yet for the love of your brother, Devim, who laid down his life for me, I will."

"Your Majesty," Elwaes appealed to Graylin. "Tell her she is needed here."

King Graylin smiled fondly at his wife, and then winked at her countryman. "I think we could manage without her Majesty for a while." He reached out a hand and fingered a strand of Keril's long hair. "Perhaps the royal tutors will be able for once to get on with the education of our children without fear of interruption."

"Graylin!"

The monarch held up his hands. "I withdraw that statement. But it has been too long since you visited your homeland, not since Sabina was born. She and Irvan will be content; they have the finest tutors in all Five Kingdoms, and I managed to rule Kishtan alone for many years before you came into my life. Go with my blessing, and take my love to your own king and queen."

Keril stepped close to Graylin, bent slightly—Rustam truly appreciated for the first time how very tall she was—and kissed him. "Husband," she said. "I love you. Have Chelmod take good care of you."

"As he has done all my life," said the king before turning his attention to the Tyr-enese. "You will be summoned when the queen is ready to leave." He sought Rustam's gaze. "I only hope you know what you are doing: Shivans have long memories and they make extremely dangerous foes."

"Your Majesty," Rustam said, "I have no idea at all, but this is something we must try, or die in the attempt. We can do no less for our kingdom."

And for Halnashead, he added silently.

"Then I commend your loyalty and your courage. May Chel's blessing go with you."

* * * * * * * * * *

In the corridor outside Graylin's study, Risada put a hand on Rustam's arm. "Rustam, I couldn't follow all the nuances, but I'm not wrong am I—you are proposing we travel into Shiva itself?"

"I am," he agreed, and was rewarded with a sudden painful stab of conscience. His outrageous idea had changed so swiftly from proposal to agreed course of action, he had given no thought to the terrors it might hold for one as magic-phobic as Risada.

There really was no other choice, and Risada was strong; she had faced death many times.

But Rustam knew it wasn't the life-threatening fears, but the little ones that nibbled constantly at the edges of the mind that were so hard to endure. He studied Risada's white face, her stiff posture. And the determined thrust of her jaw.

Risada would survive.

If only he had the courage to match. It was painfully clear to Rustam that his suggestion had been generated by fear. Not for himself—his life was insignificant in the greater scheme of things—but for Tyr-en itself, and especially for Halnashead. Without Halnashead the Kingdom would fragment into a melee of warring Houses.

Given time, Marten would be adequate to the task, perhaps even good at it. But he was still many solstices short of the coaching and experience he needed, and it was Halnashead he needed for that guidance.

Risada merely nodded and led the way back to the guest apartments they now occupied within the palace.

* * * * * * * * * * *

Doctor Hensar allowed himself the luxury of a satisfied smile. A stiff breeze whipped his cloak around his legs and spatters of cold rain clung to his face and hair, but physical discomfort was far down his list of considerations as he watched the body bounce and twist as it dragged behind the galloping horse.

Druldar, the last remaining Rees-Charlay male aside from Lord Melcard, had met his match. Over the past several years Hensar had watched Melcard's cousin closely, had even formed a grudging respect for the scheming noble. Druldar would almost certainly have made a far more formidable Family Senior than Melcard, but that was how things went. Accidents of birth and all that.

Hensar looked back towards the dark patch of woodland from which the bolting horse had emerged. Beneath those ancient trees, Druldar's guard lay with their throats cut, courtesy of two Tylocian war bands. Under normal conditions, the mountain men would have been trying to kill each other. Today, those fierce warriors were united in fear for their respective clan members held hostage by the Bastard.

They would do anything to get their women back.

Beyond the trees rose the Middle Mountains. Majestic and impassable in their white shrouds, winter had finally accomplished what Hensar himself had been unable to do: remove the threat posed by Halnashead's agents. Nothing now could cross those ranges before spring, and by then the Bastard would be securely on the throne.

Hensar permitted himself one more smile then turned his back on the open countryside and climbed back into his carriage with a shudder. The outside world always made him feel vulnerable in a way nothing else could.

He slammed the door shut and settled back into the cushions as the vehicle creaked into motion, taking him back to an environment over which he had far more control.

* * * * * * * * * * *

The wind found its way through the many layers of Rustam's garments with the same ease as had the sprite. He shivered, and gazed around the bare, rocky landscape, but no streams flowed down this bleak hillside and Rustam wondered that anyone would ever bother to come here.

Of course, that was what made it such an excellent location for one of the secret Gates into Shiva.

He glanced over his shoulder at the party behind. Besides Risada and himself there were only seven others. Elwaes rode ahead, leading the way. Queen Keril was accompanied by the moustachioed veteran General Alexi Hamd and four guards, two of whom led pack ponies carrying more camping equipment than Rustam could see need for, considering they had been told that the Gate was little more than a day's ride from Teshondra.

Swathed in grey robes and anonymous beneath hoods drawn up against the biting chill, they could have been any party of travellers and, although he had not asked, Rustam was fairly certain this was the intention. It seemed that despite cordial relations between the two kingdoms, the elves of Shiva were still unwilling for the majority of humankind to gain knowledge of places of access to their homeland.

Considering recent history, Rustam could not blame them.

Risada had been frustrated by Graylin's refusal to send the army with them so that it could be ready to travel through Shiva to Tyr-en the instant agreement was reached. If, indeed, it was reached. But Rustam understood. The presence of an army, even a Kishtanian army, camped outside the Gate was hardly grounds for building trust. Not to mention the attention it would draw to the location.

The horses crested a ridge and Rustam looked down into a desolate, weather-scoured valley which ended in a pock-marked cliff face.

"I thought they said we would reach this Gate before nightfall," complained Risada's voice beside him.

Rustam glanced at the lowering sun, but before he could comment Elwaes turned in his saddle.

"We have arrived, my Lady."

Risada's head swung as she studied the empty valley from one end to the other. "I see nothing."

"You will soon."

The elf's voice held a hint of amusement and Rustam wished he was up front, where he could watch the Shivan's eyes. There were forces tampering with their lives that he did not understand, and certainly did not trust.

At least he was more aware of their presence.

Upon reaching the valley floor, their escort began to erect shelters for both human and beast, stretching lengths of canvas between rock pillars that had apparently been used thus before, if the number of peg holes and hammer marks were any indication. Rustam stood beside Nightstalker amidst the sounds of metal biting into rock, and scanned their surroundings for signs of the elusive Gate but found nothing out of the ordinary. He was aware of Elwaes at his side, and finally canted a glance towards him. The elf's eyes twinkled mischievously but the glitter was clear blue, free from metallic taint.

"I give in," yielded Rustam. "Where is it?"

"Follow me."

Elwaes, Rustam, Risada, Queen Keril and General Hamd remounted and approached the rough but seemingly solid cliff face. Their escort continued to labour over their camp and as the Kishtanians made no effort to summon them, Rustam concluded this was the norm.

Elwaes, riding a tall chestnut that nevertheless looked like a pony beneath his rangy frame, angled towards a particularly dark patch of shadow beneath an overhang. And disappeared.

Risada swore softly but kicked her balking grey forward and vanished after the Shivan. Rustam held his breath as he entered the gloom, expecting some form of magic to swallow him up, but found instead that the shadow merely hid a jutting return that camouflaged a narrow slit in the rock face. He rode through with his knees held tight to the saddle, grateful that his mare was no wider around the girth.

Unlike General Hamd's stocky mount.

The old soldier cursed as his knees scraped along the rock wall and his horse burst forward in alarm.

"I warned you," admonished the queen's smiling voice into the darkness when their hooves had clattered to a standstill. A torch flared and Rustam looked around. The cave in which they stood was unadorned, barren of any sign of the Gate as far as he could tell, but a dark passage led onward into the bowels of the mountain and it was into this that Elwaes led.

For some while there was no light aside from the flickering of the torch, but gradually Rustam became aware of a glow in the air. It was not quite like that produced by the fungi in the *Charinsbahl* tunnels, rather it was as if the very air itself phosphoresced. Soon the torch became redundant and Elwaes doused it in a bowl of sand clearly set there for the purpose.

"The Gate," he said simply, and led around a bend.

The magical entrance stood alone in the centre of an immense cavern. It reached towards the high ceiling, gleaming with myriad moving colours that radiated outward from a central silver core. The rainbow streamers shifted and curled, intertwining and perpetually changing. Rustam found it hard to put a shape to the Gate, or even define where it ended, for the colours seemed to seep into the air itself, imparting a polychromatic luminosity to their entire surroundings.

Goddess, but it was beautiful!

Rustam's heart pulsed with excitement, seeming to match the tempo of the colour changes, and he nudged the night black mare onward, eager to join with the swirling iridescence and discover where it led.

"*Rustam.*"

Risada's strangled voice was barely recognisable. Rustam turned and felt his throat tighten as he saw her frozen face. Her wide, terrified eyes crawled with reflected colours.

"I don't think I can do this."

Rustam reined Nightstalker backward until she stood alongside the grey. The horses were not at all upset by the presence of magic; indeed the black mare seemed keen to enter the Gate and the grey was uncharacteristically docile.

Not so Risada. Her trembling hands gripped the reins like an overboard victim clinging to a life-rope.

"If you want to stay here..." said Rustam.

"I can't," she grated. "You said it yourself: this is the only way."

"Then, what?"

"Damn you, Chalice! How can someone as nice as you be so insensitive? *I'm asking for your help.*"

"Oh."

Guilt plunged his self-esteem to ever greater depths. How difficult it must have been for her to force herself this far. How much harder to ask for his help? Not so long ago he would have gloated over such a humbling of the high and mighty Lady of Domn. But now? Now he saw it for the courage it truly was, for a woman whose life had taught her to trust no one, to ask for help from one she had threatened to kill.

"I'll lead you," he offered. "Close your eyes."

Wordlessly she surrendered her reins, clutched tightly to the front of the saddle and obeyed his instruction with a desperate faith. Humbled by her trust, Rustam gently urged the horses after their companions who had already entered the Gate.

At first the colours seemed to lap around the animal's fetlocks, like gently rippling waves on the edge of a seashore. Soon they were wading shoulder deep through a rainbow, with ribbons of coloured light curling upward into their manes. Rustam looked down at himself and almost flinched at the sight of multi-hued tentacles crawling up his torso.

He was glad Risada's eyes were closed.

In front, he found he could barely see the outlines of the other riders. Their hair and clothing seemed to blend into the iridescence of the Gate, their silhouettes losing definition as they merged with the constantly changing shades until he could no longer focus on them as individuals.

Was it possible to become lost within the Gate?

Slightly panicked, Rustam urged the horses faster, but instead of seeing the others more clearly he found his vision filling with the overpowering gleam of the Gate's silver core. For a heart-stopping moment he was back inside his nightmare, pinioned by the silver eyes that brought such pain and terror. Icy fingers clutched his heart, and he struggled to draw breath—

The Gate vanished. All five members of the party sat their motionless horses in the centre of a green, leafy glade. A warm breeze caressed them, bringing with it the wholesome smell of growing things and flowers in bloom.

But it's winter, protested Rustam's dazed mind.

Unease crawled up his back. At first sight the forest clearing appeared quite ordinary, but as he looked, subtle differences became apparent. Brilliant jewel shades lent every leaf sharp, clearly defined edges, whilst the trunks themselves—Rustam smothered a gasp. Their girths were huge! Far greater than any tree he had ever seen: massive boles that must be tens of steps in circumference. Their spreading canopies interlaced overhead, hiding the sky and wrapping the travellers in what seemed to be a vast green globe. And despite the verdant growth, there was no lack of light—illumination seemed to seep from the vegetation itself.

Movement caught his eye and Rustam turned his head towards it—and then wished he hadn't. The world— precisely *what* world, he wasn't certain—spun around him, threatening to topple him from his saddle.

"Easy, my friend," said Elwaes. Rustam looked round more slowly, and endeavoured to focus on the elf through the hazy golden glow hanging between them.

"What—?" he began, but Elwaes wagged his head.

"Later, Rusty. Suffice it to say that Shivan air is somewhat different from what you are used to. You will adapt in time."

So saying, he turned away and left Rustam, riding forward to join Queen Keril where she faced a party of fierce-looking elves, all armed with javelins. Rustam swivelled his eyes to see as much as he could without moving his head. His gut clenched. They were surrounded, with no sign of the Gate which should have stood at their backs.

No retreat that way.

His stomach churned as he took stock. They were stranded in a magical land with but one friend—and Elwaes could not even be certain of his own reception, considering his petition. Added to that, nausea and dizziness had robbed Rustam of his usually excellent senses, for he had been wholly unaware of the ambush.

He turned carefully to look at Risada. Her eyes were open but glassy, as though she looked, yet did not truly see. Either her fear had overcome her, or else she was even more profoundly affected by the peculiar viscous air than he.

His only comfort came from Nightstalker, who stood calmly in the presence of so much magic, completely at ease. Rustam took this as a good sign. He had never known the mare's instincts to be faulty where danger was concerned.

Or was she under a spell?

His head full of answer-less questions, Rustam had to content himself with studying their captors, for he felt like a captive no matter that they had arrived freely, and in the company of Kishtan's Shivan queen.

He and Risada were, after all, Tyr-enese.

The elves were without exception tall, some taller even than Elwaes. They were simply dressed in tunics, some with leggings, some without, with no apparent regard for gender. The colours were the greens and browns of the forest, with some blues and greys and the odd hint of gold. No silver, noted Rustam with relief; he really had no wish to see that colour again.

Their leader, a slender girl with cascading blonde curls, appeared young enough to be Annasala's contemporary, yet Rustam knew better than to judge an elf by physical appearance.

The javelins they bore were functional shafts of wood, without the metal tips more commonly found in the Five Kingdoms. They still looked sharp enough to inflict a serious wound.

A simple hand gesture by the blonde girl lowered the javelins, and most of the elves melted away into the trees. One moment they were there, the next, gone. Magic, or just incredibly skilled woodcraft? Rustam was unable to decide. He was, in fact, increasingly unsure of how much he would ever be able to trust his senses in this strange land.

"Rusty."

He glanced sharply towards the source of his name, and again experienced the sinking nausea.

How did General Hamd manage to look so serenely unaffected? Perhaps repeated exposure inured one to the effects. Rustam certainly hoped so.

"Please come, Rusty," invited Elwaes. "I promise the effects will lessen."

Rustam nodded slowly and, after another glance at Risada's face, leaned carefully over to pick up the grey's reins.

"I can manage!" snapped the Lady of Domn. Rustam righted himself in the saddle with an effort and made an aggrieved face at Elwaes. The elf grinned in return before reining his horse round to follow Queen Keril.

21. SHIVA

"He bears the mark of Charin."

The elf who glared at Rustam was frail, the first apparently elderly Shivan they had seen. Or perhaps it was not age which rendered him so infirm that he must be supported by a strong hand beneath each elbow. Compared to the two—one male, one female—who flanked him, the only difference was in the feebleness of his body. No lines marred his youthful face and his long chestnut hair was without silvering, yet his body seemed worn out, ready to offer its spirit back to Chel.

Elwaes stepped before the venerable one and bowed his head.

"Tocar, it is good to see you. I feared I would never see any of my kind again until this one," he gestured toward Rustam, "whom I count as my friend, rescued me. It is true, he has been touched by the hand of the god, but to what purpose it is not yet clear. Certainly, he did nothing to earn this stigma."

Tocar considered Rustam afresh.

The two Tyr-enese stood, slightly unsteadily, within the circle of a small grove of emerald-bright trees. Their mounts had been led away and Rustam felt somewhat betrayed by the eagerness with which Nightstalker had followed her new attendant. Usually she displayed some temperament when parted from him, but here it seemed she could not leave him fast enough.

Maybe she senses the taint in me too, he thought dismally as he endured Tocar's close study of his face.

"Could it be, Elwaes, that your judgement has been influenced by your ordeal amongst the humans?" asked Tocar without ever taking his eyes—piercing green eyes that were sharp as a werecat's—from Rustam's disfigured face.

"Not in this. I *know* this man."

And Rustam realised that Elwaes was conveying something far deeper to Tocar then his words would imply to Risada, who stood quiescently at his side.

Tocar nodded sharply, once. "Your discernment has always been commendable, old friend. He may stay within Shiva for now. He may not, however, be a part of the embassy to the council, for without knowledge of Charin's intent upon his life, we cannot know how the god may choose to influence him."

"But—" began Rustam in protest, seeing the minute sinking of Risada's shoulders. Tocar raised a thin, bony hand. "Human, you have my sympathy for your affliction, but the decision is made. We will provide you with a guide while you remain here. Feel free to enjoy our kingdom, but do not attempt to approach where you are not desired."

Supported by his two aides, Tocar left them. Rustam began to turn toward Risada but vertigo threatened to pull him to the ground.

Enjoy this place? When I can't even move without being ill?

He opened his mouth to speak, but Risada got there first.

"It's not important, Rustam. Your support would have been welcome, and this was your idea. But it is my position as Marten's representative that is the important thing here." She squared her shoulders. "This is what I came for."

Rustam forbore to point out that her original plan had been to send him alone, and it was only Annasala's orders that had made her come at all. He could only guess what it had cost her in terms of courage to enter Shiva. Now she needed all her remaining strength to sustain her through the difficult task ahead, surrounded by more magic than any Tyr-enese would have dreamed of in their worst nightmare. Ultimately she was Tyr-en's final hope and she did not need Rustam's barbed quips to distract her.

Halnashead's voice echoed inside his head. *'You are both professionals: you will get along!'* And so, in their own fashion, they had, though he doubted that the prince would have approved. Thoughts of home brought with them a large twinge of anxiety that combined with the vertigo to make Rustam feel thoroughly rotten. He concentrated for a moment just on breathing, trying to control the nausea, and was taken completely by surprise when a rich voice spoke by his left elbow.

"I am to be your guide within Shiva," the voice said. "My name is Xindaya."

Rustam turned his head carefully, and focused on the slight figure beside him. His heart jolted against his ribcage.

Goddess! Are you taunting me deliberately?

Xindaya was gorgeous. She looked nothing like the ethereal elves, aside from her slender frame. Of similar height to Rustam, her skin was a warm shade of amber, her eyes a deep, deep brown. Finely chiselled features and a wide mouth gave her a strong yet genial appearance, and her masses of black curly hair lent just a hint of the exotic, courtesy of its slight green tinge.

Rustam did not dare ask what she was.

"Well, my friend," said Elwaes. "We'll see you later. I think we can safely leave you in Xindaya's care."

Risada glanced at him and, with a flash of the old ribaldry, her raised eyebrows begged the question: would Xindaya be safe with him?

* * * * * * * * * *

As Xindaya led Rustam deeper into the forest, he realised he'd never considered how the land of Shiva might look. He'd known it was hidden within the mountains, so this flat land of immense, bright trees came as a shock.

Distant birdsong drifted through the woods. Rustling in the leafy branches suggested a squirrel or some such, and the lazy buzz of insects droned past his ears. He imagined he would have found the land idyllic if it hadn't made him so sick.

Walking behind the oddly mobile figure of his guide—how did she manage to sway so sensuously in so many directions at once—Rustam fingered the cuffs of his new jacket, brushing his thumbs across the points of his daggers.

Something was wrong. It wasn't just the nausea and dizziness. As promised, both of those were beginning to abate. No, it was something to do with Shiva itself but— *goddess, look at those hips swing!* Glorious black ringlets curled and draped to just below hip height where their tips delicately brushed the rounded swell of the girl's buttocks.

Get a grip on yourself man, Rustam chided himself. *Where's your professionalism now? You're in a foreign, possibly hostile kingdom, parted from your allies, and you're allowing yourself to be distracted by a pert bum. Concentrate, for Chel's sake!*

What was it? He ran through his impressions so far: the quiet, the lack of people, the heavily wooded land, the scent of growing things, the hidden sky. And he had it.

Shiva's air was *luminous.*

Beneath such dense foliage, there could be no other explanation for the brightness. Confirmation came when Rustam searched for shadows. They simply did not exist. Elwaes had said that his nausea was related to the strange air. He could almost smell the brightness, taste it on his tongue, feel it whispering over his skin like sheets of gossamer fine silk.

He was breathing light.

"Xindaya?"

The gorgeous creature stopped and turned towards him.

"Is there a sun above the trees?"

"Sun?" she repeated curiously. "What is a sun?"

"That's what I thought," Rustam muttered, trying to imagine a world without a sun. "And what about dark? Does it ever get dark here?"

His guide looked confused, and then she brightened. "I have heard of this dark, from those who have been to your world. No, there is never dark here. How do you see when there is dark?"

Well, thought Rustam, *that probably goes a way towards explaining why elves don't sleep.* And he recalled an early conversation with Elwaes, about the perpetual light in Shiva. There was still one other thing bothering him. "It is beautiful here, but what about seasons? When we came through the Gate it was winter on the other side, yet it looks like spring or early summer here."

Xindaya shrugged, a peculiarly fluid movement accompanied by a slight shake of her head. "I am sorry Rustam. I have heard these words but they mean nothing to me. Come, let us sit by the pool and you can tell me all about them."

Like a trusting eager child with a new friend Xindaya reached out and grasped his hand, then pulled him through the trees at a wild run, dodging and ducking the branches with a sixth sense Rustam did not share. By the time they burst into a clearing he was breathless, somewhat scratched, and with leaves and twigs entwined in his hair. Xindaya looked around at him and burst into peals of laughter.

Affronted, Rustam scowled at her. Then he realised she was staring at the top of his head. He felt around and found a v-shaped twig sticking up from his crown, complete with gem-bright leaves. He extracted the offending article from his hair and pictured how it must have looked sprouting from his head like a pair of antlers. He grinned and began to laugh. Quickly the mirth overcame them both until they collapsed to the springy turf, alternately giggling and gasping, tears rolling down their cheeks.

When eventually they quieted, hugging their aching ribs like people who had run themselves to a standstill, Rustam smiled at Xindaya. "Thank you," he said. "I had forgotten what it was like, to enjoy a moment of madness."

She turned a dazzling smile upon him. "You should never forget how to laugh; it is one of Chel's greatest gifts. But come, you were going to tell me about sun and dark and winter, and all the other things you have that we don't."

She rose gracefully and, taking his hand again, pulled him to his feet with a strength that alarmed him.

What was this beautiful, wild, joyous creature? Did he really want to know?

She led him towards the centre of the circular glade where a raised rock formation enclosed a pool of limpid water. Delicate plants trailed over the rocks, their tiny blooms in softest shades of pink and yellow. To one side, a ledge offered them seating and a thick layer of springy moss, a cushion. Xindaya drew him down with her long, cool fingers enveloping his left hand. "Now," she said. "Tell me about the land beyond the Gate."

Rustam paused, his player's instincts cautioning him while his ego wanted to brag about all the marvels of his kingdom. But now he came to think about it, what were those marvels?

Tyr-en was certainly a lovely, bounteous land, and one that had seen peace in recent years, since Prince Halnashead had taken over as Regent upon his brother's death, continuing as head of security now that Marten had come of age.

But Shiva was beautiful and the more he looked around, the more he realised just how beautiful. He had never seen foliage of such intense colours, nor felt ground so cushioning beneath his feet. His nausea already seemed a distant memory, fading like a bad dream driven out by honest laughter, and he began to appreciate the glorious universal gilding of the lustrous air and its sweet, honeyed fragrance. The elven kingdom was undoubtedly bounteous, certainly peaceful and above all, if Elwaes was to be believed, free from the politics that marred Tyr-en's supposedly civilised lifestyle. The game was an integral part of Tyr-enese society but—and now Rustam questioned the very foundations upon which his entire life had been built—*was it truly necessary?*

He thought about the society of the younger kingdom of Kishtan. Admittedly he had not seen much. What he had seen, had been so different that at first he'd felt quite condescending. But then he'd begun to appreciate its merits. People free to think for themselves generated innovation: new dyes, new metals, new art forms, whole new ways of governance. Politics still existed in Kishtan, but in an open, participatory form; a form that his own rigid society deemed unviable.

Cold stabbed Rustam. Why was he entertaining such dangerous concepts? Was it some subtle influence, perhaps magical, of the mysterious creature beside him? He stole a glance at Xindaya, but she was gazing into the pool of water, apparently unconcerned that he had not yet answered her questions.

Could it be the elves? Were they manipulating his thoughts for some devious reasons of their own?

Unlikely. By everything he knew about elves, and despite the fact that most of his knowledge came from one source—Elwaes—he was utterly convinced that the Shivans had no hidden motives. Their only interest was in living out their long lives in as peaceful a harmony with their environment as they could achieve.

So his train of thought dared him, no, forced him to consider the unthinkable: that he really was, unprompted and of his own free will, doubting the validity of his way of life, of the lives of all in Tyr-en.

Numb with shock, his gaze drifted toward the beautiful woman seated beside him, followed the soft curve of her shoulder down the graceful arm to the slender fingers that idly traced strange sigils on the surface of the pool. Ripples spread outward from her signing and a stab of unease lanced Rustam's heart.

"What are you doing?" he said but stopped, staring past the ripples at something forming in the depths of the water. The craggy sides of the rock enclosed pool reminded him of somewhere he had seen before. Somewhere underground.

The trolls' caves? No, this was no vast cavern. This was small, roughly hewn and fronted by bars. Cold iced his spine as the image solidified, and he found himself standing once more on the winding stair peering around the corner of the brickwork into the cell where he and Risada had first seen Elwaes. The smell of dust tickled his nose, overlaid by the sharp taint of fear.

The cage held a new occupant. There was no mistaking Annasala's heavy brown tresses, but now they were dull, lank, tangled skeins falling forward to hide her lowered face. She seemed to be studying the toes of her scuffed and torn slippers, staring at the reddish-brown stains splattered on the yellow fabric.

Blood!

Rustam's heart clenched. Was she dead? His stunned gaze took in the ropes binding the princess to the chair, hands behind her, ankles one to each chair leg.

Surely even Melcard would not go that far? But Rustam's throat constricted as he realised who would.

Hensar.

The odious little creature would have no qualms—

Then she moved.

She's alive! Rustam's breath came out in a great sob of relief, only to catch in his throat as other figures stepped into view; Melcard, with Hensar at his heels.

Annasala's head lifted slowly, and the tangled strands fell aside to reveal her battered face. Yellow bruising along one cheekbone was overlaid by a fresh purple swelling half closing one eye. Her lower lip was split, dried blood spilling down her chin and onto the bodice of her pale lemon gown. Defiance glittered in her grey eyes but Rustam could not fail to see the fear, or the way she flinched when Melcard cupped her chin in his hand and turned her head to study the swollen cheek.

"Really, Hensar. I warned you against this before. You are not to mark her where it can be seen."

"Apologies, my Lord, but her highness is stubborn. She refuses to co-operate with any—reasonable—suggestions."

"But this," Melcard waved a hand at Sala's face, and frowned as she jerked her head back. "How long will the swelling take to go down? The rest can be covered with makeup, but that...?"

Hensar caught the girl's chin between his fingers, obviously pinching tighter than necessary as he twisted her head to better view his handiwork. To Annasala's credit she did not cry out, but Rustam's fingers clenched until the nails bit into his palms as he saw the tears leak from her tightly shut eyes.

"It will heal, my Lord. In plenty of time for the wedding."

Wedding? Whose wedding? Rustam wondered in confusion. Who would dream of getting married at such a time, and why was Annasala's presence required, unless...

Rustam nearly choked as the full horror of Melcard's plan became starkly clear. Once he was wed to Annasala he would have a legal claim to the throne, with only Marten and Halnashead standing in his way. As long as he could get the girl to appear to co-operate. That, obviously, was where the despicable Hensar was applying his many and varied talents of persuasion. Apparently Annasala was still managing to defy him—she was made from tough stock—but Rustam did not think she could hold out indefinitely. The tell-tales suggested it would not be long before the dwarf broke her, and Rustam could not bear the thought. He needed to do something. But how? He was not even in the same world.

In the dungeon, Melcard turned to leave. "Don't let it happen again," he snapped.

"No, my Lord," replied the doctor, and Rustam gasped at the mockery in Hensar's voice and manner. Surely Melcard could not fail to notice such blatant insubordination? But the Lord of the Fourth Family continued toward the cage door, apparently oblivious to the danger that stalked behind him on two short, stout legs. With another flash of clarity, Rustam realised that the greater danger came not from Melcard, but from Hensar. The doctor, in true Tyr-enese fashion, was playing some hidden game of his own, biding his time behind the façade of Melcard's revolution, and was surely a far more sinister opponent than the obvious one.

As Melcard stepped through the barred door, a cry tore from Annasala's throat.

"Don't leave me with him!"

Melcard stopped but did not turn. "That, my dear princess, is entirely up to you. All you have to do is agree to say your vows in public, with a willingness to convince the other Families that it is your own free choice."

"And if I should denounce you for the monster you are, in their hearing?" she demanded with a small flare of defiance.

Melcard shrugged. "Then I would be forced to execute your father."

Halnashead? Did Melcard hold him too? Rustam's mind reeled. But perhaps Melcard was bluffing. Annasala obviously had no more way of knowing than did Rustam.

The young princess slumped in her chair. "Then I cannot do either."

"In that case, your highness, I shall not see you again until you have changed your mind. And rest assured, change it you will. Carry on, Hensar."

"Noooo!" The anguished howl followed Melcard's retreat up the stairs.

Rustam held very still, unsure if Melcard could see him, but the Lord walked straight past him without so much as blinking. Hensar, on the other hand, frowned for an over long moment, staring at the very place from where Rustam watched until, with a small shrug, he turned back to the captive princess.

"Well now, my dear, shall we carry on where we left off earlier?"

All colour drained from Annasala's face as the doctor reached to lift her skirts. Her head fell back, eyes squeezed closed and she bit her lip, bright blood trickling down across the old, dried trail as Hensar's hand, holding something that glittered, slid between her thighs.

"No!" screamed Rustam and the picture broke apart, blurring and fragmenting until nothing was left but water in a rock pool.

Rustam slumped to the ground, his breathing ragged. The branches that roofed the clearing spun crazily overhead. Viscous air rushed noisily past his ears, or perhaps the buzzing was inside his head. Either way, any movement threatened to make him violently ill, and it was some while before he became aware that he and Xindaya were no longer alone.

"What have you done to him?" demanded Risada in a tone so blatantly full of concern that Rustam's befuddled brain refused to accept it as real.

"Lady Risada, we have done nothing!" That was Tocar, clearly shaken.

The spinning slowed and Rustam was able to focus again. He found a number of people, mostly elves with a few others he could not identify, standing around the edge of the clearing. And they all seemed to be staring at him. Rustam drew a deep breath, intending to speak, but another wave of nausea and dizziness crashed over him. His vision dimmed and the buzzing returned. He felt himself slither even further down until he was prone.

When the unpleasant symptoms finally receded, he found Risada's legs blocking his view.

"If you will allow me to explain?" Tocar again. Why did he sound so disturbed?

"Allow you? I demand it!" Risada was once more in her element, in a position of ambassadorial authority, and the confidence that had all but vanished when faced with entry to the magical kingdom fairly sang in her voice.

"Risada," he whispered, reaching a hand towards her. In less than a breath's-space she was on one knee beside him, and now there was no mistaking the genuine worry in her eyes.

Was that for him or the mission?

She took his face between her hands and he flinched involuntarily, remembering Annasala. Risada mistook the reason, dropped her hand away from his left cheek. "I'm sorry," she murmured. "Does that hurt? What happened?"

Without waiting for him to answer, she stood up again. "We trusted your hospitality," she began hotly, but Tocar, who had been helped forward to sit on the rock seat Xindaya had previously occupied, waved a hand across the surface of the water.

"Lady Risada, this is the *morril* pool. Your companion was granted a vision; blessed is he." The dazed tone was still there, tinged with a hint of awe.

Rustam frowned slightly, suddenly aware of an extraordinary clarity in his ability to hear emotions. One more example of how he was changing.

But into what?

Strong hands—Xindaya's—helped him to sit up and he flashed a grateful smile before his innately suspicious mind recalled those same hands drawing symbols on the surface of the water.

"And the significance of this?" asked Risada, and Rustam felt a surge of pride in her new found strength, to boldly question with no hint of fear a clearly magical phenomenon.

"Blessed is he that is granted a vision in the *morril*." It sounded like an adage. "Few are so blessed," continued Tocar, "even amongst our own people. Elwaes spoke truly. Whilst this man's life has been touched by Charin, Chel's purpose in allowing this has yet to be made clear."

A new voice rang across the clearing, sweet and with a vibrant life to it that the generally phlegmatic elves seemed to lack.

"And until it is, let us welcome our guests—all of them—as we would wish to be greeted should we visit their kingdom."

The crowd swayed aside like tall grass before a wind to permit the speaker ingress, and Rustam found himself staring in mute surprise at the extraordinary sight of a tiny girl with long black hair and pale, almost translucent skin. Woman, he corrected himself as she came closer, her rich voice and regal bearing belying her juvenile appearance. She was dressed in similar style to the majority of the elves, in a long belted tunic of lightweight, almost diaphanous fabric over figure-hugging leggings, but whilst theirs were pastel shades or earth hues, hers were of the deepest ruby red; a perfect match for the startling colour of her eyes.

"Let me introduce myself," she said, meeting Risada's gaze. "I am Leith, and as you are human and this sort of thing has significance for you, I am also King Rhe's consort."

So, thought Rustam, *the elven king survived Tyr-en's assassination attempt all those years ago*. Whether that would work for or against them remained to be seen.

* * * * * * * * * * *

Queen Leith, or just plain Leith as she seemed to be to all and sundry, took charge of the situation. She insisted both Tyr-enese rest, and then attend a feast in their honour before she would even consider convening a fresh council meeting—one to which Rustam was invited. For Rustam, despite being briefly diverted by the novelty of their accommodations inside the hollow trunk of a massive *bola* tree, the delay was almost unbearable. Not only did he fail to get Risada on her own for long enough to do more than outline the contents of his vision, but his mind insisted on going over and over the scene in the dungeon, fixating on that final moment of Annasala's anguish as Hensar resumed his torture.

In contrast to his agitated state, Risada seemed almost tranquil as they were led towards the council meeting, but Rustam knew her too well by now to be fooled. The pinched corners of her eyes and the unconsciously twitching fingers, were tell-tales that under less stress she would never have permitted to show.

And now this: King Rhe had refused to meet with them.

The Kishtanian general, Alexi Hamd, had so informed them earlier, as the feast participants had begun to disperse—they merely wandered off much as they had arrived, with no formality or ceremony—and the two queens had withdrawn, chattering together like a pair of excited children.

"So is there any point to this meeting?" Risada asked the grizzled veteran as he guided them through the trees and across yet another of the symmetrically circular clearings. Something with fragile green wings flittered across the glade and vanished into the branches, trailing a spicy odour that mingled pleasantly with the aromatic air. General Hamd shrugged. "Who can say, with elves? They make up their own minds and follow their own paths. But her Majesty, Queen Leith, despite her unusual appearance, is human and may be more disposed to assist you, though I make no promises."

Seizing on a potential ally, Risada smiled brilliantly at the general. "You know the queen?" she asked. Hamd shrugged. "I did, once," he confirmed, but volunteered nothing further.

They stepped out into one more of the ubiquitous clearings, this one occupied. A number of people were seated around a central circular table, on a ring-shaped bench. Both table and bench appeared to grow out of the ground, and as they drew closer Rustam realised that his perception was true—they had grown, though not in quite their current form. They were carved from the stump of another of the gigantic trees, the concentric ageing rings clearly visible on the waxed surfaces. The immense time span to which those rings bore testament was staggering, and Rustam could not help but feel a dispiriting sense of insignificance in the presence of the ageless elves and their enduring kingdom.

"Everything's so round in this bloody kingdom," muttered Hamd irreverently. "It's a wonder they haven't claimed the invention of the wheel!"

One corner of Rustam's mouth tugged upward and he locked eyes with the old soldier. A quick flash of teeth showed through the general's bristly moustache and a broad hand clapped Rustam on the shoulder as the younger man swung his legs over the bench to take his assigned place.

"Remind her of kin duty," suggested Hamd in a low voice before he moved away to greet the Shivan queen.

What kin? Rustam wondered, searching his memory but finding nothing useful. They had not even been aware that the Shivan king still lived, let alone that he had married a human woman.

The woman in question flicked long sable locks over her shoulder and swung her legs clear of the bench with the agility of a trained fighter. She stood up to meet the approaching general, her tiny frame coming no higher than his chin.

"Alexi!" Her voice held great warmth as did her smile. "It's so good to see you again."

Hamd bowed deeply. "Your Majesty," he said.

Queen Leith's face shadowed with disappointment. "So formal, Alexi? There was a time when I was just plain 'girl' to you."

"Things change, your Majesty."

"As do people," she observed with sadness. "Well, if it makes you more comfortable."

Hamd bowed again and moved to stand behind Queen Keril, who sat at Leith's left hand. Rustam was struck by the sorrow on Leith's face as she re-seated herself, and he wondered about the past relationship of the queen and the Kishtanian general.

The meeting proceeded with little of the formality to which the Tyr-enese were accustomed. Risada visibly struggled with the casualness and lack of protocols which Rustam, to his surprise and slight chagrin, found refreshing. As the council drew towards an end with little accomplished, Rustam's gaze drifted to the old soldier standing at ease behind Queen Keril. General Hamd inclined his head slightly as their eyes met, and mouthed the word, '*now.*'

Going with an instinct that he only seemed to have developed recently—that of trust—Rustam rose to his feet.

All eyes turned on him. Voices stilled. Into the hush, Rustam darted another glance at Hamd and received a further nod of encouragement.

You'd better be correct, Rustam thought as he turned to meet Queen Leith's ruby eyes.

"Madam," he began, unsure of how best to address a queen who had little regard for etiquette. "If all our best intentions and arguments are not enough to sway you, then I feel I must remind you of your duty to your kin."

On his periphery he saw Risada's brow furrow in confusion, but he kept his eyes firmly on Leith. *Yes, it was there!* Behind the surprise was the acknowledgement he sought.

She would help them.

Still clueless as to how he had done it, Rustam sank back to his seat, light headed with relief. Queen Leith continued to stare at him, briefly speechless. Risada, too, looked at him askance, but when she began to open her mouth to apologise for his presumption, his hand on her arm elicited nothing more than a trusting quiescence.

Rustam basked in the warmth of Risada's faith, and the knowledge that Halnashead and Annasala now had a chance.

"How did you know?" When she regained it, Leith's voice was incredulous. "After all this time, I didn't think anyone... But no matter, if it is Chel's will, who am I to argue?" Her startling red eyes moved to Risada. "*You* don't know, do you?"

Reluctantly, Risada shook her head.

"Your young king, Marten, is my nephew. His mother, Selva, was my sister."

Rustam felt Risada's struggle to control her reaction in parallel to his own. *Marten's aunt!* Then by marriage, Risada was also related to Leith, albeit distantly.

Goddess, what a tangled skein.

22. LESSONS

Nightstalker lifted her head from the rich grazing and rubbed her forehead against Rustam's shoulder. He ran a hand down her sleek neck and patted her gently as she returned to the important task of eating.

Rustam looked in admiration at the herd of beautiful horses calmly munching their way across the largest clearing he had yet seen in the forest that was Shiva.

"Glorious, aren't they?' Elwaes stood at his shoulder, looking healthier than Rustam had ever seen. The elf's face positively glowed as his eyes searched the herd and came to rest on a leggy bay stallion. He uttered a warbling cry in the strange language he had used in the mountains.

The bay's head shot up, ears twitching as he searched for the source of that call. In the instant he found Elwaes, even before he leapt into the gallop that carried him in great bounds to his master's side, Rustam *saw* the bond between horse and rider, tangible as a rope or a leather rein. It was something utterly familiar and yet he felt he was seeing it for the first time, viewing it from an entirely new perspective. *Could this be magic?*

Because if it was, then he had been guilty of practicing since he was a young boy.

"I dared not hope.' Elwaes's voice quavered with emotion.

Rustam put a hand on the elf's shoulder. "It's hard to believe,' he agreed. "To still be alive after all this time. How long do your horses live?'

Elwaes flashed him a puzzled glance that quickly cleared.

"You misunderstand, Rusty. I suppose that, by your standards, our horses are long lived. No, it's that he found his way back here—there are so few functional Gates I doubted he would find one.' He patted the stallion's crest as the soft muzzle reached out to snuff Rustam's proffered hand.

"Fleetfoot lived up to his name.'

Rustam and Elwaes both looked round at the new voice. Tocar and his aides stood on the edge of the clearing. The frail elf was lowered to sit on the ground and as Elwaes led Rustam over, Tocar dismissed his assistants with a small nod.

Elwaes, too, inclined his head. "My friend, thank you for coming.'

Rustam glanced at him suspiciously. Elwaes had suggested this visit to the herd whilst the elven council deliberated. He had failed to mention inviting Tocar as well.

"Sit, please,' Tocar invited. Elwaes sank cross-legged and, after a moment of uncomfortable hesitation, Rustam settled beside him. He endured a further detailed study of his damaged face by Tocar, and found to his surprise that it no longer bothered him.

The elf sighed, apparently unable to find what he sought. "Rustam,' he said, "Elwaes tells me you are a Horsemaster by instinct, but with no training. He has asked me to assist you.'

Rustam frowned at Elwaes. He didn't like surprises.

Elwaes smiled at him. "You know I am not much of a teacher, Rusty, and you do need help. You have seen how dangerous this gift can be without the conscious control it needs. And Tocar is the best.' He smiled at his countryman and added: "He trained me when I was a boy.'

Well, that certainly aged the other elf, even if it did not explain his frailty. Rustam bowed his head in acquiescence but before he could speak, Tocar continued.

"If Elwaes had asked this of me before you were granted the vision, I would have refused, regardless of his arguments. I could not help but wonder to what extent his imprisonment had warped his judgement. But now? I will not ask what you saw, that is irrelevant. The fact is that you were granted a vision in the pool most sacred to Chel—'

Then there are others. Rustam snatched that piece of information and stored it for the future.

"—and so, despite the mark Charin has placed so blatantly upon you, I will do as Elwaes asks. Besides,' and here a boyish grin lit the youthful face and Rustam could almost believe it was a young lad seated across from him. "it will be a challenge!'

* * * * * * * * * *

Sweat trickled between Rustam's shoulder blades and he wriggled uncomfortably. Drops beaded his brow and every once in a while one would roll down his face and cling to the end of his nose until he simply had to flick it away with a jerk of his chin.

The tiny shift of Tocar's head screamed the Shivan's frustration.

How long had they been battering away at this exercise? Whilst the elves cared little for passing time, Tocar was definitely struggling to understand Rustam's alien thought processes.

The feeling was mutual.

Apparently this was a task any child could accomplish with ease. *Grow,* Rustam willed the seed that lay cupped in his hands. *Damn you to Charin's fiery breath; grow!*

The seed promptly scorched and shrivelled.

"I cannot do this.' Tocar spoke directly to Elwaes as Rustam stared at the withered thing on his palm.

"Rustam.' Elwaes commanded his attention. "Did you swear again?'

"Ah, hell's—' Rustam stopped himself. "Yes, I did. I forgot. I'm sorry.'

"Your talent is so unruly,' observed Tocar. "Whilst I agree with Elwaes that it should be trained, I lack guidance upon how to begin. Clearly this is not the way.'

Rustam reached for another seed. "Let me have one more go. I'm sure I almost had it that time.'

"Try first to centre yourself the way I showed you,' suggested Elwaes. "You seemed adept at that.'

Rustam nodded agreement and closed his eyes, focusing inward rather than on the irksome speck of matter on his palm. As his control over his own body increased—with, he thought rather smugly, far greater speed than the last time—so he felt his irritation and tension sloughing away like the dull, dead skin of a snake peeling back to reveal the glistening creature within.

Something glittered on the edge of his inner vision and Rustam balked, a moment of frozen terror before he identified the colour as gold, not silver. He strained to see more clearly but, whatever it was, it stayed just out of range.

Uneasily Rustam glanced at the elves, but neither seemed disturbed. Perhaps it was simply some other denizen of the magical land, one that could not be seen with normal vision. Rustam gave a mental shrug and turned his attention to the seed.

Yes, he could see the tiny spark of life inside the quiescent shell, he just had to coax it into peeking outside its protective cocoon—

Gold flash. Closer this time. In and out too quickly to fasten on.

Rustam's composure unravelled, heart accelerating without permission, perception wavering between inner and outer worlds.

Get a grip on yourself, Chalice: you are not in the habit of failing and you are not about to begin now! He gathered the tattered threads of his awareness and took a deep, cleansing breath. Another.

Then jerked back with a yell.

A miniature golden dragon peered into his face from a distance of no more than a hand-span. *Goddess,* but it was *hot*!

Rustam tried to lean back away from the creature but it moved with him. Flames flickered around its tiny body and the acrid smell of burning hair wafted into Rustam's nostrils.

"Elwaes?'

"Slap it away,' instructed the elf, and now he could see Elwaes behind the flickering, flaming dragonet.

"With what?'

"Use your hand; just be convinced that you can do it.'

The skin on Rustam's nose began to blister as the creature's rapidly beating wings edged it closer. "Ouch!' he protested and smacked at his tormentor. To his horror his hand went right through it as though it did not exist. Except that he could feel the tiny hairs on the back of his hand shrivelling from the heat.

"Again, Rusty,' Elwaes urged. "But *believe* in yourself.'

Rustam searched around inside himself for the self-confidence he was certain he used to possess. He found instead, that he had become accustomed to being a victim. Since they had left Tyr-en so many forces beyond his control had batted him this way and that, manipulating him in their own incomprehensible games like the pawn he was, that somewhere along the line he had begun to accept his lack of choices.

But this was one player who liked to direct his own destiny. It was time he retook command of his own life.

Barely thinking what he was doing, Rustam raised a hand and casually knocked the fiery dragonet aside. It tumbled over and over, then righted itself at some distance, gave him a startled look, and winked out of sight.

"Well,' Rustam began, blinking to clear the bright afterimage.

"Well, indeed,' Tocar echoed. "Well achieved and well dealt with. It seems, my friend, that your talents are specific to certain forms of life, and plants are definitely not your realm.'

"What was it, and how—?'

"A salamander: a fire elemental. As to how? You must look inside yourself for your answer. Only you can know how you summoned it, and then dismissed it. Look now, while you can still recall.'

Rustam mentally recovered his steps, remembering how fire had been on his mind, first with his imprecations, and then with his perception of the embryonic plant life. Quite how he had called the elemental he could not have put into words, but he identified within himself the feeling of controlled power that had drawn it to him. Its dismissal was not even worth introspection; he just knew that he could do it.

"But I thought elementals were beyond control?' He looked accusingly at Elwaes, remembering the humiliations he had suffered in the clutches of the sprite.

"Oh, they are,' the Shivan assured him. "If they so choose. But they can be caught unawares, even trapped, though I would not recommend it, as they tend to wreak violent retribution once they regain their freedom. Use this gift wisely, Rusty. Remember that, like a young horse not yet trained to the saddle, elementals can be dangerous without malice.

"However,' and now his face split into a wide smile, "it was a good start to your training!'

* * * * * * * * * * *

Rustam prowled restlessly between the gigantic trunks of the Shivan forest. His first lesson in magic complete, Elwaes and Tocar had departed their separate ways, leaving him with yet more time to fill until the council should recall him. To distract himself from the anxiety that hovered constantly on the edge of his mind, Rustam ran over his lesson again, rather bemused that what was deemed magic seemed no different to any other technique he had learned, be it dancing, fighting or loving. No mysterious power had surged through him, no demon had subjugated his soul.

What was there to be scared of?

Whilst quite willing to admit that as a tool, magic had the potential to cause harm, having now consciously performed a magical act, Rustam could quite see why elves considered it a part of normal life. It felt so natural.

Guilt stabbed him in the gut. He should not be thinking like this. He was Tyr-enese! It went against all the cultural mores by which his countrymen lived.

So why did it feel so right?

A shape moved in the clearing ahead. Rustam's mind snapped back from speculation to wariness. In that, at least, he was truly Tyr-enese.

Pausing beside one of the ubiquitous tree boles, he studied the figure that swayed and danced alone beneath the shadeless canopy. Her movements were oddly fluid, totally uninhibited, and gloriously seductive.

Xindaya.

Rustam watched until he was certain they were alone. He was equally certain that she was unaware of him, dancing purely for her own pleasure.

She spun away between the trunks, fingers trailing over textured bark in a lover's caress, her shining green-black cascade of curls tossing behind her like leaves buffeted in a storm wind. And into the aftermath of her passage stepped Rustam, drawn like air into a vacuum.

The wild dance led ever deeper into older and older forest, the trees bigger and bigger, rough and gnarled, aged beyond imagining. Lost and disoriented, Rustam stopped, staring around himself as though waking from a trance.

He was alone.

Ambush, screamed the spy inside him.

Betrayed, screamed the lover.

"Rustam?'

She stepped from behind the twisted bole of an ancient tree, one arm trailing through the ivy that clung to the cracked and roughened bark, hair snagging in its suckers. She looked so wild, so free. So unlike the pampered, primped and perfectly presented women of Tyr-en.

Rustam"s heart paused inside his breast.

And in the same instant, rejected the idea. Why should this gorgeous creature want him? Here, there was no pool of water to reflect his hideous image, but she was gazing straight at it. He turned to leave.

"Rustam,' she repeated, voice as husky as the rattle of autumn leaves underfoot. "Don"t go.'

"Why not?' he grated, bitterness welling up like pus from an abscess. "What could you possibly want from me? There"s no need to stretch hospitality this far.'

"I want the same thing you do. Did Charin"s touch damage your mind, so that it cannot hear what your body is saying?'

He spun back to face her, pointing at his ruined face. "This! This is what"s damaged.' He thrust his numb and sagging visage close to her exquisitely beautiful one. "The only damage to my mind is caused by the prospect of having to live with this for the rest of my life.'

Xindaya"s features froze. Vindicated, Rustam turned to leave. Behind him, she burst into wild laughter.

Again, he spun round. "You think that funny?'

"No, no!' she denied. "I did not understand before.' She choked, struggling to contain her mirth.

"What? You didn't understand what?' Rustam realised he was shouting.

The wild woman gulped a steadying breath of liquid gold air. "You think I would care how you look on the outside?' she asked.

Rustam's mind swam. "What—?'

"Just look at me,' invited Xindaya, leaning back against the pitted surface of the ivy encrusted trunk. "This is what I look like, on the outside.'

And she melted back into the tree. Rustam blinked frantically, but there was nothing wrong with his vision. Xindaya had simply vanished into the ancient timber.

"There was a time when I looked better, more attractive to the eye.' Her voice emanated from deep within the trunk. She tossed her higher branches. "When I was a mere sapling, and as supple as a fish in a pond.' She emerged again. "But that was long ago.'

Rustam's mouth gaped. Xindaya stepped close and kissed him. As his body began to respond, Rustam had a second of frozen doubt, remembering the sprite. Then he dismissed it. Xindaya had spoken the truth—he *did* want this. He didn't care *what* she *was,* *she* wanted him, despite his appearance, despite his background, his hang-ups, and the tell-tale colours of his aura, which he was sure she could see. She wanted him, not for prestige, nor to alleviate the boredom of a dull marriage. Just him, for himself.

He felt dizzy with relief and excitement, and as Xindaya pressed tighter against him his mind flickered back over all his previous conquests, laying bare the shallowness of his former life. In that moment, as he realised that his looks were not, after all, his only asset, his life changed forever.

His face stretched into a fierce grin: he had cheated Charin.

He could find love, even with an ugly face.

Together the lovers sank to the mossy turf, shedding clothes as they went, uncaring if any should come upon them unexpectedly, though that seemed unlikely in this quiet arc of Shiva. Vaguely, Rustam wondered if other dryads watched from within their trunks, but he found he did not care. All his attention was for the wonderful, eager, sensuous woman who caressed him with a gentle strength that made his whole body go weak. Aside from the sprite, no other woman had ever seduced him, ever led him and given of herself in mutual pleasure like this.

The golden air no longer made him nauseous; it was like breathing liquid nectar. He drew a great lungful of the stuff, felt the luminescence seeping into his body, energising it, and rose to meet Xindaya's challenge.

* * * * * * * * * *

Much later, Rustam and Xindaya wandered, aimless and uncaring to be so, bodies sated and minds quiet, happy just to bask in the warmth of each other's company. They passed elves, others that Rustam now identified as dryads, and some besides that he was still unable to name. The dreamy quality of Shivan life no longer seemed strange or threatening, the endless glow of the air a fitting medium within which thrived a different type of life to that of the human world. Rustam felt at home.

For the first time in his life, he was at peace. No pressure to please others, no pressure to serve. Just the serenity to be himself. His whole life until this point had been driven: by the need to please others, to prove himself, to repay Halnashead.

He no longer needed to do those things. Here, no one cared who he was, what he had done or why. He was valued just for himself and, without vanity or greed, he liked it.

Here, it did not matter that he was a bastard.

He flung his arms around Xindaya and swung her crazily, round and round until he was dizzy. Then he stopped and kissed her. She tasted earthy but sweet, sweet as Risada had when he kissed her on the mountainside, in the entrance to the creeper burrow.

A twinge of guilt disturbed his peaceful state of mind: he should not have kissed his sister like that. Of course, at the time she had not yet revealed the relationship, but his conscience told him that he should somehow have known. He still found it hard to accept.

As if thought of Risada had drawn him to her—which, perhaps, in this magical land, it had—they entered a clearing and saw her sitting on the ground near a central pool of clear water. Still in a euphoric haze, they were almost upon her before Rustam saw the tears streaking the Lady of Domn's cheeks.

"Risada? What's happened?'

Reality crashed down on him. Had the elves refused to help, despite all signs to the contrary? Had bad new reached her? Were they already too late?

The Lady of Domn looked up at him, caught between tears and laughter, on the edge of hysteria. Rustam dropped to his knees, took her hands in his.

"What? What is it?'

She freed one hand, swept it over the water by her side. Only then did Rustam realise the significance. Whilst this body of water was not raised and enclosed by rock as was the *morril* pool where he had had his vision, this was nonetheless, a Shivan pool. He glanced up at Xindaya for confirmation and she answered the question in his eyes with a gentle smile and a nod.

Risada had sought a vision. Rustam's mind blanked with shock. For Risada—*Risada* of all people—to seek to use a magical device! His whole world was rocked. What could have driven her to this?

The Lady of Domn smiled weakly through her tears.

"I had to see what was happening in Domn; I don't know how Iain is coping. I just had to!'

Rustam's stomach sank like lead. What had she seen, to be in such a state—had Melcard's forces taken Domn? Worse, was Iain dead?

"And?' he prompted gently. Risada shook her head, hysteria glittering in her tears. "I tried pool after pool. Do you have any idea how many there are? Every other clearing has one, and I haven't found the edge of the forest yet. No matter how far I walk it seems to keep growing ahead of me.' The head shake came again.

"There was nothing but clear water in any of them until this one, and it will only show me what I don't want to see.'

"Which is?'

Now she laughed, the edge of hysteria tipping precariously towards insanity.

"The past. Something I never wished to think about again. That I was wrong, and half my life has been built upon a lie that I concocted for myself.' Her voice shook. "Daddy, oh daddy...'

Rustam held her while she wept, and his new found insight told him that it was not Risada, Lady of Domn that he held, but Risada, orphaned six year old daughter of the murdered Arton and Sharlanne. How long had she held onto those tears, rancid and festering inside her soul, eating away at her humanity, her ability to relate to anyone other than the brother whose disability she blamed upon herself.

How lonely had she been, all these years?

"Shh,' whispered Rustam into her fragrant hair, stroking the gleaming strands as he would the coat of an injured horse, hoping to calm it. "You're not alone. I'm here now, and while I may not be the brother you desired, I'll always be here for you.'

Risada gurgled and for one panicky moment, Rustam thought she was choking. But it proved to be laughter bubbling up through her tears, and he had to wait until she was finished before he could discover the source of her bitter mirth.

She drew away from him and sat back, looking him over piece by piece as though seeing him clearly for the first time.

"I have always believed,' she said, "that my father was having an affair with your mother. I convinced myself that it was his preoccupation with Soria that distracted him sufficiently to allow the assassin to penetrate the heart of our home. When you were born—a little early, it"s true, but still within feasible limits—my belief was proven. But now...' She glanced away from him to the pool of limpid water, and stared accusingly into the depths as though it were personally responsible for her mistake.

She looked back at him, all traces of hysteria washed away. "As I have no knowledge of the validity of magic, I cannot tell you how I know this to be the truth, but I can assure you, it is.

"Rustam Chalice,' she said formally. "You will be pleased to know that I no longer have any reason to kill you. You are not my father"s child after all. You are Prince Halnashead"s.'

23. CHEL

' Why?—

For the moment, that one thought occupied Rustam's entire mind.

' Why did you never tell me?—

He was vaguely aware that he had stumbled away from the clearing, leaving the two women behind. He could just remember Xindaya's compassionate face, Risada's passive watchfulness. Neither had made any move to follow him.

Women had always been the untrustworthy ones, the ones who let you down, who kept secrets and used them against you.

So how come Halnashead had done the same thing?

' Father! Didn't you trust me?—

He knew that Risada had told him the truth. Her belief that Arton Derano vas Domn was his father had never sat easily with him. But Prince Halnashead?

Not only did it explain a lot of things, but Rustam simply *knew* it was true.

' Father, he grieved. *' I was always your man; could you not trust me enough to tell me?—*

Halnashead's betrayal cut to his heart. Not only had he been denied the special bond of a son to his father, but the whole basis of his life's beliefs was proven to be false. Men could be as untrustworthy as women.

He looked forward through a haze of anger and turmoil to see: trees. All around, nothing but damned trees. And through those, the glimmer of water somewhere ahead. Another of those cursed pools that seemed to bring nothing but anguish. He turned aside, heading deeper into the forest, completely lost and uncaring to be so, the tranquillity of earlier hopelessly evaporated, burned away by the flame of knowledge.

And once again, the serene shimmer of water, through the trees.

Repeatedly, Rustam turned away, unwilling to risk another vision, apprehensive of what the goddess might chose to show him this time. But in the end he realised he was walking in circles. What was it that the Kishtanian General, Alexi Hamd had said? Something about everything in Shiva being round?

Defeated and exasperated, Rustam stepped out of the trees and knew precisely where he was. In the centre of the perfectly circular clearing rose a rock enclosed pool of water: the *morril* pool.

He strode defiantly up to it and stared into the limpid depths. Nothing. No vision, no message. 'Well?—he yelled insolently at Chel's pool. 'What do you want me to do now, *goddess:* go home with my tail between my legs and pretend none of this ever happened? That's a little hard to do with *this* to remind me!—

The surface of the pool rippled, distorting the image of his ruined face until it seemed quite whole. Rustam's breath caught in the back of his throat as he studied the visage that had been both his fortune and his curse.

What would he do with his life now? It was something he had never bothered to think about" what he would do when he was no longer any use to Halnashead. He could not even contemplate going back to work for the prince now.

Could he make a new life for himself here, in Shiva? He did not think he had ever been truly happy before meeting Xindaya, and it was more, far more than just infatuation. Even if she never wanted him again, for that short time she had shown him what it was like to be valued for more than just his looks.

The ripples on the pool smoothed away and his true face showed clearly in reflection. Rustam was finally able to look at his disfigured countenance without horror. He realised he could actually be happier looking like that than as he had done before. He began to turn away when something in the water caught his eye, a gleam of silver like sunlight glittering on the crest of a wave.

But there was no sunlight in Shiva.

He stiffened, tried to break away, but it was too late. The glistening motes coalesced to form lambent eyes and he was drawn inexorably back into his worst nightmare. The wooded glade receded and he stood again in the dark, facing those terrible silver orbs.

This time, however, several things were different. For one, he was free to move. Experimentally he twitched an arm, dropping an almost forgotten dagger from its wrist sheath into his palm. He wasn't certain what use a dagger might be against a god, but the feel of the cord-wrapped hilt against his skin imparted some small comfort.

Light seemed to seep from the unblinking eyes, a veil of luminescent tears touching their surroundings with a pearly glow. Slowly, more of their environs became visible and Rustam gasped in recognition: he was standing in the practice hall of his dancing Master's studio. The place where he had last seen his mother. The mingled fragrances of ondal oil and herbs brought back that moment of betrayal with a clarity that sliced his heart in two.

Glowing argent eyes watched him with a depth of compassion that made him fall to his knees.

'Chel?' he queried, his voice trembling small.

Features formed around the eyes and the radiance of the goddess's beauty smote him like a physical blow. He glanced away, staring at the polished floor where the scuff marks of a thousand dancing shoes were preserved forever beneath the wax.

'Rustam.—Chel's voice was at once the song of birds, and the sigh of waves upon the shore. It flowed over him like a healing balm and he gathered from it the strength and courage to look upon the goddess's face. Even as he watched, her features blurred, shifting subtly, reforming into a never-to-be-forgotten pattern framed by a halo of auburn ringlets.

'*Mother?*—whispered Rustam incredulously.

'My son,—said Soria Chalice, voice breaking with emotion.

'How...?—

'We are all but a part of the goddess, Rusty, as she is a part of us, even whilst we dwell in our individual forms. She feels your sorrow and anguish, even as she shared your joy earlier.—

'You were there?—

A silver sheen spread over Soria's blue eyes. 'I am with you always,— confirmed the goddess, and then faded into the background.

'Well, Rusty,—said Soria with satisfaction in her tone. 'Turn around, my son; let me look at the man you have become. You have grown as handsome as I always knew you would.—

'But" —Rustam began in protest, raising a hand to the left side of his face. His words died unspoken as he felt the perfectly smooth, taut skin of his cheek, the upturned corner of his mouth. Apparently here, in Chel's domain, Charin's disfigurement no longer prevailed.

'Why are we here?—His spy's nature could not help but seek information.

'Here?—repeated Soria. Her gaze swept the empty hall, lingering briefly upon small details; the bundles of fragrant herbs hanging in bunches along the walls, the lute propped against the chair that sat towards one end of the long room, the pile of discarded shoes in a corner. 'Or *here*?—She looked full upon her son.

Rustam shrugged. 'Either. This hall, I suppose I can guess" it was the last place we were together. So I suppose I mean, why has Chel chosen to grant this little interview?—

'Rusty!—Soria sounded hurt. 'Are you not as pleased to see me as I am you?—

'You can ask that? When you were the one who walked out on me?—As he said it, all the old bitterness welled up. 'You *left* me. You went away and you never came back. Why should I be pleased to see you now?—

'I never intended it to be so, my Rusty. It wasn't that I didn't want to come back to you, but I could not. I was murdered.—

'*What?*—

'It seemed such an innocuous mission at the time" the first information we had gleaned about the Royal Bastard in seasons. We had no idea it would be any more than unfounded rumour. But he found me before I found him, and he murdered me. Poisoned me, and then watched to see how long it would take me to die. I tried so hard to live for you, so very hard.—

Soria's blue eyes sheened with tears, hardened into a glittering silver staring from a mask that made Rustam's whole body cringe with remembered pain.

Charin smiled down upon him.

'Amazing sensation, isn't it?—whispered the hatefully seductive voice of the god. 'Discovering that the very foundation of your life is a lie. Your mother was never to blame" it was your sire all along. He ordered her to that mission, and when she died he never told you, just used you as though you were nothing to him.—

The sharp, masculine countenance of the god blurred and once again Soria's blue eyes watched him from auburn-framed elfin features. Rustam stared at his mother, seeing her as if for the first time. Which, in a way, he was. All his recollections were those of a small child, without any knowledge of the twisted convolutions of the Tyr-enese game.

His voice croaked into being. ' You're one of them, aren't you? Child of a forced union between a human and an elf. That's why magic is so easy for me, why I'm not afraid of it. Is that where I came from too?—

Halnashead, force himself upon Soria? Revulsion crawled between Rustam's shoulder blades at the thought but, even with all he now knew, and with all that Charin obviously wanted him to think, he could not find it within himself to believe the prince" his father" would be party to such perversion.

His mother was quick to confirm his feelings. ' Never! Hal and I loved each other. It was he who rescued me from that abomination of a breeding programme.—

' And yet he could never bring himself to tell me the truth.—

' Rusty, my son,—said Soria gently. ' He did it for your own good, and the good of the kingdom. There are those who, if they knew, would use you" —

' *He* used me!—Rustam protested with a last burst of long festered bitterness.

Soria smiled sadly. ' He uses everybody, even himself, for the good of Tyr-en. You know that" you are proud of him for it.—

Finally, Rustam let the last dregs of rancour seep from him. He gave his mother a wry grin. ' You know me too well.—

The glowing colour of Soria's hair began to fade and desperately Rustam searched her face, trying to fix forever in his memory this new image of her, an image formed with the love and understanding of maturity. Soon, she was gone, and it was Chel's visage that hung before him. But Soria was forever stored now within his heart and mind.

' My son,—said the goddess. ' You have learned much in a short time, and your life can never return to the way it was. The question now becomes, in all that is yet to pass, will you trust me?—

Rustam was shocked. 'You are my goddess" how could I not trust you?—

'You have shown little trust for women in your life so far.—

'I trust Xindaya,—he protested, 'and Annasala.—After some thought he added in surprise, 'and Risada.—

As he said it, he knew the last to be true. He knew also that Chel already knew.

'You just wanted me to admit that, didn't you?—

The goddess smiled gravely. 'To yourself, yes. It is important that you know how much you have changed.—

Suspicions curled uneasily around Rustam's stomach. 'You're going to use me, too, aren't you?—

'Your choices are your own, my son, but the pattern is already drawn. It simply remains to see where you will fit within the weave. I ask you again: will you trust me?—

Rustam bowed his head. 'I will.—

His heart stopped as icy fingers touched his brow. He squeezed his eyes shut, holding himself rigid as arctic fire retraced the path of Charin's touch from temple to jaw. Merciful numbness followed the fire, and no stench of scorched flesh assailed his senses.

'*Follow your conscience, my son.*—

The voice whispered around him on a distant breeze and he could not tell if the voice was Chel's, or Soria's. The ground seemed to fall away from beneath his feet and he staggered. Reaching out to steady himself, his fingers met rock and he opened his eyes to find himself back in Shiva, beside the raised body of water that was the *morril* pool.

He slipped the half-forgotten dagger back into its sheath, then fingered his left cheek, delighting in the taut skin and renewed sensations that rewarded his palpations as the deadness evaporated. He smiled and felt both corners of his mouth lift equally. His probing fingers found roughened skin where Chel's touch had traced a line down his face, and he looked curiously into the water.

The ridged seam of a scar split his cheek from top to bottom, like the legacy of a knife fight.

Or a disagreement between a god and a goddess.

But Charin's taint had brought him to where Chel wanted him, so could that really be considered a disagreement? Rustam shook his head; the motives of deities were beyond his desire to understand.

He set out in search of Risada.

* * * * * * ** *

' I see you have settled your dispute with Charin,—observed Queen Leith.

' I had a little help.—

' As have I, in the past.—

The human queen of elves sat cross-legged on the ground beside yet another of the Shivan pools. Rustam had happened upon her whilst searching for Risada, but doubted it was coincidence he had found Leith instead. He wondered if she, too, had been seeking a vision.

' Come, sit beside me,—Leith invited. ' You can tell me about my nephew, young Marten.—

Rustam sank to the mossy grass and drew a deep breath of the fluid golden air. It no longer made him in the slightest bit unwell, rather he savoured every breath and wondered how he had survived on the thin, insipid excuse for an atmosphere that existed in his own world. *But this was his world too.* At least a portion of him belonged in Shiva, and the longer he was here, the more at home he felt.

Unease rippled through him. He still had a duty to his Kingdom, to his father.

'What would you know?—

'How old he is, what he looks like. Will he be a good king?—

'Marten is a good king already. He was crowned two solstices past and has displayed none of his sire's poor qualities. As to his looks, he's a personable young man with brown hair and eyes, but with a distressing tendency to blush. Have you never met him?—

Queen Leith shook her head. 'No, I haven't. It's hard to believe he's so old already. Living here, it's easy to forget about time.—

She stared away into the distance, her strange red eyes seeming to cut through the thick air like a sharp knife through flesh. Her alabaster skin was flawlessly white against her long, sable hair and, despite her unusual colouring, Rustam found her incredibly alluring. Yet at the same time totally untouchable.

Must be living amongst all those elves for so long.

'You can't be that much older than Marten yourself.—

Leith's pale skin coloured ever so slightly. 'You flatter me, Master Chalice, but I think you reckon without the benefits of living in Shiva. Whilst it is true that Shivans themselves live longer lives by nature, it is also sure that those few human folk who have settled here enjoy a far greater span than those of the Five Kingdoms.—

'But if I understand correctly, you will all die at some time? There are no true eternals?—

'Eventually, we all return to the goddess.—She looked straight at him, and Rustam found her deep ruby eyes almost as disturbing as the silver of the deities. 'Will you stay now and delay that return,— she asked, 'or does Tyr-en so command your loyalty that you are prepared to risk hastening the day?—

Rustam barely paused. 'My prince needs me, as does the king we both serve and the people of a kingdom who deserve a more peaceful existence than they have had in recent years.—

Queen Leith nodded her approval. 'Patriotically said. My nephew is fortunate indeed to have subjects such as you.—She glanced up and included in her speech the Lady of Domn, who was just entering the clearing accompanied by Elwaes.

Rustam sprang to his feet, noticing as he did so how energised he felt. Bearing in mind what Leith had just said about extended life spans, he suspected that the glorious golden air was at least partially responsible. As he felt it must also be for the miraculous return to health of the sickly elf they had hauled almost as baggage across the mountains and into Kishtan. Elwaes positively glowed with vigour, his skin no longer sallow, his still tufted hair shining and his frame filled out to the elegance it had always promised.

This last gave Rustam pause" how long had they been here, in Shiva? As Leith had just said, it was easy to lose track of time within this magically enclosed land.

Urgency suddenly reinstated itself. 'How long have we delayed? Has the council agreed to our request yet? When can we start moving troops?—

'She hasn't told you yet?—Risada's voice was so brittle Rustam barely recognised it and when he looked, he found her face to be almost as white as that of his hostess.

'Told me what?—he asked, heart sinking.

Beside him, Leith rose to her feet. 'I have not told him because there was more I wanted to know.—

'What difference could it make?—asked Risada bitterly. 'Your king has refused passage to the troops we need. There is an end to it.—

After all this! Rustam despaired. *I really thought I'd found a way.*

'Rusty!—Elwaes exclaimed. 'Your face!—

Risada's head snapped round. Then she groaned. 'I don't want to deal with this anymore. I want to go back to a world where magic doesn't happen every few seconds. Not,—she added hurriedly, 'that

I'm not pleased for you, Rusty. Even with that mark, it's a huge improvement. If we still had a kingdom to return to, you'd probably find yourself even more in demand than you were before" scars always add a certain mystique and maturity to a man.—

' But King Rhe has refused?—

My prince—father—I've failed you, thought Rustam in anguish. Then: *Sala! My sister, what have I condemned you to?*

' I can still help.—

Both Tyr-enese regarded Queen Leith in confusion.

' Surely,—began Risada cautiously, ' You would not go against your King and consort?—

Leith shook her head. ' You misunderstand. We are not able to help you in the way you requested. We simply do not have the strength needed to open a large enough portal to convey the sheer numbers of troops you were proposing.—Seeing their lack of comprehension, she explained further.

' Whilst certain Gates exist in scattered locations about the mountains, there are none near enough to where you need to go. We can, if needs be, open a new one. But the larger the Gate, the greater the sacrifice of strength on the part of our elven mages, and since the wars with your Kingdom, there are precious few of those left to us. Tocar is one, and you have seen for yourself the devastating effect of overextending mage power as he was forced to do at Larn.—

An image of Tocar's wasted body, supported by his two indispensable aides flashed before Rustam.

Leith accurately read Rustam's expression. ' So, you understand. You can also understand then, why my husband will not ask that of his people, particularly to aid Tyr-en.—

' But?—

' But *I* can still aid you.—

' How?—Risada asked, sounding sceptical.

Leith smiled, a particularly predatory smile that made a trickle of ice run down Rustam's spine.

'It has been a long time since I last rode into battle,—stated the tiny, raven haired queen. 'But I have not forgotten how to fight.—

* * * * * * * * *

'I still don't see how this is going to help us,—grumbled Risada as they gathered their few belongings and stuffed them back into their saddle bags. Rustam checked the interior of the hollow tree to ensure nothing was forgotten. 'What difference can two dozen elves make against hundreds of Tylocian mercenaries?—

Elwaes stood in the door arch. 'Lady Risada, you have never seen elves fight.—

'I haven't,—she agreed, 'but whilst I have heard of their skill and ferocity, I still cannot ... *Oh goddess!*—She turned a stricken look upon Rustam. 'We're going to bring *magic* into Tyr-en!—

The thought had not even occurred to Rustam. By now he was so comfortable with the idea of magic as a part of everyday life that it took a moment to readjust to the Tyr-enese view of the arcane.

'Surely at this stage, any form of help will be acceptable. We've been gone for so long now there's every likelihood a small assault team may be more effective than mere numbers of troops. And we stand a chance of moving that small a number without detection, considering the distance we'll need to travel from the nearest Gate.—

'But Rustam" m*agic?*—

He shrugged, finally out of patience with the whole Tyr-enese mistrust of a naturally occurring gift. As Elwaes had once suggested, you might just as well ban fire. 'You can always refuse.—

Risada looked hurt. 'That's hardly helpful. We're supposed to be on the same side, though lately I have been unsure of where your heart lies. Remember what I've said before, Rusty: you will need to shed your affiliation for the black arts once we return home.—

'*Rusty?*—echoed Rustam. Risada shrugged, a slightly embarrassed grin twitching the corners of her mouth. 'It suits you,—she admitted, then added sternly, 'but don't expect such familiarity when we're back in Tyr-en.—

'Goddess forbid! It wouldn't fit with the natural order of things. I can quite see that.—

She glanced at him obliquely. 'You really don't like our way of life any more, do you? I've watched you changing, and I'm not sure you can change back again. You are, however, the prince's man, and you will do your duty. Of that I am sure.—

Risada Delgano vas Domn pulled the last drawstring tight on her pack and straightened up. She turned to Elwaes. 'Lead on then, Sir Elf. We have a kingdom to save. Even if they won't thank us for the way we do it.—

Elwaes swept an elaborate bow. 'My Lady, we are yours to command.—

24. BLOOD

They emerged on a hillside deep within the foothills of the Middle Mountains, almost ten days ride from Darshan.

This Gate was hidden behind the silver curtain of a waterfall, at the head of a barren, rocky valley. The first rays of a low winter sun were just gilding the black and grey outlines of the jagged peaks at their backs. Rustam shivered in the chill air, and pulled his cloak higher around his neck. The abrupt change of season between Shiva and Tyr-en was a sharp reminder that there was more than just distance between the two kingdoms.

As was the insipidly thin air.

He studied the others in their party. Risada was still mounted on her grey despite the offer of a Shivan horse.

'We ve been through so much together," she d explained. ' And I feel Greylegs and I have reached an understanding."

' *Greylegs*?" queried Rustam.

Risada had looked slightly embarrassed. ' Well, I felt he deserved a name."

Rustam approved, but felt the real reason was more to be found in the Lady of Domn s mistrust of the magical nature of their escort s steeds. He restrained himself from saying so with surprising ease.

Elwaes was riding his beloved Fleetfoot, Leith on a gigantic grey stallion that looked too massive for her to have any hope of controlling, yet she appeared utterly in command. Strapped diagonally across the queen s back was a huge sword, and Rustam wondered if she handled that with the same ease she displayed in governing her outsized mount. Some twenty more elves, all clad in greens and browns, rode with them, astride the Shivan bred horses that were tall enough to carry their long limbs with ease and grace.

Not quite what we had in mind when we set off on this venture, mused Rustam. Despite his confident words to Risada, he wondered if they were on a fool's errand.

Darshan was due north of the Gate but, in accordance with plans already made, they headed east by north east towards Rees-Charlay, in the hope that Melcard would not already have marched upon the capital.

'Either this is a mild winter," observed Risada, looking at the height of the snowline on the peaks, ' Or else we have not been gone for as long as I believed."

'Time has a habit of behaving differently in Shiva," offered Elwaes.

'How so?" asked Risada.

Queen Leith joined their conversation. 'The flow of time in Shiva is rarely related to that in the Five Kingdoms, my dear. For instance, whilst you know that Marten's mother was my sister, I doubt you realise she was six years younger than me."

Rustam felt his eyebrows vanishing into his fringe. If he had been asked to guess, he would have put Leith's age at close to his own, somewhere around twenty. Not twice that.

He could see Risada struggling with the idea.

'Is there not a constant difference?" asked Rustam.

Elwaes shook his head. ' No. Not that it's ever bothered us" you know we take little notice of passing time. I believe that some humans have tried to understand it, but no one yet seems to have found a way to predict it."

'But time always passes more slowly within Shiva?"

Again, Elwaes wagged his head. 'Not always. Most often, but on rare occasions it has been quicker."

'That's ludicrous!" Risada objected.

'No, my Lady," corrected the elf. 'It's magic."

* * * * * * * * * * *

Later, and in more privacy after Elwaes and the queen had ridden ahead, Risada broached the subject of fathers.

'Rusty," she began, sounding almost tentative, embarrassed.

'Mmm?"

'I had no idea, you do realise that, don't you?"

'Pardon me? Ah, you mean my august parentage."

'Well," she qualified, 'that's not quite how I would put it" you're still illegitimate, after all. But yes, that is what I mean. I was so utterly convinced you were my father's, I never considered any other possibility. And now I find that not only are you not my brother, but I have no basis for a grudge against your family either; your mother must already have been pregnant when she came to Domn. What a hateful little girl I must have seemed to her."

'I doubt she viewed it that way. You witnessed the brutal murder of both your parents; you needed an outlet for your grief, and she would have known that."

'Even so, I wish I could tell her how sorry I am."

'I think you just did."

Risada looked startled, then frowned. 'You're not going mystic again, are you? I've warned you about that."

'It's just that..., well, in my vision..."

'Go on," prompted Risada.

Not, *its magic' I don't want to hear about it.* Did the Lady of Domn have any idea how much *she* had changed?

'I spoke with Chel. And with my mother."

'You spoke with the *goddess*?" Risada sounded awed but not disbelieving. She nudged Greylegs closer to Nightstalker, until her leg rubbed against Rustam's.

Very aware of the physical contact, Rustam turned to look into her eyes, and nodded. 'You weren't the only one to make unfounded assumptions about a parent, you know. I'd always believed my mother abandoned me. But she didn't. She was murdered too."

Risada's hand shot out, gripped his thigh as her eyes rounded in horror.

'*Rusty*! How?"

'Poisoned. By the Royal Bastard. Oh yes," he continued as Risada's expression changed. 'He does exist. But I don't think he's left many witnesses alive to vouch for it."

'What does he look like?" Risada asked eagerly. Rustam blinked. He hadn't thought to ask. *Stupid*, he berated himself. *So stupid. Suppose he takes advantage of this coup? We may not realise until it's too late, because we have no idea who we're looking for.*

Despair sank through his guts. Risada would think him an imbecile, and suddenly he found himself wanting very much to retain her favour. But there was no way out.

'It didn't occur to me to ask," he admitted.

Risada's fingers gently squeezed his leg.

'Under those circumstances, Rustam dear, I doubt many would have."

He looked at her in blank surprise. She grinned and shrugged. 'We'll just have to keep our wits about us."

Their eyes locked, and it seemed to Rustam that his time sense was stretching away into oblivion. He struggled to draw breath, but then Risada's face jerked away.

'Look," she said in a curiously thick tone, and snatched her hand away from his thigh to point into the distance. It left a small, cold patch on his leg.

' Does that hut look familiar to you?"

* * * * * * * * *

Three days later, they stood on Rees-Charlay land. The mansion nestled quietly inside its formal gardens where, not so long ago, lords and ladies had strolled and picnicked, and Rustam had walked with Princess Annasala, his sister. Now those gardens were as deserted as the farms around the estate had proven to be.

It appeared they were too late.

' It was only ever a slim chance," said Risada. Rustam was unsure whether she was trying to console him, or herself.

' *Look!*"

One of the elves pointed. Rustam sighted along the out-thrust finger and saw what had aroused the Shivan-s interest. Smoke. Clearly the mansion was not totally deserted.

' Melcard would hardly have taken everyone." Risada-s tone was somewhat acerbic. ' There are bound to be staff, and other Family members still in residence."

As if to prove her point, a troop of guards marched around the corner from the direction of the stables. The low glare of winter sun bounced off their silver helmets and buttons.

' I agree with your Ladyship," said Elwaes. ' But why are the guards not wearing Melcard-s livery?"

Stunned silence prevailed as all present absorbed the implications of the black and silver uniforms. As far as Rustam could recall, this was a colour scheme belonging to none of the nobility of Tyr-en. ' Could Melcard have adopted this for his pretension to the throne?" he suggested hesitantly.

' I doubt it." Risada was equally as dubious.

'No," stated Elwaes. The others regarded him in surprise. He stared back, daring them to disagree. 'I know how attached Melcard is to the idea of adopting the royal purple. He even spoke of his plans one night, when he and Hensar came to visit."

That last was spoken with such irony that Rustam winced, recalling what he had witnessed the night he had been an uninvited observer at such a visit.

But if those were not Melcard's men, whose were they?

He glanced towards Risada and knew she had the same suspicion.

The Royal Bastard.

The man who had murdered Soria Chalice, and countless others over the years to protect his identity.

'It appears my long term quarry may have made his move at last," murmured Risada. Rustam guessed her words were intended for his ears only, but Queen Leith proved that not only elves had sharp hearing.

'And he might be...?"

Risada had the grace to look embarrassed. 'The bastard son of King Belcastas, your Maj" " The diminutive queen held up a hand, and Risada corrected herself with difficulty. She had been brought up with formality and tradition; to address a monarch so informally went against her cultural conditioning. 'Leith. That makes him Marten's uncle, but somehow I doubt he has the best interests of the king at heart. Rumour at the time implicated him in the death of your sister, although there was no proof it was not an accident."

Leith looked grim. 'But you don't think it was?"

Risada shook her head. 'There were too many coincidences. No, I think he's been plotting treason for a very long time, slowly removing the obstacles between himself and the throne." She gestured towards the troop of guards now disappearing around the further corner of the mansion. 'That suggests to me that he now feels confident enough to move openly. But I wonder why they are here, unless..."

'Melcard is still in there." Rustam finished her thought. 'But why would the Bastard leave him alive?"

'Perhaps this Bastard of yours has some use for him," suggested Elwaes, then his voice roughened. 'But it won-t do him any good. There won-t be enough of Melcard left for anyone to do anything with by the time I-ve finished with him."

Rustam knew his next suggestion would go down poorly with his elven friend.

'Surely, if Melcard is a prisoner, no matter by whom, we need not waste time breaking in to deal with him now. It would be more sensible to follow the pretender and attend to him first. Melcard will still be here when we come back."

Always supposing we are alive to *come back*, Rustam added, but only silently, to himself. To his surprise, Risada disagreed.

'You are overlooking something, Rusty: we have no idea *who* the Bastard *is*. There-s every chance that, by now, Melcard knows. I think we should ask him."

* * * * * * * * * * *

They entered the mansion the same way they had left it" via the sewer. Rustam expected some complaints from the elves but once their goal was set the Shivans turned grim and silent, moving with such stealth Rustam could almost forget they were behind him. It was like working with twenty assassins, not just one, he reflected with a shiver.

The horses had been secreted in nearby woodland and left with instructions not to move from the area unless discovered. Risada had looked a touch askance at the idea of leaving the animals with no one to guard them, but Rustam doubted anyone meaning them harm would live to tell the tale. He had seen the intelligence in the eyes of Leith's huge stallion, Moonwind, and left Nightstalker confidently in the care of the elven steeds.

Wading hip deep in the freezing, reeking, vermin-infested water with his boots and leggings held aloft, Rustam wondered briefly how they would tackle the climb up to the garbage disposal room. In their flight, they had not stopped to study the wall with any thought of returning, and he had no idea if it was smooth or rough, if there was any way of scaling it.

It turned out not to be an issue.

Once they stood below the jagged hole in the brickwork (not quite smooth, but slick and slippery certainly) two of the elves hoisted a third aloft. With the extra reach of their limbs, the lofted one had no trouble slithering through the hole and very quickly a rope snaked its way down to the waiting party. In quick succession they shinned up it" even Queen Leith with her massive sword still strapped to her back proved to be as agile as the two trained players" until all twenty four of them had gained the interior of Melcard's stronghold. Rustam was drawing his boots back on when he realised that there were only ten people still with him.

' *Damn!*" he muttered. ' They really don t hang around."

' If you have no desire to hang, you ll move quickly too," hissed Risada close beside him. She had her boots on already, but she had climbed up before him.

' I just hope the smell doesn t give us away." Rustam wrinkled his nose and Risada tapped it lightly.

' You always were an old popinjay," she teased.

' Less of the old, thank you."

The corridors were as empty as before, and infrequently lit. Lakes of darkness spread between puddles of light at intersections, and no one disturbed them as they made their way towards the dungeon. A single guard stationed by the door at the head of the stairs, stood splendidly illuminated in the centre of the single well-lit passage.

Risada gestured those behind her to retreat. Rustam presumed she was intending to confer, but before she could do more than open her mouth, she flinched and glanced wildly around, staring wide eyed into the darkness at her feet. Something scuttled over Rustam's boot. He snatched it away and joined Risada in her frantic search, before he noticed that none of the elves seemed at all disturbed. He followed the direction of their gaze, and watched in horrified fascination as the darkness extruded itself beyond the confines of their unlit passage.

Ragged fingers of shadow reached towards the unsuspecting guard, travelling along the creases where wall met floor and, when Rustam glanced up, where wall met ceiling. Faint rustling and the odd high pitched squeak told Rustam what he was seeing and he tapped Risada on the shoulder, drawing her attention to the unfolding scene.

The black-clad guard glanced uneasily around. The rustling was unmistakable now, like autumn leaves in a strong breeze. Something dark dropped from the ceiling onto his shoulder.

He shrieked and batted the lump of shadow away. A large rat flew across the passage, to be swallowed up by the incoming tide of vermin. Trained soldier that the guard was, his first instinct was to draw his sword but it was barely halfway from its sheath when his nerve broke and he bolted. Straight onto the point of a Shivan blade.

'Ugghh.' Risada shuddered. Even as they watched, the rats dispersed and vanished into the gloom. 'I suppose that was Shivan magic at its most useful, may Chel protect us.'

Rustam forbore to point out that Chel was as much goddess to the elves as to humankind.

The dungeon key was still attached to the dead guard-s-belt but, as Rustam bent to retrieve it, the tall figure of an elf intercepted him. He straightened to find himself facing Elwaes, but an Elwaes he barely recognised. The Shivan-s-eyes were burnished silver, his fierce beauty almost too terrible to behold.

The mask of the goddess.

’That,“ he said in a voice that promised death, ’is mine.“

Rustam spread his hands wide and stepped back.

’Elwaes,“ said Risada, and the elf turned shining eyes upon her. Rustam watched proudly as, with a barely visible effort, the Lady of Domn controlled the fear that once would have gripped her to face the magic without flinching. ’Just remember,“ she cautioned, ’we need answers from him.“

The elf nodded. ’I will remember.“

’Ware!“ cried one of the Shivan warriors. Rustam heard the thunder of many boots in the same moment, and spun to see black uniformed troops emerge from the dark corridor behind them. He whirled round, but they were coming from the other direction as well. The Shivan party” the fourteen that were now with them” split smoothly into two groups, half facing in either direction. They moved as though unheard commands whispered inside their heads, drawing weapons in unison and forming formidable barriers to either side of the dungeon door.

’Go!“ ordered Leith in the last second before swords clashed deafeningly.

Elwaes lunged for the door and slammed the key home. Screams of rage and pain shrilled above the clatter of blades, but the lines held and Leith pointed imperiously into the gaping darkness at the head of the dank stairwell. Elwaes stepped forward and was swallowed by the gloom. Risada followed. Rustam hesitated until the elven queen shoved him after the others, and then positioned herself in front of the open door with her huge sword gripped between her two tiny hands. Rustam marvelled that she had the strength to hold it at all, but she did so without apparent effort, and it seemed to Rustam that the metal hummed eagerly, almost as if it were keen for battle.

With a shudder left over from his Tyr-enese superstition, he realised what it was: a legend. *Rhesmett,* the most feared sword of the Shivan Wars" a magical weapon reputed to have a fearsome life of its own. He was hugely grateful that it was at his back, not facing him as he descended the spiralling stairway. The crash and screech of metal upon metal followed him down, and he was round the last turn before he realised there was also fighting below.

' Rust" "

A sword sliced towards his neck. He jerked back and the blade bounced off the wall. Stone chips flew and Rustam yelped as one stung his cheek. His own sword slithered from its scabbard and up to parry the next blow but there was no pause in which to change his time sense and he was forced to fight like a normal man. Still standing on the bottom step, he at least had the advantage of height.

The floor space between the base of the stair and the iron bars of the cage was small, and it already held five combatants. As he dodged another slice, Rustam caught a glimpse of Elwaes wielding a light sword against a black and silver uniformed guard, and Risada struggling at close quarters with a heavily built Tylocian, clearly distinguishable by his swarthy skin and long dark hair and beard.

The fifth was his own assailant whose backswing came through at ankle height, forcing Rustam to leap in the air. His head cracked against the lintel at the base of the stairwell and colours sparkled before his eyes, but even through the dazzle he spied an opening and seized it" in taking such a wild sweep, his opponent was overextended and exposing his left flank.

Rustam abandoned both his height advantage and his sword, and flung himself forward. Daggers slid smoothly into each palm and onward, imbedding themselves between the enemy s ribs. One slithered out again but the other stuck and, as blood spurted from around it, the man staggered backward with a look of astonishment and fell against the bars of the cage. His hands clutched convulsively at the metal railings like those of a drowning man grasping at driftwood. He slithered to the floor. Over his head, Rustam locked eyes with the occupant inside the cage.

Melcard.

Still as handsome as ever, the Lord of Rees-Charlay was, however, no longer the suave sophisticate of the Royal Court. Bruises shadowed his face and his overly elaborate, lace-edged shirt was torn and stained. His usually emotionless eyes smouldered with rage, the first signs of life Rustam had ever seen in them.

Images from the Shivan Pool, of Annasala in terror and in pain at this man s orders, washed over Rustam and he felt his lips break into a wolfish smile, his new scar stretching tight across his cheek.

The sound of fighting continued above, but down in the dungeon a dangerous quiet descended. Glancing round, Rustam saw three bodies on the floor, none of them his companions. Elwaes was relieving his opponent of a ring of keys, and Risada was propped against the wall beyond, cradling her left arm with her right.

' How bad?" Rustam rushed to her side. The Lady of Domn grinned fiercely back, not yet feeling the wound that Rustam could see through the rip in her sleeve. It extended almost from shoulder to elbow and bled freely. Rustam s whole body went cold. He could not gauge how deeply the blade had cut, but a mere scratch would have been enough" Tylocian knives were almost invariably poisoned.

The same knowledge shone in Risada's eyes as she said, 'I'll live. At least, long enough to see this traitor die.'

'Traitor?' grated Melcard's voice and all three looked round at him. 'You call *me* traitor? I had only the interests of our people at heart, to slice away the infection that is the Royal Family before its newest incarnation could fester with the sickness of his forebears. How dare you call me so, when you are willing to sully yourself for Halnashead?' He glared at Risada.

'What?' The Lady of Domn's outrage burst from her lips and carried her across the floor until only the bars separated her from Melcard.

'You know to what I refer,' he sneered. '*Magic*. You have debased yourself with the vile art to maintain a monarchy that should have been torn down generations ago.'

Risada drew herself up. 'I don't know how you came by such a ludicrous idea,' she said with dignity, but swayed so unsteadily on her feet that Rustam put a hand beneath her elbow. She leaned against him. '*I* have never used magic. *You*, on the other hand, employed a sadistic meddler with more than a passing talent for the arcane, and the willingness to use it in support of your insurrectionary goals.'

Melcard scowled. 'My conscience is clear. Hensar's methods were beyond my knowledge, and as we now know, it was not to my ends that he worked.'

Elwaes fitted a key to the gate and swung it open. Melcard's composure slipped when he recognised the face of his erstwhile victim.

'*You!* But you're *dead!*'

The elf smiled, argent eyes flashing as he advanced. Melcard took a step back. And another.

'Keep away from me, spawn of Charin.'

But Elwaes kept advancing, and for a brief instant Rustam almost felt sorry for Melcard. The Shivan towered over even Melcard's tall frame, and his lithe, deadly tread recalled that of a werecat. Not for anything would Rustam have traded places with the Lord of Rees-Charlay.

A scuffle ensued but Rustam's attention was diverted by Risada sagging against him. 'I think I'm going to faint," she whispered, and he had just enough time to catch an awkward hold on her shoulders before her body turned boneless. He staggered as her limp weight dragged them both down, then gave in to the inevitable and dropped to his knees. He propped Risada against himself with her head lolling loosely on his chest, his arms protectively around her.

At this level, the stench of death was overpowering and he swallowed convulsively, turning his face away from the carnage that surrounded them and back to the cage. Elwaes and his former captor were struggling in the gateway, though the elf appeared to have the upper hand, with one of Melcard's arms twisted up behind him.

'Demon spawn!" screeched Lord Melcard, and his furious, terrified eyes fixed on Rustam. 'See how low your precious Royal Family has fallen, assassin? Were I you, I would guard my back. Magic may strike from the most oblique angle, and when you least expect it. Do not think even you are safe from its foul blade."

Assassin? Rustam blinked. Melcard believed *he* was Dart, and Risada some form of magical practitioner. Was there a way they could use his misapprehension to their advantage?

Risada stirred in his arms and both he and Elwaes were momentarily distracted. That moment was all Melcard needed.

Jerking out of the elf's grasp, he flung himself upon the body of the man Rustam had killed, plucked the knife that still protruded from between the ribs, and spun back to face them. The short bladed weapon wove threateningly to and fro, dripping gore.

'Now we are on more equal terms," said the Lord of the Fourth Family.

In front of Rustam, Risada sat up. He loosened his hold on her and felt her flinch as she shifted her injured arm. His stomach clenched in sympathy" he knew the sharp pain of sliced skin and muscle.

'Hardly that, traitor."

Her voice was strong, though Rustam could feel the effort it cost her. She jerked her chin towards the stairs. 'Whichever side wins up there, you lose. Why are you still alive anyway?"

Elwaes drew his small, light sword and took a step forward. Melcard brandished his knife and the elf stopped but did not retreat. Melcard's eyes swivelled back and forth, and then he smiled lasciviously. 'Hensar is saving me for his private amusement. I'm sure he will be delighted to add you to his planned diversions, my Lady. He has a taste for beautiful women."

Rustam stiffened, his vision of Sala's torment burning across his inner eye. 'I've seen his perversions," he spat. 'But they were at your command."

Melcard met Rustam's angry gaze. 'Hensar was efficient. It was unnecessary for me to know his methods."

Rustam choked. '*Unnecessary?* You delude yourself. You knew. Or you would not be so scared of being his next victim."

Melcard's eyes flashed. 'Scared? I don't know what you think you've seen, but if you had any real idea.... But I doubt I'm anywhere soon on his agenda. He has a wedding and a coronation to organise."

'Whose coronation?" demanded Risada.

Elwaes edged closer.

'You don't know, do you?" Melcard's tone was surprised, then gloating. 'You *really* don't know. How delightful. Then I shall not be the one to spoil the surprise. I" "

Elwaes lunged forward, sword aimed for Melcard-s-knife, trying to knock the small but deadly weapon out of the traitor-s-grasp. With the strength of desperation, Melcard hung on grimly even when the Shivan-s-blade sliced the tops from his knuckles and embedded its point in his upper arm.

' *Nooo!*" screamed Rustam as, unbidden, his time sense stretched.

Pinned in place by Risada, he watched helplessly as Melcard-s-bloody hand swung inexorably forward beneath Elwaes-s-extended arm. Like viewing a sluggish vision with the detached sense of not being physically present, Rustam saw the dagger point" *his* dagger" touch his friend-s-side and slid in, moving relentlessly upward and inward, stopping only when the hilt kissed his skin.

Soundless, Elwaes curled forward. A scarlet fountain blossomed from his open mouth to drench Melcard-s-feet. The Shivan toppled sideways by degrees and slithered slowly, oh so slowly down the bars of the cage that had defined so much of his life.

Time paused. Numb with anguish, Rustam-s-eyes wandered distractedly over the interior of the cage. Little had changed since Elwaes-s-rescue. The bed and the faded hangings were perhaps thicker with dust. The table had been moved further to one side and ropes still dangled from the chair where Annasala had been tied, but essentially the dungeon remained the same. Ironic that after all their adventures, the elf should die here, back where it all began.

Silver blue eyes pleading for liberation...

Rustam shivered. At least this time Elwaes would be truly free.

The Lord of Rees-Charlay turned his flushed, triumphant countenance upon the pair on the floor.

' And so, none of us wins, but I can at least rid the Kingdom of two more heretics."

Emerging fury overwhelmed Rustam-s-mental paralysis. Risada shifted her weight to free him and he lunged to his feet as Melcard bent to pluck the dagger from his victim's side. As the traitor's fingers closed around the hilt, he froze, his whole body a petrified image of horror. Elwaes's hand closed over his own.

A bloody mask dominated by two glowing silver eyes stared full upon Melcard.

'Make that just one," came a harsh whisper. Rustam did not even try to identify the voice" Chel, Charin or Elwaes himself, he would not have cared to guess. Once again he watched, rooted to the spot as his dagger slid between ribs, clutched in Melcard's own fist with the Shivan's hand curled tightly around it.

This time the blade found its prey's heart. Melcard dropped to the floor. His lifeless eyes, at last truly devoid of emotion, stared sightless from the relaxed, handsome features.

Rustam stumbled forward and dropped to his knees. He lifted Elwaes's shoulders to his lap. A radiant, silver aura surrounded the elf, fading even as Rustam watched, and when their eyes met, Elwaes's were the clear blue of his friend.

Words choked in Rustam's throat.

Elwaes put a bloody hand on his arm. 'Do not grieve for me, my friend." Tiny red bubbles frothed on his lips. Using a corner of his sleeve, Rustam wiped them away. 'They say" " Coughing took him, scarlet spittle staining Rustam's hand. 'They say revenge is a bitter victory, but I've had mine, and it tasted sweet." The elf grinned and coughed again, a steady flow of bright blood trickling from the corner of his mouth. His head moved slightly, eyes roving the cage beyond the bars, then back to the spreading red puddle on the stone flags.

'So much blood," he whispered dazedly. 'It was always about blood, here..."

The last word turned into a long sigh, and his body relaxed, leaving a slightly puzzled expression on his beautiful, bloody, dead face.

* * * * * * * * * * *

' *Goddess!*"

Rustam looked up. Leith stood on the bottom stair. Her face was, if anything, whiter than usual" bloodless. Behind her, two other elves descended, looking equally as shocked as they viewed the slaughter. Their eyes lingered on Elwaes, lying in Rustam-s-arms.

' Risada, you-re hurt!"

Leith crossed quickly to the other woman, kneeling beside her to inspect the injury.

Risada shook her head. ' It-s-just a scratch, really." Her voice quavered.

' If that-s-a scratch, I don-t-want to see a real wound," said Leith, slipping a pouch from her belt and decanting the contents. She picked something out of the pile. ' Here, swallow this."

Risada looked at her vaguely. ' What" ?"

Leith-s-anxious eyes met Rustam-s-over Risada-s-head. Panic stabbed him in the gut.

' I think the blade was poisoned. Please Risada, swallow what you can."

Obedient for once, Risada held the small phial to her lips and downed the draught in one gulp. Leith poured the contents of another into the top of the wound. Risada gasped.

' Sorry," muttered Leith, and began binding the arm with a small roll of fabric.

' Please," said someone quietly beside Rustam. He looked round. The two elves were kneeling beside him.

' Let us take him into the light and air."

Rustam nodded, unwilling to trust his voice. Elwaes-s-body was lifted from his lap and borne away. He sat, silent and hurting.

' He would not want you to grieve," said Leith, looking up from her bandage.

'He was too weak," grated Rustam. 'We should never have brought him with us. He needed longer to recover from all those years of abuse."

'It s not your fault, Rustam."

He shook his head angrily.

'Rustam!" Leith snapped.

Startled, his eyes snapped up, blinked as he met her blood red gaze.

Her face softened. 'Did he seem weak to you, in Shiva, or on the journey here?"

'No," Rustam admitted grudgingly. 'But" "

Leith wagged a finger at him. 'No buts. He had just one thing left to do in this phase of his life, and this was it."

'How can you be so sure?"

'You saw his eyes." Statement, not question. 'That must have happened even before you reached Shiva."

'It did." Rustam remembered the night in the guest house in Teshondra. The first manifestation of the silver aura. And the metallic taint in the Shivan s eyes the next day. 'What did it mean?"

Leith took a deep breath and sighed. Rustam noticed gratefully that Risada seemed more alert, following their conversation.

'In a way, Melcard almost had the truth of it. Blood *is* an elixir of life, but only to the one who owns it, and they took too much of it from him." The elven queen s ruby eyes bored into Rustam s. 'Elwaes was already dead, long before he came here."

'What do you mean?"

'Seek the goddess for your answers, Rustam. I m sure you will find the truth." She rose to her feet. 'I ll send help down."

She stepped over a body and vanished up the stairs, leaving the two Tyr-enese alone.

'I m not even going to try to make sense of that," declared Risada, her voice stronger. She looked at Melcard s crumpled body.

'Tell me, Rusty, knowing what his future held, whichever way things turn out" was that really revenge, or was it a mercy killing?"

The silver eyed mask of the goddess hung before Rustam's vision. He shook his head.

'At the end, I·m really not certain."

25. PRISONERS

The scene at the top of the stairs was even bloodier than the one below. Two elves lay dead, each liberally smeared with blood, though how much was their own was not readily apparent. Attended to by their kin, they lay peacefully with their eyes closed and arms folded upon their breasts. Elwaes lay alongside them. He looked as if he were simply asleep, and Rustam half expected him to wake and sit up at any moment, as he had done so many times during their journey.

Glancing away, trying not to acknowledge the tightness in his chest, Rustam forced himself to look to either side of the dungeon door, where human bodies in black and silver uniforms lay in heaps. Rustam estimated approximately three soldiers to every elf in the fight, including the dead.

He allowed himself to be impressed. Apparently the Shivans' reputation was truly earned, and not just the rumour-mongering of magic-shy Tyr-enese.

"I'm fine, really. Leith, call off your..." Risada's voice, preceding her up the stairwell, trailed off as she was carried through the doorway and into the midst of mass death. Bearing in mind the Lady of Domn's profession and her composure on earlier battlefields, Rustam swiftly concluded that her pallor and the sheen of sweat on her face were not due to an assault on her sensibilities. She was patently not fine.

At Leith's indication, the elf carrying Risada settled her to the floor beyond the pile of corpses, and another held a flask to her lips.

Leith drew Rustam aside.

"The blade was poisoned," she said. Rustam nodded in mute agreement. "I have herbs that will help, but only if she rests."

"For how long?"

Leith shrugged. "Days, possibly weeks. You must convince her to stay here."

"She won't," Rustam stated flatly.

"Then she may die." Leith was as uncompromising. "Activity will spread the poison through her body. If that happens, I'm not sure I can help."

Rustam grimaced, the sinking feeling of inevitability settling into an indigestible lump in his stomach. "I'll try," he said without hope.

* * * * * * * * * *

"Stay here? Have you finally lost your mind?"

"Risada." Rustam knelt down at her side and took her cold hands into his own. "This poison can kill you. Do you want that now, when we're so close to success? What about Iain?"

She glared at him. "That was low," she said, then paused and cocked her head. "And what makes you think we're close to success?"

Her breath was a little too fast, her eyes a touch too bright.

Rustam glanced away, looking round at the elves. "They do," he said, struggling to keep his panic in check. "Look at what they've done here. They are the ultimate stealth force—like a whole troop of assassins. And whether you like it or not, they have magic to call upon. Something no Tyr-enese should have a defence against."

Except perhaps the Bastard, by way of Hensar's services. But why mention that when things sounded so promising.

"We still defeated them in the last war."

"Superior numbers and that good old Tyr-enese tradition of treachery. But we're not talking about a war. We're talking about infiltration with the purpose of killing just one man. The Bastard. This situation is radically different to the one we left. He's no Melcard, with a whole Family waiting to step into his shoes. He's one man and without him the whole thing falls apart. We can do this!"

"We don't yet know the situation in Darshan. His security may be so tight we may not be able to get anywhere near him."

"Ah." The heat of anger swept through Rustam and he grinned savagely, feeling the scar stand proud from his cheek. "But he has both a wedding and a coronation to attend. Even at its best, there will be loopholes somewhere in the security of such public events."

Risada eyed him up and down. "You have this all worked out, haven't you. But I'm afraid the answer is still no. I started this play, and one way or another, I will complete it."

Desperation clawed at Rustam's heart. His fingers tightened around hers. "You always were senselessly stubborn. Should I tell Iain that, when I deliver your body to him?"

Risada looked away, and then turned pleading eyes back upon Rustam. "I have to do this, Rusty, for Iain's sake. I couldn't live with myself if anything went wrong, and I could have fixed it if I'd been there. If we don't stop this, Iain will be one of the first to die, straight after Marten and Halnashead. If they're not dead already. Annasala will only live until she's borne an heir, if he even decides that's necessary. Bastard or no, he bears Royal blood himself and may decide that's sufficient once he has the throne firmly in his grasp."

Images of Rustam's newly acquired sister flashed into his mind. Followed swiftly by thoughts of his father. Was Halnashead still alive? He had to believe so, for he had things he wanted to say to the prince.

He bowed his head and surrendered to the inevitable.

"You will promise to rest as much as possible?"

She slipped one hand from his grasp and ran an icy finger along his jaw line, cupped his chin and drew him close until the warmth of her breath mingled with his own.

"As much as possible," she whispered with her lips against his cheek.

Rustam's throat tightened against the sob that threatened to bubble up. And then their lips met, and such a shock ran through him that his mind blanked. He was intensely aware of her body against his; the soft swell of her breasts, the fevered heat of her skin. The sweet taste of her mouth.

She was finally his, and she was going to die. They both knew it.

Leith's voice spoke close beside them. "We're moving out now. Can you stand?"

Her abrupt manner startled Rustam and he looked up to search the queen's anxious features.

"What's wrong?"

"I'm not certain, but my scouts have failed to return. We should move." Deftly, she fashioned a sling from cloth and immobilised Risada's injured arm. "I'm sorry, but you'll have to walk."

"I would expect nothing less if our situations were reversed."

What Rustam would once have taken as arrogance from the Lady of Domn, now sounded like courage. Leith smiled tightly and turned to lead the way, the great sword *Rhesmett* in her hands.

"Is that what I think it is?" Risada asked, sounding awed as Rustam helped her to her feet.

Rustam nodded. "Yes, it is."

* * * * * * * * * *

They passed through the remainder of the unlit passages without encountering another soul. The building was eerily silent and the corridors smelled of dust and disuse. Rustam guided the party with whispered directions as he recalled turns and junctions until they reached a door that he knew opened into a little used passage leading to the smaller guest apartments. Cautiously, Leith cracked it open and they all stood, breathing lightly, listening.

Nothing.

Leith shouldered the door gently open and took a step forward.

"No!" yelled Rustam as his dark-adjusted eyes made out the fuzzy shape of a loop on the ground. *Too late.* Leith's right foot planted solidly in the circle's centre and, quick as a breath, it snagged closed and wrenched her off her feet. She yelped in surprise, putting out one hand to break her fall and, even before Rustam could leap forward, her other wrist was seized by a huge fist and *Rhesmett* shaken from her grasp.

Rustam and the others froze in the open doorway. Before them, Leith's life hung in the balance, a large set of fingers curled tightly around her throat.

The swarthy Tylocian to whom the fingers belonged grinned happily through his bushy beard and took a step back, keeping the queen firmly between himself and Rustam's daggers. From the corner of his eye, Rustam saw Risada fractionally raise her right hand.

"Uh, uh," forbade Leith's captor with the slightest shake of his head. In his grasp, Leith gurgled, and Risada subsided.

More Tylocians appeared from behind the door, others at their backs. They were urged forward. Rustam had barely taken one step before he was wrestled to the carpet, his weapons wrenched from his fists and his clothes torn apart in search of others. He gagged on the stench of unwashed bodies and sour ale. When his clothes were in tatters barely sufficient to hang together, his assailants moved away, leaving him trussed and helpless but able to see what was happening.

Leith still dangled in the grip of the largest Tylocian Rustam had ever seen, and Risada lay on the floor beside him, bound and obviously in pain with her eyes shut and sweat trickling down her forehead. Rustam's heart ached for her. If only he could *do* something. Her clothes were rent beyond modesty, but with a tiny stab of hope Rustam wondered if they had truly found all of her assassin's tools—it had taken him long and patient searching, that day beside the lake in the mountains.

The elves were receiving the same treatment and Rustam tried to count them, hopeful that some at the rear of the group might have escaped. It was hard to see from a prone position, but he was fairly certain that at least two, if not three besides the missing scouts were unaccounted for. Nevertheless, it had been a well conceived and largely successful ambush.

"Just as the Master promised," declared the giant in charge. Gold neck chains glittered through the bushy length of his beard, and the hand around Leith's throat was studded with heavy gold rings.

Now that the others were secured he let go of Leith. She crumpled to the carpet and lay in a heap, gasping.

"You two," he said, leering at Rustam and Risada. "He wants you two. I wouldn't be in your skins for all the gold in this Kingdom."

He returned his attention to Leith as she stirred to a sitting position. Her head was downcast and she rubbed gingerly at her neck.

"This one, though. He didn't say nothing about this one." He sneered as he took in her Shivan clothes. "Elf lover," he spat. Then his eyes were drawn to *Rhesmett*, lying away to one side.

"Little girls shouldn't play with big weapons," he said, thrusting his hips suggestively towards Leith's averted face. Rustam strained impotently against his bonds.

The brute bent to pick up the weapon, but as his fingers closed around the hilt blue sparks spat and he dropped the sword with a clatter.

"Charin's balls! A demon sword!" He turned back to Leith with a calculating expression. "And I wouldn't mind wagering you're the only one as can handle it."

So, thought Rustam. *Superstitious, but not stupid. Dangerous.*

Reaching down, the Tylocian hooked a grubby finger beneath the queen's chin and lifted her face to get a better look. She opened her startling, blood-coloured eyes and glared at him. He sprang back, as shocked by her eyes as by her sword. Swearing mightily, he regarded her from a safe distance. When nothing untoward happened, a slow smile spread across his broad face.

"The Master will be thrilled! To have you too is a bonus he could never have anticipated. Brask!"

The one named Brask lumbered forward. Heavily built as all Tylocians, he stooped a little, as if the weight of responsibility was too great for his shoulders. The intelligence that shone from his captain's eyes was, in Brask's, decidedly dimmer. The perfect lieutenant.

"Load these three onto the wagon. We're ready to leave."

"What about them?" Brask glanced anxiously at the remaining elves. "Don't want none of them callin' magic down on us."

"Don't you worry about them." The captain raised his voice to ensure the elves could hear him. "The Master left instructions on how to deal with that, and we're to leave them locked down below. Master has new associates coming from the mountains to tidy things up. Promised them a feast, he has."

Rustam shuddered in comprehension as he was hauled like a sack of vegetables down the corridor, recalling the sick look on Elwaes's face when he explained rock trolls' preferences for live elf meat. As to the other, he also remembered hestane, the drug Elwaes had needed; the one that blocked arcane powers.

The Bastard had thought of everything.

* * * * * * * * * *

The wagon was just that: a large cart that Rustam guessed was probably used for bringing produce in from the fields. Chains secured the captives to the metal framework supporting the rough planks upon which they lay. Two huge, shaggy draught horses pulled them along at a steady pace, following a second pair and wagon laden with supplies. The Tylocians themselves walked. Having now experienced travel through the mountains, Rustam could understand the clans' lack of affinity for riding animals—really quite impractical in their domestic situation.

The Tylocian captain, Hext-al, came to see them at dawn every day to administer a dose of hestane to each of the women, but it took Rustam's depressed and grieving mind several days to work out why he was exempt from this treatment. Eventually, he realised that Melcard himself had told them. Risada was believed to be the magic wielder whilst he, although thought to be an assassin, would not be expected to employ arcane abilities.

On the one hand, he nursed the knowledge of their mistake, whilst on the other he fretted about the effect of the drug on Risada who seemed to grow weaker every day, drifting in and out of long periods of unconsciousness.

Leith's herbs lay crushed underfoot back in Rees-Charlay, and none of the Tylocians seemed in the slightest bit interested in treating either Risada's festering knife wound or the effects of the poison. Rustam even tried threatening Hext-al with the Bastard's retribution should Risada die before she could be delivered, but the huge Tylocian merely smiled deep within his beard and kept his silence.

At least she was resting.

With nothing to do other than shift his body at intervals in an attempt to find a position that was a little less uncomfortable—impossible on the bare wooden boards, but it didn't stop him from trying—Rustam found his mind relentlessly picking at the painful memories of this Charin-dammed quest, and wishing he had never left Tyr-en.

"I'm sorry, Rustam," Leith said suddenly, distracting him from his self-indulgent misery.

"Rusty, please," he corrected. "And for what?"

"For stepping into that stupid noose. I'm out of practice at skulking around the countryside; it's been years. And yes, before you ask, I do remember years. Despite my appearance, and the time I've lived in Shiva, I am still human."

"Leith, if you don't mind my asking, where have you met Hext-al before? He obviously knows you, and you scare him."

Leith grinned and Rustam was uncomfortably reminded of Elwaes's vengeful expression when he knew Melcard was within his reach.

"Oh, we've never met, but they all know who I am. Have you ever seen anyone else with my colouring? It's pretty distinctive. So they know I have contacts in their mountains. That I'm one of a very small number of people able to call directly upon the gemeyes."

Rustam scowled at her. "Oh, come on. I know I've had to accept a lot of things on this trip that I thought were myths, but you can't truly mean that the gemeyes are real— they're just a children's story!"

"Poor Rusty. Don't you realise yet that myths have their origins in fact? What will your countrymen say when they know you've spoken with Chel herself? They may think you insane."

"Mmm," Rustam concurred. "Gemeyes? Really?"

"Uh huh," Leith nodded.

"So why don't you call them?" asked Rustam, wondering if the insanity theory was perhaps not so far from the truth. Leith simply waited until he answered himself. "Of course you can't. They've given you hestane."

The Shivan queen nodded.

Risada moved stiffly and opened her eyes. "You should be grateful," she said.

Whilst relieved to find she was not too ill to join in their discussion, Rustam was confused by her statement. "Why?" he asked bluntly. "I should have thought you'd have welcomed some help at this point."

Her sharp blue eyes bored into him, belying the weakness of her body. "Imagine the consequences of bringing magical entities into Tyr-en, even if they were intending to help. It was bad enough that we came with elves—no disrespect to your people, Leith—but I was hoping we could keep their involvement secret.

"Tyr-enese society is built upon our rejection of the arcane powers that forced our ancestors to risk the Crossing, the main reason we have little truck with those Kingdoms that still allow it, no matter how carefully controlled. The very nature of Tyr-en's isolation by the surrounding mountains and, until recently, our superiority in numbers have been the only things that have allowed us to maintain our Kingdom as it is. If you now prove to our people that they cannot be saved without magical intervention, you destroy the basis of our society. We must not bring magic into this."

Her last words were accompanied by a very intense look, directed at Rustam. He was used to hearing the warning by now, but had never had the consequences so clearly laid out for him.

As if she had delivered the last of her strength with that admonition, Risada subsided once more into oblivion.

"At least she's not noticing the accumulation of bruises the way we are," complained Rustam and shifted onto another part of his anatomy.

"No, indeed she isn't," Leith agreed. "But I am concerned about the dosage of hestane they're using. Too much can be lethal, and I have no idea how carefully they're measuring it."

"Well," said Rustam sourly. "If they get it wrong they'll have Hensar and his new Master to answer to. I wouldn't envy them that at all."

* * * * * * * * * *

The wagons moved through a nightmare landscape of burned dwellings and smouldering fields. The acrid stench seared the travellers' throats and Rustam was not sure whether the tears that rolled down his cheeks were caused by the irritation to his eyes, or by his sorrow for the once beautiful land.

Since leaving Rees-Charlay the sight had become ever more common, testimony to those who did not support Melcard's—now the Bastard's—attempt to overthrow the Royal Family. Many had probably not even seen beyond the fact that Tylocian outlanders were being used to supplement Tyr-enese troops.

Rustam wondered how it was that the Bastard thought he could convince the Families to accept him as their ruler when he resorted to such methods. If he planned to kill all the dissenters, he would be left with a very small population indeed.

Of course, there was the matter of Chel's Casket.

If the Bastard was truly a son of Belcastus, then the box would open for him as it did for any of royal blood. Would that age old ritual satisfy the Families? Would they accept him despite his illegitimacy, if he were the only member of the Royal Family left alive aside from his wife, Annasala. Rustam guessed the Bastard was relying on that last detail to be the clincher.

Rustam Chalice smiled at the irony. Although nobody would ever know it, the box would open for him too. Somehow he did not think anyone would accept him as king.

Turning his attention outward again, Rustam watched little oases of unspoilt country slide past. Each untouched estate proclaimed a traitor Family, and Rustam logged their names away for future use.

If, indeed, he had a future.

* * * * * * * * * *

Five days after leaving Rees-Charlay, Leith's elven scouts attacked. They chose a narrow track through a heavily wooded valley. Ideal conditions for a guerrilla attack.

Rustam raised himself stiffly to his knees—as far as his chains would allow—at the first yells from up ahead. Three elves had engaged the leading guards, and other Tylocians were rushing forward to help. The huge bulk of Hext-al was clearly visible, yelling instructions as he struggled to squeeze between the leading wagon and the thick branches that scraped its sides.

Leith sat up. Her face showed no surprise, but was set in an expression that at first Rustam could not read. Her disturbing red eyes flickered down to Risada's prone form and back up to meet Rustam's gaze. Then he understood.

There would be no rescue. No matter how skilled Leith's warriors, the Tylocian troop was far too large for them to overcome, and Risada was a helpless, dead weight. They would not even make it into the trees.

As if to confirm his thoughts, Brask appeared beside him and gave him a rough shove. Manacled and perched awkwardly on his knees as he was, Rustam slammed onto his side. His breath whooshed out as already bruised flesh smacked heavily onto the bare boards at the bottom of the wagon. He lay rigid and gasping, fairly certain that the agonising grinding sensation in his side meant a broken rib or two to add to his discomfort.

Lying there, unable to see, he jerked with surprise when an elven face peered over the wagon side. Fire shot through his ribs and shadowed blots danced before his eyes. Through the rushing sound in his ears he heard Leith urgently giving instructions.

"... back to Rees-Charlay. Rescue the others—they've been given hestane. They're in the dungeon and there's a troll pack on the way. Oh, and the horses..."

The blots before Rustam's vision merged together into blackness and increasingly loud buzzing swept all sound away. When consciousness returned—painfully—the face peering down at him was that of Hext-al. The Tylocian captain glowered.

"Cost me three good clan brothers, you have. I'll not forget it."

After that, there was no more food, only water. With the pain of his broken ribs, Rustam doubted he could have kept anything down anyway.

Only two days journey left to Darshan.

* * * * * * * * * *

Flowers showered into the wagon. Rustam jerked awake, startled by the soft touch of petals on his face. Pain stabbed his side.

Beside him, Leith and Risada also jolted out of sleep.

"What—?"

"They're not real," pronounced Leith. Rustam looked closer. She spoke truly—coloured bits of paper cut and pasted to resemble flowers littered the wooden boards and their bodies. They all looked up as another cloud filled the air and descended upon them.

"Oops!" voices beyond the wagon giggled and in the twilight of late afternoon Rustam saw that they had entered Darshan. The wagon jounced and rattled over cobbled streets and houses loomed warm and inviting to either side. The sweet smell of wood smoke tickled Rustam's nose.

Beyond the Tylocian guards who marched alongside their transport, they could see festive crowds dressed in finery surely reserved only for the most important of occasions. Children rode high on their father's shoulders, tossing the paper blooms enthusiastically for the sheer fun of it. The adults' pensive expressions were out of sorts with their gay clothing, and their voices were muted against the shrill piping of the excited children.

Rustam's heart sank all the way into his boots. Somehow, even trussed and captive as they were, he had cherished the belief that they would still win in the end, but the evidence around them could mean only one thing: they were already too late.

The failing light darkened further as the wagon rolled beneath a stone arch. Voices shouted directions, and Rustam realised they had entered the palace grounds. He recognised the approach to the east wing stables—the very yard where Nightstalker had so often been stabled.

His mind fled briefly back to Rees-Charlay, wondering what had become of the abandoned horses. Would the elven scouts rescue them before the trolls hunted them down for meat? He had the feeling the trolls would come off worst, but he could not be certain.

The rich, well loved aromas of horse filled the air. Torches flared into life as the light failed, and the wagon ground to a halt in the middle of the familiar yard. Lads, some of whom Rustam knew but who would not, now, meet his eye, swarmed over the horses, unharnessing them. The tailgate was lowered and the three captives dragged onto unsteady feet. Rustam gasped at the pain from his ribs and arched his body protectively over to that side, trying to find a stance that lessened the hurt. He held his breath, swallowing nausea.

Prodded into motion, the three tripped and stumbled over the uneven cobbles, shivering in their tatters of clothing. Rustam saw everything through a thick veil. The very familiarity of the scene lent a nightmarish quality that only worsened as they were hustled through corridors he had trodden all his life, but now barely recognised.

Gone were all the well-known wall hangings, the nick-knacks on the hall tables he had picked up and fiddled with over so many years. The display racks of family weapons.

Instead, bare walls glared impassively back, and soldiers in the stark black and silver of the Bastard stood on guard at regular intervals. They emerged from the building and crossed a garden courtyard, richly decorated with lavish canopies and hangings where servants all in black were busy clearing the debris of a celebration. Rustam was so bemused by the fact that he could not place the garden that he simply stopped when Halnashead's private entrance loomed in front of him.

"Move!" growled the Tylocian who had bumped into him.

An elbow jabbed him sharply in the back, directly into one of his many bruises. With his hands still bound behind him he lost his balance and stumbled. Pain lanced through him and he cried out, falling to his knees in front of the guard who stood at the entrance.

"Up you get," instructed a well remembered voice. Rustam's head jerked up. Above the black and silver uniform was the familiar face of Dench. Horror crawled icily through Rustam's gut.

What a supreme position for an opposing player! Rustam's mind ran swiftly back over the years, wondering when Halnashead's trusted guard had started working for the enemy.

Dench smiled down at him, as urbane as ever. "Good to see you again, Master Chalice, after all this time. I do hope you are well."

The chilling sarcasm took Rustam's remaining breath, and he gasped a strangled: "Why?"

"Why?" Dench gave a different smile. "Revenge, Master Chalice. Simple revenge. Halnashead killed my parents. I was ten years old and I still remember them going off on a mission for him, but they never came back. He thought he could make it up to me by paying for my upbringing and then taking me into his service—as if money could ever replace what I lost. I've devoted my life to this moment."

Their Tylocian captors hauled Rustam back to his feet, and steadied him briefly as the world spun blackly. Then he was pushed back into stumbling progress.

The painful journey only worsened as they were marched past Halnashead's study, the door wide open on a bare, empty space. Rustam ached for the well-known smells of ondal oil and leather, but the atmosphere was sterile, devoid of comforting familiarity. Even the great tapestry was missing.

Rustam's eyes met Risada's. Here was where they had first met, where it had all begun. And here, it appeared, it would all end.

* * * * * * * * * *

The cells in Halnashead's private wing were a place Rustam had had no cause to visit. He knew the prince had secure facilities for a small number of prisoners—in his capacity as chief of security it had been necessary—but how often they were occupied, he had no idea.

By the state of them, they had seen considerable use in recent times. Dirty, straw stuffed mats littered the floor, and the only sanitary facilities were a reeking, half filled bucket in one corner.

To Rustam's surprise and chagrin, the three of them were shoved in together. He could not decide whether this was because the others cells were all full, or because they were considered such a minor threat it wasn't deemed worth splitting them up. Either way, apart from the lack of privacy for the women, he was glad.

Risada tottered over to one of the mats and collapsed. Leith knelt beside her and Rustam had no trouble reading the concern in the queen's ruby eyes.

"How is it?" he asked as Leith peeled Risada's sleeve back to reveal angrily swollen, purple flesh.

"No worse than could be expected," said Risada through gritted teeth. She glared up at Rustam. "I am still here, you know. And I don't appreciate being talked about as if I wasn't."

Rustam hunkered carefully down. "You know I'm just worried about you. I didn't drag you all this way just to have you die on me now."

"You," Risada struggled up, propped herself onto her good elbow. "Drag me? How dare you—" She broke off and stared at him, then shook her head. "Oh, very good. Yes, I am still well enough to get indignant."

"Good," said Rustam, and planted a swift kiss on her lips. He straightened carefully, breath held against the pain. The sound of keys in the lock heralded a visitor. "But I don't think you should let *them* know that," he murmured without turning.

Risada smiled and nodded, subsided to a prone position and closed her eyes. She needed to make no great effort to appear very ill indeed.

With his arms wrapped protectively around his ribs, Rustam rose to meet their caller. He was not surprised when Doctor Hensar entered the cell.

What did surprise him was his own reaction.

He began to tremble, every fibre in his body battling with the urge to leap forward and tear the miserable little dwarf to bits, piece by exquisite piece. The guard with the drawn sword in the open doorway was just barely enough to keep him from such a stupid move. He also recalled his abortive attempts to assault Risada during the earlier days of their journey, and found he had learned that lesson well. He would bide his time.

Hensar read his body language differently. His look of contempt dismissed Rustam as a threat, gloated over the supine form of the Lady of Domn, and then froze in astonishment as his eyes lit upon the third member of their party.

"Lady Leith!" His fat pink tongue moistened his lips eagerly. "What a truly, unexpectedly pleasant surprise! Oh, I suppose it should be 'Your Majesty', shouldn't it? But in the light of recent events, I don't think we need use such formality, do we?" His head tilted as thoughts ran swiftly behind his eyes. "This could not have been more fortuitous. Your presence will add the finishing touch to tomorrow's ceremony, and I will finally be able to rid myself of the last of your family."

His face took on a hungry look. "You will plead for your life, won't you? I have such wonderful memories of your sister. She grovelled on her knees for hours, begging at the last to be spared, even as she went beneath the waves. It was—" He paused, licked his lips again. "Exhilarating."

Rustam looked aghast at Leith. The Shivan queen sat quite still, he face chalk white, barely breathing.

Hensar had killed Marten's mother. Everyone had suspected King Saimund, the boy's father, although the drowning could just conceivably have been the accident it had appeared to be. No proof had ever been tendered, and the gentle queen had been mourned by the kingdom, if not by her sot of a husband who had retreated ever deeper into his bottomless tankard.

"And you." Rustam jerked back to find the dwarf's pitiless gaze upon him. "You have caused me endless irritation. It will be a pleasure to see you lose your head alongside your master and his puppet king. I suppose I should have anticipated the trouble you would give me; you are a product of the same experiment as I am, after all. Oh yes, don't look so surprised. Did you really think a

Tyr-enese would willingly mate with a dwarf, except for the purposes of the game?

"But you could never have hoped to be my equal. Your blood is too diluted with human weakness, being one generation beyond mine. I may have to think of resurrecting that experiment..."

His voice trailed off but Rustam clung to the one piece of important information he had given away—Marten and Halnashead were still alive.

Hensar waved a guard into the cell, indicating Leith's removal. She moved woodenly, hardly seeming to notice the rough hands that dragged her through the door and out of Rustam's sight. Hensar turned to go.

"I take my leave of you." The tip of his tongue travelled round the perimeter of his mouth. "I have a wedding celebration to conclude. Until tomorrow, then."

So saying, he swept out and the door clanged shut behind him. Rustam's anguish increased as the doctor's words slammed home. A wedding. Annasala's wedding to the Bastard. And they still did not know who he was. Poor Sala. Tonight she must endure. He shook his head; he did not even want to think about it. He refused to speculate upon Leith's fate either. For now, he must cling to hope: his father and the king still lived.

But he had no idea what he was going to do about it.

26. BASTARD

Fresh winter greenery garnished the Great Hall. Long strands of ivy festooned the rafters, cascaded down the acres of tapestries and curtains, trailed across the steps of the dais and over the two thrones situated there. Clumps of white and red berries clustered at irregular intervals in bright bursts of colour against the polished wooden walls and the rough beams overhead. Rustam reckoned that a small forest must have been denuded to so richly garnish the cavernous hall, and the sweet smell of freshly cut vines made him long for Shiva's endless glades.

As he staggered beneath the weight of his shackles, still Rustam ached to help Risada. Flushed with fever and barely able to stand, the Lady of Domn had been spared the shackles, but only because her arm was so swollen it was no longer possible to fit a manacle around her left wrist. Both of them wore gags above the tattered remnants of their filthy clothing, and the bitter taste in Rustam's mouth brought his nausea nearer the surface.

Hundreds of still faces watched their laborious progress up the central aisle, urged on by four burly soldiers in the Bastard's black and silver livery. At Rustam's best guess, the audience comprised representatives, if not whole Families, of each of the Twenty Great Houses, and many lesser nobles as well. In all important respects, the entire Kingdom was there to witness their humiliation.

A number of the men, most of whom Rustam recalled from the Rees-Charlay fest, were dressed in finery that looked as though it had been slept in for several weeks. He caught a glimmer of defiance in one or two eyes, but the majority looked so cowed as to be beyond rebellion.

Of the women some wept with pity and some, revenge, whilst a small number of couples—apparently the ones who knew, or *thought* they knew, what was going on—gloated with satisfaction. True to his profession, Rustam memorised the faces of those who had willingly colluded with the traitors. Then he returned his attention to their surroundings.

Guards stood by every one of the many exits, at the end of every second row of seats, all along the first step to the dais, beside the twin thrones and the small table upon which rested Chel's Casket. Honour guards they were surely meant to be, but their swords were loose in their scabbards and Rustam doubted they would hesitate to use them. The old taboo about drawn blades in the presence of royalty would not apply now anyway—the pretender could hardly be classed as true royalty any more than could Rustam himself. The only full blooded royal was likely to be Annasala, and indeed just as he thought about his half-sister she appeared from the rear of the dais, led forward on Doctor Hensar's arm.

The dwarf positively swaggered, dressed in a white leather military style uniform embellished with silver buttons and medals. A blue crystal pendant hung on a chain around his neck. Rustam thought he looked ridiculous.

So just where *was* the Bastard? Rustam had yet to see him, to see if he would recognise the face of the lifelong enemy of whom he had been only distantly aware. He had always been there in the background, a minor brief—pass on any information gleaned but don't do anything about it—always someone else's mission. But now it was personal. Now Rustam knew him to be Soria's murderer, and the one who had violated his sister and imprisoned his father. Somehow, despite the shackles, despite the guards, Rustam was going to do *something* about it.

Annasala was seated upon the smaller throne. She simply sat where she was placed, hands limp in her lap, glazed eyes focussing on nothing. Carefully applied make up lent colour to her face, but still she looked wan, her beautifully dressed hair dull beneath the weaving of flowers and ribbons. In traditional Tyr-enese styling her gown was full, high in the neck and long sleeved. Rustam cringed at thought of the injuries that concealing fashion no doubt hid from the eyes of the Kingdom.

The guards on the first step parted to allow the prisoners to ascend. One step below the top they were ordered to halt, and forced to their knees. Rustam's eyes swept the dais and his skin chilled with shock.

In the furthest left hand corner, hidden from sight until now, knelt Marten and Halnashead, shackled as Rustam himself, but also chained to the floor by weighty links attached to thick metal collars. They too, were gagged. His father's bleak eyes met his, and then slid away as his head bowed beneath the weight of iron. Marten's head never lifted.

Risada stirred beside him. Her breath hissed in sharply and Rustam jerked his attention back to the thrones.

Approaching them now was Hensar, leading a child dressed in crimson. Rustam felt his brow furrow in confusion. What was Hensar playing at? Then recognition came.

The child was no child at all. It was Queen Leith, clad in child's clothing, her sable hair in two long plaits adorned with scarlet ribbons. She looked fragile, doll-like, and the vivid shade of her dress only served to accentuate her extraordinary colouring. Hensar led her, meek and un-protesting, to the front edge of the dais where all could gain a good view of her.

What *was* he up to?

"Greetings to you, loyal citizens of Tyr-en." Hensar's eyes swept the crowd and the mutter at Rustam's back died to a breathless hush. "You have gathered today to witness the start of a new era for our glorious Kingdom. One that is free from the taint of the vile magic that drove us from our homeland and across the hostile sea."

Hensar's hand pointed towards Halnashead and Marten, chained and helpless but still a threat to the Bastard whilst they lived.

Unless it could be proven they had been using magic.

The plan was suddenly all too clear to Rustam. If the Bastard was successful in convincing the nobility of just that, there would be nothing left to prevent him from executing the entire Family under their own laws. Rustam had to admire the man's cunning and audacity—a populace grateful for their rescue from the hands of liars and magic wielders would be so much easier to control than one held entirely by force.

And somehow Rustam, Risada and Leith had provided him with the proof he needed.

"Halnashead," said Hensar, voice dripping with disdain, "has deceived you for decades. He has hidden from you the truth that magic is being used today. Not just in the barbarian Kingdoms, but here, in the heart of our very own Tyr-en!"

A murmur like waves rushing upon the shore made the skin between Rustam's shoulder blades crawl. Hensar was accusing Halnashead of the very crime *he* was committing! And gagged as they all were, there was no chance to refute his allegations or make counter claims.

"He and his puppet king are using the proscribed arts," Hensar proclaimed with another flourish of his hand towards Tyr-en's chief of security and the youthful monarch. "Worse, they do not only use *magic*, but consort with the demon Charin and his creatures!"

The doctor signalled, and a guard—a particularly tall, robust individual—came forward to take Leith by the shoulder. He pulled her down the first step, onto a level with Rustam and Risada. Against the soldier's solid frame she looked like a child of about twelve years old. She now also appeared considerably shorter than Hensar's dwarfish stature.

This whole performance had been carefully choreographed.

"Allow me to introduce you to Leith de Garon, *older* sister to Marten's mother, the late Queen Selva. Look well upon her, citizens. *Look at her.*"

Rustam could feel the shock emanating from the crowd behind him. He knew well how Leith would appear to them: bizarrely coloured, with eyes a shade no human should possess, dramatically accentuated by the crimson gown in which Hensar had dressed her. The dress, too, was designed to make her seem child-like. But if Marten's mother had still been alive, she would have been thirty six by now. And Leith was older.

She was also thoroughly drugged beyond any ability to speak for herself.

Hensar's face took on a glow of triumph, and Rustam groaned inwardly, only able to imagine the expressions of the populace.

"You see, my countrymen? Not only has Halnashead used magic behind your backs, but he has bred it into the line. Some of you may still remember that it was he who arranged that marriage for his brother, King Saimund.

"As you can clearly see for yourselves, this *woman*—aunt to Marten—is no more a natural human being than an elf." He waved forward another soldier. This one carried a cushion held gingerly at arm's length. As the man approached, Rustam made out the shape of a sword lying on the fabric. Not just any sword, but the legendary Shiva blade, *Rhesmett.* Hensar waved his hand again and the guard, his face screwed up in anticipation, hesitantly put his hand to the grip. It was no surprise to Rustam when blue sparks crackled and spat. The sword fell with a clatter to the steps beside him.

The onlookers were silent.

Under Hensar's instruction, Leith's guard propelled her along the step, clamped his huge hand around her tiny one, and placed her palm to *Rhesmett*'s grip. He enfolded her fingers in a meaty fist, and lifted the weapon, clearly quiescent in Leith's grasp.

Now the crowd gasped.

"You see?" crowed Hensar. "She even possesses a magical elven blade, one of those that was used to such devastating effect against us during the Shivan Wars. This can only confirm the taint in Marten's blood."

Moving swiftly on, not giving anyone a chance to think, let alone question, Hensar turned his attention to Risada.

"And this one? You have known her all your lives, but is she truly all she seems? For years, behind the acceptable façade of crown appointed guardians, she has been the real ruler of her Family, despite there being a male heir. Did not many of you wonder at the delay in appointing Iain Merschenko vas Domn to leadership of his own Family? Did it not seem odd to you that wherever he was, there also was his sister—his *unmarried* sister? Unmarried, at *twenty six* years of age, and with surely the richest dowry in all Tyr-en."

Hensar paused briefly, to ensure everybody considered his words. Then: "It should not come as a surprise to you to learn that Iain Merschenko vas Domn has been ruled mentally incompetent."

Rustam's heart wept at the anguish seeping from Risada. From the corner of his eye he could see tears rolling down her cheeks, and her face seemed to crumple in on itself.

"And *why* should this be of no surprise to you?" continued Hensar relentlessly. "Because Risada Delgano vas Domn is a *magic wielder*! She used magic to control the duly appointed guardians to her brother's estate. She used magic to damage her brother's mind so that he would be unfit to rule. And she has used magic for years in the service of her cousins, those members of this disgraced royal Family you see before you today."

Voices rose in confusion behind Rustam. Doubts, protests, fears all mingled together in a hubbub over which presided an immensely satisfied Doctor Hensar. Had Rustam been free to move he would have strangled the monster with his bare hands in front of the entire ruling class of his Kingdom, and damn the consequences.

As the babble died down, one question could be heard over and over from many different voices.

"Are we safe? If they can use magic, are we safe?"

Hensar held up his hands for quiet. It came slowly, reluctantly, but it came.

Into it, Hensar pronounced: "Yes, you are safe. During the years in which I have painstakingly gathered the evidence I now put before you, I came also upon knowledge of a drug that may be used to control magic wielders. With great difficulty, I managed to obtain some specifically for this purpose, and for the moment they are all incapable of calling upon their obscene powers. But I warn you, it will not last; this matter must be dealt with swiftly."

"What of him?" called someone from the rear of the hall. Rustam was unable to place the voice. Jealous rival, cheated husband or Hensar's creature, it did not matter, the question was what mattered.

Hensar managed to look pained. "Chalice? His crimes are lesser, perhaps, though he, too, is proof that Halnashead believed himself not subject to the same laws as everybody else." The doctor paused dramatically, eyes travelling the hall, judging when he had brought them to just the perfect moment to shock them the most. Then he announced: "Chalice is the Royal Family's assassin."

The tumult that erupted was so layered with indignation and outright anger that Rustam flinched, expecting at any moment to be dragged from the step and torn limb from limb. He could not see behind him, and had no assurance that the guards would prevent the mob from doing just that. Not that he really had anything else to look forward to now, anyway. Executions were assured for them all, if the howls of the crowd were anything to go by. Trials were unlikely and Hensar had already given a reason for swift decisions. Rustam looked despairingly toward Risada.

Only to find her oblivious to the reactions unfolding behind them. Her gaze was riveted upward, to where Hensar stood on the step above them. She was staring at the underside of the dwarf's jaw. Rustam looked, and saw what she saw.

A jagged, raised scar, running the length of the underside of Hensar's right jawbone.

Underneath! Not where she had always searched for the tell-tale mark along the side of the assassin's jaw-line, but underneath!

Clarity exploded in Rustam's mind like a bright flash of white light—no, *silver* light. The eyes of the goddess swam before his inner vision. *Will you trust me, my son,* Chel had asked him. And: *follow your conscience.* He had done that, and it had brought him to this moment. That must mean there was a solution to this situation, somewhere, somehow.

Staring up at the scar on the doctor's jaw, Rustam realised how Risada had made her error. She had been searching with the eyes of an adult. *But when she saw this monster murder her parents, she had been six years old. And much smaller.*

Her mind had ignored the fact that her perspective would change, altering the memory as she grew, until the wound she had seen her mother inflict had seemed to occur much higher upon her assailant's face. And finally, she was faced with her mistake.

Rustam too, recognised his own misconception.

Hensar did not work *for* the Bastard. Hensar *was* the Bastard.

Utter calm descended upon Rustam. The raging crowd behind him, the glowing triumph on Hensar's face, the numb, bewildered expressions of Leith and Annasala, all receded to leave him in a tiny pool of tranquillity. He glanced towards Risada, knowing without question that he would find her within the haven too. Their eyes met, total understanding passing between them without the need for words, and briefly Rustam recalled longing for just such a level of communication, never expecting to achieve it, and certainly not with Risada, of all people.

The Lady of Domn fractionally moved her unfettered and uninjured right hand and at last it was clear to Rustam where her tiny jewelled dagger was concealed – lying beneath one breast, incorporated into the structure of the boned bodice she wore beneath her ripped gown.

In full awareness of the consequences of his decision, Rustam composed himself to perform magic—at least, the one piece of magic he had learned so far. If he was successful, he would never learn any more. For, although he might yet save his kingdom, he was condemning himself to death. With the others under the influence of hestane, he could be the only possible source of arcane power.

He found that he was, after all, willing to make that sacrifice. For both his kingdom and his family. His conscience demanded it.

With a swift prayer to Chel, he composed himself and centred his mind. It came easily now, even in the midst of an angry crowd howling for his blood. Had they torn him apart in that moment, he doubted even the tiniest wisp of ire would have risen through the peace that enfolded him. He rested briefly in the balm of total serenity, truly at one with himself, aware of how every action and reaction of his life had drawn him inexorably to this place. Even the machinations of Charin had served to strengthen him, and now he would claim his place in Chel's tapestry of life before he joined her in death.

He reached back, drawing out his memory of the Shivan meadow, of Tocar's patient frustration, of Elwaes's encouragement, and summoned the feelings that memory evoked.

A scream split the air behind him. Other voices rose in panic. Calmly, Rustam twisted around until he could see. One section of the crowd was milling frantically and in its centre, a shrieking noblewoman tore at her flaming hair. The flames leaped sideways to her neighbour, catching his beard alight.

Was there something *inside* that finger of flame?

Bedlam took hold of the rear ranks, whilst those further forward watched in frozen astonishment. Then another, closer voice shrieked above the rest and an older Lady gesticulated frantically towards the rear of the dais.

Rustam turned his head forward again. Sure enough, flickering amongst the drapes and tapestries was not just one, but five salamanders. Their tiny golden fiery bodies darted to and fro and everything they touched caught light.

Hensar's triumphant expression faded into confusion whilst around him his guards stirred and turned anxiously, trying to identify a threat they could address. Behind, the crowd stampeded for the doors.

Overhead, clusters of berries exploded, spitting hot juices out like miniature missiles. Some of the beams began to smoulder. Most of the curtains were spotted with glowing holes as the tiny elementals played hide and seek through their folds.

Discipline withered in the heat of the salamander's flames and soldiers began to break ranks.

Hensar, his plans going up in flames around him, narrowed his eyes and glared at Rustam. Comprehension dawned and his pudgy features contorted with fury.

"*You!*" he screeched.

With all his attention concentrated on Rustam he strode menacingly forward, stroking the blue gemstone that hung on a chain around his neck. Brilliant azure light flooded the hall, overpowering even the glowing orange of the fires. The fleeing populace paused and turned to stare. Rustam grinned fiercely.

The Bastard had declared his true nature to the Kingdom.

Oblivious to his mistake, Hensar took another step forward. The blue glow intensified. One more step. He descended the first stair.

And a look of utter astonishment wiped his face clean of all other emotions. Bewildered, he let go the pendant and raised his hand to his throat where a tiny, emerald encrusted hilt protruded from his skin. His wide eyes turned to meet Risada's fever-bright gaze.

The Lady of Domn rose to her feet, the gag she had worn dangling from her unfettered right hand. "That was for my parents," she hissed as she reached out to grip the tiny hilt. "And this," she jerked the blade sideways and blood gushed, drenching them both "Is for Iain."

The doctor's hands fluttered frantically against the miniature of the dagger that had scarred him so many years before, and then clutched at the tatters of clothing hanging from the body of his nemesis as he slithered to the ground.

A roaring sound brought Rustam back to full awareness. He blinked like a sleepwalker awakened, confused by the brightness around him. With a mighty sizzling, a huge rope of flaming ivy arced across the dais before him, setting light to the greenery that festooned the steps. Rustam found himself on his feet, but with his hands still shackled behind him. Risada fumbled one handed with the knot of his gag. As it fell from his mouth he spat, gasped in a deep breath, and coughed on the acrid smoke. Pain stabbed his side. He pressed his arm against his aching ribs and turned urgently to

Risada.

"Keys?"

The Lady of Domn sank to her knees beside Hensar's body, her one good hand groping for the ring of keys that hung from his belt. Her arm shook violently and Rustam knew she was at the very edge of her endurance. She scrabbled clumsily, trying to detach the ring from the belt. Just as she succeeded, she froze.

Horrified, Rustam saw Hensar's hands shoot out to clutch Risada around the throat in a deadly grip. Over her head, Rustam could see the wound in the Bastard's neck closing even as he watched. *Of course!* Hensar had been experimenting for years in his pursuit of the elixir of eternity. No doubt many of the potions he had tested along the way had proven efficacious in producing other effects, if not the desired end result.

Terrible cracking noises overhead distracted Rustam long enough to glance up. The beams above were burning fiercely and thick smoke roiled in the gap between rafters and roof. Soon it would descend to choke those who survived the flames. Waves of intense heat washed over Rustam. Even the metal bindings on his wrists were becoming uncomfortably hot.

He aimed a foot at the side of Hensar's head and put all his fury behind the kick. He cried out as pain lanced his side, but the Bastard's head snapped round and his hands flew open. Risada fell back gasping, her fingers still clenched around the all important key ring. Rustam felt sure he must have broken Hensar's neck, but the doctor's head swung back, eyes glaring madly at him. As if in a bad dream, the stocky figure began to rise—

With a whoosh and a roar, the beam directly overhead collapsed. As it crashed down, Rustam caught a brief glimpse of Hensar, hands raised as if in hope of fending off the huge timber, disbelief of his own mortality plain on his face.

Then he was gone. Great gouts of flame erupted from the burning greenery and Rustam was forced back, up the step onto the dais. He lost sight of Risada in the smoke and heat haze. She was on the other side of a wall of fire.

"Risada!" he yelled, "Ris—"

He broke off, coughing, and for a moment the agony in his side took all his attention. When the pain subsided, he glanced around and saw to his dismay that Marten and Halnashead were still kneeling, chained to the floor. Their eyes were fixed in desperate, silent plea on Rustam. To his right stood the child-like Leith, looking small and lost with the great Shiva sword dangling passively in her tiny hands. Behind, eyes wild with a look that was half insanity, half hope, was Annasala.

Something flew through the flames. Instinctively, Rustam ducked, the missile missing his ear by a mere hand span. It clattered to the dais and skidded along, coming to rest against the toe of Sala's elegantly embroidered silk shoe.

The ring of keys.

"Sala?" Rustam spoke carefully, coaxingly, wondering if she was still capable of reason. *Annasala. His sister.*

"Sala. Pick up the keys."

Her wild eyes swung his way and Rustam watched in horrified fascination as sanity and madness warred for dominion. Neither seemed able to prevail but slowly, painfully slowly, a fragile balance was struck.

And all the time it was getting hotter, and harder to breath.

In a dreamlike state, Annasala bent slowly down to retrieve the keys. Hopefully, Rustam turned around and presented his manacled hands to his sister.

Nothing.

Twisting round, he found her staring fixedly at the keys.

"Sala. Please?"

Rustam's eyes began to water. He glanced up. Smoke curled downward. Leith coughed, then the princess herself. Sala gazed vacantly at the fires raging all around them, the ruddy glow reflecting in flashes across her eyes. She looked back at the ring of keys resting in her hands and suddenly her head snapped up.

"Rustam?" she quavered, voice barely audible against the crackle of the burning building.

"The keys, Sala. Please, free my hands."

Again, he turned his back and this time felt her timid hands trying keys, turning them in the lock until with a *snick*, the manacles fell off.

"Thank you," he said and took the key ring. "Look to Leith," he instructed, and pushed Sala gently towards the drugged queen.

Dodging little heaps of flaming ivy, and batting aside a curious salamander, he crossed the dais in six steps and dropped to his knees beside his father and Marten. Desperately, he searched for a key to fit either of the collars. Both prisoners were shifting uncomfortably, reddened patches forming beneath the hot metal where it lay heavy against their skin.

"Dammit!" swore Rustam. "These don't fit."

He tore Halnashead's gag off, did the same service for Marten whilst the prince—his father— gagged and spat. "Where are the keys?" Rustam demanded.

"I don't know." Halnashead's voice was heavy with a defeat Rustam had never expected to hear from his prince. Marten coughed. "One of the guards had them," croaked the young king. "He ran away."

"Save the women," Halnashead instructed as Rustam freed his hands. The manacles, at least, all had the same key. "Save Annasala, Rusty, please."

That note of pleading was foreign to Rustam's expectation too.

"I'm not going to leave you."

"Rustam, that is an order!" Halnashead tried to bark, but his mouth was too dry and his throat too raw from the smoke. It came out as a croak. Rustam just shook his head.

Hooking his fingers inside the collar to alleviate some of the pressure, the prince glared at Rustam. Their eyes locked. Despite the crash of another descending roof beam, Rustam stared stubbornly back. Halnashead's expression changed.

He recognised the knowledge in his son's eyes.

"Save your sister, Rusty. Please."

A sudden idea burst inside Rustam's head. He sprang to his feet then gasped, clutching his side. Awkwardly, one hand pressed against his ribs, he staggered back to the women. Annasala was tugging at Leith's sleeve.

"She won't move!" Hysteria edged Annasala's tone.

"Sorry," muttered Rustam and, with one eye on the sword still dangling loosely in her grasp, he slapped the queen hard across the cheek. Was there a flicker of reaction?

"Rusty!" protested Sala.

Knowing what his sister had endured at the hands of a man, Rustam cringed inside, but struck Leith again. This time there was definitely an angry glow, deep inside the ruby eyes. Rustam took her by the shoulders and shook her.

"Fight it, Leith. I need your help."

The light in those odd eyes died away.

"*Come on!* Fight."

Catching his breath, Rustam put a hand to the Shiva blade.

No sparks. Nothing at all. Or—a faint vibration, a warmth that was nothing to do with the fire.

Leith turned to Rustam.

"What do you need?"

Her voice was slurred, and came as if from a great distance. With a shudder, Rustam realised it was the sword, speaking through its human counterpart.

"Those chains." Rustam pointed. "Can you break them?"

Leith turned and strode across the platform. The sword rose and fell. Both chains parted with a screech of protesting metal.

The two men staggered to their feet and Rustam looked wildly about for a way out. The roaring was too loud for words now and smoke billowed towards the little group from behind the dais. Indicating that they should link hands, Rustam took the lead and staggered into the choking dark.

Do I trust you, Chel? Yes, I do.

Staying head on into the air current, he stumbled through pitchy gloom, holding his breath and moving as fast as his shaking legs would take him. He just hoped that no one would let go.

Thunder crashed behind them and the roof fell in. Debris struck them from all sides and several voices cried out in pain but they were out, the clouds parting before them, fresh air ready to be drawn into aching, scorched lungs.

Rustam glanced back: Annasala and Leith, Marten and Halnashead emerged behind him, choking and bleeding, reddened skin beginning to blister, but they were all alive.

They staggered across blackened grass, and into the cool shelter of the portico surrounding the king's own private wing. In silent accord, they all turned to watch the burning palace.

No words were spoken, but Rustam knew the same question was on all their minds.

Where was Risada Delgano vas Domn?

27. THE PRINCE'S MAN

Prince Halnashead's private wing of the palace was far enough from the burnt out Great Hall to have suffered no structural damage, but the acrid smell of smoke pervaded everything from cushions to wall hangings. After locating all his furniture heaped higgledy-piggledy in a small waiting room, the prince's study had been restored to an approximation of its former state, although the great tapestry was nowhere to be found. Someone thought they remembered Hensar burning it.

Rustam slouched in a padded, smoky-smelling chair, across the enormous desk from the prince. Even now, five days later and with his ribs firmly strapped, he was still finding new bruises.

To add to his discomfort, he did not know what to say to his father.

In the days since the fire, Halnashead had been terribly busy, and it had been deemed inadvisable for Rustam to show his face. Consequently, they had barely seen one another. Now, after so much time to think and so little time left in which to talk, still Rustam could not find the words he wanted. Neither, it would seem, could Halnashead. Silence stretched, uncomfortable and charged with unexpressed feelings.

Rustam shifted again, finding yet another sore part of his anatomy. He had been in and out of this study all his life and knew every corner of it, but his abiding sense of familiarity jarred uncomfortably with the reality of bare walls, missing clutter, and a prince who was a mere shadow of his former robust self.

Halnashead's clothes hung from his wasted frame, held in place with hastily taken tucks and a belt several notches higher than he could ever have hoped to tighten it.

Rustam acknowledged wearily that whilst some things might recover with time—Halnashead's girth amongst them—much would never be the same again. His relationship with the prince was one of those casualties. Now that he knew the truth, there was no going back. A fact of which he was sure the older man was as keenly aware.

Best to stick to other things, at least for the moment.

"Risada," said Rustam. "How is she?"

Prince Halnashead looked at his son with a ghost of a smile. "You two finally made your peace, didn't you?"

Rustam nodded. "We reached an understanding. But I haven't been allowed to see her, and now I hear she's left Darshan."

"Quite, quite. Gone to Domn. Refuses to rest any longer. Says if the poison hasn't killed her by now it isn't going to."

Rustam smiled. He could picture the Lady of Domn laying down the law to her doctors, saying just that. He would always be able to hear her voice now, inside his head.

"But how did she escape the hall? She was barely on her feet when I last saw her." He scowled. "I haven't been allowed to see anybody I could ask."

Halnashead's expression turned anxious. "You do understand the necessity for that, don't you?"

"Yes. I don't have to like it, though."

"No, you don't. It does nothing to make me happy either. But to answer your question, you have a secret admirer, m'boy. One with courage and conscience."

Rustam raised a questioning eyebrow. Halnashead's mouth curved into the merest hint of a wicked grin before continuing. "Betha Fontmaness. Sweet, fragile Betha. Stayed to try and help you. It was she who threw the keys. She who helped Risada escape the hall."

Rustam shook his head, both singed eyebrows lifting incredulously. "Who would have thought it? Little Betha. I don't suppose her husband was too thrilled about it."

"Herschel died of a heart seizure some weeks ago. Betha is a widow now, and Lady of her own House."

"Ah."

Silence threatened to regain control. Rustam fidgeted, and then plunged on. "But Risada's going to be fine, isn't she?"

"Yes, yes," confirmed the prince. "She may lose some of the mobility of that arm, but as I'm sure you've seen for yourself, she has many abilities that will not affect. And due to your selfless actions, her positions in both society and the game have been safeguarded. Personally, though," the prince paused to consider, then looked straight at Rustam. "She's needed at Domn to pick up the pieces, and to see to Iain. Her brother is not well, and it is uncertain whether of natural causes or some evil legacy that dwarf has left us."

"At least she had her revenge."

"Quite, quite."

The uneasy quiet prevailed again, and once more it fell to Rustam to break it.

"And Leith? I heard that last dose of hestane was pretty near the mark."

"Indeed," agreed the prince. "As I understand it, Hensar made no provision for her recovery. He appears, however, to have been without intimate knowledge of the magical nature of the relationship between Queen Leith and her sword." Halnashead looked a little uncomfortable at the knowledge himself, and muttered, "It's hard to believe that an inanimate piece of steel like that..." He shuddered.

"Well, whatever it is, it wouldn't let her go. For two days she lay as though dead, with that *thing* gripped in both fists. No one was about to try prising it away from her. Then she simply woke up. She won't talk about it and, to be honest, I think that's just as well."

"Is she back on her feet yet? I haven't seen her either."

"Yes, yes. She's out with Marten, becoming acquainted with the Families, smoothing things over in regard to Hensar's accusations." Halnashead looked rather impressed. "She's good at it, too."

Rustam gave a small snort of amusement. "You mean, she's good at it considering she's a reigning monarch. You don't expect a queen to be a diplomat, do you?"

Halnashead's return smile was slightly embarrassed. "Well, no. That's not how it works." He cocked his head thoughtfully. "Useful though, isn't it?"

"Indeed," mimicked Rustam. Halnashead choked, and then roared with laughter. The tension between them lifted and for a moment it felt to Rustam like a return to older, simpler days.

He took the plunge.

"Did you love my mother?"

Startled, the Prince's face dropped into a mournful expression. The deeply etched lines betrayed how often he had worn it over the years.

"Of course I did!" he protested, and regarded his son with a peculiar mixture of indignation and vulnerability. "Do you really consider me so stupid as to have physical relations with a woman who meant nothing to me? Do you think so little of me?"

Rustam shrugged, but the bitterness he had expected to feel seemed to have been left behind, in Shiva.

"I don't know what to think. All these moons I thought I understood you, then I find out you are my sire, and you never bothered to tell me. Nor to inform me that my mother had been murdered."

Halnashead stood up and began to pace. For the first time in his life Rustam found the habit annoying. "Please, father. Don't be evasive. Thanks to your manipulation of the law, we don't have much time left."

Halnashead rounded on him. "Would you rather be executed? There is no precedent for what you did. We are all exceedingly grateful for your self-sacrifice, but with the whole kingdom to witness your arcane abilities? Under the circumstances, exile is the best I could achieve."

"And I am grateful for my life, believe me. But before I leave, I want some answers, some truths from you."

Halnashead sat down again, his expression softening. "And you shall have them, my boy. I owe you that much, and I know well that you can hold your tongue."

Rustam regarded him obliquely. "Did you not know that, before?"

It was Halnashead's turn to shrug. "Rusty—son—a prince must have no skulls in the kennels, especially when he is in charge of security. No one knew, only your mother and I. While you were young, you would not have had the discretion. When you were older—" He shrugged again. "It just never seemed necessary." The prince began to rise, hesitated, and then sank down again. "Rusty, you have no idea how many times I imagined this conversation over the years, but never like this. As time went on, the longer I left it, the more difficult I knew it would be. How did you...?"

Rustam smiled secretively. "Let us just say, the goddess spoke to me in a vision."

The prince looked mildly offended. "Well! If you don't wish to tell me I'm sure you have your reasons, but I need your assurance that it will go no further."

"Risada knows."

"Mmm. She can be relied upon. Annasala?"

Rustam shook his head. "No, but I wouldn't put it past her to figure it out. How is she doing?"

Halnashead's mouth turned down, the mournful expression reasserting itself. He steepled his hands and rested his forehead against his fingertips for a moment to regain his composure. Rustam's heart sank.

"She will recover, won't she?"

His father's eyes glistened with unshed tears. "Physically, yes. It will take time but the doctors assure me none of the damage is permanent. Mentally? I have seen stronger characters crack under far less than she endured. We can only hope that she will find a way to cope. I just wish..."

"Don't! You could not have prevented it. It was her strength of character that led her into the situation, and it is that same strength that will pull her through. She is her father's child."

"As are you, Rusty. I have often wished you were legitimate. You would have made a fine successor."

"Speaking of successors, did it never occur to you to think that Risada might believe me to be *her* brother?"

Halnashead looked utterly stunned, and was speechless for some seconds. "*Rusty!* I— No." He shook his head. "Now you suggest it, I can see why she might have thought so, but it never crossed my mind. *Goddess!* So *that* was her problem with you." Halnashead went white beneath his beard. "She might have killed you!"

Rustam grinned wryly. "She nearly did, on several occasions, some of which I may have deserved. But I have to admit, there were times when I wondered at your motive for pushing us together like that. It's hard to credit, after your lifetime of experience in the game, that you might have missed that one."

The prince shook his head, hands spread wide. "I was so wrapped up in my guilty secret, I never considered it. Arton was my best friend and utterly devoted to Sharlanne. I'm amazed that anyone, least of all his own daughter, would have thought him capable of .... Well, there we are. That explains many little comments and attitudes from Risada over the years. Another example of my fallibility."

Rustam reached across the desk, put his hands around his father's and squeezed gently. "It makes you human." Then he laughed. "Not, of course, that those of us who are not quite human are any better than you."

Halnashead cuffed Rustam lightly on the side of the head, leaned back in his chair and roared with laughter. "Now," he said and gasped for breath. "You sound just like your mother! What you *really* mean is, you don't want us to *realise* how much better you are, hmm?" He sighed. "Ah, Rusty, I would give anything to have her back. I have missed her every day we've been parted, and now I'm to lose you too."

"Oh, I'll be around. Even if I can't enter Tyr-en, you can always come and visit me."

"Where will you go?"

Rustam sat back to consider. For the first time in his life he had free choice. And absolutely no idea what to do with it. Vague plans drifted through his mind.

Kishtan would bear some study, with their creativity and progress, and their strange ideas of involving the populace in their ruling decisions. Perhaps he could find a job somewhere on the fringes of the court—even Kishtanians needed dancing Masters. And then there was Rylond. The skills he had learned as a player in Tyr-en would surely permit him to make his way in life as a merchant.

And, of course, there was Shiva.

What he *didn't* want to think about was what he was leaving behind. Blood family, so newly discovered and now forever beyond his reach; a kingdom in turmoil, much of it caused by his actions.

And Risada. Arrogant, self-serving and annoying beyond belief, but *goddess*, he was going to miss her so much. His chest grew tight and his breathing shallow.

Was this what it was to love?

He gave himself a mental shake. It could never have worked. No matter who his father was, he was still a bastard and she, a Lady of the Second House. The fact that she had gone without coming to see him first, proved that her overriding concern would always be her Family. And rightly so, he told himself, particularly with Iain unlikely to produce an heir. In the aftermath of the rebellion there was of necessity going to be a major rearrangement of the noble Houses, and Marten needed all the support he could muster from the strongest remaining Families. Risada's ultimate loyalty would always be to her kingdom.

Rustam's mind settled to a decision. The best thing he could do now for Tyr-en and for Risada would be to embrace his exile as an opportunity, and remove himself before his very presence muddied the political waters.

He put on his most flippant expression.

"I think, at least for now, I'll head back towards Shiva. First, I need to find my horse. Then there's this dryad......"

Epilogue

DOMN

Risada Delgano vas Domn studied her brother's unquiet face as he tossed in fitful sleep. He looked careworn, with deep frown lines scoring his brow, and his brown hair shot through with silver strands. In his waking moments his mind seemed to have reverted to a child-like simplicity far earlier even than his perpetual juvenile state. Still the doctors could not tell her whether this was some evil legacy of the dwarf's manipulations, or simply a natural progression of Iain's condition.

Risada sighed and lifted her head, glancing around the bedchamber until her eyes came to rest upon a plump, over-stuffed sofa squatting before a heavy tapestry. Behind there was the hidden door she had used as a child. Her eyes travelled up the wall to where she knew the spy hole was located. Even knowing where it was, still she had to search the ornate carving carefully before she could pinpoint its exact position.

How different things would have been had she not stood there that night.

She rose and walked over to her mother's dressing table. On Risada's orders, the furnishings had never been moved. Throughout her childhood and adolescence she had haunted this room, replaying her parent's deaths over and over in her mind, deepening her resolve to avenge them with every passing day.

Now, it was done.

She gazed into her mother's glass and tried to remember Sharlanne's face. Her own hair was the same, she was sure of that. Even as a small child, people had commented on how alike the colour and texture. But her memory of Sharlanne's features had blurred with the years and she was no longer certain if she looked very much like her.

Irritably, Risada hitched her sling into a more comfortable position. She wriggled her still swollen and discoloured fingers and sighed again. The doctors had told her that whilst she was lucky to be alive, her arm would never be the same again. They argued over how much use of it she would regain, but in truth only time would tell.

Of one thing she was sure: her days as an assassin were over.

Her mother had been this age when she was murdered, and had already produced two children to secure the future of her husband's House. Risada turned to look back at Iain. It seemed that task must now pass to her.

She sat down on the padded stool before the looking glass, and let her mind drift back over the past months. Despite her best attempts, the political face of Tyr-en had been irrevocably changed by what she had allowed to happen. Whilst she recognised the futility of trying to think how she might have done things differently, still she felt it had been her fault. She resolved to help build the new Tyr-en stronger than the old. Strong enough to stand against the other, magic-wielding Kingdoms.

For the first time in her life, Risada began to think about a future beyond revenge.

Always, before, the other kingdoms had seemed irrelevant. She had the basic knowledge of them that any player needed, but had never expected to use it. The journey to Kishtan had forced her to revise her opinion. Not only had it become abundantly clear at what a disadvantage Tyr-en might be should one of the magic using kingdoms decide to invade, but there were other lacks as well.

Whilst Risada could not bring herself to approve of Kishtanian society, the technical advances they had made in such a short time were alarmingly impressive, and she coveted them.

Perhaps she would suggest to Marten that he should develop more open diplomatic relations with their neighbours, and as a consequence, trade negotiations. Such a step would require careful preparation, as the Families would undoubtedly balk at the suggestion. But now was the time to set change in motion, to elevate some of the lesser Families who might be more willing to support progress. In the aftermath of the revolution there were significant gaps in the hierarchy which Marten would be eager to fill with younger, more forward looking Houses. He would need to be careful, of course, because his own position, whilst not as precarious as it might have been, was by no means as assured as it once was.

It was time Marten started thinking about marriage, too.

Risada picked up her mother's silver hair brush and began systematically brushing her long locks. It was soothing, resurrecting memories of sitting here as a child, with Sharlanne stroking the brush along the kinked waves that emerged from her plaits. She had never allowed anyone else to brush her hair, no maids or dressers. It was a cherished feeling that she clung to, like a little piece of her mother that could never die. She wondered if Rustam had a similar memory of Soria.

Thought of Rustam made her throat tighten. Her image in the glass blurred and she brushed angrily at the moisture overflowing onto her cheeks.

Guilt was a new experience for the Lady of Domn. She had never needed to justify her actions to anyone before, least of all herself.

She put down the brush, stood up and stalked across the room, back to Iain's bedside. She dipped a cloth into the bowl of water on the stand beside the bed and wrung it out with savage intensity.

It could never have worked. Even if Rustam's parentage should become known, he would always be illegitimate, with no social standing. Certainly not an acceptable husband for a lady in Risada's position.

She scowled. She should have seen him, face to face, and pointed all this out. Of course he knew already, but still, she should have done it.

She had intended to but, standing at the end of the palace corridor, looking at the guard outside his room—as much for his protection as to prevent him from leaving—her nerve had failed her. Risada Delgano vas Domn had fled Darshan in shame, too afraid to face the man who knew her better than anyone in this life and try to tell him why she couldn't love him.

She swallowed hard and used the cloth to scrub away a tear-track.

Trouble was, she *did* love him. He understood her as no other man ever could. They had shared more than a married couple were ever likely to. He was compassionate, strong and faithful. And he made her laugh. Not many people in her life had been able to do that. Keeping him at a distance was probably one of the hardest tasks she would ever undertake.

Oh, and he wasn't bad looking either.

Risada wasn't sure if she loved him more as the brother she had believed him to be, or as a potential mate. But it didn't matter either way because she could never have him.

For a brief, luxurious moment, Risada allowed herself to flirt with the idea of leaving Tyr-en, of abandoning her responsibilities and her heritage and following Rustam into exile. They could go anywhere, be anyone. With their combined skills they could surely invent a new life for themselves in one of the other kingdoms.

But those other kingdoms were not magic-free, and no matter how much Risada had changed, she knew she would never be comfortable living within such easy reach of the arcane.

Clamping a solid vice of reason onto her imagination, Risada turned her mind back to the real world. Her duty now had a new goal: a husband, suitable to secure the future of the Second Family.

Sorting through the eligible possibilities, she found little to her liking. If she couldn't have the man she wanted, she was at the very least going to have one she wouldn't murder within the first six months. None of them compared favourably to Rustam—damn, but she must stop thinking about him, about those long, lean thighs and the way they wrapped around that black mare of his—no!

Iain shifted restlessly in the huge bed and moaned. Grateful for the distraction, Risada bent to wipe the sheen of sweat from her brother's brow.

She didn't need a lover, just a husband.

And the answer came to her. She couldn't have Rustam, but his father was single, a widower. What better match could there be for the Second House? And more than that, she could make for herself a fresh role within the game, and help to shape the new kingdom her actions had spawned. Her mind could be fully engaged whilst her body performed those duties necessary to perpetuate her Family.

Her heart, though, would always be somewhere else, beyond the mountains that had changed their lives.

Wherever *he* chose to live.

NOTE FROM THE AUTHOR

Thank you so much for spending your time reading my words. If you liked what you read, would you please leave a short review on Amazon.com or Amazon.co.uk?

Just a few lines would be great!

Reviews are not only the highest compliment you can pay to an author, they also help other readers discover and make more informed choices about purchasing books in a crowded space.

Thank you!

If you'd like to read more about the Five Kingdoms and novels yet to come, find me at:

Blog: www.deborahjayauthor.com

Facebook: www.facebook.com/deborahjay

Twitter: www.twitter.com/DeborahJay2

If you would like me to notify you when the next book is released, please contact me via my blog and I will add you to my mailing list.

About the Author

Deborah Jay writes fast-paced fantasy adventures featuring quirky characters and multi-layered plots. Just what she likes to read. Living mostly on the UK south coast, she has already invested in her ultimate retirement plan - a farmhouse in the majestic mystery-filled Scottish Highlands where she retreats to write when she can find time. Her taste for the good things in life is kept in check by the expense of keeping too many dressage horses, and her complete inablility to cook. She also has non-fiction titles published under her professional name of Debby Lush.

Read more at Deborah Jay's site.

37112186R00257

Printed in Great Britain
by Amazon